"Sergeant?" It was Kellehay's voice from below, hushed, strangled.

Kellehay never called him "Sergeant."

Matusek hung over the edge, motionless, waiting.

"You better get down here, Sarge—fast!"

Matusek hitched up his belt and thrust himself into the blackness below. Rocks chattered out of his way, spraying into distance. He stopped short on an impenetrable piece of darkness—Kellehay.

"Whoever called wasn't dreaming, Sarge. This is gonna be a rough one, really rough. Look."

The piece of blackness that was Kellehay trained a shaft of light on the bottle-littered ground, illuminating a swath of tattered Hamm's beer labels, shattered brown glass and something large and pale and star-shaped lying on the brittle carpet of refuse.

"Ho-ly Christ!" Matusek extended the words into several awestruck syllables. "I hope she's dead."

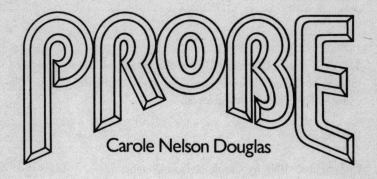

PROBE

Carole Nelson Douglas

A TOM DOHERTY ASSOCIATES BOOK

This is a work of fiction. All the characters and events portrayed in this book are fictional, and any resemblance to real people or incidents is purely coincidental.

PROBE

Copyright © 1985 by Carole Nelson Douglas

All rights reserved, including the right to reproduce this book or portions thereof in any form.

Special thanks to Bob Seger and Gear Publishing Co. for permission to reprint lyrics from *The Distance* album. "Roll Me Away" © 1982 Gear Publishing Co./ASCAP; "Comin' Home" © 1979 Gear Publishing Co./ASCAP

First printing: July 1985

A TOR Book

Published by Tom Doherty Associates
8-10 West 36 Street
New York, N.Y. 10018

ISBN: 0-812-53585-5
CAN. ED.: 0-812-53586-3

Printed in the United States of America

For my husband, Sam—again,
because he is
the best

The Finding
August 31

Chapter One

"Ten to one this is another crank call."

Sergeant Biff Matusek implanted perfectly fitting dentures deep in the mushy guts of a Big Mac. Special sauce ran down his outjutted jaw and he automatically slapped it off his double chin with the swipe of a paper napkin. "Should have gone ten-seven *off* the air, then we wouldn't be chasin' our tails around on every Friday-night fracas in town."

The in-dash Motorola squawked sudden agreement.

"Jesus! Squelch that thing. Man can't even eat in peace." Matusek was silent while stuffing fingersful of limp fries into his mouth.

At the wheel, his young, mustached face lit from below by the dashboard lights, rookie John Kellehay glanced regretfully to the quarter-pounder congealing on the seat beside him. The veteran sharing the squad car's front seat with Kellehay jammed his empty fries sacks into the McDonald's bag, stretched his six-foot frame in a practiced little buck and, out of some obscure habit, tightened the belt underlining his prominent Milwaukee goiter. Required standards of police physical fitness had not yet reached Crow Wing, Minnesota. Anyway, a red-necked old-timer like Matusek would have snorted at the idea of a weight loss or regular exercise.

Kellehay smiled, looking even younger with his choir-boy crop and closely trimmed mustache—all the hairiness allowed uniformed officers.

"Say, Sarge, this might not be so bad. Could be something hot up on the overlook. Usually the kids want us to stay

9

as far away as possible; dispatcher said these sounded pretty shook.''

"That old hen is dreamin'. Only thing hot you'll find up there is the Friday-night neckers,'' Matusek predicted. "Do a hell of a lot more than neckin' nowadays. But Christ, that ain't nothin'. You can see it at home on TV a lot easier. And you'll find out after you've been in police work longer, kid, that shinin' flashlights into lovers' lane cars is a kick that don't last. Hell, I've spent more time on that damn overlook chasin' nothin'— Watch out; this road's a bitch for night drivin'.''

Matusek glumly watched the black-and-white's headlights flush vivid green patches of bush and pine from the night undergrowth for a few moments. His bulk bucked uncomfortably again on the sticky vinyl upholstery. It was warm for late August in Minnesota.

"The big zero. Nothin','' he pronounced. "You'll see.''

The Plymouth hummed steadily up the tortuous incline. Going down the road at murderous speed was a favorite postmidnight summer sport of local hot-rodders expressing high spirits after a few hours of bluff-top necking and Sergeant Matusek's "a lot more.''

It was not quite midnight now; a bright full moon bobbed in an August sky clad in scarves of fast-flying clouds. The Crow Wing bluff was a remarkable earthen upthrust from predictably flat Minnesota farm country. Tough native clay fueled the pottery plant that had made the town famous; that same carmine earth shaped the plateau Indians had once used for lost ceremonials. Now, it served mainly as a stage for starlit clandestine necking or daytime sight-seeing, a setting composed of rock, dirt and what random greenery amateur climbers hadn't trampled. The squad car rolled to a stop near a limestone wall that ringed the official overlook. Matusek lumbered out to stretch again.

"See, Kellehay? Quiet as a cat up here. Even the kids don't need the place; nowadays they got them fancy vans they can park pretty as you please in Mommy and Daddy's driveway.''

"Nice night," the rookie agreed, getting out to study the ghostly sky and the few bright barbs of stars visible behind the scudding cloud wisps. "Maybe even a little spooky." He grinned at the sergeant, who snorted, then placed a perfect arc of spit on a nearby limestone slab.

"Take a look around, Kellehay. I'll, uh . . ." Matusek stretched back into the front car seat, grunting, and surfaced with a white bag. "I'll finish your burger before it gets cold."

Kellehay got the powerful flashlight from the trunk and shook his head as he probed the darkness with rhythmic sweeps of the beam. He was a farmer's son, but he had a college degree from the outstate branch of the University of Minnesota, and he knew men like Matusek were a doomed breed. Modern police work was filtering down even to isolated towns like Crow Wing. And modern crime. Crow Wing saw its share of rapists and child murderers now, as well as the occasional spectacular crime of rural isolation—the farmers who went berserk and killed their wives, children, dogs and selves seemingly for the sole purpose of bringing a plague of big-city press down on the boondocks.

Kellehay dug his heels into the incline and worked his way below the bluff profile with a seesaw gait. There was a lower outcropping, a sort of earthenwork balcony, that the kids liked to scramble down to. It was usually carpeted with broken beer bottles. . . . Kellehay's foot stubbed on something; he heard shattering glass chime on the rocks below a second later.

"No drinkin' on the job, Kellehay," Matusek bellowed jocularly from the bluff lip above.

The rookie didn't answer; he was too busy trying to slow what had become a breakneck rush down the treacherous surface.

11

"Find anything?" demanded Matusek. "Told you so," he added into the continued silence.

The silence prolonged past what was acceptable. Matusek crumpled the cardboard shell of the devoured quarter-pounder and threw it aside, debating pulling his gun and going down. Forty years of simple instinct was suddenly hound-dog keen. The hairs on the back of his hands rose to attention.

"Sergeant?" It was Kellehay's voice from below, hushed, strangled.

Kellehay never called him "Sergeant."

Matusek hung over the edge, motionless, waiting.

"You better get down here, Sarge—fast!"

Matusek hitched up his belt and thrust himself into the blackness below. Rocks chattered out of his way, spraying into distance. He stopped short on an impenetrable piece of darkness—Kellehay.

"Whoever called wasn't dreaming, Sarge. This is gonna be a rough one, really rough. Look."

The piece of blackness that was Kellehay trained a shaft of light on the bottle-littered ground, illuminating a swath of tattered Hamm's beer labels, shattered brown glass and something large and pale and star-shaped lying on the brittle carpet of refuse.

"Ho-ly Christ!" Matusek extended the words into several awestruck syllables. "I hope she's dead."

"Better have a look," said Kellehay, not moving. The flashlight beam shook a little in the pooling darkness, but the figure it spotlighted was unforgettable.

It was a woman, clothed only in the yellow light that revealed her. There was nothing prurient about her nudity; it was too awful. Her body was flat, paper-doll-thin, the dead whiteness of the skin blotched with a leprosy of filth. The face. Dirt-caked until the features looked half-eaten. The eyes. Open, glistening like beer bottle shards. The mouth, open too, distended, stiff, frozen into a death camp grin.

"What kind of pervert . . . ?" Kellehay spoke in a dazed

12

singsong. Sergeant Matusek suddenly punched him on the arm.

"Come on, kid. We don't think. We get her topside and then we call the white-suit boys. Well, come on! You was the one so damn hot for there to be something here. Well, there is. There sure as shit is. Take her feet."

"She's dead, ain't she, Sarge?" Kellehay asked the dark as he scrambled up the bluff face. He felt that his hands, curled around bone-hard ankles, were about to sink into something resembling rotted marshmallow. The older man only grunted. The white body bridging them hung slack and amazingly heavy. Kellehay couldn't see anything of Matusek except his dark shoulders.

They lay the body down not far from the squad car; Matusek straightened over it slowly. "Best answer your own question, John," he said seriously. "You got all that up-to-date training. I'll call for the hospital meat wagon."

The sergeant turned away while the younger man reached a reluctant hand to the woman's neck. The face, the awfully grinning face, thank God, had fallen looking away from him. Kellehay's fingers fluttered on the cold skin, then pressed resolutely on the carotid artery. Behind him, the squad door opened; Kellehay could almost feel its dawning yellow interior light fall like a warm blanket across his back. The Motorola barked once. He felt, against all likelihood, an answering flutter under his fingertips. He pressed harder. His own pounding pulse, it had to be. . . . He glanced toward the horrible visage turned nearly away. A slick white glisten caught the moonlight or some vagrant ray of headlight. The face swiveled slowly toward him—stiff, expressionless except for the savage staring eyes. Pity conquered his revulsion. He put a palm under the short matted hair and lifted the head that seemed so heavy on its fragile neck.

"Hey, Sarge," he yelled over his shoulder. "Tell 'em to come quick. She's alive!"

He looked back to make sure she hadn't died even as he

spoke. The catatonic grin was unchanged, but the glassy eyes were widening with comprehension, with growing terror. The head in his hands swiveled sharply to the car with its door agape and Sergeant Matusek leaning into its illuminated interior, the mike in his hand like a dark lollipop trailing coiled licorice. . . .

Kellehay's hands fell away, but her head remained half-raised as her fearful stare focused on him for a moment. Her eyes shifted rapidly to the squad car as if drawn by the mechanical buzz of its two-way radio.

"You're a hero, kid," Matusek was saying with the mike poised in front of his mouth. "You'll get a citation if she's alive—"

The mike exploded into flame in Matusek's hand, fanning into his half-open mouth as if he were eating it. Matusek was thrust back against the front seat, his dark uniformed figure as detailed as a spider's against a fire. The car's yellow light reddened, then the whole interior exploded out and back, just like Matusek. Everything was swallowed in a curtain of red-orange flame that shook like a clothesline blanket in a fall wind.

The force of that interior explosion started the car rolling toward the bluff edge. Kellehay saw Matusek's foot dragging along the ground out the still open door; everything—trunk, roof, hood, wheels—blazed into flame. The gas tank finally ignited with a crimson burst that pushed the burning frame farther down the incline. It rolled remorselessly to the edge, paused on the rocky brink, then teetered over in a shower of shooting flames.

Kellehay ran numbly to the drop. The car was bouncing—a small, bright ball—down into the darkness. Kellehay wondered what words to what song he should sing as it touched earth each time, then rebounded on to the next note. . . . His stomach was gripped by a sudden spasm of—hunger? Whatever it was, it grabbed his guts and held on. He turned back to the bluff-top. She still lay there. Her eyes were closed. He prayed she wasn't still alive.

14

Chapter Two

The phone rang into his sleeping consciousness with the insistency of a dentist's drill. He hated dentists.

Kevin rolled out of the smooth warm sheets, and patted the nightstand in the dark. He was pretty good at it, midnight phone calls being the price of his profession. His groping hand hovered over the mouth of his before-bed Heineken, moved carefully around his expensive Swiss watch—don't want to knock that sucker down—and finally closed on the barbell of the standard-style receiver. Just try and wring extra bucks outa me for one of your fancy phones, Madame Bell. . . .

"Hello. Blake here," he mumbled into the mouthpiece, hoisting himself up against his once perfectly piled pillows. He punched them into the semblance of a back support and waited for what would be either news of Dora Culver's latest suicide attempt or the successful snatch of a cult member or—

"It's Cross," a perfectly wakeful baritone throbbed into the receiver. "Wait'll you see what the Lord dropped down on a plateau in Crow Wing. We've got a triple-priority case here at the hospital. Better get down."

"What time is it?" Kevin muttered ill-naturedly, groping for the lamp switch and snapping on a blinding flash. He blinked at the eighteen-karat-gold hands of the Swiss watch and nearly dropped it. "Four A.M.? Come on, Cross, nothing's that priority it can't wait three goddamn hours."

"Neither rain nor sleet nor dark of night . . ." Cross chanted in an acerbic monotone. "Believe me, Doctor, you

15

wouldn't want to miss a minute on this one. Also, she's in pretty tough shape. I don't want her waking up without you here from moment one. This one is worth your beauty sleep. I'll see you as soon as.''

The phone clicked off, settling into a drone Kevin left at his ear a minute. It was almost enough to push him back over the edge into sleep, but Cross was his boss . . . and often right, which carried even more weight. He swung his feet to the floor and snapped on the watch, a parental gift on his graduation from Harvard Med School. Four-*ten* A.M., Cross, to be precise.

She. Crow Wing? Tough shape. There was no speculating on the last phrase. If Dr. Norbert Cross said she was in tough shape, she was at death's door. Cross was one of the most conservative diagnosticians at the University Hospitals, which was probably why they'd pushed him into administration.

And why they left the risky stuff to young Turks like himself. Kevin grinned as he jammed on jeans and moccasins and wriggled into a sweater. Preppie he wasn't—Harvard only proving that even a Minnesota boy can get good grades but no class. It was a damn good thing Probe needed him. What else would they do about mysterious ladies left on hilltops in Crow Wing?

''You took your time,'' Cross noted out of habit, his eyes flicking to the bland white moon of the hospital clock. ''That fancy watch of yours must be running slow.''

Kevin raised a propitiating hand. ''Look, all present, white coat, washed behind the ears, honest. And it's only five. Five A.M.! Sometimes, Dr. Cross, I think your generation gets a secret pleasure from getting mine up at ungodly hours—''

''That's because we know what yours has been up to the night before. That's *our* major form of recreation,'' Cross rejoined. He turned and walked briskly down the hospital hall with its colored visitors' guide ribbons streaming away on the

16

floor ahead like a rainbow-brick road through an institutional forest of monotone green walls and ceiling.

Cross was in his late fifties, a man of thinning hair and thickening middle. His watery gray eyes could grow sharp with command, though, and he was a hell of an analyst. Cross stopped outside a broad pale wood door. Kevin noticed the name slot was empty.

"This one's got 'Jane Doe' written all over her," said Cross, observing his glance. "She was briefly conscious on admission, but no one could get anything out of her."

Kevin took the clipboard Cross extended. "These her stats?" He whistled softly through his teeth while he studied it.

Cross studied him as intently. Shaggy, somehow Kevin Blake's generation always managed to look shaggy and friendly as an Old English sheepdog. Thirty-something. Bright as surgical steel but all geniality. This particular model had longish brown hair, a not too offensive beard, an endless propensity for blue jeans no matter what the occasion, matching blue eyes that were sharp as a tack and twice as penetrating, and a totally laid-back manner over one of the keenest psychoanalytical intelligences Cross had ever become infuriated with: too damn radical and too often right.

Kevin glanced up suddenly and gauged the intensity of his scrutiny. Cross didn't bother to hide it.

"Why does a brilliant young shrink like you get into a cul-de-sac like Probe?" Cross asked abruptly. "We all know why I ended up a desk jockey. But you . . . The money's comparatively rotten and you don't like our sponsors and the cases are usually downers."

"Why do some doctors specialize in cancer? It's the thrill of the remission, maybe."

"Hmmmm, and the agony of defeat, as likely. Interesting personality type, the against-all-odds doctor. Strong ego."

"Healthy ego, Doctor," Kevin corrected, returning his eyes to the medical report. He flicked the top sheet. "You haven't officially tagged her a Doe. I can see why. If she lives, it'll be a miracle. A hundred and one pounds, suffering from exposure . . . Found on a scenic overlook in a quiet little rural Minnesota town. Signs of sexual attack?''

"Nothing obvious.''

"What's this? Mention of rictus sardonicus. A corpselike grin. Mysteriouser and mysteriouser. I assume the lady is no longer smiling now that Probe's got its hands on her.'' Kevin glanced up and nailed his boss with a look. "I stay in Probe to lend some humanity to your little military-industrial-funded mind-unraveling unit, Doctor. The best research in the world means nothing if you don't put it into a human context.''

"Lord, Dr. Blake.'' Cross laughed suddenly. "Our favorite argument, even at five A.M. You're made for this work. And you are the best with these fragile cases, you know. This one will take all the humanity you've got, Doctor. I have a feeling that when you find out where this girl's been, you won't believe it.''

"Then let's get on with it,'' suggested Kevin, tucking the clipboard under his elbow.

Cross's hand halted Kevin's white-coated arm just as he was about to push his way into the hospital room.

"Wait a bit on the Doe. There's . . . I'd like you to see the police officer who found her first. He was sent down here with her in the ambulance. Actually, in front of her in the ambulance. Wouldn't ride up back even though she was unconscious. There was a tragic accident when they found her, delayed getting her medical attention even longer. Squad car exploded. This man's partner was killed. At the moment, he's a worse trauma victim than she is. . . .''

Kevin's hands jammed into his lab coat pockets in mock resignation. "Gee, you get me all ready to meet my blind date and then pull a substitution. Look, Norbert, accident survivors don't need Probe-level attention. Couldn't one of the house shrinks see him?''

"I'd like you to be in on this all the way, Kevin. The guy might know something, and I have a feeling it's going to be a long haul before you can pin any name other than Jane Doe on her."

Chapter Three

Cross and his ominous croakings left Kevin at another anonymous door down the hall. Kevin pushed his way into the darkened hospital room. It was a double with only one occupant—a man who seemed absurdly young and healthy for a sickroom.

Checking the chart at the bed's foot, Kevin read both his name and that of the tranquilizer now acting in him. Damn, why were they always so quick to tranq an interesting case? He liked the undrugged psyche better; it could cure itself a lot faster.

"I'm Dr. Blake." Kevin came around to stand by the bedside. "Officer . . . Kel*lee*hay."

"*Kell*ehay," the man corrected. It never failed, mispronounce people's names and they get all interested in rectifying your mistake and forget what was upsetting them. Of course, you couldn't do that with a Jane Doe. There wasn't even that recognition factor there.

"I understand you've had a bad shock," Kevin said conversationally, apparently much more interested in taking the pulse than hearing the answer.

"Shock," Kellehay repeated with indifferent, tranquilized bitterness. "Matusek dead, blown up like a firecracker, and that grinning thing, her—with her wild eyes and so thin and dirty, like someone dead. She is dead, isn't she, Doctor?"

19

He sat up, agitated despite the drug. "She ought to be dead."

Kevin's pulse-taking hand tightened powerfully around Kellehay's wrist. "Lie back, officer. You'll be all right. I understand your partner died—an explosion . . ."

"Yes. An explosion. Two, actually. One when she looked at him. Then the gas tank blew. I knew about that, about shorts in the taillight and your gas tank'll go. I didn't know about her. I wish I hadn't of said stop at McDonald's and we can stay ten-seven on the air; I wish we'd of gone and eaten at the damn greasy spoon on Main Street. . . . Someone else would've gotten it—the call. It was nothing. The big zero. There was nothing up there, Doctor, nothing. Except those eyes, that smile. . . . Hell, it sounds like some goddamn golden oldie. Hey, I'll be all right. I gotta get outa here, back home. Good ole Sarge. I don't even think he saw it comin'. Zapped by a dead woman. I'll never forget her face—so filthy and strong. Someone made her that way. That's the crime of the thing. Awful, it was awful."

Officer Kellehay put his face in his hands and wept.

Kevin went to the window. It wasn't much use questioning a drunken man, and strong emotion combined with strong drugs produced a sort of psychic drunk. He drew the imitation-slubbed-silk beige drapes open. A pale morning glow was turning the Mississippi slightly molten as it curved past the University of Minnesota. Kevin could see the white, wedding-cake bulk of the theater department showboat softly riding the mellow water.

What was it like to have a partner and have him die like a shish kebab flambé? What was it like to have to go out at night and find starved, naked, dirty young women in the bushes, victims of who-knows-what barbarity? It struck him that Officer Kellehay was a kind of probe, too, an ill-prepared investigator of the body human at its most inhumane. No wonder the emotions fractured like bone under too much pressure. . . .

20

Kevin turned back to the room. Kellehay was watching him now, awaiting judgment. His young face was faintly pink; he needed a good dose of Crow Wing without Jane Doe.

"You'll be all right, officer," Kevin pronounced with physicianly confidence. "You've had a shock. . . ."

"Are you going to see *her,* too?"

"Yes. It's my case."

"Then you're going to have a shock, too," said Officer Kellehay with sudden stabbing maliciousness, as if resenting all the white-coated confidence that sprang from the hospital environs like a whiff of carbolic acid. "That's *my* diagnosis."

Kellehay lay back; perhaps having delivered this curse transferred it. He lay back calm and collected and Kevin went out into the corridor with a twinge of foreboding. How could one unfortunate, helpless young woman spawn such unlikely venom?

He found Cross waiting at the nurses' station.

"Well?"

Kevin shrugged. "Guy's had a shock. He'll pull out of it. A bit obsessive about our Doe, though. Know why? And by the way, when do I get to see the main act?"

"Now," promised Cross, starting down the hall. "She was a mess, you know. Naked in name only she was so covered with caked-on dirt, stiff with exposure—a holy mess. No wonder she scared the boy." Cross paused at the first door again, oddly hesitant. "Don't let her scare you."

"No chance," Kevin said, pushing through the swinging door, his hand spread on the brushed aluminum plate that prevented fingerprints. . . . But he felt a certain unpleasant tingle, as if he'd just been invited to take a personal inspection tour of Auschwitz. Nobody relished the results of man's inhumanity to man, or, more commonly, woman. Being a doctor, being a psychiatrist, was no shield against just plain seeing too much of it. . . . He was curious to see her now, yes. . . . Curious, and a bit reluctant.

Another double room, another lone occupant. He drew the drapes again, halfway, to let a bright bar of morning light fall across the bed with its plain, pale hospital linens. The form that lay there was pathetically flat, the sharp promontories of bones carving shadows in the thin bedspread. He braced himself and went to regard the face on the pillow.

She lay like an Egyptian prince in a sarcophagus, head perfectly centered, hands crossed on her stomach. Her eyes were closed. He studied her with increasing interest. She was thin, in the almost neurotic way that ballerinas are thin—all hollow beneath the bone, a sexless sort of aesthetic thinness that would set a fashion photographer slavering. . . . Her hair was dark, but cropped very short. Her breathing, remarkably, was regular—the long, delicate hands moved slightly up and down on a shallow rhythm. Her color was poor, whitewashed, but her nails weren't blue. They were short, like the nails of those who chew them off past the top moons. But these weren't bitten; they were smooth-ended, as if they'd been manicured. An IV dripped silently into her left arm. He worried about her circulation and put the arm down at her side. It immediately returned to its folded position. He studied her face again—straight nose, well-molded forehead, chin and, of course, cheekbones forever. Her eyelashes were quite short and thick, or perhaps simply looked that way on her candle-wax complexion.

She reminded him of nothing so much as Joan of Arc about to be carried to her burning pyre—but that was the cropped hair, of course, and the ascetic's thinness. . . .

He was suddenly aware that what was abnormal was his reaction to her, rather than any abnormality in her. Despite all he had heard, all he had reason to dread, he found one overpowering impression wiping out every circumstance of her existence and her condition.

She was beautiful.

Her eyes opened slowly, under the curve of heavy lashes.

22

"Hello, Jane," he said. "I'm your doctor. Dr. Blake. I'm going to take care of you."

He knew even before he said it that there was no possibility of her being anything other than a Jane Doe; that there was no name he superseded in her consciousness by giving her this clichéd baptism of anonymity. And he felt impelled to extend her some instant rope of recognition, so he could watch her personality flounder in its amnesiac sea with his scientific conscience at peace.

"Jane," she said flatly, like a person savoring something perfectly tasteless. "Jane," she repeated. Her eyes shut again. She would think about it.

It wasn't until ten o'clock that Kevin got a chance to think about the new Jane Doe, and that was over an uninspired tray of watery vegetable soup, egg custard and coffee in the hospital cafeteria.

"Contemplating your navel, Doctor, or only what experimental vat your lunch came from?"

Kevin looked up. "You can do better at the cafeteria line, you're welcome to try. Danish? Not exactly nutritionally recommended, Kandy. It's gonna ruin your lean athletic build."

"Eat your heart out, Captain Carrot." Martin Kandinsky, a human pretzel in a white lab coat with an incendiary beard and hair the texture of crepe hair tied back into a ponytail, jackknifed his angles onto the molded plastic chair next to Kevin's. He bit sensuously into the half-inch-thick white goo frosting an obscenely outsized pastry.

Kevin laughed and pushed away his lukewarm soup; at least the coffee was steaming hot. He leaned back and watched Kandinsky consume. Kandinsky was fascinatingly ugly—the typical picture of a socially maladjusted shrink with a dash of sixties lack of couth mixed in. It was a strangely trustworthy façade the combination produced. He was known as Kandy to patients, friends and probably his landlady. More formally, he was called the Czar Confessor.

23

"What's got you here at this tender hour, Kevin?" Kandy finally asked, wiping frosting from his generous lips with a napkin.

"You know damn well I've been here since five A.M. on a new Doe. What else would bring you over from those fascinating Saturday admission sessions at student health?"

"Yeah, sure. We heard about her over there. Weird, man. The rumors are thicker than Mississippi mud, but any Probe case stirs up the natives. You're the glamour shrink around here, you know; all the distraught coeds would love to get on your case list."

"Bullshit. You know my bedside manner can't match your gloomy Ukrainian mesmerizing. . . . Seriously, Kandy, how much is out about her? She's in really bad shape; I'd like to keep the press off this one a little longer than the deprogramming victim—that one nearly blew Probe out of the water."

"Just the usual. 'Cept word around the halls is this one's a jinx. The 'Killer Doe,' they're callin' her."

"Je—sus." Kevin slammed his coffee mug down on impervious Formica. "Superstition lives at U Hospitals. God, I think of that pathetic frail creature, and I've got to go into and unravel her brain like a plateful of spaghetti and the 'normal' creeps out there decide *she's* dangerous. . . ."

"They didn't say she was dangerous, Kevin; just jinxed. I thought you should know. Ambulance crew is makin' points describing her as a 'mask of death' when they picked her up. 'Ghoulish,' they said. The white skirts are getting goose bumps everyplace but where it counts over it."

"That does it, then; extra wraps on this one. The last scoop involving Probe nearly got the whole program dumped. Deprogramming cult members is chancy enough when Ted Patrick does it; when a respectable shrink at an eminent medical facility tries it, there's hell and headlines to pay," Kevin added a bit bitterly. "Thanks for the tip, I'll go tighten 'security.' "

"Hey, that's all right. But don't flatter yourself—"

"Huh?" Kevin paused in leaving to see Kandinsky hovering over his untouched egg custard.

"Respectable?" Kandy arched one shaggy eyebrow over the curve of his thick, rimless glasses. "Nobody as smart as you is ever respectable, kiddo. Can I have your custard?" he asked consideringly, his spoon slicing the cinnamon-dusted surface with surgeonly precision.

"You can have it framed, for all I care," retorted Kevin with a backward wave; he was already bolting for the cubbyhole of his office. If he wanted absolute control of this one, he'd have to make a good pitch for it at the special Probe intake meeting at four. . . .

He stopped by the unlabeled room; it was dim still and resonant with the even breathing of the unconscious and the slow melodic drip of the IV's clear plastic tunnel. Jane Doe was in the same position as he'd last seen her. He took her pulse, maybe just to convince himself that she was real. Slow and steady, almost mechanically rhythmic. He let out the breath he'd been holding and put her left arm down by her side.

It automatically folded itself back across her stomach.

Chapter Four

"Okay, Kevin, what have we got here?"

Cross chaired the meeting, but Kevin knew there was no kidding himself; what Matthews, the Probe internist, and Swanson, the Probe research psychologist, thought was equally important. Kevin decided to try a judicious bit of overkill.

"Trouble," he answered weightily. "We've got trouble right here in River City. It rhymes with 'T' and it starts with

'D' and it stands for 'Doe.' Enough musical comedy. This is a delicate case; we've got to keep this Doe under wraps until she's strong enough for a full Probe work-up.''

"Hmmm." One of Cross's typically incisive responses to challenge. "What do you think, Roger, you're the only one who's had a real look at her?''

"A cursory examination at best, Norbert. Just to get the geography right so we could treat her. She's weak, but should survive—physically, I think. No signs of what you'd call foul play, drugs . . .''

"No, only three-quarters dead,'' Kevin murmured to his yellow legal pad, making blue ballpoint spirals in the shape of DNA molecules.

"You want to sit in on the rest of the examinations, Doctor?'' Roger Matthews asked sharply.

"Kevin? . . .'' Cross took this case seriously; he was being even more formal than usual about these staff fandangos.

Kevin shook his head. "I'll rely on your reports, Roger. If I'm going to crack through the Great Wall of China in her head, I've got to leave her some physical room, some privacy; otherwise she'll have no ground of her own on which to meet me. Her memory may be a blank screen up to now, but from here on, we're day one.''

"Bravo, Dr. Blake,'' seconded Swanson, a wire-brush-scrubbed-looking woman in her midforties who usually did all she could to disagree with him. "It's nice to see one of you medical detectives resisting the urge to poke and probe at all opportunity. I take it you want total responsibility, as usual?''

"Right on, Swannee,'' said Kevin with a grin. "You do read my mind. No wonder you're our crack parapsychological researcher.''

Swanson laughed a little self-consciously and jammed her pen back into the pocket of her lab coat.

Roger Matthews slid him a glance and a comment. "Your mind isn't that hard to read, Blake.''

26

It never failed; Matthews had to drag his feet out of the sheer perversity of seniority, and Swanson, that highly educated piece of medical starch and structure, longed for the benediction of med school camaraderie. Usually Kevin didn't stoop to applying any; but the Doe was too important for mere pride. He looked at Cross. What he decided would sway the others, if Cross would only decide. . . .

"You want to see this one totally through, then? It's why I called you in on it. . . ." Cross appeared to be reconsidering even this already accomplished step, his pale lips puckering rhythmically.

"What sort of police help can we count on?" Kevin asked impatiently.

"They're sending a city detective down to Crow Wing, that's all. We can't show foul play, which Roger pointed out—"

"Cop is dead," Matthews barked, as if annoyed at having his name invoked. "That's foul play right there."

"An unrelated accident. . . ." Kevin interjected quickly.

"Nothing to do with *our* investigation, surely," added Swanson frostily. Jeez, maybe he'd have to ask her out for a drink, after all.

"All right." Cross detected a majority opinion forming and rushed in to take advantage of it. "She's your baby, Kevin."

"Kevin's Baby Doe," smirked Swanson suddenly with a high-pitched giggle.

He flashed her what he supposed was a good-natured grimace while his pen arched triumphant spirals all across the page.

Matthews slapped his manila folder shut. "Well, I've got to give this baby a good going over before Dr. Blake can get his hands on her cerebellum. I'll let you know when I think she's strong enough for therapy."

Kevin nodded, careful not to say anything subversive while Cross and Matthews left, their conversation turning to their

27

golf handicaps and the condition of the greens at the Minikahda Club.

"Kevin, may I see you a minute?"

"Sure, Swannee."

"You know," she began, sitting against the table beside him before he could stand up. She took off the farsighted glasses that made her pale eyes swim like carp in the thick bowl of her lenses and tucked them in her breast pocket next to the pen. "We tend to get a bit too involved in our cases as cases here at Probe, Kevin. I'm concerned about that. A good part of our function should be pure research. It's the application of what brilliant young psychiatrists like yourself learn from exploring the most concealed regions of the human mind and its memory function that matters; not merely 'detective' work for the sake of it. I sometimes think you get too high on solving these people's problems, Kevin. You're doing it all for a reason, you know."

"I thought I knew the reasons I was doing it."

"Oh, maybe you do. But they might not be the same as the Probe program's. Or mine. With government funds dwindling, we've got to make sure that Probe does nothing that smacks of the, well, the lurid, the sensational."

Kevin's careful deadpan broke into another grin. "I wouldn't think of digging up anything lurid or sensational for your computers, Swannee. You'll have to find it on your own. May I suggest an adult bookstore?"

Her broad, pale face tightened, if that was possible. Out came the glasses and back came the enlarged floating eyes. Out also came the ballpoint. She jotted a meaningless squiggle on her notepad.

"Yes, well . . . I think you should have the go-ahead for now, Kevin, but I really can't endorse a prolonged investigation here. We've seen John and Jane Does before. There isn't that much to learn from the average amnesia victim. The Russians are into astral projection, remote viewing and telekinetic movement of objects. All you're trying to move in your Jane Doe is her memory, and that really only means something to her, doesn't it? Probe is not a charity, Kevin. Dr. Cross is too kind sometimes to point out certain realities to the younger doctors. You will take my intervention in the right spirit, I hope."

She finished, straightened, blinked brightly at him and smiled, colorless lips parting stiffly over yellowish teeth.

He stood soberly and took her hand.

"Dr. Swanson, I can only thank you for your advice, and your support. Pure research to the end, I swear it." He swept her fingers to his lips, bowed and ducked out of the room with his notepad carefully tucked doodle side in.

It was five o'clock and he was beat. He decided to avoid a last check on Jane Doe; he'd gotten her lock, stock, barrel and soul at the meeting, at least for a while, and he didn't want to blow it with too much mother-henship.

He did stop at one bland, unmarked door, though. His splayed fingers pushed it slowly open. Curtains wide, bed made and empty. Real relief played tag with his half-empty stomach. Good, released to the curative environs of Crow Wing, Officer Kellehay. Kevin felt momentarily guilty; perhaps the poor guy needed more than a quick dismissal. Finding a near dead girl and losing your partner in the same night weren't exactly soothing to the psyche. Still, policemen were trained to undergo that kind of unexpected stress and Kellehay was young. Young and bitter at the moment and likely to say irresponsible things about his irrational dislike of the Doe . . . Kevin's Doe. Kevin's Baby Jane Doe for as long as Swanson and Matthews and Cross would let him have control of the case, which might not be long enough.

Kevin swung out into the busy hall, long strides taking him past nurses rustling to and fro on their crepe soles to the rhythm of the bedpan. He passed the room where she lay without a glance. He nodded to passing people he knew—nurses, orderlies, the maintenance man.

He knew only two things: he was dead tired, and he was somehow more reassured by the departure of Officer Kellehay than he was by the fact that Jane Doe remained, and remained as his patient. If he hadn't been so tired, he would have worried more about it.

Chapter Five

He hadn't gone.

It had been so easy. Hospitals are like that; they don't expect their rules to be broken. They don't expect patients to leave without being discharged, and they don't expect discharged patients to *not* leave. . . .

He had avoided the visitors' cafeteria, the lobby, the end-of-hall lounging areas, anywhere he might encounter Blake. Blake was the only person who might recognize him, tie him in with—her. Blake was the only one who might suspect something. He was sharp, that doctor, but not sharp enough to see through *her*.

Right now he was fairly safe on the emergency stairwell. Anyone who used it would find just a uniformed officer on a brisk tour—not an unusual sight in a hospital that housed a whole floor of the violently mentally ill, not to mention a psychiatric trauma unit. All that high-powered hardware, and yet all they could give him was a pill and a pulse-taking and a pat on the head. Matusek hadn't gotten even that. Why couldn't they *see*? She was wrong, all wrong. He was only a hick cop, but he'd sensed it from the first. Now, he was someone to be shoveled out of the way while *she* hogged the spotlight.

Kellehay sat on the second from the bottom step at the

landing between floors four and five and hugged his knees. It had been hard to think since the shocks of the Crow Wing bluff, less than twenty-four hours ago. It was always the same. Matusek had warned him. But no, he hadn't listened, not with his college degree and his up-to-date liberalism. Matusek had been right. They always took the side of the "disadvantaged"—of the crazy and the clever and the colored and the alien—against a cop. Have a little trouble with Cuban refugees at the internment camp near Crow Wing, and it's police brutality. Bust some smirking drug dealer and it's insufficient evidence. Stumble over a goddamn human bomb who blows your partner to kingdom come—and it's poor Jane Doe; she's harmless, and what's the matter, officer, strain of your job getting to you?

His hands were wringing each other and he carefully separated them. He was hungry. Hadn't had anything since lunch yesterday. Matusek had eaten his quarter-pounder. . . . Matusek. Kellehay checked the big serviceable Timex on his wrist. Almost time. Two-thirds through the seven P.M. to three A.M. shift should do it. He didn't dare risk even a raid on a candy machine. He had to keep out of sight. So what if he was hungry? They said the big cats hunted better on an empty stomach. Maybe he would, too.

"How's she doing?" asked the night desk nurse.

"Same. But Blake'd have my head if I didn't check on her anyway."

"That's one M.D. who could have *my* head anytime."

"He wouldn't want it," returned the floor nurse, leaning on the elbow-high counter. "He's too smart to fraternize with nurses. It sure ain't like the soap operas." She sighed, tucking her flaxen hair absently under her cap. The night floor nurse was a buxom young Swede, and did just fine with most of the hospital staff, from panting orderlies to the younger doctors. The night desk nurse was plainer, older and liked to dream about the impossible.

"Still," she went on, "you're baby-sitting his prize patient; he's got to notice you."

Neither of the women basking in the fluorescent glow of the nurses' station and their own incandescent daydreams noticed the navy shadow that slipped through the door under the lurid red "Exit" sign at the hall's far end.

Like most hospital hallways, this one was wide and echoing, but Officer Kellehay walked with silent rapidity, clinging to the mint-green institutional walls. Every so often he ducked into the shadow of a doorway while the door's hospital-soft hinges *whooshed* him in—and out again after a quick perusal. He was nearing the once distant nurses, but their capped heads were bowed together in mutual boredom. The floor nurse was advising the night desk nurse to get her brown hair streaked. The word "frosted" drifted to the advancing shadow.

They were all nicely sleeping-pilled, the patients; Kellehay's stealthy appraisals didn't even stir them. It would be different with the nurses, if he had to go too near . . . He slipped into another shadowy room, so like the one before it, and focused on the figure on the bed—yes! And drugged like the others. He tiptoed to the wide window, naked of the skyline of floral offerings that had decked the other rooms. Who would send flowers to *her*? The single visitor's chair was bulky and heavy. Kellehay had just made the police height requirement, so brute strength wasn't his long suit. Still, he managed to lug it to the door without banging its legs on the bedframe or the ajar bathroom door. He jammed it under the doorknob with relief and turned to the room again.

It was by her unbelievable thinness he had recognized her. No other patient made so flat a profile in the hospital linens. He went to the window and pulled back the drapes. The night hissed open before him with theatrical suddenness, fluorescent pools of light glowing UFO-green in the parking lot below, on the building's shrubbery-set brick corners. An equally fluorescent full moon rode the top of the big rectangular window. It was a bright night, a city night—not nearly as dark as it had been out on the Crow Wing blufftop . . . Kellehay turned, bracing himself for seeing her—it—better.

She was light-bathed all right; he could even see her breathing stir the light cotton-weave blanket tucked with nurselike care up to her neck. She wasn't grimy anymore, but white as the linens around her. A thin translucent snake charmed its way from her left arm up to a bottle hung from a stand. For her, the thin thread of life; for Matusek, fiery death. For Kellehay, dismissal. He stepped nearer, bracing himself for the glint of teeth between caked, stretched lips. No smile this time. His hands uncurled.

They clenched again when he saw that she had two pillows. There. So easy. She was in bad shape; he'd heard the murmur of it out in the hall. So natural that she'd be took sudden in the night. Happened all the time to old folks. Then he wouldn't have to worry so much about what had happened on the bluff, about what he had found. . . .

He gently pulled one end of the extra pillow to him. Only a corner was actually under her head, which rolled a bit as he tugged. Kellehay froze, his heart hitting his chest wall in great, uneven thumps, like a big, angry fist knocking. But she was drugged. This time she wouldn't wake, look, do anything. He had only to press the limp pillow to her sleeping face and keep it there. There probably wouldn't even be a struggle. He leaned across the serving table that projected an ironing-board-like arm over the bed. It was in the way a bit, but he wouldn't move it until he was sure the pillow had begun to take effect. He would do his duty and go home and there would be no questions. He pressed down on both sides of her face, forcing the pillow to meet its mate under her head, moving his fists closer once she was safely shrouded from his sight by three inches of polyester batting. . . .

He felt it the instant the cotton pillowcase touched her skin, an almost electric sensation, charged, just an odd little tingle up his straining arms. She knew.

The serving table arm spun into his gut with vicious force, rolled him right across the tiled floor and slammed him against the wall, his head ramming into a framed print hung there. He heard the glass grind into a shattered web behind his head and felt the blow's instant headache begin.

One arm clutched to his bruised stomach, he shoved the table away and waited for his breath to come in something better than ragged bursts. Damn bitch had caught him napping and kicked the cart at him. Who would have thought she was that strong?

The pillow was off her head, thrown to the floor, but he couldn't be sure he hadn't done that himself in his surprise. . . . She was lying as before, a pale figure on a paler rectangle of bed lit by moonlight. But her eyes were open, her damn staring eyes. He saw the white glisten and wished he could use his gun.

Kellehay pushed himself off the wall with one arm and edged warily to the other side of the bed. Her eyes followed him. She might have been paralyzed for all the movement she showed. All right. Good enough. It was tougher to drown a kitten that looked at you, but if it was for everybody's good, including its own . . .

"What did you do to Matusek?" He was surprised to hear the question explode from his mouth. He expected nothing from her, unlike Blake, least of all answers. "You did something," he accused, and felt better for it in some dim way. "How did you get Matusek?"

Her head had turned on the pillow to watch him, an even, slow rotation that unnerved him. She watched him like a dog that waits for its master to make clear what he wants, except there was no question in her eyes, only watching.

But he couldn't keep from edging closer, couldn't stop the questions. He wanted to know—before. He was insane maybe to do this, maybe they'd get him for it, but it had to be done. So it would be nice if he knew—there, his breath was back to

34

normal, he was up to doing what he had to do again. Maybe an answer wasn't so important.

His foot stumbled against the steel leg of the IV stand; he bit his dry lips to hold back the automatic curses. He shoved it away with his foot, brushed the thin plastic tube from her arm like a cobweb he was dislodging. Her arm moved then, at the shock of separation, and he caught her bony wrist in his hand, hard.

"You won't need that where you're going, back to wherever you came from." He had the other pillow, eased from under her head, and she wasn't that strong; her wrist felt like it would crumble in his fist—

The warning shock thrummed up his arm, like an injection of energy. His lips opened to mouth a protest. The metal IV tree came crashing down, hard against the side of his nose. He was on the floor, his face numbed and throbbing, the unit tangled in his legs. He got up slowly, keeping his eyes on the bedstead's even white horizon.

She was sitting up now, as stiff and unreal as a corpse come to life, her dark eyes pits in her hollowed face. For the first time, Kellehay was afraid of her for a reason he could out-and-out name. He thought she could kill him. But how, how?

He stood and watched her, his head lowered, hands loose on coiled arm muscles. A rush—now?

This time he didn't even get near enough to touch her. The familiar shock repelled him; he was slammed sideways against the bathroom door, the knob punching into his kidneys. This time his fall made an untidy noise as the door rebounded against the doorstop.

He lurched forward again, intent on wringing her skinny white neck until her staring eyes bugged right out of her head. He was utter rage and certainty and no restraints now. There was only one consequence he feared: that she should live. He charged the bed, ignoring the oncoming chatter of alarmed nurses.

She was finally shrinking against the high hospital head-board, looking pathetic and innocent, but it was too late for self-defense. Her eyes were as wide and watching as ever.

He wondered why she didn't scream.

Chapter Six

Kevin was hunting, which was odd, because he hated blood sports. But then, this was a dream, and even as he recognized the inappropriateness of the activity, he accepted it. He carried a long gun, but somehow knew it was loaded with tranquilizer darts, not live ammunition. If he remembered the dream when he awoke, he could analyze the nicety of his subconscious for putting harmless ammunition into his dream gun.

He was in the north woods; black-green trees fenced him in and brittle, needleless pine branches crackled underfoot. He was stalking something, something that always rustled a bit to the right and ahead, out of sight. He was afraid—no, anxious.

It sprang into his dream range of vision, like a trap springs on an unsuspecting animal—poised, unmoving except for the quick, animal panting of its furred sides—the deer. Deer stood as still as rabbits when alerted to danger, their neat, white-lined ears flicked back, the liquid eyes as calm and regal as a sphinx's. . . . This deer had a particularly liquid brown gaze; its delicate face and legs seemed carved out of some satiny wood. Kevin raised the rifle to his shoulder, aimed between the slanted watching eyes and pulled the trigger even as he wondered why he took such lethal aim with so harmless a weapon. . . .

A dreamy sort of recoil, then blue smoke—but tranquilizer

guns didn't spout smoke, few guns did nowadays. . . . The deer was gone; from the undergrowth an enraged pheasant spiraled up into the looming pines, shrieking outrage again and again. . . .

It was still shrilling its warning when he realized that forest and gun had melted away and that he heard instead the siren song of Ma Bell at his bedside table. Kevin managed to both check his watch and catch the phone before it rang again. One A.M.? Not again.

"Yeah?" Sitting groggily on the bed's edge, his shoulder stiff. Maybe that's why he had been dreaming about guns and recoil.

"It's Sylvia McClusky, the night nurse on the fifth floor, Doctor. You better come down right away. There's been a bad accident."

"Accident?" He was disoriented, catapulted back to his medical residency days of twenty-four-hour emergency call.

"I'm sorry, Doctor; we kept a regular eye on her. It was quite a freak thing. . . . It's your Jane Doe."

The woman sounded shaken, he could tell that now. Kevin jammed his legs into the crumpled jeans at his feet and started working them up as he stood, wedging the phone between his shoulder and jaw.

"What is it? Damn it, what's happened?"

"That's just it. We, we don't know for sure. You'd better come over—"

He was hanging up before she finished, forcing his feet into the nearest shoes—tennis, it happened—and throwing on a T-shirt. The car parked behind his restored condominium was his one sop to a doctor's vanity—a sleek 1976 Jaguar, forest green. The color reminded him momentarily of his dream. He hurled himself behind the wheel and gunned into the night, unmindful for once of neighbors' ears. It only took minutes to arrive at the hospital lot, full as usual. He screeched the Jag into the nearest yellow zone and wrenched down the

37

visor with its special medical parking permit attached by rubber bands.

Rotating red lights washed the back wall of one hospital wing. The ambulance, its backward letters made for seeing in rearview mirrors branded on his brain like ominous hieroglyphics, throbbed before the side entrance. Its rear backed up to the sidewalk and narrow strip of grass alongside the building, no hopeful sign of false alarm.

Kevin felt anxiety wash from his throat to his feet. He stared up at the fifth floor and saw a black ragged hole in one window. It looked like lake ice does after something has gone through it.

Adrenaline pumped through him before the immobilizing worry could surge back up through his legs and drown him. He ran straight for the ambulance, and around it, dread tightening its grip on his throat.

The men convened around an empty circle on the ground; not empty—a chalk figure was sketched on the grass that looked half-black in the artificial glare. Two attendants were wheeling a sheet-covered stretcher to the ambulance. Kevin knew with a physician's certainty that no live body could lie in quite that assemblage of angles. He stopped them with a gesture and put his hand on the sheet top. He could almost see a puff of blue smoke before his eyes, could feel some emotion recoiling into his left shoulder with stunning force. . . . Lost, so soon. He remembered that he wasn't left-handed and yanked back the sheet and stared down.

It was Kellehay, looking placid and dead with his bones clearly smashed to smithereens in their sack of flesh.

Kevin wordlessly waved on the attendants. After a moment's shocked pause, he bolted for the door and up the stairs, not even bothering to go into the hall and ring for an elevator. They were notoriously slow, anyway. He exploded through the door into the fifth floor to find a dark official figure on duty halfway down the hall.

"Hey, wait a minute! Where do you think you're going?" it demanded as he tried to spring past.

Kevin gestured beyond the policeman.

"Inside. My patient." His words came in breathless gasps. He saw the officer take in his T-shirt—Christ, it was the marijuana one—his jeans, his beard. "I'm Dr. Blake—"

"Oh, yeah." The man's hand, pressed to his chest to restrain him, dropped away from the legend "Cannabis Rex." He jerked his head toward the room. "They called you. G'wan in."

Kevin edged past into a room made tiny by the number of people in it—three men by the window, a nurse by the foot of the bed and on the bed . . .

"Oh, my God."

One man turned at the sound of his involuntary exclamation.

"You Blake?"

"That's right."

"Don't be so impatient," said the man, somehow detaining Kevin from rushing to the bed by the force of his presence. "I've got a few questions. Detective Smith, downtown division. This your patient?"

"Yeah, since about this time yesterday."

"What do you mean?"

"Look, this is a psychological trauma ward. The patients on this floor are all very—delicate. I need to examine my patient."

The detective narrowed his eyes for a moment, then folded his notebook shut and nodded. Kevin moved quickly to the bedside, the nurse automatically in his wake.

"You found her like this?" He glanced at the nurse and recalled her, recalled the customary diamond flash on her left hand. "Mrs. McClusky, isn't it?"

"Yes, Doctor. I'm always on nights, so we haven't worked together. . . ."

"It looks like we will now, Mrs. McClusky. And?"

"This is how I, we—Kristin Johrdahl was with me—found her. We heard a terrible noise . . ."

"What kind of noise?" interjected Smith.

"If you don't mind, I'll do my medical interrogation first," said Kevin crisply. "Yes, Mrs. McClusky? . . ."

"It was about forty minutes ago. The room was a mess, the window broken, and she was like that."

"With the IV torn out of her arm?"

"Yes. The stand was knocked over."

The detective came to the foot of the bed. They were all silent as Kevin gently picked up a wrist and held it for the sweep of a second hand around his gold watch face.

The detective shook his head. "She looks like that Quinlan girl is supposed to. Same thing?"

"No," said Kevin abruptly. "No coma. And she was all right—well, much better—earlier."

They stared at the figure on the bed. She was curled into a fetal position against the headboard, fingers curved into her palms, arms jackknifed into her body, narrow legs drawn up. Her eyes were closed and she was unconscious.

"Look, I know this is a hospital, Dr. Blake, but I'm a cop and there's some guy outside as limp as a bag of French fries and I gotta find out how he got that way."

Kevin didn't take his eyes from the bed. "There *was* a guy outside," he said absently. "They were hauling him away when I came. . . . I've got to get her to another room," he decided.

"Wait just a minute there. I'm not sure I want this room disturbed. I've got a photographer coming. . . ."

"The room will still be here."

"But *she* won't—"

"For God's sake, do you think she'd make a reliable witness, the state she's in?"

"She might be more than a witness, Doctor."

Kevin faced the man. Smith was big and beefy with blunt features, typical prime-time television, big-city cop. He didn't look dumb, though. Kevin lowered his voice and stepped nearer.

"I'm just concerned about doing my job, same as you. She's an amnesiac in a state of malnutrition, weighs barely a hundred pounds; she's been in this hospital less than twenty-four hours. If there's anything she's involved in, it can't have much to do with your man outside. Let me get her cared for, and then I'll cooperate until you OD on it."

The detective nodded and Kevin shot the nurse a glance.

"I, uh, imagine, Doctor, we'll have to find some orderlies," she responded, "and a gurney. I doubt we can straighten her out enough for a wheelchair. If you'll just wait, I'll—"

Kevin snorted and leaned forward to gather up the Doe. Slight as she was, she was heavy; he wasted no time in brushing by the stunned nurse and backing out into the hall.

The commotion had attracted a minor crowd of staff. He strode through them, aware that he was adding to the Blake legendry; it was a severe breach of hospital etiquette to move a patient so directly, no matter what the circumstances. Kevin shouldered his way through the first unlabeled door and brought the Doe to the empty bed, furious at hospital hideboundness, sick at the deterioration necessary to have caused this physical shrinking into herself, always the worst possible sign of mental retreat. . . .

Her limbs had relaxed a bit against him. As he transferred her weight to the bed, he noticed with relief that her body fell into a more normal position. Startled, he glimpsed her dark eyes as he bent over, an actual, deliberate glance at himself through veiling lashes. She looked as sleepy and self-satisfied with herself as a kitten; then her lids closed again, leaving him strangely disturbed.

McClusky had summoned sense enough to follow him with the IV and came clattering in, trailing equipment. Kevin pulled the light cord above the bed.

"Oh, she's looking much better already," breathed the nurse.

41

"That's why I wanted her out of that room. Upheaval can distress a fragile patient—even when unconscious," he emphasized. But he was not so sure she was completely unconscious. That one look had been as perfectly timed to strike him just as he laid her down as if it had been engineered by a Southern belle. It nagged at him. It was the equivalent of a wink. It was knowing, that was it, and by definition, a Jane Doe knew nothing.

"That's all right, Mrs. McClusky. You need to get back to the desk. I'll hook her up." He reinserted the IV, taped it down, pulled up the covers. If she wasn't totally unconscious . . . He leaned closer and put his hand on her face.

"It's all right, Jane. It's Dr. Blake. You're going to be all right. I'll take care of you." Perhaps some message of reassurance would leak through. But there was no response of any kind, not even a tremor of those thick lashes. He sighed, straightened, started thinking about what to tell the detective, adjusted her arm atop the covers. He paused, chilled.

There were the beginnings of several bruises around her wrist, the flesh just starting to discolor. It wouldn't have shown up so quickly except for her extreme thinness and translucent skin. Kellehay *had* touched her, attacked her in some way. It wasn't just simple suicide and simply coincidence. . . .

Kevin carefully put the bruised wrist under the covers and turned off the light before leaving.

Chapter Seven

"Any place around here a man can smoke?" was the first question on Smith's mind.

Kevin led him to the grouped vinyl-upholstered chairs at hall's end, where Smith sank into one until the cushion exhaled a protest under his bulk. He lit a filter tip and shook out the match. "Should quit. Smoking. Know it's bad for you, but we all gotta do something bad, right, Doctor?"

"That's more your line of work than mine." Kevin lounged in the corner of a tweed-covered sofa.

"Both of our lines of work get us out at all hours, I guess," Smith mulled, blowing smoke past lazy hazel eyes.

Kevin leaned forward. "Look, uh . . . what do I call you—Detective Smith, Mr. Smith? . . ."

"First name's Lucius." He grinned. "Folks had to make up for the Smith, I suppose. I go by Luke. What's your first handle?"

"Kevin." This Smith carefully noted down. "Blake, spelled as in Robert."

"Oh, yeah. *Baretta*. See the reruns. What's your title here?"

"I'm a resident in psychiatry, University of Minnesota Hospitals, attached to the Probe unit."

"Probe . . ." Smith exhaled thoughtfully. "That's the outfit was in all the papers—yeah, the *Star-Trib* had a big thing on it. That cult member whose parents had him snatched and brought here to deprogram. Hey, was that you?"

"I worked with that patient, yes. . . ." Kevin smiled boyishly, a strategy equally disarming to both sexes, its success owed to honest blue eyes and long study of the devious human psyche. "That's another time our professions crossed swords. The legality of the parents' right to take the young man got to be quite an issue. The police finally were involved."

Smith squinted, maybe to atone for his lack of comment. "Now on this case, Doctor. We got a guy took a dive out the fifth-floor window in a policeman's uniform. None of our boys recognize him—"

"They wouldn't. He's from outstate. Crow Wing."

"You know the deceased?"

"Officer John Kellehay of Crow Wing. He was in the hospital briefly about twenty-four hours ago, suffering from shock after the death of his partner in a squad car explosion. . . ."

Smith leaned forward to smash out his cigarette in the oversized ceramic tray.

"Crow Wing, sure. We heard about that. Tragic accident, veteran officer. Say, that gal in there, she wasn't that naked woman they found up in Crow Wing?"

Kevin winced and tried not to show it. There were worse things to call women than "gals"; he supposed it was better than "broad." It was hard to think of the Doe as anything so commonplace, yet emphasizing her rarity was dangerous now.

"Yup, that was Probe's latest Jane Doe. We haven't had much time to work with her; that's why I was so distressed that this accident had worsened her condition."

"You think it's an accident?"

"What else would it be?"

"Killing."

Kevin was silent awhile. "And the Doe was the only one in the room with him. . . . Look, Smith, I haven't had a lot of time to think about this." He rolled his wrist to check his watch and saw the gold of it impress the detective as nothing else on his person had. "Less than an hour ago I was asleep. But I'll tell you what I think happened, based on my experi-

44

ence of the human psyche, and my brief exposure to Officer Kellehay's particular variation of it."

Smith's felt-tip pen was poised as Kevin stretched out his denimed legs and folded his hands over his stomach under "Cannabis Rex." But he spoke with a doctor's authority, and Smith listened intently.

"Kellehay was upset over his partner's death, so much so that he was sent with the Jane Doe in the ambulance to the Twin Cities to get some psychological first aid. I saw him. He was pretty racked up. Understandable; it was a violent explosion and there was nothing he could even try to do. . . . Guilt can be a sort of parasite of the psyche. I released him, told him to go home, take it easy, think it out. I'm afraid he was more unstable than I thought. I think he somehow associated the Jane Doe with, uh, being a witness to something he couldn't face. So I think he came to her hospital room and, in his confusion and despair, made her a witness to his suicide as well."

Smith nodded, mulling it over. He shut his notebook, capped the felt tip.

"Yeah, it fits. Funny thing, though; most jumpers are fussy about opening windows before diving through 'em. You'd think a few cuts wouldn't faze them when you figure what's ahead of 'em. But it does. Those that go for the windows would never use a razor or a gun. . . . Well, thanks, Doctor." Smith stood, the action pulling Kevin to his feet, too. "You're probably right. But I'll have to go the full route. Talk to your Doe tomorrow."

"If she's better tomorrow, sure. But good luck."

"Oh?"

Kevin looked amused. "I haven't gotten more than one word out of her yet. I'm not altogether certain that she does talk."

"That's okay." Smith's smile showed a chipped tooth. "That's another thing our jobs have in common; I'm used to getting my patients to talk, too. Night, now."

Smith ambled back to the room where lightninglike flashes indicated photographs were being taken. Kevin wouldn't have been surprised to hear thunder, too. Something was building up to quite a storm. It would take delicate handling to keep his Jane Doe from getting caught out smack in the middle of it.

Chapter Eight

"Got a minute?" Roger Matthews's thinning-haired head poked around Kevin's office door, a telltale manila folder in the hand that hesitated on the doorjamb.

Kevin swiveled his chair from the window, where he'd been ostensibly contemplating a blue-skied September day; he'd been on pins and needles all morning about this report. "How did things go?"

"Great." Matthews edged into the room. "Your little pep talk must have done some good. Meek as a lamb, and as silent. Little No-Peep. How're you going to get anywhere if she doesn't say anything?"

Kevin laughed. "You ever worked with a catatonic case at the state mental hospital? Well, I did, during my year's residency there. Jane Doe could outmotormouth Phyllis Diller compared to that. Sit down."

Matthews paused, flummoxed. Kevin's office was just like all the Probe offices, from Cross's on down: same mint-green walls—institutions must have that color custom-blended by elves in hollow trees, Kevin often railed; same battered battleship-gray metal desk and files; same air of semipermanent transience. Except for the seating. Matthews eyed the rosewood-and-leather Eames chair and its matching ottoman

46

askance before pulling a university-issue chair from its stiff position by the door and sitting on it.

"I always feel I should be sipping Chablis in a chair like that," Matthews apologized, eyeing the Eames again.

Kevin shrugged. "Theory of mine. A couch intimidates, and those molded plastic jobs cut off circulation. You figure the average patient spends sixty to a hundred hours in a chair spilling his or her guts to you—more if it's a Probe case. The least you can offer for sure is some physical comfort. Me—I get the bottom desk drawer if my blood kinks," Kevin finished cheerfully, pulling out the drawer in question and propping up his feet. "Well?"

Matthews mutely extended the manila folder.

Kevin studied it. "Weight up, huh? Good. Blood count okay. Did you do a T-four to see if hyperthyroidism explains the emaciation?"

"That's down at the lab for analysis. As you see, all the gross signs are pretty normal. Nurses say she's eating solids now."

"Ye gods! If she goes on like this, we may have to put her on a diet. Up to one hundred and six pounds already. She looks like a basically healthy girl, whoever she is."

"Too healthy."

"What do you mean?"

Matthews rose, grasped his chair back and leaned forward with professorial ponderousness. "Did you notice anything, any pattern, in that report? I know you shrinks don't see physical exams that often—"

"I've seen my share, and made them, Roger. What are you getting at?"

Instead of answering, the man went to shut the door. "Perhaps we'd better keep this confidential."

As Matthews turned back into the room, a surrealistic Rolling Stones poster of a fleet of lascivious flying tongues slid scrimlike past his shoulders. Kevin kept the poster there as a background for his more pompous colleagues; it was a favorite game to maneuver the door open and the poster out of sight before the innocent visitor could spot it. For once, he cared more about what his staid colleague had to say than about sticking his—or the Rolling Stones'—tongue in cheek out at anyone's pretensions.

"What's the problem?" Kevin paged through the forms. "All the numbers are normal. She's doing great. No reason not to begin my sessions with her—"

"No reason," agreed Matthews, sitting again. "Maybe it's what's *not* there."

"Look, we're doctors. We ought to be able to make a clear diagnosis. Quit dancing around and spit it out."

"Well, for one thing, look at the note on dental health."

Kevin flipped the page. "Yeah . . . nothing much wrong."

"Wrong, Doctor. *Nothing* wrong. There's a difference."

Kevin leaned his elbows on the desk and scrutinized the page. He glanced up at Matthews, at a smug Matthews, but what was new? "No cavities at all? You're sure?"

Matthews nodded portentously.

"Hell, Roger—this is great. You estimate she's what— twenty-three, twenty-four years old. And no cavities. There're only a few places in the country where there's enough natural fluoride in the water to give protection like that. We've got a lead on where she's from."

"How many places with good water also refrained from routine inoculation twenty-five years ago, Dr. Blake? That ought to narrow it down even more."

"Inoculation? Everybody got inoculated. If not against smallpox, then diphtheria, influenza . . ."

Matthews's head shook sourly. "Not our Doe."

Kevin frowned. "No inoculations? What about birthmarks, scars?"

"Not a mark on her. No inoculations, no chicken pox scars, not even a pierced ear or two. Oh, and her vision's twenty/twenty as well." Matthews sighed. "It looks as if nothing's happened to her since she was born."

48

"Except semistarvation, abandonment, memory loss," Kevin enumerated sharply.

"Abandonment and memory loss is your bailiwick, but I'm not sure even those should be taken at face value in this case. She wasn't starving; she'd never bounce back this way, otherwise. Thin, yes. Say her metabolism was running on idle for some reason. But not to the point of bodily abuse."

"How can you tell?" Kevin jumped, determined to rattle Matthews in turn. "I had a patient once who'd been kept prisoner by a group of devil worshipers—I wouldn't even tell you what they did to her. Sat there"—Kevin indicated the empty Eames chair—"in a polyester print dress and finally found her way back to remembering and telling me about it. Abuse doesn't advertise, Roger."

"You still think this one's a victim of some kind of abuse? Sexual?"

"I don't want to. . . ." Kevin flipped the folder shut. "But when women or children turn up in suspicious shape, there's usually that behind it, yes."

"Forget it," advised Matthews.

"Forget it?"

"I told you; no one's laid a hand on her—except for a few bruises some orderly probably put on her wrist in transport. No one; there's one last . . . perfection . . . not mentioned in the report. No blank for it. Her hymen is intact."

"You did a pelvic?"

"Not past that point. It sort of seemed like breaking the shrink wrap on somebody else's record, if you'll pardon the pun." Matthews was on a roll now, enjoying Kevin's confusion. "I haven't seen an intact hymen in so long . . . well, only if I've got to examine a pubescent—like that case of hermaphroditism you were treating." Matthews's head shook gravely. "Tragic. How'd that finally come out?"

"Surgery and lots of psychoanalysis. Fine." Kevin dismissed what to Matthews was freakish anomaly and what to him had been business as usual. At least today hermaphrodites could be eased into one side of the sexual mainstream or the other, and weren't left to sideshows. But too much perfection, now *that* was an anomaly.

"If she's a virgin—" Kevin began. Matthews rolled his eyes. "Okay. No argument. She has a hymen, ergo . . . Still, there's no reason a twenty-four-year-old virgin should be a dying species. I mean, it has happened, that a girl . . . woman doesn't—"

"Be realistic, Kevin. The point is, a woman can be a virgin until twenty-four or forty-two or the end of time. But even with virgins the hymen usually is gone by the time of her first routine pelvic. Tampons, usually, or these days, even a little self-experimentation. You just don't see hymens anymore. They're socially extinct. When'd you last see one?"

"Med school. But then they went out of their way to dig up the abnormal."

"My point, Kevin, is that I don't think that stock answers will work in this case."

"Cross did say he had a feeling I wouldn't believe what had happened to this girl; instead, I can't believe what *hasn't* happened to her. Well." Kevin stood, slapping his hands on the closed file. "I'll just have to get out my voodoo apparatus and start peeking into her virgin mind, if her body refuses to give any clues. Isn't there some North Dakota town with decay-preventative water? Might be a good place to have the police start once they get off the suicide case. . . ."

Kevin had edged behind Matthews and was easing the incriminating door open. Rows of lolling tongues dwindled to a raw edge of formless red.

"It's certainly safe to begin talking with her." Matthews rose and turned. "You know, what's in that report is a lot less telling than what isn't recorded. I can't see drawing the rest of the unit's attention to something that . . . calls for more questions than answers. We can keep this between us, if you like."

"Thanks. No use muddying already murky waters. If you

need a second in a meeting sometime . . . It was sharp of you to pick up on it.''

Matthews smiled thinly. ''Sometimes we old medical war-horses are good for something.''

Kevin frowned as the other man moved over the threshold, then his face brightened. ''Thigh! Hey, that's it, Roger!''

''Beg your pardon?''

''Lots of parents had their baby girls inoculated on the *thigh* years ago. Supposed to show less than on the arm when on the beach. Did you check there?''

Matthews looked insulted. ''No . . . besides, with what women wear for swimsuits these days, the thigh is hardly a discreet site.''

Kevin suddenly grinned. ''Little did the parents of twenty-five years ago know. But that may be it. So simple. A leg inoculation. I'll check it out. And the teeth could tell us where she came from. Good detective work, Roger.''

Matthews recognized flattery when it was oozing over him. ''And the hymen?'' he insisted.

Kevin shrugged. ''That's for Jane Doe to know and me to find out. It's no good being a mystery lady without a few secrets.''

Kevin wasn't so cocksure when he stood over her bed a half hour later. The nurse had left with an empty food tray, burbling nonsense about good appetite and clean plates. Jane herself was alert and grave as a sphinx, her secrets securely locked behind her eyes, her mouth, her mind. Why did Egyptian imagery always surface when he thought of her?

''I hear you were easy on Dr. Matthews this morning,'' he told her. ''You and I can start talking tomorrow. But first, I'd like to check—''

He reached for the shoulder of her voluminous hospital gown. Something told him to stop short of touching her. Everything flared—her eyelids, pupils, nostrils. The reaction passed in a millisecond and his hand descended almost with-

51

out pause. He pushed the gown down, his mind cataloging them bones, them dry bones, as if he were studying some dusty med school textbook. And the clavicle leads to the scapula; the scapula leads to the humerus . . .

All her bones still seemed painfully prominent; his fingers were gentle as they rotated her upper arm. Slender, smooth, unmarked by the white rosette of scar tissue most adults of a certain age take for granted. The other arm was clear, too, and when he asked her to roll over, which she did, without question, he parted the hospital gown on thighs thin enough for Christie Brinkley to envy. And no inoculation on either one. He decided to take Matthews's word on the hymen.

She had rolled back and lay looking at him with her grave, unquestioning stare.

"We're going to talk, Jane," he told her. "Tomorrow and every day. We're going to find out who you are, and where you came from, and why you forgot all this. You do want to know, don't you?"

She was silent long enough for a chill to creep over him. Perhaps there were worse things than working with a catatonic. Perhaps a calm, uncaring amnesiac was one of them. Frozen, fatal, like a deer. And he was the man with the gun.

Jane's Bambi-like gaze dropped to her still hands on the sheet. "Yes. I want to know; I want to know everything." It was the most he'd ever heard her say; her husky voice, a Brenda Vaccaro–style contralto rumble, surprised him. He had expected her to have no peculiarities, no touch of anything identifiable, specific, personal.

He found himself reaching out to pat her pale hand, as his old GP had done to his once childish paw so many times. He had hated such awkward, inarticulate adult gestures then, and had despised the old coot.

But Jane looked up and smiled, actually smiled. "Thank you, Dr. Blake."

Contact. Breakthrough. It was going to be all right. He had a name; she would have one. Eventually. It was just a matter of time, therapy and his usual messianic skills, right, Dr. Blake?

He kicked resurgent ego aside and smiled back.

It lay—floated really—where it had always seemed to be. What buoyed it, water or air, it couldn't tell, but it recognized them as elements, although one seemed no more threatening or welcome to its existence than the other.

It was merely an organism upon which other organisms acted. It had little sense of size or shape; at most times, no hearing, and its vision was clouded at best. It knew what sight and hearing were, though, and thought it had once done both a great deal better than it did now.

For now, it floated, vaguely conscious. Some see-through shell separated it from a larger place. As it bobbled—insensately, aimlessly—in a circle, its senses focused enough to notice that. More detailed flashes of the place beyond its own glimmered through—vast, occupied by rows upon rows of tall, hovering structures, by a gleaming architecture of metal, by more of the vitreous compartments like its own, by a great glittering array of instruments that hummed and buzzed and clicked and sometimes flashed . . .

Its unguided motion brought some portion of itself up against the translucent barrier. Vibrations began and multiplied. Yes, the place still hummed, only now it couldn't hear that low buzz. It suddenly envisioned itself uncontained and loose within the larger place, with all its senses intact. It could . . . recall . . . such an occasion, which pricked the surface of its consciousness now and again.

The place belonged to those others, the ones that moved. It recognized it had named an action perceived by the sense known as vision and was vaguely self-pleased. That proved that it had been once, might be again, more than it was now. It felt incomplete, but no alarm at this insight, merely a dreamy sort of certainty.

Constant drifting rotated it. Above, through the clear barrier and close enough to penetrate its cloudy vision, a fellow floater also lay jellied within some convex vessel.

The other's physical presence was swollen and inchoate, a pulp of faint pink empurpled here and there along its curled, bobbing shape. A large bulbous knob on one end was centered with a vivid blue-red blossom of tissue. Extremities, clawlike in their waxy white passivity, curled against the dormant body. These projections numbered four, clearly visible as the shape bobbled to a rhythm matching the watcher's.

It felt quite pleased with itself, that dreamy, less than half-conscious observer, for so thoroughly identifying its amorphous neighbor. It felt it functioned, however briefly. There was no curiosity toward what it observed, no sense of identity with it. It was merely an observer. Its neighbor buffeted gently out of range. The observer resettled into its own lulling motion, the dark shadowy shapes beyond its view distorting as it moved, through the curve of the surface between it and them.

It floated, content to wait—and dream.

The Probing
September 10

Chapter Nine

She was probably the one patient who could drive him crazy. That was the only sure thing Kevin Blake, M.D., D.Q.C. (Don Quixote Complex), knew after his first session with Jane Doe.

He sat in his comfortable leather swivel chair, at his ugly gray metal desk, tapping a pen on the glass desktop and staring at the jeering posterized tongues of Jagger and Co. The Eames chair was vacant again; it might as well have been vacant two hours before, for all he had learned from Jane Doe.

Kevin jerked open the upper-left-hand desk drawer, the one nearest the Eames chair. It was empty except for the two tools of his trade he most despised, a Kleenex box and a notebook. He loathed the ubiquitous tissue box in its floral dress-up best, an icon that decked most head tenders' offices. It was insulting to expect people to wring out years of accumulated sorrow into tufts of supermarket disposables. He only resorted to the tissue box when the leather looked in for a good dampening.

And the notebook. He flipped over the spiral-bound cardboard. The notebook was as empty as the Kleenex box was full, except for a cryptic string of letters in fresh felt-tip black. Notebooks were another way to distance doctor from patient, to put the already wary psyche on guard. If a shrink couldn't remember what was important . . .

Two hours past. The squirrels were shaking the upper elm boughs visible from his window in their fall scramble for food and nesting materials. The Eames chair was waiting, as he was; an internal anticipatory edge sharpened itself on his stomach acids. The stage was set. All he needed now was the girl. A knock, then a nurse led in Jane Doe.

"This is where you'll be seeing Dr. Blake, dear. Every day at this time. You think you can find your way here again on your own?"

Jane nodded solemnly, her eyes scanning the room's many unfamiliarities before resting on its one known, him. She didn't look like someone who needed to be addressed as "dear," but nurses seldom noticed that kind of thing.

"Come in, Jane," he encouraged.

She advanced a couple of steps, a frail, self-contained figure in an oversized hospital gown.

"Have a seat."

She studied the Eames chair, then sat primly on the edge.

"You can put up your feet. Relax."

Her pale, narrow legs, covered with a light down of hair, swung obediently onto the ottoman. Paper slippers on black leather. He always forgot about the damn paper slippers. Maybe he could get some real slippers from someone. She'd be here for a while, and she deserved better than Kleenex and paper slippers. Any patient did.

She settled into the cradle of soft leather without the wrigglings most gowned patients underwent—twitching to get the coarse back ties away from any sensitive spot, writhing to close over their posteriors the three inches of gaping robe that seemed designed to resist modesty and instill embarrassment. Jane Doe seemed neither uncomfortable nor embarrassed—and incapable of either.

"Anything you want to ask me? About your condition, about what we'll be doing here?"

She shook her head no. Great start.

"You said you want to know. Everything. Where shall we begin?"

"What is this place?"

58

"This? My office. In a hospital complex at the University of Minnesota in Minneapolis. Have you been in the Twin Cities before?"

She looked blanker than usual, if that was possible.

"Saint Paul and Minneapolis are called the Twin Cities," he explained, guessing at the reason for her confusion—she wasn't necessarily a local product simply because she had been found nearby. "They sit next to one another. Sort of. Maybe you're from Crow Wing. That's where you were found."

"Crow Wing." She tasted the words, as she had sampled the new name her anonymity had conferred a few days before. "Are there crows there?"

"There are crows everywhere. So Crow Wing doesn't ring a bell either?" Blank, blanker, blankest. "It doesn't sound familiar?"

She shook her head.

Christ. Psychiatrists who do all the talking are listening to an idiot.

"Let's start then with what you *do* know. Tell me."

Amusement tautened her contained features, as if she recognized a game. "I am . . . Jane. Jane . . ."

He waited, but she waited longer. "Doe," he finally finished.

"Jane Doe. And you are Dr. Blake. There is Dr. Matthews, who must touch me. And the nurses, who give me food and baths. Anderson, Milnar, Yamato, Sweeney, Phalen, Young—"

"Good enough. Nothing wrong with your memory now," he joked, then switched gears. "Are you worried about not remembering your past?"

"Worried?" She was so deliberate. She seemed to smell, taste, weigh each word, each concept, before consuming it. "No."

"Then I'll have to do the worrying for the both of us. What kind of person do you think you are? Who is Jane?"

59

"I am . . . I." The lyric she unwittingly had quoted ran on melodically in his mind. "I am I, Don Quixote, the man of La Mancha . . ." Terrific. She was leading him right back to his own inadequacy.

"What is 'I'?"

"I is, I am . . ." She was reaching, trying to please, to respond. "I am—a, a . . . amnesiac." Triumph imbued her intonation. A nine-year-old at a spelling bee, answering by rote. A-m-n-e-s-i-a-c. She'd overheard it, of course, and shouldn't have.

He sighed. Her head tilted curiously. "What's the first thing you remember?"

"Screams."

He straightened, startled. His easily betrayed interest prodded her on.

"Screaming and screaming and screaming. Far away. Forever. It was the, the ec, ec-na-lub-ma."

"The . . . ecna—?"

"The ecnalubma. I saw it written at the top."

Opening the hated drawer, he drew out the virgin notebook. "Can you—write it?"

She took the felt tip, laid the notebook on her lap and rapidly drew a series of block capital letters.

He studied the handed-back hieroglyphs, perplexed, tidbits of Russian and Greek script colliding in his mind. **ƎƆИA⅃UᗺMA** Foreign? Or even foreign born? But her English was so perfect. Or—too perfect, as Matthews said everything else about her was. No identifying marks, not even in the teeth. A foreign agent, a double agent, gone bonkers or escaped from the CIA. Kevin spun to the window to examine the senseless symbols in good light. Nuts. He was going certifiably nuts. Listen to him. There had to be a simpler explanation. The most simple. Usually the right one.

If you reversed the first symbol you had an E. Then C, N, A, L, U, B, M, A. Ecnalubma, if you had to coin a pronounceable word for it. Ecnalubma . . . Simple, so simple!

He spun back. "Ambulance. You heard the siren of the ambulance bringing you from Crow Wing to the Twin Cities."

"Then why do they write ecnalubma over the window?"

Kevin smiled. "They don't. That's how you reversed the letters so you could pronounce it. It's ambulance reversed, so drivers ahead can read its name right in their rearview mirrors."

Her face wore the first purely human expression he'd seen on it yet. Annoyance. They'd changed the rules and hadn't told her.

"I kinda like ecnalubma better," he teased.

She relaxed—into the same maddening serenity. "It *is* a more interesting word."

"And that's the first thing you remember? The ambulance siren?"

There was a long pause. Although her expression remained impassive, Kevin had a hunch a lot was going on behind the drawn brown shades of her eyes. "The first thing," he prompted.

"A man . . ." she began. "Touch—" Her eyes widened with fear, then her face jerked hard and cold and shut. "Many men. Screams. Flying. Fast. Fire. Night. Endless night. Endless stars. Cold. Men. Women. Here. You."

His sheathed pen tip traced invisible letters across the glass. Ecnalubma, all the nonequilateral letters reversed. Some learning defects caused the mind to reverse letters. But then to rearrange them mentally, spell them into sense and pronounceability? No defect there, or mystery once the word was translated. He took ambulances' backward ways so for granted it had never occurred to him to note the new word created.

As for Jane's mystery, all he had was a string of perfectly ordinary—perfect again—words. Night and stars, flying and fire, speed and people, and the dead end of Probe. He threw down the pen and picked up the phone.

Chapter Ten

"So? How's it going with the mysterious Miss Doe?"

Martin Kandinsky nipped a pinchful of fries from their papery nest and transferred them to his waiting maw.

"So-so. We've only had one session."

"Aha! Case solved. The mighty Blake strikes again."

Kevin turned his beer halfway around on the varnished tabletop. Above him, around him, The Police droned one of their sinister hits at amplified wattage.

The Improper Noun was a typical campus hangout—from its cutesy name, dark stained-glass-lit interior and uneven-legged tables to its baskets of calorie-and-cholesterol-laden burgers, deep-fried mushrooms and kosher dill pickles. Kevin nibbled at what the menu had christened the Yellow Submarine—roast beef and mustard on a kaiser roll; Kandy dived uninhibitedly into a pile of meat, mayo and onions disguising a pumpernickel bun.

"The mighty Blake strikes again—and out," Kevin mumbled over the sandwich and the music. "I don't know when I've had less of a handle on something."

"The lady's not for spilling her guts? Too bad."

"Oh, she's cooperative. Like a phone-answering machine. Clicks off just when you think you might get somewhere. Sorry, message not received."

"Come on, Kev. Since when could one lousy session get you down? You know you were panting to unravel this one," said Kandy, washing down his aromatic mouthful with a gulp of Miller Lite beer.

Kevin idly massaged the condensation-dewed neck of his

barely touched Heineken and smiled. "Anyone ever tell you that you were the quintessential oral personality, Kandy?"

"Yeah. My analyst." He dived back into his food basket for a second tour of duty. "Why d'you think everybody loves the lad? You can't help adoring a glutton; we're so harmless. So what's your problem?" he asked, chewing enthusiastically. "Isn't it only a matter of pushing the right button? One, two, three—bingo! The girl remembers. Great scene. Sainted shrink to the rescue. Sell a million."

Kevin was laughing in spite of himself, his mood. "Look. You take over. The poor woman will remember everything in self-defense."

"I'm not the messianic type. Leave it to you and Bishop Moon."

"You think I've got a savior complex?"

"Every shrink's got to have an Achilles' heel—or an ingrown toenail or an Oedipus complex. But what's got you so worried about this case? You usually slip right through the average mental disaster area to the scene of the crime. Psychic Superman. Run into some kryptonite?"

Kevin sketched several letters on his napkin. "What do you make of that?"

Kandy's sharp shoulders shrugged. "Jibberish. What's this, anyway, some new Rorschach? Don't tell me! You're working on an experiment for your favorite parapsychologist. Swanson is eavesdropping on everything we say and is right now transcribing that scrawl as the secret key to KGB's international code, right? Long-distance telepathy or whatever."

"Kandy, you don't get serious, I'm gonna start eating your fries."

"So all right. I'm all ears."

"It's just that . . ." Kevin sighed, then heard himself. He hunched over his beer and got analytical. "I've never seen anything, anyone, like this. Most people under stress get uptight. Sure, some *act* in control, but the tension is there, under the calm. This one is just, just calm. That's all she wrote. I get the feeling she doesn't *need* to know who she is. Without that, I'm excavating a cipher. She doesn't seem to *need* the stuff we take for granted.'' Kevin gestured at Kandy's ketchup-stained basket. ''French fries. A pet cat. Uhhh, a little rock 'n' roll. Any human connection. She's disconnected, that's it. Perfectly rational, perfectly healthy, if you come right down to it. Perfectly content the way she is.''

Kandy leaned back and wiped his mouth with a paper napkin. He smiled slowly. ''The perfect patient. Doesn't need help. No wonder you're having a nervous breakdown. But look, you said yourself some really weird things could have happened to her—the psyche can retreat from ugly reality right into the semblance of normality sometimes—''

''I never said 'normal,' '' Kevin interrupted. ''Besides, Matthews did a thorough physical. There are no signs of abuse, present or past, but why the memory loss then, if her past wasn't so terrible to be worth forgetting?''

''No beatings, forced screwings, signs of physical restraint?'' Kevin shook his head.

''Curiouser and curiouser. Maybe we're looking at a lifetime of mental abuse here. You know, Mama or Daddy kept her out of school, locked in closets, underfed—and she only just now got away.''

Kevin pointed to the napkin. ''You still haven't figured that out. Try reversing the letters. . . .''

''Oh, sure. Silly of me. The familiar ecna-LOOOB-ma.''

''It's 'ambulance' spelled backwards and reversed, like she saw it written above the front windshield the night she was wheeled in. She remembered and reversed it. Half-dead, they said. But she noticed that. She's not illiterate.''

Kandy's lips pursed on the problem, as if about to deal with it by devouring it. Instead, he *tsk*ed consideringly, something Kevin saw rather than heard over the restaurant racket.

''Why don't you tape your sessions? Then you could chew them over later. All the big boys did it.''

"I hate that. Warmed-over insight is a sop to make the psychiatrist think he's doing something. It's what happens in session that counts, interaction—"

"You don't get interaction without insight, and right now you don't have a clue to who she is or where she came from or why she forgot herself. Anyway, if you had it on tape, you could run it by a sympathetic fellow shrink."

"You?"

"Know anybody more laid-back, insightful, analytical?"

"Ravenous . . ."

"That, too. It's a wild case, Kevin. I get a little bored with all those bad trips and unwanted pregnancies and NODOZ dreamers at Student Health sometimes. Let me in on this one. You won't be sorry and I'll let you take all the credit."

"I don't know, Kandy. On anything else, sure, but—"

"I know." Kandy's long-fingered hand swiped the check to his side of the table. "She's your baby. You always were a one-man operation, even in residency. They must have loved you at Harvard."

Kevin laughed. "They hated my guts. But I got a damn good education—my way."

"Then you'll just have to bend all that academic artillery on Jane Doe. Poor thing doesn't stand a chance."

"Kellehay didn't think so," Kevin muttered as they stood to leave.

"Who?" Kandy shouted into the din.

"Nobody," answered Kevin, threading his way to the door. "Nobody now."

Chapter Eleven

Something besides tissues and notepad occupied Kevin's upper-left-hand desk drawer now—tape cassettes. He liked them even less. Yet he had to admit the new, paperback-size Japanese tape recorder was a classier desktop accessory than a Puffs box.

Today when Jane Doe arrived, he'd have more than naked skill to offer. Technology. The transistorized shrink.

The knock was eerily familiar. One, then two, softer. Kevin expected the same nurse as yesterday, but Jane entered alone. As she turned to close the door, the slickly leering poster swung past. She ignored it—or appeared to—and went to the Eames chair.

"Kind of a dreary day," he mentioned. Even in therapy, the weather made an infallible opening gambit.

Her face turned interestedly to the window, where raindrops dribbled dolorously down the pane against a dampened background of gray-green trees and sky.

"Dreary," she repeated.

"Or don't you find rain depressing?"

"I hadn't noticed it. . . ." She rose to walk to the window on paper-sheathed feet and stare silently out. He pictured her viewed from the other side, a white-robed waif whose rain-veiled face looked out on a rippled world.

Now would be as good a time as any to get things rolling. . . . Kevin leaned forward to push the recorder on. His chair squeaked, a comforting rainy-day sound. The button snapped and Jane Doe whirled from the window. Kevin couldn't tell which had come first—the mechanical whine of

66

protest from the tape or Jane's quick whip around. Either way, he was pushing buttons—too small, damn lilliputian machines—trying to stop a tape cassette that twirled hysterically from left to right and back again, squealing like one of the three little pigs all the way home.

"*Damn* innovations! Don't know what's gotten into this thing. Sit down, Jane, I'll get it fixed in a minute—" Kevin sensed rather than saw her return to the chair, but he finally pressed the right button. The wild rewinding stopped. So much for subtly introducing a tape recorder into their sessions.

"My new toy," he apologized. "Haven't got the hang of it."

Her hand hovered tentatively to touch the black plastic edge with one fingertip. The gesture, languid yet deliberate, recalled something, he didn't know what. But he'd never seen her reach for anything yet, and was as absurdly pleased as the proud father of a newborn. Man's reach must exceed his—or her—grasp, and all that, but first, there must be reach. . . .

"I thought I'd tape-record what we say, for study later. You don't mind?"

She stared at the little black box and, like a good shrink, he shrank. It was an invasion of privacy, an intrusion of technology. He'd always relied on establishing purely human relationships, and now he'd frightened his most wary patient with a piece of imported hardware, with his own clumsiness.

"I'll take it away."

Her fingertip lifted, imperiously. "No. It's all right now."

"Oh, sure, the malfunction's stopped now, but, believe me, I could push the wrong button and set it amok all over again. . . ."

Her head shook "no."

"Okay. I'll try again. You're sure it won't upset you?"

A suspicion of a smile tautened the corners of her mouth, reminding him suddenly of the Mona Lisa. She cast her dark eyes down with some unspoken retort, but he couldn't read minds, merely unravel them sometimes. It wouldn't upset her, that he knew. And more than that, he sensed that she found the idea of it upsetting her ludicrous.

He rewound the tape, Jane ignoring the high-speed burble, his own motions. She had decided not so much to accept the tape recorder as to dismiss it. It was while his forefinger hovered over the STOP button that the image of her gesture of moments before took visual shape in his mind. Sistine Chapel ceiling. The Creation. Hand of Adam reaching for the hand of God. Or vice versa. Jane Doe breathing obedience into a tape recorder. Or vice versa? He was getting technology happy, reading volumes into a grain of silicon.

Kevin settled back into his chair and began gently directing the conversation into more productive channels, forgetting the rain, forgetting the tape recorder.

It was only later, when he replayed the cassette in the comfort of the overstuffed sofa in his condo, a glass of sherry warming his hand, that he realized he might just as well have recorded the rain. She was as limpidly transparent as water, as relentlessly noncommittal as a meandering raindrop, as emotional as a puddle. Their conversation was just that, patter, full of sound and serenity, signifying nothing.

"How's your Doe going?"

Swanson seemed pleased with herself for asking after Kevin's latest project. Kevin just looked around the table with cautious confidence, or what he hoped resembled it.

"Good, good." He nodded with shrinklike sagacity. "It's going to take a while to get to the bottom of the well, but she's cooperative in session, uh . . . doesn't seem to have any taboo areas of discussion—"

"You getting some insight on the circumstances of her finding?" interrupted Matthews. Kevin set his teeth. Matthews was as curious as a teenager about that hymen.

"Not yet."

"Any memory return?" demanded Cross.

"No." Conceded reluctantly, too reluctantly. "But it's early yet. The—incident—she experienced before she was found must have been intensely traumatic."

"Any clue on what happened physically?"

"No. Roger's exam revealed surprisingly little damage; she's still underweight, but gaining daily. Anything show up on that T-four, Roger? The lab find a high count, any hyperthyroidism?"

Matthews shook his head. "No, the numbers were normal. Perfectly normal. Right dead on normal." Only Kevin blanched at the clear double meaning in Matthews's response. Perfect again. Too bloody perfect.

"Any word from the police?" Once Cross found a sentence structure that worked, he stuck with it.

Kevin squirmed. "I've, I've been holding Smith off." He caught their common eye. "Detective Smith. Minneapolis's finest are once again interested in a Probe client." They squirmed, too.

"Why hold off, if she's coherent, healthy?"

"She is, Norbert. It's just that . . ." Just that she's too coherent, too healthy, too obviously a suspect physically able to push a Crow Wing policeman out a window—now.

"It's just that Kevin hates to share his patients," slid in Swanson.

"I just don't happen to think, Carolyn, that the mind in trauma is the ideal subject for parapsychological experimentation."

"Of course it's the ideal subject! Stress opens gates usually guarded by the subconscious. But you're so convinced your patients are all precious . . ."

"All our patients are precious," said Cross benignly. "I know you resent that Dr. Blake has never seen fit to release one of his patients to your parapsychology program, Dr. Swanson, but that's his prerogative."

"But he gets the most interesting patients, the ones whose minds are most open to the out of the ordinary! Like that cult member—the ones most suitable to my experiments, the ones most—"

"Vulnerable, Swannee?" Kevin interjected in a dangerously invulnerable tone.

"You make me sound like a witch doctor!" she retorted, her pale eyes blazing magnified indignity through the thick lenses. She looked like an angry carp trapped behind an ill-fitting fishbowl.

"We're all witch doctors," soothed Cross, "and there's no way to tell which doctor is right."

Kevin groaned. Matthews chuckled. Swanson simmered, but she was such a washed-out personality, all her passion driven into her work. that it was an oddly cold kind of simmer.

"I respect your work, Dr. Swanson," Kevin conceded. "Your results are remarkable. But you get enough subjects via referral; you don't need my basket cases."

The meeting unwound normally after that. They were an odd team; Swanson the academic, publishing passionately in a field most of her peers ridiculed; Matthews the physically grounded doctor, lethargically pursuing the relationship between body and mind just doggedly enough to get his grant renewed. Cross the uneasy administrator, still excitable, still gripped by the idea of the human mind and all it can grasp, and lose a grip on. And Kevin, the lone stranger, daring to boldly go where no shrink has gone before—and earning headlines and resentment because of it.

Cross interrupted Kevin's terminal reverie. "Hold on a moment, Dr. Blake." The others, filing out, gave him the look reserved for classmates asked to stay after school.

"Usually you're bursting with theories, no matter how wild, by now, Kevin."

"Sometimes theories aren't enough. I told you she'd take time—"

"Time's not normally a problem at Probe. We have a free

70

hand on that. Results, now that's different. But you don't have to worry about results; you always get them.''

Kevin flashed his superior a rueful look. ''You setting me up in a failure-success bind?''

''No. But that city detective has been calling. I wish you'd let him see her—soon. And . . . the local press has been on the line, too.''

''Dammit, no!'' His hand slapped rosewood veneer, then stung. ''Aren't the damn news stories enough?''

''Maybe if Smith gets a photograph for the papers to run—''

''Oh, great, now I've got a police photographer all over her. There's no evidence yet that any crime has been committed against her—''

''There's Officer Kellehay, Kevin. Who knows, there might be a link between her, him and Crow Wing. Maybe she saw something out there that night. Maybe he did, too.''

Kevin looked away. All his instincts told him that Jane Doe had been the way she was, which was turning out to be not so abnormal—on the surface—for a long time.

''Norbert. I don't think so. There was no Mafia hit on a Crow Wing bluff top, and she happens to witness it and gets conked on the head and loses her memory, and the mob blows away the two cops that found her because they unwittingly witnessed something. . . . You've been watching *Mike Hammer* too much.''

''Let the police have their time with her, Kevin. You're acting as if she's your private property. She isn't. She's a question mark on the face of the community, and we ordinary officials have as much right to search for an answer to her as you do.''

''I'll call Smith tomorrow.'' Kevin went to the door, and paused with his hand on the knob and his white-coated back to Cross. ''But the media can take a flying leap to the moon!''

Behind him, Cross chuckled softly. "And after all they've done for you . . ."

Kevin stormed down the hall, past Matthews talking to two interns at the hall crossroads. The heel of his hand rammed open Jane Doe's door. Then he was inside, with the calm. She was sitting in the chair by the window, looking out. It was odd; she did nothing, but never seemed bored. Or rather, she was given nothing to do. That would change now.

His anger flared out with a last, primitive surge, revealing the underlying fear that fueled it. That was the psychiatrist's crown of thorns, analyzing one's own emotions all too accurately. He was afraid of Detective Smith and his mild-mannered ways of getting people to talk. He feared the police photographer's skill in capturing a recognizable face for the sunset final. He feared the media and their awesome, casual reach into every middlesex village and town. He was afraid one or all of them would find her, claim her, before he could.

He sat on the radiator and stared down at Jane. He wasn't afraid of her, though Kellehay had been.

"You won't be seeing just me tomorrow," he told her. "There are—others—who'll need to interview you. Do you think you can talk to them? Can you tell them what you know of . . . yourself, of the man who fell from your room?"

"I don't," she said solemnly after a moment, "know anything."

He smiled. "That's not a very good start for a girl who wants to know everything. But it'll do just fine for the people you'll talk to tomorrow."

His hand briefly clasped the wrist so languid in her lap, closed around the loose plastic hospital band with "Jane Doe" printed in faint blue ballpoint across it. Let Smith go head to head with that calm indifference, that majestic ignorance, and come up with anything self-incriminating, including an identity.

Sometimes, came the bittersweet thought, one man's frustration can be another man's failure.

Chapter Twelve

One summer Kevin's younger sister had found a stray cat, a skinny, semibedraggled, collarless, unprepossessing tabby. Tammy had begged passionately to keep it, found a box and stuffed it with rags for a bed, collared the creature with a bell and named it. Bellarina. Kevin, in the way of ten-year-old brothers everywhere, used to call it Bag-o'-Bones and squirt the hose at it.

Then one day a family came, with its own little girl, and took the stray away. The Blakes, being orderly parents, had advertised the find and someone, incredibly, had claimed it. Tammy had threatened to never forgive their parents, when, red-eyed, she'd watched Bellarina vanish forever into an alien car.

Tammy had two kids now, a career as a law librarian, and she got along with Kevin as well as any mutually fond adult sibling could. But she'd never gotten another cat, and Kevin wasn't sure she'd ever forgiven anybody anything.

Now Kevin stared at the one-column sketch in that morning's *Star-Trib*, lower-half front page, about as prominent as one could expect. Only wanted mass murderers got their sketches above the fold. It was a striking likeness; obviously, the police artist, used to erecting faces on such foggy foundations as verbal descriptions and sketchy recall, had relished doing a portrait from life. Kevin, who'd insisted on a sketch rather than a photo, could almost picture Jane Doe's grateful parents requesting the original shortly after claiming their daughter, and hanging it above their quilted floral sofa in one of those 3-D, boxy plastic frames. There probably would be a maple coffee table in front of the sofa. And TV trays on a cart in the living room corner. . . .

Kevin threw the *Strib* facedown on the desk. Only eight A.M., but already the day was jaded and the thought of the next session was haunted by haste, by the specter of someone rising up to name Jane Doe. He whiffed the lingering, long dead odor of Tammy's betrayal coming through the open window on the breeze that stirred gilt-tipped elm leaves. Fall was coming. Mornings started out cool to the warming day. Old claims were being reasserted on all fronts, the seasons freezing the veins of nature in every leaf and bough, reason chilling his psychoanalytic passion for sole possession of an interesting case to the bone. It was getting to be a T. S. Eliot time of year.

So he welcomed the brash ring of the desktop phone, the ugly, flesh-toned model that institutions love to inflict upon their employees.

"Blake."

"*Dr*. Blake?"

"Yes." Impatient. An uncertain caller meant a waste of time.

"This is Mary Ann Cleaver at the Kimball Library. Is this the Dr. Blake who has a, a patient named . . ." Awkward pause. "Jane Doe," she finally blurted. "That's what she says. You are on staff, aren't you, Doctor? I mean, we found her. This morning, first thing. I don't know *how* she got in. But she isn't wearing anything! Just a, a gown. She's been going through the books. Piles and piles of books. They're all out of sequence," added the voice of librarianly annoyance.

"Wait a minute! You're telling me you've got a UM Hospitals patient AWOL in your library? Kimball's halfway across campus—"

"I know where it is, Doctor. And apparently your patient did, too. She *is* your patient?"

"Shouldn't be there, though. Look, uh, I'll be right over. What's your name again?"

He jotted it down, still stunned. "It'll take me a few minutes. Just, um, just let her read. That *is* what she's doing?"

Another pause. "Not exactly, Dr. Blake. You'd better come see for yourself."

Kevin hung up and headed for the door, already calculating how long it would take him to get there. . . . He stopped, turned back and wrested his ID badge off his white coat, just to prove he was who he was supposed to be. It'd be great if they *both* ended up loony bin bound. . . .

"Got an emergency. Errand. Be back in half an hour," Kevin told Bridget McCarthy, Cross's secretary across the hall, who answered all their phones if needed. He started down the corridor, then stopped. "Bridget. You, uh, wear a coat today?"

"Just my trusty raincoat."

"Can I . . . borrow it? I'll explain later."

"My raincoat?" Kevin's car keys chimed impatiently. "Okay, but do I get an explanation?"

"I need it for an exhibitionist I'm treating," he said deadpan. She paused in handing the bundled beige poplin over the desk. Kevin winked and Irish-green eyes rolled. "For a psychiatrist, you sure are a pathological liar."

"I tell you true; I swear. But let's keep it just between us, right?"

He took the five flights down to the underground parking area at a dizzying clip. You had to say one thing for Jane Doe and the surprising phone calls she generated: she did wonders for the cardiovascular system. He hated to back the Jaguar out of its sweet niche near the elevators. Sure to be snapped up while he was gone and he'd have to spiral halfway to Hades to find another open spot later. Campus parking was more precious to faculty than straight A's to students.

Oh, well. . . . Kevin and the car burst out of subterranean dimness into full fall sunshine and a pedestrian-mobbed street.

Traffic progressed at a crawl, but he really couldn't see escorting Jane six blocks across campus on foot, even in a raincoat. Although evidently that's how she'd made her way there.

The Church Street light took forever, and class-happy students surged into the crosswalk long after it had turned in his favor. Such ardor to get to class; more likely a bridge game at Coffman Union. He drove the people-thronged curves, avoiding jaywalkers but cursing them roundly, if only mentally. There'd be hell to pay if word of a Probe patient's . . . jaunt . . . got out. But how? And when? And why? The same old questions that always surrounded Jane Doe.

Kimball Library sat on the opposite side of an inner quadrangle. Kevin jammed down the visor to display his parking permit and jogged across sidewalks slicing still-green lawn into pie-shaped pieces. A few early-fallen leaves snapped like insect husks under his soft soles. He was glad he'd worn his corduroy jacket; under the trees, the morning air felt chilly. When had she come here—last night? Early this morning? In only a light gown?

Kimball, like all campus libraries, was marbled, vaulted, echoing and somehow deserted-looking, despite the seated students lining its corridor walls, eating and studying. The information clerk told him Mary Ann Cleaver was in general reference and so she was, a trim Molloy-success-suited young woman waiting by the main desk as impatiently as he hurried toward it.

"Dr. Blake," Kevin identified himself, surprised to hear he sounded slightly winded.

"She's over here; in a back section, luckily. I just left her there. She didn't seem interested in leaving."

Kevin could see what the librarian meant. It was Jane all right, standing at a long table heaped with books. She had the top one on the pile open, and was turning pages rapidly, like a speed reader. She didn't notice—or perhaps she just didn't acknowledge—their approach.

76

The librarian paused with Kevin to watch her. "Lost, just lost. That's how I found her. I'm first in, except for the maintenance man. He hadn't noticed her. But no locks are broken. We can't imagine how she got in. She's been like that ever since, simply turning page after page, not even reading. She dragged all those heavy books out herself. You work in the psychiatric department, don't you, Dr. Blake? That's all she would say. Your name. And—hers, when we insisted. What's wrong with her?"

"Did you get a *Star-Trib* this morning?"

"Of course. It's back at the desk."

"Get it," Kevin said softly. "I'll watch her."

She was back in a couple of minutes, turning the paper in her hands as she came up. "Oh." She'd found the sketch.

"Think the likeness is recognizable?"

"Amazing. Then she's the girl without a memory. Poor thing. But why come here, why the books?"

"Maybe she's hoping to see something that triggers a memory. It can happen that way with amnesia victims—they see something in passing and, bingo, the whole forgotten past returns."

"Poor thing."

"I'll take her back. Sorry if it caused a problem; she shouldn't have been able to slip away like this. But she's . . . harmless."

"That's okay. It must be pretty unsettling to have nothing to remember."

Kevin advanced slowly on Jane, obliviously captive amid her towers of books. "Good morning. Boning up for our next session?"

She looked up, perplexed but calm. He swiveled the top book toward himself, flipped the cover shut to see the title. "*The Physics of Belief: A Metaphysical Approach to Science.* A bit dry, isn't it?"

Her fingers stroked the page and then she rubbed her thumb across the tips; she'd taken him quite literally.

77

"Here. Put this on." He held up the raincoat until she thrust one arm into a sleeve, then the other. She was, if possible, more docile than ever. He led her to the librarian.

"Could you possibly find time to list those books—just title and author. I know it's a chore, but it might give some clue; she probably was looking for a picture, something recognizable, not reading at all—"

"Of course. Who could read at that rate? No wonder she didn't pay us much attention. We must seem like ghosts to her."

"My number's in the campus directory," he reminded her.

"At least she remembered your name. Aren't you the one who worked with that guy from the nutsy cult?"

"Right."

"It must be fascinating." The librarian's smile was dazzlingly personal. "I'll call you with a list as soon as I can."

"Great. And if you could . . . keep this quiet. The less attention drawn to her case, the more chance I've got to crack her memory."

"I understand. There's nothing missing; no need to call the campus police. She must have hidden away yesterday evening."

"Thanks a million." Kevin flashed his own smile and steered Jane down the hall. In the coat, she looked as ordinary as the average U student, maybe more so. Except for the feet. He stopped her at the top of the stairs.

"Where are your slippers?"

"Slippers?" She seemed dazed, or—more correctly—abstracted, as if she'd been lost in another world.

"Those stupid paper shoes they make you wear. Where are they?"

She smiled comprehension and agreement. "Oh, those. I don't know. I think they blew away."

He escorted her quickly to the car. Busy students ignored them, even her bare feet overlooked. No wonder she'd been able to wander unchallenged halfway across campus in her

78

hospital gown. Everything and everybody was accepted on a campus with fifty-five thousand students ranging from punkers to Hare Krishnas.

"You mustn't skip out like this again. It could get you into trouble, Jane," he lectured in the car. "It could get *me* into trouble." He turned the key so hard the engine squizzled uselessly until he winced and let up on it.

Kevin was silent on the way back to the hospital; so was she. It gave him time to reflect glumly that she volunteered nothing and that all of psychiatry was based on patients being emotionally needy enough to betray themselves.

Once inside the parking ramp, he hustled her up the back stairs, taking away the coat. By the time they reached the familiar corridors of floor five, she looked her perfectly normal ward self. Except for the missing slippers, which no one would notice; they were too easy to lose, damn flimsy clodhoppers.

In her room, he sat her down on the bed. "Here, better warm your feet. How long were you gone?"

"Since morning." For one of her unswerving literalness, that would be when the sun came up at six. At least she hadn't been out and on her own all night. He shuddered to think what dangers lurked on the deserted campus.

"You mustn't leave the hospital, go anywhere, without my permission; do you understand, Jane?"

She nodded seriously. It was all too easy to treat her like a child, to order and confine and assume that silence was a form of acquiescence. It wasn't with a child and it had less chance of being so with her. He started to leave.

"Dr. Blake?"

"Yes?"

"Do I still come for my session this afternoon?"

Kevin leaned against the doorjamb. "Do you still want to?"

"I just want to know . . . what's expected of me."

79

"And I just want to know what you expect of yourself. I guess you'd better come. I'm not angry with you, Jane."

"No, but you . . ." She stopped, her face smoothing out the tiny frown that had puckered its center.

"See you later, Jane."

He spun into the hall. Jane had never showed uncertainty before, never a hint of reading someone else's reaction. Progress, a baby step of progress. Bridget McCarthy watched him approach with her chin tilted on her palm. She was a freckled redhead who usually worked too hard and fast to show her sense of humor. Now, she had a suitable object.

"Well, if it isn't Dr. Blake and the well-traveled London Fog. What was the matter, one of your overnighters get locked out in her skivvies with the funny papers?"

"Just think of yourself as a modern-day Sir Walter Raleigh. Plus you get the coat back unmuddied. And you know better than to ask a shrink awkward questions; I could have you analyzed."

"Heaven forbid! It's bad enough to work around here; I should be analyzed for that"—her voice dropped—"if you'd do it."

"I only take hopeless cases, remember? The great Cross in?"

"He's got a big meeting with some honchos from Washington in ten minutes. I don't know if I should let you in."

"All I need is ten minutes, for a modest proposal."

"Kevin Blake, the only thing modest about you is your salary."

But two minutes later he was in, and eight minutes after that—and some vociferous arguing with Cross—he was out, a petty cash voucher in hand.

Kevin flourished it at Bridget.

"Six hundred dollars out of *petty* cash?" she demanded. "You ever consider being a lawyer? How'd you talk Cross out of that, and what for?"

"You wouldn't want to know," Kevin said modestly. "When can I get it?"

She shrugged. "Two days. You want cash—or traveler's checks?"

"Cash will do fine. Believe me, I'm sticking around."

He headed back to his office, whistling.

In half an hour he had talked the head of the nursing school into okaying the second half of his plan. Then he called the dorm to set up a meeting for the next day. Next was lunch in the cafeteria with Kandy. And then the session with Jane. He managed to keep his mouth shut on his plans at both appointments—not so easy with Kandy, a mere matter of following suit with Jane.

Their session wasn't productive; he got little out of her about her early-morning escapade and less about how she'd gotten into the library or what she wanted there. He remained as serene as she; he had a bigger surprise in store for her than she had laid on him yet.

At four Mary Ann Cleaver called. "I've got the list, Doctor. It was quite a job. The range of subjects alone—theater to topology, that's a form of speculative mathematics; geography; social history; the life of Marconi. Fashion . . . It's bizarre. There's no focus to the subject matter. An almost random selection, I'd think. Even a genius would specialize more. If you want to drop by for coffee, I'll go over it with you."

Ah, sweet mystery of unilateral attraction. "I'd like that, but I'm up to my cranium in paperwork. Could you just drop it in the intercampus mail? Thanks a million. You've been a great help."

The books interested him less now than his scheme for taking arms against a sea of suspicions with one stroke. If his plan worked, Jane would be deposited safely where she was less likely to attract overt attention and would be forced—gently—to let him into more of her mind than she had so far.

81

It was an inspired idea, he thought, catching himself smoothing his mustache in thoughtful self-satisfaction—bold, simple, unpreditable. It would both protect Jane Doe and disarm her. It was—in a word—perfect.

Chapter Thirteen

"Sit down, Jane."

She perched gingerly on the overstuffed chair, her Calvin Kleins clinging like navy paint to her long legs, and faced them mutely.

"We came out perfect on the sizes," Hazel Bellingham chirruped.

Kevin had forgotten that there were still women named Hazel out there, but here she was, in the pink, wrinkle-traced flesh: widowed, white-haired, benign—the perfect dorm mother.

"I just gave you height and weight," he said. "The rest is your doing. But are you sure the, uh, jeans aren't too tight?"

"Get with it, Doctor," chided sixtyish Hazel Bellingham. "You said to dress her like one of the student nurses. Melanie Masters here was my technical consultant."

"Everything's right on," said the girl lounging in the doorway. "Those are my best jeans." Melanie was a tall, lean blonde who looked like she should have been in high school—was he getting that old?—jean-clad, too, with a sky-blue sweater that matched her eyes, its long sleeves pushed up to the elbows. "What d'you think? Jane looks great, doesn't she?"

He glanced again at his charge, finally dressed, albeit in borrowed clothes. He saw her for the first time as an ordinary young woman. Her hair had grown out extremely fast, and now brushed the shoulders of her yellow sweater. Her frame had filled out to slender but normal proportions. She still watched him—them—solemnly, as noncommittal as ever. Even as he thought that, her eyes slid to Melanie. Jane pushed first one long yellow sleeve, then the other, up to each elbow.

"Terrific," Kevin agreed. "But it's just the beginning. Did you get that list together?"

Melanie handed him a sheet of paper. "I can't guarantee you'll come in under budget, Dr. Blake. But it's everything the girls on the floor could think of. Get this, and she'll be set."

"Thank you. Thanks a lot. Everybody in the dorm understand the situation?" He turned to Mrs. Bellingham.

"We had a group powwow on it. They're really excited. It gives them a chance to see firsthand something most nurses don't encounter in a lifetime. They'll take good care of her, I promise."

"Okay. Good." Kevin patted his corduroy jacket over the inner pocket where Cross's—or Probe's—$600 rested. "We're ready. Let's go shopping, Jane."

He put out his hand and she came to him on silent, tennis-shoe-clad feet.

"Adidas. Hey, they're treating you right."

"Doctor." Melanie stopped him at the door of the lounge, a knot of brown material in her hand. "She'll need this. If she's trying on shoes."

Confused, he crammed the mysterious ball in his pocket. He hoped when he produced it the clerk would know all about it. Certainly Jane wouldn't. . . . They left the dorm.

Willhelm Hall was a vintage, 1930s redbrick building that begged for ivy. Its floors were slightly tilted and its furnishings worn, but it had a solid, mahogany-and-lace-doily air and it wasn't coed, as most dorms were. He felt good about entrusting Jane to such a bastion of the traditional.

She slipped into the Jaguar's low front seat like a pro. If she encountered something once, it was enough. An awesomely quick learner, Jane Doe.

"How'd you like the nurses? Melanie seems nice."

"She was . . . fine."

"And Mrs. Bellingham?"

"They call her Ma Bell when she's not there. I heard them."

"Well, you call her Mrs. Bellingham. I'm not sponsoring a Valley girl at Willhelm Hall. She does have that Ma Bell look, though."

"She's very friendly."

"Will you like living there—better than the hospital?"

"Will I still . . ."

"Of course." He knew what concerned her. She had imprinted on him, despite her aloofness. "You'll still come over every day for sessions. But you'll be among well people, girls about your own age, and no more stupid paper slippers, huh?"

Jane absently pushed up the sleeves again. Interesting, how she'd picked up that detail and imitated Melanie. It smacked of wanting to belong—or of being highly adaptable to stimuli and situations. A pang of sympathy shot through him as he shifted into low and turned left onto busy University Avenue. He was catapulting her into normalcy—into people and traffic and clothes and fashion fine points. She had been found naked and disconnected; now, he would camouflage her, provide the connections, the clothes to create the appearance of an ordinary person. And in the process, he would study her reactions, gather clues to her past, tap her unconscious as it acted. And, perhaps, if she appeared normal, she wouldn't stir the wrong kind of curiosity, the dangerous kind that comes from police detectives and hostile colleagues. . . .

Sometimes, naked wasn't the best disguise.

The Dayton's ramp was fairly full; they spiraled up and up

84

in shoes. He studied the list. The dreaded "underwear." But he was a veteran now and guided them right to the "sheer nothings" department. Here, he pushed the list into Jane's hand and indicated a clerk tending the counter. "Remember. You've been in the hospital. Tell her you need help with the sizes."

He could only loiter in the aisle, pacing past lushly dyed sets of flimsy underthings—burgundy and grape, silver gray and gold, pale peach and faint aqua. He kept an eye on the arch leading to the forbidden fitting rooms. when Jane and the clerk emerged, he joined them at the computer, money ready.

The clerk was stuffing Jane's purchases into another bag, but Kevin noticed something.

"Wait a minute." The clerk looked up politely. "These are all, all white."

"That's what she said. White."

Kevin waved at the kaleidoscope of seductive color behind him. "What about all those?"

"We have these styles in every shade, sir. But the young lady insisted on white. Actually, it's harder to find white these days."

Kevin stared at Jane, who stared back. All white. All these colors to choose from, to be tempted by. And she chose white.

"Will that be all, sir?"

"Um, yes. Here." He quickly checked the sales slip and handed four twenties across the counter. Over $60, for the smallest bag yet. Shopping was crazy.

All white. Colorless. Why? They had wandered into the stream of shoppers, Jane following Kevin's lead as mutely and automatically as a dog. It chilled him, her utter lack of lust for the frivolous. She ought to *care* about something; instead, her shopping spree had all the passion of a trip to the dentist. Of course. The nurses wore white. Jane see, Jane do. She was utterly programmable. He checked the list numbly.

Winter coat. Winds blew colder, leaves turned yellow, and Jane would probably still be in treatment when the snowflakes swirled. And he probably would be no closer to solving her mystery. How to depress a shrink: Take one unrevealing amnesia victim and shake well . . .

Outerwear was in full winter gear, its mannequins huddled into hoods and scarves. Jane examined the rows of coats with the same lackluster interest while Kevin counted his remaining twenties, setting a limit of $180; that ought to buy *something,* even these days. If nothing else, he'd learned a hell of a lot about women's clothing.

Jane was gone.

He looked around, sure he'd hallucinated her absence; she'd been at his elbow all the time, except when he left her with some clerk. His eyes flicked frantically across the endless stream of customers—looking for . . . yellow sweater, that was it. He swung into the traffic, brushed strangers' arms, went a few steps, turned, doubled back. Lost. Lost again. But she knew his name, knew hers, such as it was. She'd told the librarian. Would she have the sense to tell anyone now? Or would she just merge with the mob and wander, calm as crystal, into the rush-hour streets, into downtown Minneapolis, vanishing as oddly as she had been found?

His blood throbbed anxiously; his mind applied the cat-o'-nine-tails of guilt with a vengeance. How could he have lost her, how could he? He circled back to outerwear, frustrated, fearful, almost hoping time would reverse itself and serve the Jane of minutes past to him on a platter.

Only the same deserted department. Apparently not everyone had a winter coat on her fall shopping list. Against the far wall, the expensive furs lurked behind their glass sliding doors; here, the same wool coats that had failed to excite Jane hung, with no one to reject them now. . . .

"Do you want to try that on, dear?"

Simple sentence, half heard. And somehow familiar. "Do

you think you can find your way here again on your own, dear?" Deer/dear; they always, instinctively, called her "dear."

He was plunging through the racks of coats as through a forest, their close, woolish scent reminding him of trees, of his dream. Lost, lost in a cashmere jungle and there, a glimpse of red-gold fur, something wild . . .

Jane was there, her face buried against a sleeve of thick fur, her back to a hovering, expensively dressed saleswoman.

"It's hooked to the rack; I'll have to unlock it if you want to try it on," the saleswoman was saying in a voice as hard and lacquered as her high-piled hair.

Kevin stepped up, put his hand on Jane's arm, drew her attention. The saleswoman eyed him—shoes first, then jeans, jacket. Her glance rested on his watch and remained there a full three seconds. A predatory smile dawned.

"She seems most taken with the opossum, sir. Were you looking for a coat?"

"Yes, but—" Kevin looked uncertainly over his shoulder to the cloth coat forest behind him.

"A fur coat is really a wiser investment for a Minnesota winter. And these are on preseason special." She was unleashing the thing from its hanger, unfolding its satin lining to slip it over Jane's shoulders. "Perhaps the silver would better complement her coloring, but this will give her a feel of it. Come to the mirror, dear."

Jane went, her hands driven into the deep fur at her arms, holding it on, holding herself within it. She turned before the triple mirror, as the saleswoman said, her expression transfixed.

"Let me get the silver," the woman suggested smoothly, reaching for the coat. Jane's hands tightened and held, her face grew cold and taut in the mirror.

"Oh!" The saleswoman's hands flared back, open, as if she was in a bad play and were showing surprise. "A shock. Quite a nasty one." Her face had grayed. She took a few deep breaths. "It's these carpets, you know. The management insists on carpet in the fur salon. But it's so easy to pick up static electricity. . . . I've never had a shock quite like that.'' She glanced to Jane and the coat again, nervously.

Kevin stepped behind Jane in the mirror, so the saleswoman saw only him. ''I think she likes this one. How much is it?''

''Only seventeen ninety-nine,'' she trilled cheerfully.

Kevin watched Jane in the mirror. Her hands stroked the coat, her eyes warmed to the fur and admired it. She reminded him of a cat preening, cleaning, grooming. And he had thought her unreachable. She adored the coat; she had eyes only for the coat. For $1,800 of dead animal pelt.

Her eyes suddenly met his in the mirror. They glowed with excitement, sparkled with mute appeal. Kevin reached for his wallet. The MasterCard he seldom used lay in its appointed slot. He couldn't remember whether his credit limit was $1,200 or $2,000, but he guessed he'd find out soon enough.

''We'll take it.'' Jane dropped her cheek to the collar and rubbed it there, her eyes on his still, satisfied and therefore registering an expression he'd never seen on her face, never expected to see—sensual.

He turned away while the saleswoman brought the sales slip for his signature. She glanced over his shoulder at Jane, questioningly.

''We'll, uh, take it with us,'' he said. ''No box. We already have enough to carry.'' He nodded to the bags heaped around his feet. The woman arched one darkly drawn eyebrow, then smiled her brittle marzipan smile. ''Of course, sir. I hope your lady enjoys the coat as much this winter as she does now.''

Jane followed him down the string of escalators leading to the first floor, wrapped up in her coat both literally and figuratively. Well, it was what he had wanted—to see her taken with something, to see her react positively to something. God, $1,800. Not bad for a fur coat, he supposed, but too much to put on the Probe account. He'd just have to pay for this little brainstorm out of his own pocket.

But it wasn't the money that bothered him, or how nuts he'd look to anyone who knew he'd bought it for her. It was her obsessive reaction to it. She was either turned off or on, one or the other. Nothing moderate, nothing in between. She'd been ready to claw that saleswoman for possession of the damn coat—but then she hadn't had to. The lucky accident of the static electricity had prevented a scene. Or was it lucky? He turned back to watch Jane, still intent on caressing her new pet. She sensed his glance and looked up, her eyes full of trust and pleasure.

She was silent, as usual, on the drive back to campus. Still consumed by the coat, she let herself be led away as Mrs. Bellingham and Melanie descended on Jane, murmuring over the coat and peering into the packages.

Kevin left the dorm unnoticed and stood at the top of the steps, looking across the campus. The landscape was reassuming its peaceful academic isolation now that the daily tide of people ebbed as the campus clocks neared five o'clock. Normalcy. That's what he'd wanted for Jane, a camouflage of normalcy. Now she had a whole wardrobe of it, including what every woman supposedly wanted—a fur coat. What did that tell him? That Jane Doe was female? That he knew. But what else was she?

Chapter Fourteen

"You're right, Dr. Blake."

"In what regard?"

"There *is* a North Dakota town where tooth decay is practically unheard of. Must be the only thing the state's got going for it."

"For shame, Detective Smith, that's Minnesota chauvinism if I ever heard it. Any luck identifying the Doe there?"

"Nope. Tried Montana, too. Good teeth there."

"What about . . . her sketch in the *Star-Trib?*"

"Not yet. Lots of calls. Mostly nuts. You know how it is."

Kevin relaxed, tilting back his chair. He was glad Smith confined contact these days to the odd call now and again; he'd hate to be under visual surveillance when asking such questions as: Has anyone come forward to claim Jane Doe yet?

"Any progress on Kellehay?" he ventured.

The phone sighed profoundly. "That's a tough one. Everything on the kid from Crow Wing comes up routine. No history of mental illness, that kind of thing. You still holding to your theory that he snapped when he saw his partner fry?"

"That's grounds for snapping, even in Crow Wing."

"Maybe especially in Crow Wing. Your gal spilling anything yet?"

"All she remembers is the ambulance, and we're lucky to get that, considering the condition she was in."

"But she's doing okay now physically?"

"We're, uh, cautiously optimistic."

"You doctors always are. She looked pretty good for her portrait session the other day. Maybe we should've gone with a photo. Too bad you were so against flashbulbs. But people tend to study sketches; they know sketches only run for wanteds and other interesting stuff. A photo in the paper is just another photo to be ignored, unless it's a murder victim, if you know what I mean?"

"I know exactly what you mean."

"Well, take it easy and let me know if you get anything from our Doe. I'll be in touch."

Kevin let Smith hang up first, dwelling on the casual "our Doe" dropped in at the end. Smith wasn't letting go, even though he had nothing more than air to sink his teeth into. Cops and shrinks weren't that different.

He'd barely laid the receiver in its cradle when the phone rang again.

"Dr. Blake? It's Hazel Bellingham."

"Yes, Mrs. Bellingham." His shoulder muscles tensed again; he was waiting, he realized, for something to go wrong.

"I just had to tell you, the girls have been having so much fun with Jane and her new clothes; it's like they've got a doll to dress up.

"And Jane . . . well, Doctor, it was so cute this morning. I peeked in on her, and she was *sleeping* with that new fur coat of hers, just like with a teddy bear. She's even given it a name. Don't you think that's progress? I mean, she's fitting in so well. Some of the girls bring their old stuffed animals to the dorm, you know, sort of a security blanket. And now Jane has this fur coat. Isn't it wonderful?"

"What name did she give it?"

"Oh, I don't know. Something funny. Zyunsinth. No clue there, unless baby talk. Maybe she's reverting to her child-hood now that she's with other girls and out of the hospital."

Everybody was an amateur shrink these days—security blankets and reverting. Kevin wished he had a security blan-ket he could revert to. "That's great, Mrs. Bellingham. I appreciate these reports. I'll ask Jane about that in session."

"So glad to help, Doctor."

Zyunsinth. Typical baby babble, sure. Just like ecnalubma. Much too sophisticated a collection of sounds for your aver-age eighteen-month-old. But at least the oddities were in context now, in an environment where those around Jane had an unconscious stake in arranging what she said and did to fit their own frame of reference.

Jane gone girlish; homesick Jane, clutching her new fur coat at night like any lost freshman hugging her pink, floppy-eared stuffed dog. . . . His job would be to never accept her

93

on those terms, yet make everyone else accept her at face value—and make the Probe team think she was still an interesting enough case to justify its time. Kevin Blake. He led three lives.

And still he expected—he knew in his bones—that something was about to go wrong.

He pulled out an article on amnesia victims he'd unearthed in the subterranean metal shelves of the medical library, a repository for obscure Ph.D. theses and long-lost back issues of medical journals.

This time his in-house line rang. Shit. If it was Cross or Swanson . . .

"Bridget at the desk. There's someone here to see you. A Laurel Bowman."

"My calendar's clear today—"

"She says it's important. About your Jane Doe."

Everything stopped. His senses buzzed. This was it. The going wrong. "Okay. Show her in."

Laurel Bowman. It didn't sound like the name for a nemesis. . . .

He greeted her at the door, shoved the chair Matthews liked over to the desk. No Eames chairs for potential problems.

"Thank you for seeing me, Doctor." She looked around, quickly, but thoroughly, and she didn't like what she saw—the tacky office. Her eyes registered the most approval when they paused on the Eames chair, the second most when they came at last to him.

He studied her as well. Slender, dark-haired, in her thirties. Adolescence had pitted her cheeks with souvenirs of hormonal upheaval, but she used makeup well and dressed better—expensive emerald-green sweater, pearls, well-cut black suit. She adjusted herself in the chair, legs crossed, slim calves angled left, and set a large black calf bag as business-like guardian on the lap her legs pointed to. Nervous as a Bengal tiger, but channeling it into intellectual energy.

"You handled the Larsen cult case, too, Dr. Blake."

He nodded.

"You seem to get the brain teasers, don't you?"

"I ask for them."

"I'm not surprised." Her smile was nicer than he had thought it would be. "Mind if I smoke?"

He shoved the big olive-green glass tray toward her. Chain smoker. He'd bet a case of Heineken on it.

She lit up expertly, inhaled hungrily. "I've come about your current case. The one in the *Strib*."

Strib. She knew this town. Couldn't be from North Dakota, home of holeless teeth, not in that outfit, anyway. Dark-haired, slim—no, thin. Sister? Damn. He didn't want easy answers walking in on him on a Thursday morning without an appointment.

"I'm interested in Jane Doe, very interested," she said.

"So am I."

"Perhaps we can work together, then."

Work? What the hell—

"I've done some medical reporting—you know, ordeal stories for the national magazines. 'Liver Transplant Tot Blooms Again,' that kind of thing. I thought—"

"Look. I wouldn't let the *Star-Trib* do a story, why should I let some free-lancer?"

"I'm not 'some free-lancer.' I'm a damn good reporter. I've got an application in at the *New York Times* and a good shot at it, but I need a big story, an exclusive story. Jane Doe could be it."

"Lady, Morley Safer called my boss. *Sixty Minutes* wanted to do it. I turned it down."

She sat back, her eyes narrowed through an exhaled veil of smoke. Her smile was satisfied. "All the better. I knew it could be a big story; I don't like to share, even with *Sixty Minutes*."

"Does the *Times* hire chutzpah?"

She nodded, still smiling. "You bet. Look. I'll do it your way. You're the doctor. Just let me be there. Watch. Maybe

95

interview you—and her, when you think she's ready." Laurel Bowman leaned forward, the pearls shifting against their flat-chested field of green, yet somehow shouting her sex out loud. "It might help her find her past. And—it might make you a national figure, Dr. Blake. You're young, attractive—charismatic enough to cure a cult member. *People* magazine is panting for altruistic types like you, the talk shows—"

"My patients cure themselves," he said sharply. "That's what it's all about, you know. Jane Doe and I aren't going to be any media dog and pony act."

She shrugged and squashed out the cigarette. Her fingernails were gnawed to the quick, but her hand motions were graceful as a pantomimist's. "The medium can be as hot or cold as you like it. I'll just do the story, then. There's nothing more dignified than a *New York Times* Sunday front. Cold type. No lights, no heat. No halo for Dr. Blake. That better?"

"No!" He leaned forward. "Negative. Forget it. I'm not interested in publicity. I'm not interested in advancing your career."

"It's not a career, Doctor, it's my goddamn survival!" She was leaning forward, the anger he sensed under the surface steaming from her very pores, her intense eyes. He could almost smell the acrid, bitter odor of it. "I've got two kids to support; the papers aren't hiring; my damn ex-husband has a sweet job at the *L.A. Times* and still can't get his support checks out on time; and I've got to pay the rent. Don't I need help just as much as some lost soul from Crow Wing County? I'm a crack reporter. I quit when I married him and he left me to try to get my seat back on a train that's booked full. I'd do a good job. Better than anybody. Give me a chance."

"I didn't ask for your personal history," he said gently.

"No." She sighed and sat back, pulling out another cigarette. "But you've got a nice face." Her features hollowed as

96

she sucked the lighter flame deep into the raw end of her cigarette.

"Nice is not a synonym for easy."

"You take your job awfully seriously."

"Someone has to."

"Are you so . . . hard . . . off the job?"

"How about you?"

"You'd be surprised." A long blue smoke stream sailed in his direction. "But on the job . . . It's a free country. First Amendment, etcetera. If a reporter runs into an immovable object, she can always write around it. Interview ambulance attendants, the police, nurses, other doctors—"

"Probe people don't talk."

"Not only Probe people have dealt with her, seen her. I could do a poignant sidebar on the young Crow Wing policeman who died after finding her, for instance. On the series of jinxes that seem to follow her—anything gone wrong in your life lately, Dr. Blake?"

"I see perfectly well what you *can* do. I suppose there's no way I can talk you out of it. I'm only concerned for my patient's long-term good, that's all."

"You could—" The silken slither as she uncrossed her legs drew his glance to her hose. They weren't Jane's bland brown gray, but a sheer black shade. "You could take me to dinner and talk it over seriously. At least I'd know you hadn't rejected me out of hand."

Rejected her. Yes, of course. She wanted a story. And something else. Always. She had to win something, having concluded that life had somehow cheated her—of a job or a husband or financial security. He was on her want list, she'd decided. And she wasn't the type to walk away from anything empty-handed.

"Dinner . . . ," he stalled. "Any preference where?"

"You name it."

"Geppetto's all right?" It was Italian, trendy, expensive.

97

Money was one thing that could soothe that inbred resentment. Money, and a currency more personal.

"Per-fect." She blew out the word with her last mouthful of smoke. Her eyes twinkled as they both stood and she extended her hand for a mock businesslike shake. "I'll meet you there. Tonight. Seven?"

"Fine."

"Kevin at seven," she noted piquantly. "It'll be hard to forget."

Jane sat on the Eames chair, straightening the pleats on her new gray skirt with melon-pink-tipped fingers.

"Your nails . . . How'd you come by that stuff?"

She fanned a hand as if seeing it for the first time. "Melanie did it. She said it would match my blouse."

"It does," he agreed shortly, startled by how her neat, perfectly cropped nails had grown long and strong without his noticing it. The fur saleswoman had been luckier than she knew.

"Don't you—like it?"

"I'm just surprised, that's all. It only matters what Jane likes."

But that one, calculatedly feminine touch on a person previously stripped of all such artifice had tainted the session. It conjured visions of Laurel Bowman, who had been wise enough to avoid enameling her rawly truncated fingernails, but whose scent—musky perfume overlaid with stale smoke— still lingered unhappily in his office that afternoon.

His overimaginative mind had cast Laurel as Jane's sister for one ugly moment. The camouflage he'd so carefully engineered for Jane only enhanced that linkage now, he realized as he studied her. It was working too well, and he didn't like it. Perhaps, like any mentor, he didn't want his protégée to grow up, grow independent.

"You like your new coat, too, don't you, Jane?"

Her eyes stayed downcast. "Yes."

"You like it so much you keep it with you at night."

She looked up, startled. He'd never seen her surprised by anything. "It is . . . with me."

"Any particular reason?"

"I . . . like it."

"Of course you like it. It's soft and warm. That's what it's there for—to keep you warm. But you have blankets at night; you don't need the coat—"

"It's mine!" she interrupted fiercely, her painted nails convulsing on the skirt material. "My Zyunsinth," she murmured. If he hadn't heard the word before, he wouldn't have recognized it.

"What is—zyunsinth?"

She looked confused and stared at him as if expecting him to define it. "What I call it," she said finally. "That's all."

"Do you remember why you call it that?"

Her head shook calmly, control restored. "No. I don't remember anything, Dr. Blake. Except the . . . ambulance, and the people, the bed, the dorm, the chair. You. And the paper slippers."

He smiled. "The paper slippers are the one thing worthy of forgetting."

"Do I have to remember?" Her dark eyes were troubled; he felt he was dealing with a slightly confused, slightly rebellious twelve-year-old. Perhaps Mrs. Bellingham was right; Jane Doe was regressing.

"Yes, Jane. We have to try. I think, from now on, I'll try a different approach. . . ." The idea was off the wall, but then this case was bananas. And he wanted some answer to "zyunsinth."

"Tomorrow?" Was there a hint of anxiety in her tone? Afraid of a change in therapy? Afraid of ending therapy? Pick your answer; nothing was working either way.

"Tomorrow," he said absently, already thinking ahead to his unwanted tonight with Laurel Bowman.

Jane's hands tightened on the abused gray wool again, hiding the bright nails in ripples of fabric. He noticed, but ignored it. For once, Jane Doe was not his central problem.

99

Chapter Fifteen

Geppetto's was darker than the belly of a whale. The tiny tabletop lamps barely lit the menus, though their rose-tinted shades cast flattering light on the diners, who came there more to be seen than to see.

The restaurant occupied the below-street-level floor of the latest high-rise condominium ringing Loring Park, once the exclusive domain of the proud and the gay. Now, fashion had expelled the fashion-conscious forerunners; fevered heterosexuality threatened to become the neighborhood's ruling sexual preference once again.

Kevin waited in the foyer, observing the young singles schooling in the calculated Stygian darkness of the bar. He felt old himself, having traded his jeans for cords and donned a leather sport coat to pass muster in these halls of Ivy League. Preppie was the pervading style now.

Laurel was late, purposely, he guessed. He waited unperturbed. Shrinks loved to people-watch and this place was a test of eyesight as well as insight.

"Sorry." She came sweeping in wearing a coat full enough to sweep with her. "The kids."

"No problem." He moved them into line at the podium, where the maître d' held forth in black tie over a tiny lamp, looking like the Devil at a reading of "Don Juan in Hell."

Their table proved to be located in the dimmest, most intimate corner. Laurel slid in next to him on the velvet banquette, verifying his instincts. She would order a gimlet, he decided, tart and strong.

"Tom Collins, straight up," she told the waitress. Close enough.

"You don't look like a Scotch man," she commented when their drinks arrived.

"I drink by color—beer, Scotch, sherry."

"The blond school," she noted. "You have anything against brunettes?"

"Not a thing. But that would confine me to Black Russians."

"Not healthy, confining oneself, is it?"

"I'm just your average shrink. Healthy . . . is in the eye of the beholder."

"Well, my eye is on your case." The waitress came for their order, and Laurel gave it without checking the menu. She'd been here before, often. Kevin ordered veal scallopini and waited.

"I've been thinking about our talk this morning," she went on, already draining the ice in her glass. "There must be a reason you're so against my doing a story on Jane Doe."

He sipped his Scotch. "Would a good reason change your mind?"

"Maybe." Laurel was retreating behind her nicotine smoke screen again; it haloed her against the dimness. She wore something black, slit needle-narrow from throat to lower sternum, where her pale skin flashed though like a long thin fang of flesh.

Dragon lady, he thought. Dinner with a hungry dragon lady. How do you disarm a dragon? Show it a chink in your armor.

Kevin turned his glass contemplatively, watching the heavy crystal indent the padded tablecloth. "Maybe the reason is fairly simple." He looked up. "I'm not getting anywhere with her, Laurel. Nowhere. Zip. There's no story, because there's no triumph of mind over matter. It wouldn't be worth a classified in the back of the *Loring Park Tattler*."

101

She leaned away, both to assess him and let the waitress deliver an oval plate of linguini.

"You're telling me the wunderkind is striking out?"

"Something like that."

"That's hard to believe."

"Nobody's perfect."

"I guess."

"Look, Laurel, I'd like to help you out. I know you're a top reporter—you did the first piece on the U heart transplant program."

"You remembered that?"

He smiled disarmingly. "I had Bridget look up some of your stuff."

"Well." She was flattered. "And what did you think?"

"I thought you'd be perfect to do a story—if there was one. There isn't. I didn't want you to think my refusal was a professional reflection on you. . . ."

"Isn't that getting a little personal, Doctor?"

"Kevin. And it means a lot to you personally, I see that. So I thought you deserved an explanation."

"It's tough," she said suddenly, pushing aside the half-empty plate and lighting another cigarette. Kevin methodically ate his overcooked veal and did what he was so good at, listening.

"It's not just Ted's running off with that ninny from the Arts page. Then they both get jobs on the *L.A. Times,* like honeymooners. The *L.A. Times*! When I can't land a PR job. And it's not just having the kids to worry about. They're darlings; I love them both wildly. I wouldn't let that stinker have them even if he wanted them. I can make enough money here and there to keep us going, maybe not as nicely as we used to, but enough. It just gets lonely, when you've got nobody to talk to but grade-schoolers. You've never been married; you don't know what it's like to be out there alone again, surviving."

"You check me out?" he inserted into her monologue.

"Hmmm? Oh, the married bit." She toyed with her empty glass as Kevin flagged the waitress for another. His Scotch had barely ebbed, thanks to melting ice cubes. He began to feel a bit guilty for being such a ready victim.

"Yeah, checked you out, Dr. Blake." She smiled, meaning to signal intimate interest, not empty desperation. Her finger tapped his hand. "You have a very good track record, you know that? With your cases." She traced a tendon from his knuckle to his wrist. "If I had something wrong with me, I'd come to you for treatment. Just like—if you had a story, you'd let me do it. Mutual professional respect, right?"

"Mutual something," he agreed.

She put her glass to her mouth and kept it there, sipping slowly, eyeing him over the rim. "No more games. We're too modern, right? Your place or mine?"

Something flashed over his expression before he could control it.

"The kids are at a sitter," she added quickly. "That's why I was late. Dropping them off."

Kids dumped; place clear. She loved them dearly, but woman does not live by maternal instincts alone. Kevin signaled the waitress for a check. He had a feeling he was going to hate himself in the morning.

Chapter Sixteen

Leaves rained by the window in a relentlessly unpredictable rhythm, like drifting yellow confetti from a party long over, hypnotic and sad. Kevin spun from the scene, feeling sheepish for a couple of reasons. One occupied the surface of his consciousness, embarrassing as a five-year-old's puddle. That one he could skirt. The other, more immediate shame lay deeper, submerged, and he wasn't ready to dredge it up yet. First he had to deal with a crucial step in the treatment of Jane Doe.

She was due any moment. Kevin tapped his fingertips together, then pulled the watch off his wrist, turning the time contemplatively in his fingers. Three minutes to two. She always arrived on the dot. Kept perfect time, like a metronome, like a pendulum—his mental imagery was dwelling on precisely what his emotions wanted to dance around.

He watched the second hand make its graceful golden sweep three more times, then looked up. Jane was standing in the doorway, watching him gravely, as she always did.

She came in, turned to shut the door, then paused as the poster slid by.

"Mick Jagger is really cool," she observed.

"That your opinion—or Melanie's?"

"Glenda's." She perched matter-of-factly on the Eames chair, not swinging her legs up on the ottoman, but sitting with her hands folded as for prayer between her jean-clad thighs. Her sky-blue sweater sleeves were pushed up to the elbows. He found himself wondering if her legs and underarms remained unshaven.

"She played me some."

"Who?" Speculation had derailed sequential conversation.

"Glenda."

"On her tape player?"

Jane nodded.

"I bet Glenda didn't have the problems with her machine I had with mine," Kevin joked, tapping the box where the tiny mechanism unreeled rapidly through the Plexiglas window.

Jane didn't quite look at the tape recorder—or him. "No."

Kevin frowned. Was this what she was learning among so-called normal people? Evasion, a stock set of reactions—pushed-up sleeves and the Rolling Stones are cool? What was

104

wrong with that? Why else did he have the poster if not to advertise his tastes? Why shouldn't she? Maybe because she hadn't come with any tastes, his inner voice answered.

"Relax." Kevin indicated the full sweep of chair, and she pulled her hands reluctantly from between her legs as she changed position. Was she cold? "Jane—your nails . . ."

"Yes?" She looked at them.

"You didn't have to change . . . I mean, take off the nail polish. Was it because I said something? I was just surprised. You're supposed to do what you feel like."

"Why? Hardly anybody does in the dorm." Her look was frank, confused. "Do you do what you feel like?"

He smiled. "Sometimes." That other thorn prodded him. "Sometimes not. But nail polish is such a little thing. . . . You don't have to take it off because you think I don't like it."

She fanned her hands to study them dispassionately. "I didn't," she announced. "They grew so long I cut them off. The color went—snip, snip—into the sink. Melanie gave me a manicure set with a little scissors. . . ."

"They grew—when?"

"Last night," she informed him solemnly, contentedly. "They were so long by morning, I had to cut them all off."

He was speechless as she curled her fingers into her palms, then stretched and settled into the leather. "What are we going to talk about today, Dr. Blake?"

"Something new I'm trying. Have you ever heard of hypnosis?"

Her eyes paged sideways to a recent memory. "Oh, yes. In a book. It taps the unconscious," she parroted. "But no one really knows how it works."

"True, but it might 'tap' some of your lost memories. I need your permission to try it."

She nodded blithely.

"It shouldn't be stressful; I can tell you to forget if you remember anything too . . . upsetting."

"I thought it was important for me to remember?"

"It is. But in your own time, your own way. With hypnosis, I can perhaps learn things that will help you remember on your own."

"All right."

She looked at him, calm, pliant, expectant. He felt foolish. Damn B-movie scheme. Look into my eyes; you are getting sleepy, sleepy . . .

It wasn't like that. It was merely a matter of telling her quietly, firmly, that she would be slipping into a deep sleep, that she would hear his voice and answer him, that she would not remember what happened during the session when awake again. That she would respond with a hypnotic state when he said a certain word.

Her expression didn't vary as she sank into an easy, open-eyed trance; it was already blank enough. The key word he planted was one she was unlikely—certain not—to hear elsewhere. Ecnalubma.

"Jane."

"Yes."

"Jane, I'm taking you back. Back to the Crow Wing plateau, where you were found."

She stirred uncomfortably on the cradling leather.

"I know it's dark and damp, and you don't feel very well. But these things don't touch you now. You're just there. Alone. What do you see?"

"Dark. My eyes are too heavy to open."

"Why? Are you tired, weak?"

"Sleeping."

"Sleeping?"

Her head nodded heavily. "A long time. Sleeping."

"Now you're not alone. A car is coming. You hear the wheels on the road—it's not coming fast, but it's coming."

"Yes. The car."

"What happens then?"

"It, it stops, the car sound. . . ."

106

"So you hear?" Again, the slow nod. "But you don't see?"

Her head shook from side to side. "It's stopped. I hear stones, crunching. Voices, far above."

"What do they say?"

"I can't make out the words—"

"But they're coming closer."

Her face tightened. "Yes, closer. He says, yells—'No drinkin' on the job, Kellehay!' "

Kevin leaned forward. He'd never expected to hear that name from her lips, an invitation to open up the matter of Kellehay's death in a later session. . . . "What happens then, Jane?"

"Rocks. Falling on me. Someone is there, in the dark above. They're talking, and then . . . light, so bright. Hot. On my eyes. I open them . . ."

"And see . . . ?"

"Sun, sun in my eyes!" Her head jerked away, eyelids squeezed shut.

"It was just a flashlight, Jane. You're not supposed to look directly at it. What happened then?"

"They, they touch me." Her voice deepened. "Not safe. Men with metal touching me. The sun shines inside my head. I'm very far away, but they are there and they have touched me and their machines are buzzing and clicking . . . I must, I must . . ."

Jane's head rose from the leather cushion, turning sightless staring eyes to the left. Her face reflected horror, revulsion, panic, terror. Kevin fumbled too late for a smooth transition from the violent emotion evoked by the relived moment. Her mouth froze in a silent scream. She looked left, at the desk, seeing something far more exotic.

"Talking! Talking to the machine. Must defend, defend—"

"Jane . . . Jane, time has passed—"

The recorder on his desk exploded with a whirl of motion, a screech of fast-unreeling tape. Kevin punched buttons desperately, watching Jane. Smoke sifted up from the machine's interior; its mechanical shriek grew ear-piercing, loud enough to attract people from the hall, from Cross's office—holy shit!

"Jane! You're in my office. Dr. Blake's office. It's Friday. Today. The plateau is far behind you. You're alone with me. There are no men. . . ."

"Burning," she announced triumphantly, even as he intoned his headlong incantation to return her to the present. "Burning . . ." Her face turned away from him, fell almost, as if she were irresistibly drowsy.

The tape snapped, its wild motion ended. Smoke dissipated into clear air. No one came. Psychiatrists' offices were expected to emit odd sounds occasionally. Kevin's hands shook as he swept the recorder into the drawer with the Kleenex and the notebook.

Jane was breathing rhythmically again. He watched the slow rise and fall of her chest, almost mesmerized by the peaceful cadence, wishing his own respiration would return to normal. She wasn't out of the trance yet, just moved to psychic cold storage until he gathered the strength to recall her waking persona. Kevin rested his bearded chin on the fork of his thumb and forefinger, watching her float in the unconscious world he had evoked. He felt like a magician who had managed to levitate the girl in the star-spangled suit and now he didn't know how to bring her down without the wires showing.

" 'There are more things in heaven and earth, Horatio, than are dreamt of in your philosophy.' " He softly quoted Swanson's favorite, clichéd response to skeptics of her own arcane line of psychology. "But you didn't mention what in hell to do about it, Mr. Hamlet," Kevin added chidingly.

He supposed he could begin by telling Jane to forget what she'd seen, done, remembered . . . and to wake up.

*   *   *

108

Kevin made himself into a human hammock on the old Victorian sofa in his living room—feet up on one sturdy armrest, neck cradled in his laced hands on the other—and contemplated his sins both professional and personal.

It was a hell of a way to spend a Friday night, but a Bob Seger tape was booming into the high-ceilinged room and a glass of pale sherry was positioned carefully on the Oriental rug fronting the sofa, so things weren't as bad as they felt.

That afternoon's session with Jane still unnerved him. He'd tried to run the tape, but it degenerated into inarticulate whines just as she relived the moments after her finding on the Crow Wing bluff. Still, the words had imprinted in his brain: . . . they touch me. Defend, defend. Men and machines. And a machine had—apparently—killed one man then and there, a berserk squad car radio; Jane, to hear the late Officer Kellehay tell it. And the late Officer Kellehay? What had killed him? There were no machines in Jane's hospital room with him. Merely one foggy-minded, helpless patient.

"Roll, roll me away, won't you roll me away tonight . . .
I too am lost, I feel double-crossed . . ."

Atta boy. Kevin reached for the sherry placed just where his hand swung down to meet the floor. No more Jane. He had enough Jane daily in his office.

And those nails . . . Easy to overlook in the excitement later. She'd *grown* them out, as if her body had rejected the bright polish and simply pushed it away, at the mere suggestion of his distaste. What'd that tell him? She was highly suggestible—at least from him, not unusual with patients—and she had . . . unsuspected talents. Swanson-style talents. Wow.

". . . met a girl and we had a few drinks and I told
her what I'd decided to do.
She looked out the window a long, long moment, then
she looked into my eyes. . ."

Laurel Bowman. Kevin cringed mentally. A cynical, self-serving incident, if ever there was one. He'd never slept with a woman he had disliked before, and he felt—bring on the clichés—cheap.

But she was a bulldog for what she wanted—a story or . . . He'd sensed it instantly; you only needed the perceptions of an amoeba to see it. Laurel was one of the few women in the world actually in need of a good screw to set her right for a while.

He played back the previous evening, like a punishing tape of himself. He thought it would be easy at first, sex between consenting adults, a tacit contract: one hand washes the other. . . . He should have known you don't come away clean from a woman whose emotional needs are as raw as Laurel Bowman's.

Kevin stared at the high white ceiling with its recessed lights beaming down on him. Laurel's apartment had been mean-ceilinged, nondescript, cluttered; abandoned little children's shoes made a bread-crumb-like path through the combination living and dining room. An attempt to shovel broken-spined books and plastic toys into vacant corners only emphasized the kids' existence, their calculated absence, Laurel's last-minute efforts to transform a careless family nest into a site suitable for casual sex.

"It's a mess," she apologized. "Kids. They drive you nuts. It's a good thing they're so adorable."

The photos on the upright piano of uneasy faces edged in lank brown hair were not adorable.

"Sit down. An after-dinner drink?"

He nodded numbly, wishing he hadn't come, hoping he was right that being here would buy her off his case, off his Jane Doe. The coffee table was quality—oversized, good walnut—obviously a refugee from a big house, a home with two working professionals and enough money. Like her clothes.

Laurel was in front of him, a doll-sized cut-crystal liqueur

110

glass winking brandy-colored in her hand. "B and B all right?"

He nodded and took it as she plopped down beside him, her body twisted toward him, skinny legs crossed at the ankles, an elbow propped on the sofa back. It was one of those deep-cushioned suckers you sank into and couldn't get up from.

Laurel chimed rims with him. "To our collaboration."

"Not on—"

"I know your terms, Dr. Blake. Do you know mine?"

She leaned forward to loosen his tie, undo the top buttons of his shirt. He might as well enjoy it, he thought, setting down the B and B while he tried to psych himself into the mood. He had an awful feeling he was about to get a firsthand taste of the feelings of women patients who felt they had overdemanding husbands. Not that he had anything against the mutual consent of a one-night stand. Laurel was simply so predatory, so single-minded, so openly hungry it turned him off. Maybe hubby had fled for the same reason. Or maybe the hunger had come after.

Kevin knew what to do. He took hold of her meandering arms, turned his face to hers, kissed her, harder than he really wanted to, but maybe strong sensation would quiet her, disquiet him . . .

She murmured against his mouth, drowning his senses in a heavy nicotine swell, her face twisting hard against his, her hands still worrying his clothes. He attacked her zipper and hooks in turn; maybe performing the mere motions would provide the still missing motivation. . . .

Her excitement overheated the wool of her dress; it smelled like it was being ironed. His fingers slid off a designer label at its neck, then eased the dress over her shoulders, narrow, sharp shoulders heaving into his hands, as her small pointed breasts were heaving against his half-open shirtfront.

They went to the bedroom soon after, Laurel leading him down the hallway to a shade-drawn room. Here the order was

111

offputting. The bed freshly made. Too ready. But he let his clothes slide to the floor with hers and moved to the cheerily floral surface of the sheets.

He didn't feel like preliminaries, but she didn't seem to need any. They joined quickly, almost furtively, as if she expected the ghosts of her children to be peeping around the corner. Kevin had his own ghosts, and they weren't children. He moved fiercely, simulating hard desire, perhaps releasing repressed hostility, not caring enough to be careful. Laurel matched him pelvic thrust for pelvic thrust, her hands digging into his shoulders, her lost face thrashing on the pillows.

Was she orgasmic? He didn't know, but he willed a climax on her as he drove at her in a relentless rhythm. Over with. Over with. His own climax was rushing irretrievably forward, nature overcoming the niceties of conscience with its usual self-serving impetuosity. He wanted it over. . . .

Laurel moaned, clutched at him with all her muscles contracted. He felt the wrenching spasm of her vagina wring him dry. They collapsed, apart at last, each satisfied for vastly different reasons, in a bed reeking of mingled smoke and sweat and semen.

Laurel, of course, lit up afterward.

"How was it for you?" she asked, watching him through smoke-slitted eyes.

"Great." He hated reporting verdicts on intimate acts, he hated the nicotine that her very pores exhaled, he hated the look and feel of her and hated himself most for all the preceding hatreds.

She wriggled into the linens, pulling the top sheet up to her armpits, over the aggressively small breasts. "I thought we'd be a good team the minute I met you."

"It's not a long-term thing, Laurel," he warned her.

"I know." She seemed insulted that he felt it necessary to spell it out. "Strangers in the night and all that." A contemptuous stream of smoke funneled ceilingward. "I don't want continuity any more than you do, Doctor. I've had it with

112

men, their selfishness. It's time I got mine. But—'' She glanced archly his way. ''If you ever get the itch, you know where to find a good scratching.''

And that had been it, except for dredging his clothes from the floor, reassembling the shards of his ego and making what passed for a graceful exit.

Now Kevin let his eyes savor his own place. The condo was a lovingly balanced blend of old and new, an 1890s building gutted and restored. One long living room wall had been opened to its spine—sand-blasted red brick; the woodwork had been stripped and restained to the mellow sheen of a Stradivarius. But recessed lighting spangled the new white Sheetrock ceilings, and a bathroom skylight spilled starlight down on the claw-foot porcelain tub set in a retiled niche.

Kevin had showered in the glassed-in cubicle in the tiny guest bathroom after coming home, until the steam obscured the mirror over the sink, glad he hadn't brought Laurel here. It was where he lived, and its relative affluence would have sat like a greasy meal on her stomach when she returned to the apartment he had seen. She would have been even more vindictive toward him than she was by nature. And no matter what, she needed to use him more than he needed to use her.

Kevin got up and went to the long bookshelves on the brick wall, where the stereo and speakers rang out another relentlessly poignant ballad. ''Comin' home . . . You've been gone so very long. Comin' home . . .''

The condo had its own resident ghost, and Kevin didn't share it casually. He took the last photo from its resting place behind some books. Framed. The only one he'd kept. Shadow and light defining a lithe neck and limbs, a torso as taut as a bone, small head in profile. The pose artificial, frozen in the proud impossibility dance demanded of its practitioners. The beauty one saw in this motionless moment was mere cultural conditioning, Kevin knew, for he no longer admired the attenuated limb, the gravity-defying contortions. He saw them as that, contortions.

113

But Julie never had, not even at the end. She couldn't even see her own contortion into suicide. Graceful as a gazelle, dead as deer in a dream from a slow-motion tranquilizer dart. "Mine eyes dazzle; she died young." He'd heard that line at a Harvard play his senior year, from some Elizabethan tragedy. It had rammed home, forever imbedded. He'd always thought it written for Julie.

Kevin returned the photograph to its semiobscured position, where it belonged.

Chapter Seventeen

Again, the forest. Thick, engulfing dark. Himself, crashing through, something cocked over his left shoulder. A spray of small creatures across his path—startled rabbits, squirrels. Something large, bounding, leaping, stretching across the distance just ahead. A dancer, elongating into an air-suspended deer, arms thinning and stretching, fingernails widening and merging. Delicate hoof and hock, sleek withers and flank and great, staring doe eyes . . . Gone. Only the bushes whipping to and fro in token of the passage. And blood on the track. Kneeling, dotting fingertips in the sticky red . . . Nail polish, rose-scented, bursting into flame, into ashes, into smoke finally. Stale, blinding smoke, and the crash of panicked animals all around.

Kevin sat bolt upright in the dark, staring at the pale blots of window on the darkness, identifying left, right. Yes, bedroom. Same place. No change. The dream left a smoky ring of anxiety looped around his throat. No reason for it, except a tiny tingle of something. Of knowing something he really didn't know yet.

The phone rang.

It jangled his nerves so much he pounced on it, catlike, and wrenched it to his ear. "Blake."

"This is Mrs. Bellingham, Dr. Blake. I hesitated to call you so late, but—thank God you're in. Most of the girls are still out."

"What time is it?" he mumbled, still patting the night-stand for his watch.

"Twelve-thirty, Doctor. I was taking a midnight look around when I noticed the ruckus. I'm afraid it's Jane Doe's room. I don't know whether to call the police or—"

"I'll come first. What's wrong?" He kept himself from adding "this time."

"Not a bad injury. I cleaned her up already. Really, very minor, but . . . she was where she shouldn't have been."

"Be right there. Just keep things as normal as possible."

He went through the same clumsily efficient motions that had seen him through med school, that were becoming SOP again. Thrusting himself into clothes and out the door, down to his car, driving dark streets as fast as he thought he could get away with. Racing onto campus, not to the hospital this time, but to the nearby dorm. Running up steps, down halls, looking for Mrs. Bellingham.

"Dr. Blake!" The woman stood in a doorway, beckoning him up a wide set of turning stairs, then down an even wider hall. The building was old and echoing; their footsteps clattered noisily, but Mrs. Bellingham seemed unconcerned.

She opened a door stained almost black with age. It was Jane's room. He never had thought to wonder what it would look like. Painted pale yellow, almost taller than wide, thanks to high ceilings. A pipe in one corner, painted yellow, too, in hopes it would disappear. It didn't. Dark old bureau, desk. Architect's lamp. Narrow single bed. Jane on it, wearing something not on their shopping list, a floral-print flannel nightgown. Probably some dormmate's unwanted parental gift bestowed again.

The fur coat lay across the counterpane, over her knees. She looked white and wary, but—what else?—calm.

"You said an injury?" He looked bemused at Mrs. Bellingham.

"Oh, not to *Jane*. But I thought you'd want to see her first. To see that she was safe."

"She looks safe to me. Everything okay, Jane?" She nodded solemnly, her hands pulling the coat closer. "Well, good night, then."

She nodded again, and he withdrew, perplexed.

"Mrs. Belling—"

"You've got to understand. It's very upsetting when anybody unauthorized gets in. And I'm not usually on night duty. Oh, she seems to be what she says, but . . . who knows? If it hadn't have been for the accident, I might never have known she'd gotten in."

"Who, Mrs. Bellingham?"

The woman looked at him strangely. "She says you know about this, about her talking to Jane." Mrs. Bellingham nodded grimly as he shook his head in denial. "You should talk to her, Doctor. Besides, someone with medical training should see her. She's in this room. I didn't want to leave her unsupervised. I've got to get down to the desk. My girls will be checking in. It's Friday night, you know." Happy to deal with more normal concerns, she tripped away down the hall.

Kevin opened the door to a tiny lounge. A silent TV occupied a table faced by empty chairs. Except for one.

"Laurel."

She slumped in one of the hand-me-down armchairs, her elbow on its arm, her face cradled on her hand, half-obscured by falling hair.

"What's the matter? What are you doing here?"

The hand in her lap raised something in listless demonstration. He came nearer and saw it was a small tape recorder.

"You came to interview Jane Doe, didn't you?" Her laugh

116

as he realized what she'd done was bitter, vacant. "But you said, you promised—"

"Oh, Dr. Blake. Oh, lover. You should know better than to believe what a reporter promises. I wanted a story; I needed a story. I'd have said anything—"

"*Done* anything? . . ."

"Anything not too unpleasant. I figured you wouldn't be so vigilant if you thought I'd succumbed to your charms." A movement of her eyes glistened. "I was right."

He sat on one of the vinyl-upholstered chairs. It reminded him of some hellish inversion of O. Henry's "Gift of the Magi"—he had let her seduce him to keep her from Jane Doe; she had let him think she had seduced him to get closer to Jane Doe. And all for nothing. He wondered who had disliked it more.

"So—what went wrong?"

"Dumb—damn—machine!" Laurel shook it at him, her eyes glimmering feral through strands of limp hair. She suddenly hurled it straight at his chest.

He caught it, cradled it like a pet and slowly turned it over. The shattered casing radiated cracks, as if bullet-struck. Shards snapped off into his hands. Laurel went on.

"Should have taken notes, like in the old days. But I was in a hurry. I knew I'd catch hell if anybody found me. But eleven o'clock on a Friday night—who's around a dorm? Except the star invalid. I'm surprised you were snug in your bed at home, Doctor. No date?"

"What happened to the machine?"

"It, it exploded; it bloody exploded. Right in my hands. Didn't get to question one."

"Would she have . . . given you what you wanted?" he asked curiously.

"How the hell do I know? Didn't even get a chance. I walked in, told her who I was, that you had sent me—yes, I lied—and she was to answer a few questions. And then I

117

turned the thing on and it whirled and whined and flew to smithereens in my hands, my—''

Kevin sat on the chair near her. He pushed away her hair, delicately, as if defusing a bomb. Laurel's head finally came up to face him, a dozen scratches making a jigsaw puzzle of her features.

"I'm sorry, Laurel. Mrs. Bellingham said she'd cleaned you up—"

"Sure. Rubbing alcohol. Damn, it hurts. She said the plastic missed my eyes. . . ."

She sat still while he turned her ravaged face to the feeble rays of a table lamp and studied it. "Looks like it. All superficial cuts. Be healed in a week. You're lucky. Shattered plastic can cut; must have been some explosion.''

Laurel rolled her eyes, still avoiding his. He tightened his grasp on her chin.

"You lied to me. I told you I didn't want you bothering my patient and you sneak in on her at night. You got off lucky. I'm not going to call the police, as Mrs. Bellingham wants. But I don't ever want you anywhere near Jane Doe or the dorm or the hospital. Or me. You are persona non grata, get it? I'll get you out of here, but that's it. And if you try to come around again, with or without a recorder, I'll have Mrs. Bellingham hit you with trespassing charges.''

"Nice.''

"Nice doesn't mean easy, I told you that. Just because I ran your way once doesn't mean I'm a total fool. Now, c'mon, go down to Mrs. Bellingham's desk and wait for me.''

She watched resentfully as he went back down the hall to Jane's room. Jane had settled back in the covers, the coat up to her chest.

"That woman shouldn't have been here; you know that, Jane. You weren't afraid?''

"No. She said she—''

"I don't care what she said. She was wrong. You won't be

118

seeing her again." He bent down to tuck the coat around her chin, disturbed at yet another disruption of the atmosphere he wanted to blanket Jane with, one that would let her trust and remember. . . .

Jane suddenly smiled up at him, a smile disturbingly conspiratorial. Her hand touched his. "I'm glad you don't like her, either," she confided, her husky voice wavering between childish innocence and utterly adult intimacy.

Chapter Eighteen

"I'm taking you back, Jane. As far back as we can go, to when you were very young. Just a child. But you'll remember and report with all the perception you have today. You're relaxed now, and you'll stay that way, no matter what memories surface. They'll be like a movie, and you're the viewer. And you'll tell me all about it."

Bullshit. No matter how many calls for calm he implanted in her hypnotized mind, if his probing scratched some subconscious sensitivity, she'd be agitated accordingly. But he'd invoked his gods of rationality, and his conscience would rest easier.

Kevin leaned back in his chair, watching Jane carefully. One thing he knew for sure—she had to have been *somewhere* for twenty-some years. Now, he was about to play a dangerous game of psychiatric Pin the Tail on the Donkey, stabbing wildly in the dark direction of her ambiguous past, hoping to strike some clues to her present condition. If he were unlucky enough to score a bull's-eye on the period that caused her amnesia—with no hint of how to handle it—she could react with utter mental withdrawal.

"You're four years old, Jane. Just four. Where—are you?"

Her face puckered in puzzlement. Four was a fairly uncomplicated place to begin, since most people had several childhood memories dating to that age. It wasn't as if he was reverting her to unremembered infancy. She should have registered something.

"It's the day after your fourth birthday. What's the weather like outside? Cold? Warm? In between?" A birthdate could help uncover her identity.

Her head shook. "Four . . . What is four? I'm not four."

"What *are* you?"

"I—don't know."

"But it's a long, long time ago. You're very young. You don't remember much because you haven't experienced very much. What were you like—at the beginning? When you first began to know you were you?"

"I. I—was sleeping."

"At night? Or in the day? Is it a nap?"

Her head shook, slowly, implacably. "No day. No night. Nothing. Sleeping, just sleeping. Always."

"Did you have any . . . dreams?"

"Long ago. No dreams. Just—"

"Yes? Tell me, tell me whatever floats through your mind." He was leaning forward, and now she answered his urgency.

"Floats. Yes. That was it. Floating. Away from things. From *them*. But not Jane. Not I. . . ."

"They wouldn't have called you 'Jane.' Something else. Some other name. . . ."

"No name."

"You must have had a name. Remember. It will be the word that feels right. . . ."

"No name. Just floating. And the others, far away."

"What others?"

"The formless ones."

"Formless? But you saw them?"

"Not saw—sensed, I think that's it. Yes. Long ago I sensed them. But I was very . . . young. More than young. Not me yet."

"When did you become 'me'?"

She was quiet for a long time, but Kevin didn't prod her. Her whole face registered concentration. She was mentally paging through the blank book of her mind, looking for a mark that was hers alone. He waited, like Poe's mad lover, for some word of his lost Lenore. . . . The last thing he wanted was a croaked, "Nevermore," but he got his own personal version of it.

Jane's face smoothed with a smile, with the success of finding. "Zyunsinth," she announced triumphantly.

"Your *name*?" He was glad incredulity couldn't penetrate the fog of her hypnosis.

"Not mine!" She seemed irritated to have been pulled back to this place, this time by his stupidity. "*No* name. But Zyunsinth. Name. That's when . . . I . . . begins." Her hands curled around her upper arms, hugging Jane to herself, perhaps hugging someone present only in the Morse code of her responses. No name. I begins. The others.

Kevin sighed and shut off the small recorder, glad for once that Kandy's off-the-wall idea had proved useful. He'd listen to it again tonight, mull it over and get nowhere. But at least he had recorded his failure for posterity. Zyunsinth. No doubt a mythical beast, like the fearsome, screaming Ecnalubma. Jane, Jane, Jane . . . What was it backward? Htnisnuyz. Sounded bizarre, Egyptian . . . Reincarnation? Oh, come on, Dr. Blake. Hit too many blank walls and you're liable to start painting any insane visage of possibility on them.

Jane remained calm, even reflectively happy. At least *she'd* gotten something out of session today. "Okay, Jane. Bridie Murphy you're not. But you'll wake up now, feeling good—and—you'll remember what you remembered. Whatever it was," he murmured as her aspect shifted slightly into normal consciousness.

Usually hypnotized patients were curious for reports on their behavior under the influence. Jane never was. But her amplified serenity clung. It scared him suddenly. Her smile was as emptily, as imbecilically happy as a cult member's—or a presidential assassin's. What memory had he dredged up?

She smiled beatifically as she left, pausing only to tilt her head at the Stones' poster. "Today was nice," she said on the threshold. Her hand stroked light farewell down his arm.

Kevin shivered after she'd gone, staring at his forearm. He'd worn his sweater sleeves pushed up to the elbow—an affectation no doubt unconsciously learned from the same student nurse who taught Jane the trick. His arm hairs stood erect—as if a wave of static electricity had rubbed them the wrong way. Kevin donned the white jacket he normally kept on its office hook as often as he could get away with it. Maybe he needed the badges of office when dealing with a patient as volatile—as plain unpredictable—as Jane Doe. He shrugged into the starchy garment and slouched down the hall to the Probe meeting.

It floated, awake and not awake. Aware and not aware. The others, empty now, floated with it, ever-changing, as it was. Ever the same. Silent, withdrawn; there and not there. It was not the same.

Floating. For a minute it throbbed with a response that made its world, vague as it was, tremble. Floating. On something. In something, some *state*. A state remembered. And forgotten. A state about to assert itself, then fading away. Floating in sleep. Sleep was a new concept, a thought from the past—or future.

Confusion buffeted it more than the buoying element it couldn't name but depended upon for existence. It felt dislocated, duplicated. It felt it floated in many places at once—awake, yet submerged by the unfamiliar one it called sleeping. And plunged into a new state, in between awake and sleep, with another new word guarding its misty boundaries. Ecna . . . Gone, lost in the floating environment, a mere piece of driftword. So many new words, swirling around, twirling past to be drawn into its being. To be devoured. And regurgitated.

New words, new thoughts. And an old one, remembered when it should not be remembered. Zy . . . The word slid away, floating, with the formless ones.

Ah, but *it* was not formless. Not any longer. Now, it had a shape to be mirrored in those well-formed others around it. Hands. Hair. Toes. Many beings all together, shaped by hair. And these beings wore more than mere shape; other properties. Warmth. Nearness.

In the beginning, there was darkness and cold all around, and sleep was not. Then the itchy, hot press of the others. Around the hot red flutter. Far away, the gleaming globules of polished rock. Sitting on rock. Rock. Earth. Sky. Cold, then heat. Alone, then accompanied. Mute, then speaking. Empty, then overflowing with sights, sounds, words.

Thoughts. It was uncertain whether it dreamed or slept or saw. But it knew it thought. And it no longer thought of itself as "it." It was something else. The one that saw the others as apart, even as it gratefully pressed against them to form a greater whole of many parts. It was "the one." Yes. And the one seemed to be merging the memories of many "the ones."

And now—a name. A name for them—the furred, the gathered, the friends. A name they conferred upon themselves in throaty barks. Zy . . . Zy-un-sinth. It repeated the sounds to them, and they nodded, grinning to show their gleaming white—teeth, another new word.

So many new thoughts and words. And now it had one for itself, though it was the briefest, oddest, most mysterious new sound of all. Perhaps it was its name.

I.

123

Chapter Nineteen

"I must be nuts. I can't make head or tail or midsection of it," Kevin complained.

"And the truth shall make ye modest," intoned Kandinsky, drawing contemplatively on his beer.

Kevin punched REWIND. The recorder reel burbled its way back to the tape's beginning. "Robust little sucker," he noted.

"Huh?"

"If you'd taken the pounding this little machine had, you wouldn't still be blithely rolling backwards."

Kandy leaned forward on the forties armchair Kevin had rescued from Goodwill. "That's right. You did say your Doe has an empathetic effect on equipment. Maybe she's a case for Swanson and her remote viewing legions—a biological TV."

"Perish the thought. And I'm not sure it's equipment, per se. So far, it's only been tape recorders. And maybe a two-way radio."

Kandy leaned back, bored. "Told you, old boy. Case for the spooks. She's a goddamn spy, programmed to wipe our MX missile tapes clean and abscond to the Kremlin with the dope. You sure 'ecmalubna' isn't Russky?"

" 'Ecnalubma,' " Kevin corrected automatically. "Maybe the spy theory isn't so weird. So far I've got reincarnation . . . um, cult stuff, espionage and telekinesis to explain the thus far inexplicable. And she's wild about fur coats. How does that fit?"

Kandy unfocused his eyes at the redbrick wall opposite.

124

"I'm thinking. She's, she's—a throwback. Somehow un-frozen from a slice of million-year-old ice like a resurrected TV dinner. She misses her furry little playmates."

"She doesn't look like an apewoman."

"You said she was as natural as wheat germ. No Lady Schick had nicked that hairy epidermis . . . ."

Kevin grimaced. "Not anymore. The student nurses have remedied that oversight, too."

"Busy little beavers," Kandy said admiringly. "But that's what you wanted, right? Camouflage for an anomaly. Blend her right in with the native wildlife. I still say you're looking too far afield. I bet the answer is a lot closer to home. Right under the proverbial nose."

"There's never been a nose long enough to inspire a proverb—unless it's yours. 'Nother beer?"

"Why not?" Kandy slid onto his spine and laced his fin-gers over his concave stomach while Kevin vanished into the adjoining kitchen. "You haven't got a pizza in the freezer?" he shouted hopefully.

"Nope. You ate the last one last time."

"And you didn't rush out and get another? Bad sign. Shows indifference to social stimuli. You're becoming a regular hermit, man."

"They had their reasons." Kevin dropped the beer into Kandy's waiting hand and threw himself full length on the sofa while he nursed his own. "I feel like a twentieth-century Sherlock Holmes with a whacked-out Dr. Watson in tow. I keep wanting to say, 'Quick, Kandinsky, the game's afoot!' or, 'By George, I think I've got it!' But all I've got is the beginning of a mystery without an end and a middle."

"Keep playing the tapes. There's got to be something in there. Or maybe it's what she *doesn't* say. It's pretty weird to not have a childhood identity. No birthday parties. No playmates except 'the formless ones.' Maybe she really was kept in a closet."

Kevin washed his face with dry hands. "I told you, the

125

abuse profile just isn't there. She's too self-contained. I'm beginning to think she's the shrink and I'm the patient. . . ." He sat up. "Honest to God, it's getting unreal. I snapped at Cross in the Probe meeting today. If it'd been Swanson or Matthews— But Cross. Christ, he's the guy who's kept my little crusades going in his own spineless, muddling way. . . ."

"That's what I love about you, Kevin. You never let personal loyalty interfere with your incisive analytical mind. What do you say about me behind my back?" Kandy rose, draining the bottle in an awesome display of Adam's apple work.

"Same thing I say in front of it. You're a flake, but you grow on a person. Like dandruff."

"Yeah, well, I'm gonna flake off if that pathetic tape is your idea of Friday night entertainment. You wanta hit the hot spots?"

"Campus bars aren't my thing."

"This is a great place." Kandy looked around with cheerful envy. "Don't get hooked on it, okay?"

Kevin only nodded as Kandy let himself out. He knew what Kandy was saying. How long had it been since Kevin had let anyone or anything untidy into his neatly compartmented life? Work and—work. He began playing the tape again. Jane not sure when she began to be—whoever she was. The formless ones. It sounded like bad Stephen King—or good Stephen King, which was usually the same thing. Kevin drove his fingers into the hair at his temples, braced his elbows on his jean-clad knees and listened, listened, *listened*. It was supposed to be what a shrink did best.

"Wild weekend?"

"Huh?" Kevin had poured his customary mug of morning coffee from the community pot by Bridget McCarthy's desk. Bridget herself was watching him stare into the caffeine-laden circle of pungent darkness filling his cup like water from a dark, prophetic well.

"You always get into your morning coffee so intensely?"

"Just thinking, I guess. Or what passes for it. Did you want something?"

"How about being useful and pouring me a cup?" Bridget's dimples were gum-deep and the Irish was up in her eyes. Kevin shook off the Monday morning fuzzies and brought her a Styrofoam offering.

"Thanks, Doc. You're an absolute *angel*." And she giggled.

He shrugged and went into his office.

He'd started a doodle file in the notebook, so he pulled it out for review. Ecnalubma in Jane's kiddish block letters. His own less legible scrawls came next. Ego-disassociation. Brilliant. Any fool could see that a patient with no strong I-dentity had a lower level of ego involvement. Why had he bothered to write down such grad-school gibberish?

For lack of anything constructive to do. He was reacting to terminal frustration with the classic pattern: boredom. He decided to take a turn through the ward, even though he had no patients there now that Jane was squirreled away in Willhelm Hall. He would ask for any new case that came Probe's way, broaden his horizons. Put Jane Doe back in her proper place. Just another patient with another problem he could fix, would fix, eventually and infallibly. . . .

The phone rang, and he caught it before the second ring. Man, was he itchy for something.

"Dr. Blake? Mary Ann Cleaver. She's back."

"Back?"

"Your Jane Doe. In the library. This is—"

"Of course." He smoothly interrupted the mildly miffed tone developing in her voice. "I haven't forgotten you."

"Have you made any progress in discovering her identity?"

"Some. But you say she's back in the library."

"I'm looking right at her. Oh, she's dressed like Katy Coed, but there's no mistaking the stack of books. She's going through them like sixty. I asked if I could help, and she said, thank you, no; she'd found what she wanted."

"I'll come collect her."

"You want me to list the books again?"

"Yes . . . no, never mind. I'll just skim 'em when I get there. Oh, and thanks a million for calling."

This time he walked. Fall leaves sprinkled the ground like brown sugar, and crunched underfoot. This time he'd give Jane heck for her escapade. She was formally "his" now, identified with him; he'd be the campus laughingstock if his pet patient kept turning up AWOL. . . .

This time Mary Ann Cleaver looked a lot less tolerant; maybe he should have had the damn cup of coffee with her. She led him to a different section, but the scene was the same: a quiet corner, a leaning tower of tomes, and Jane whizzing through them like a speed-reading robot. It was different this time, though. He couldn't call her to task as if she were a delinquent child. She looked too normal now. Too adult.

Kevin edged up to her while the librarian hovered nearby, and stuck his hands in his jean pockets. He felt like Tom Sawyer about to embark on a little con job involving a fence.

"You stop here on the way over to my office?"

"The library isn't on the way to your office; it's three blocks north and west," she observed without looking up.

"That's what I thought I was getting at. How did you get in?"

"It was open." Jane's eyes finally met his, as darkly limpid as his morning coffee, black with honesty.

He flipped the top book shut. "But you don't have a library card. I can get you one if you want to take out some books. . . ."

"Take out? No. They're so heavy."

He laughed. "You noticed. Look, they get upset around here if someone is where he isn't supposed to be."

She looked bewildered. "Who? You?"

He. God, making a feminist point was beyond an amnesiac, he'd think. "Not where *she's* supposed to be. You."

128

"Oh. Well, I'm done." She pushed the book aside and he jumped to keep the whole tower from collapsing.

"Wait for me by the entrance," he suggested, "and I'll make it right with Madame Librarian."

Jane glanced to the waiting woman. "She isn't supposed to talk to me, either?"

"She's not like that woman," he quickly assured her; all he needed now was a telekinetic book-hurling. "But she is in charge. I'll smooth her feathers and be right with you. Then we'll—we'll take a walk along the river. Look at the leaves. How'd you like that?"

"I've seen the leaves." Jane looked even more bewildered. She left him and the books as if they'd both developed a sudden blight. Mary Ann Cleaver moved in.

"She looks quite . . . normal now."

Kevin nodded, then smiled. "But then we all do, don't we?"

"I suppose so. Have you had a chance to skim those books? Her taste in reading material appears to have shifted dramatically."

He ignored the new snideness in her tone and began separating books into piles, rapidly scanning the titles. After a few, he slowed down, then speeded up. The librarian announced the titles for him anyway.

"Masters and Johnson, *Human Sexual Response*. Comfort, *The Joy of Sex*. Penney, *How to Make Love to a Man*."

"Isn't this a rather—catholic—collection for a campus library?" The best defense is a good offense, Kevin figured.

"We, of course, have many psychology students. And then, we have an extensive pop sexuality section—"

Kevin laughed, so loudly that studious heads lifted across the vast room. "Sorry. Pop sexuality, huh?"

"You want to take notes—" She indicated the scattered books.

"No, I think I get the general idea. Thanks for the call."

"I'd say think nothing of it, but really, Doctor, I've got

129

more to do than lug your patient's books back to the proper shelves.''

"It won't happen again," Kevin promised as he retreated.

Once outside, he and Jane angled across campus, through an indifferent meld of students. It was a late October, Indian summer day. The air was still, in perfect tune with body temperature, as if the human organism was in sync with its environment for once. The sun, distilled by either the light ruffle of clouds or the way it fell through semidenuded trees, felt neither hot nor chill. Such days were rare, a tease from the oncoming winter to make its impact sharper. Mummified leaves crackled under their tennis shoes as loudly as if they wore boots.

Soon dignified brick campus buildings gave way to the undistinguished three-story concrete-block bunkers that served as cheap student apartments, then more interesting but less sound stucco houses that had long ago lost the battle to remain residential and had been hacked up into even cheaper student quarters. Along the drowsy Mississippi, students walked, jogged, biked and sat on benches to pretend-study. The river was unimpressive here, hardly visible in the deep gorge it had carved. On the opposite bluff, trees the color of burned broccoli rolled into the distance.

Jane was silent beside him, and for once Kevin felt no need to interrogate her, to continue his ceaseless probing. He was silent, too, having decided to let her speak first. He wondered if she would.

She stopped walking first at least. "I'm tired. Can we sit?''

The nearest bench was occupied by a long blue-jeaned frame—possibly but not definitely male—sleeping under the light shade of a jacket. Kevin headed for the low limestone wall that meandered along the bluff top, and straddled it. Jane sat beside him, watching the parade of too lean runners pound past along the streetside dirt path. He ought to investigate the psychology of runners; now there was a social pathology if he ever saw one. . . .

"I went to a—party—this weekend."

From anyone else the comment would have been banal. Kevin's attention snapped back to Jane. "Did you like it?"

"It was . . . strange. Glenda and Karen took me, but they didn't stay with me long. It was noisy. There were so many people."

"Were you frightened?"

Her gaze was level. "No. I was . . ." She blew out a frustrated snort of air. "It made me sleepy."

"You were bored."

"There was nothing to see, do."

"Weren't the other people doing things?"

"Not really. And they did it for the longest time."

Jane was complaining now, and Kevin smiled. He knew the student nurses' parties. Wall-to-wall bodies. Popcorn and cracker crumbs crunching underfoot. Smoke and body heat. Loud music, loud people—people crammed onto sofas, people crushed against walls, people necking. It would look like a Fellini nightmare to anyone not acclimated. No wonder she'd rushed to her nearest campus library for a quick course in human sexual behavior. . . .

"Nobody, uh, bothered you?"

"Why would they? No, I just watched. Then Glenda and Karen finally came back for me. They were very strange, laughing all the time, and they took me back to the dorm. I missed Zyunsinth."

Name. It was a name. Kevin's lazy fall day senses surged into full alertness. "But you were back with . . . Zyunsinth and it was okay?"

She nodded. "Zyunsinth makes me feel—peaceful." Her arms wrapped herself close despite the tepid embracing air as she rocked slowly to and fro, her eyes glancing left, where daydreams lurk.

Kevin slid nearer along the limestone, careful, wanting to

both remain part of the pleasant October background and yet intrude his questions into her self-lulling state.

"Jane. What is Zyunsinth? A thing? An animal? A friend?"

Her brow knit, strong dark eyebrows darting together and staying there. "I don't know. I'm not supposed to know anymore. . . ."

"Jane. The day is making you very tired. Sleepy. You know when I say the word, you'll move into a state where you can remember. When I say—ecnalubma."

She was under with her customary ease of trance, waiting for his lead, his questions. They could have been fellow students, quizzing each other quietly on trigonometry in the fall sunshine. The beat of running feet pounded faintly from the street, like a pulse. An occasional leaf gave up the ghost and fluttered noiselessly to the ground. Kevin concentrated on Jane.

"It doesn't matter what you're supposed or not supposed to know, Jane. You want to know everything, remember? You told me so."

"Yes. Everything. I must know everything."

"Tell me about—Zyunsinth."

Her smile was warm as melted caramel. "Zyunsinth," she crooned, rocking slightly again. "Warm. Strong. Safe. Soft. Zyunsinth."

"Who is Zyunsinth?"

Her forehead corrugated. "Who? Zyunsinth many. All are Zyunsinth. Fine Zyunsinth."

"All right. You're with Zyunsinth. Where are you?"

"Under the silver sky. With the fires flaring. So warm. Away from the chilling daggers. The basalt domes gleam like black raindrops in the distance. It's cold, but the stay-fires burn and Zyunsinth is everywhere. Dancing, the flames dancing on their golden hair. I feel wrapped in Zyunsinth. I feel warm and soft and safe. Stay. Stay with Zyunsinth. Stay!"

He caught her reaching hand by the wrist; instead of dispelling her mood, he felt enwebbed by it. She rocked still, and his body echoed that primitive motion. Her hand curled warmly around his own wrist, so they were linked, wrestlerlike. But her fingers stroked his skin rhythmically, hypnotically, over and over.

"Jaaa-ane." Saying her own name seemed an effort. "Jaaa-ane stay with Zyunsinth. Stay here. Please."

Stay. Here. Where? Under the silver sky? With black basalt domes and stay-fires? Sure. In Xanadu did Kubla Khan a stately pleasure-dome decree, with Zyunsinth and golden flames all dancing madly 'neath a tree . . . Maybe they'd given her something at that damn party and he was tapping secondhand opium dreams. Cocaine on the rocks. Those damn nurses were supposed to look after her. Giggling? From what?

"Stay." Warm fingertips, circling persuasively. He was half-ready to leap into some dark recess of his own mind and find the fabled fires of Zyunsinth, to go where Jane would stay, where it was warm and soft and safe, a womb of the psyche where the I could disappear under the smothering presence of Zyunsinth, whatever the hell it was, they were.

He loosened his grasp on her wrist, pulled away his hand, feeling a sense of loss, as Jane apparently felt for the lamented Zyunsinth.

"You're going to wake now, Jane. You won't remember what you saw or felt. It's just Monday, and you're by the river with me."

She woke up, still smiling.

Chapter Twenty

He walked Jane back to the dorm, told her to skip their usual afternoon session and hiked back to his office, kicking leaves savagely all the way. He didn't know if he was more relieved or aggravated that his most provocative hypnotic session yet had occurred without the corroborative witness of a tape recorder. But he played back the key phrases mentally. Zyunsinth, of course, hairy little buggers. Or big buggers, for all he knew. The landscape out of an opium dream, strangely poetic. And Jane's feelings, perhaps the most important part of the puzzle.

The key thing was that she once had been somewhere where she felt she belonged, where the essential childhood needs for physical safety and emotional security had been met. That was progress of a sort; it meant that she was vulnerable to such feelings now, no matter how aloof she seemed. And feelings were the building blocks of memory.

He took the elevator to his office; he wasn't used to hoofing all over campus. This damn case was wearing him out. At least cult deprogrammees stayed where they were put.

A few stray nurses eyed him as he went by. Apparently they were hung over from the same Sunday night party that Jane had attended, for they giggled as they passed, their laughter-sheened eyes, polished as agates, rolling in his direction. Was everybody nuts? Or just him?

Bridget waved a note at him. "Laurel Bowman called."

He went into his office to tear his white jacket off its hook and shrug it on over his bulky sweater. He crammed Laurel's call into the same brittle nest the others made in his pocket. Maybe he'd call her back. Someday.

"Off on your celestial rounds?" Bridget inquired archly.

"More likely hellish," he said, ignoring whatever obscure jibe she was offering. "I'm descending to the employee cafeteria for the usual abysmal late lunch, then it's on to the Cross and Cronies Show at four."

He ate alone, but not unnoticed. Nurses bussing empty trays ambled by, sidelong glances mixing admiration and mockery. He was used to a certain amount of female attention; unmarried doctors always were. This was more unnerving, like entering a room just after the joke's punch line has been delivered and trying to grin along with everybody else.

By the time of the Probe meeting, he was jittery, expecting something. And he got it.

"Running late, Kevin?" Cross pointedly eyed his Seiko, a brass-and-chrome affair with the circumference of a golfball.

"Sorry." Kevin slipped into the chair nearest the door, all eyes upon him, all—was he getting paranoid?—filled with the same secret merriment. No, not all. Just Swanson's. And it wasn't really merriment. It was smugness. "Did I miss anything?"

"You're the star attraction, Doctor." Swanson smiled serenely. "We all know nobody wants to hear my probability statistics on squares, stars and crosses."

Silence ruled while everybody tried to think up an appropriate pun on Cross's name and couldn't.

"Anything new on Jane Doe?" Cross himself finally asked.

"Well—" They relied on him for easy entertainment. Usually Kevin was euphoric with insights at this point in a case. He'd never thought of himself as a dancing ape in a white lab coat before. Better deliver. "Quite a lot. A breakthrough of sorts."

Shoulders around the table stiffened with interest.

"It doesn't mean much yet. But she, apparently, was with a . . . band of— This sounds weird, but there's got to be a

135

grain of reality in it. Anyway, they sound like hairy people who, um, dance around fires. It's bizarre, but so is her history so far.''

Silence. Furry flashdancers they hadn't expected.

"What do you, er, conclude from this?" Cross didn't quite look at him, like a teacher whose star pupil has just pulled the world's worse boner.

"I haven't concluded anything yet, but it reminds me—of that case of the satanists shaping that girl's mind to whatever they wanted. There was ritual there, and people in goat-skins . . .''

"Satanists, eh?" Cross brightened. "And you think she's been programmed to forget these, er, incidents?"

"Exactly." Imply you were on the track of counterculture brainwashing, and the Probe machine was right behind you. Modern science, for some reason, was fascinated by ancient arts. "But it's a subtle, complicated process. I'll need time to sort it all out.''

"You certainly have fallen, Kevin," Swanson put in, "from the sublime to the satanic. If your Doe *has* been in occult hands, it might be doubly interesting to try my para-psychological battery on her.''

"Maybe." He made it sound like "over my dead body." "But I'm on the track of something bigger here. Say a *sub*—subconscious, almost on—or below—the racial memory level. That's why her amnesia's so hard to crack.'' He was beginning to believe himself and get excited.

"Could be." Theory was Cross's cup of tea, but sometimes he just wanted to keep cases bubbling along and the Daddy Warbucks who sponsored Probe happy. And there were other things to discuss. Swanson offered interminable reports on various of her remote viewing, out of the body, clairvoyant and telekinetic experiments until five.

"You can see that even with so-called normal subjects—like the student volunteers—I'm getting a percentage of accuracy slightly higher than probability, which is significant,''

136

she concluded. "Washington was most intrigued by my last summary."

"What did Lincoln think?" Kevin quipped.

"You may scoff, Doctor, but the fact is that, spectacular as some of your cases may be to the press and other sensation-seeking elements, my work has far more practical applications."

"Yes, yes." Cross's hands patted air, urging harmony with a well-recognized gesture. "Most commendable, Dr. Swanson. I won't keep you from your work any longer. Matthews, come into my office. Some record keeping. . . ."

The two doctors drifted out, at home with problems of paperwork as they never would be with people. Swanson lingered, watching Kevin through her disconcerting lenses.

"I'm glad we have a chance for a tête-à-tête."

"Yes?" Kevin tilted his chair back expertly and jammed his fists in his lab coat pockets, a hostile gesture whose effect was not lost on Swanson. If anything, her face became more maddeningly bland. She was married, to go by the narrow gold band and stingy diamond on her plump left hand. Kevin thought someone should analyze that particular astounding fact of human behavior. Who on earth would marry Swanson?

"You know, Kevin, many of my subjects—since I'm so dependent on *volunteers*—come from this campus."

"You soliciting me, Swannee?"

"Hardly. I doubt you have any concealed psychic talent. Not one to hide your light under a basket, are you?" She leaned against the table, her own hands crammed in her pockets. Mirroring body language usually signified accord; in this case, Kevin assumed it was mutual loathing. But Swanson wanted something, and worse, was pretty damn sure she'd get it.

"Most of my subjects," she went on, "are volunteers. Even some of the student nurses from Willhelm Hall. That way I not only get unprejudiced, young subjects, but they keep my ear to the campus grapevine. That's the advantage of working with students, as Drs. Cross and Matthews sadly have no opportunity to discover.''

"So, you're the Pied Piper of Psych One and Two. That's great, but I—''

"You have something to worry about, Kevin. They're talking about you again. Oh, of course, they always talk about you. But this time . . . A patient can be a two-edged sword. Especially an unpredictable one like Jane Doe. First they call her a jinx, say things happen around her—'' Kevin started to respond, but her implacably moving yellow teeth and unblinking steel-gray eyes held him silent. "Now they're talking about you, the sainted Dr. Blake. I think you're in for a rather nasty fall, and all of Cross's horses and all of Cross's memos might not be able to put you back together again—*if* I brought the campus gossip to his attention.''

"I don't know what you're talking about.''

She studied him. "No, you don't. And that's the real danger. But some interspecialty cooperation could persuade me not to bring anything—awkward—to Dr. Cross's attention. He's a harried man. Let's keep it between us. You make Jane Doe available to me three hours a week for my experiments . . .''

"What experiments?''

"Telekinesis,'' Swanson answered. "I hear that girl has a way with electrical things. Student grapevine again. I'll work with her alone; no one need know—for now. If I get the results I hope to, I'll want to publish, of course. Later.''

"You don't look like a blackmailer.''

"You don't look like a . . . well, I'll leave that to your imagination. That's your department. Me, I'm just a pure, empirical scientist in need of a challenging subject.''

"You're just a pure—'' He broke off, not wanting to waste a good obscenity on her. "I don't know what you're getting at, but if you're so wild to have Jane for a few . . . harmless . . . ?'' She nodded. "Experiments, okay. No threats

138

needed. Just ask nicely. No hints on the supposed ax you hold over my head, I gather?''

She just smiled in answer, and he left, feeling, in badly mixed metaphor, that he'd bought a pig in a poke by shaking hands with the devil.

It was clear the nurses had something to do with it; they were smirking at him, he noticed with sudden clarity as he traversed the halls to his office. He tapped the last cup of coffee at the community pot.

''Bad day?'' Bridget paused in sheathing her Selectric for the night.

''Just—not good.'' He sipped the bitter bottom of the cup. Not good? Hell, he was hot on the trail of Zyunsinth. What more did he want? ''Bridget, what's up around here? I keep getting weird vibes.''

''Oh, Kevin, you still don't know, do you? Look, I'm not going to be the one to tell you. It's just kinda funny.''

''Let me in on the joke.''

''You better try the dorm.''

''Willhelm?''

''You had anything to do with any other dorm recently?''

''Not for years, thank God. . . . Thanks for the tip.''

He got there at five-thirty just as trusty Mrs. Bellingham was coming off day duty.

''I can see if Jane's at supper,'' she offered.

''Forget Jane. I wanted to see you, ask how things are going.''

''Beautifully, Doctor. I can't tell you how Jane has fit right in. No wonder you love your work; it's so rewarding to see someone simply blossom and become, well, normal.''

He nodded encouragement. ''But has anything she's done lately caused comment? She isn't quite normal, you know.''

Mrs. Bellingham's glasses rappeled on their black cord to her shirtwaisted bosom. Her pastel face sprouted a thousand hairline wrinkles of concentration.

''Well, Doctor, there was that fuss she caused when *Star*

Wars aired the other night. Everybody was in the lounge to watch, and I peeked in. Never'd get to see what these kid crazes are about, if it weren't for the TV,'' she confided. "Jane was . . . most peculiarly taken with that giant ape character. Chew, Chewbacca. But she's like that. Nothing to worry about, I'm sure. Odd little things take her now and again. Notions. Like last Thursday night, watching *Magnum, P.I.* Oh!''

Mrs. Bellingham's cherubic cheeks pinked suddenly. Kevin had it, he knew, if he could get it out of Hazel Bellingham.

"Yes? It could be important.''

Her white head shook softly. "Oh, no. Not this. This was just—cute. It was so cute. I hope you won't take it personally, Doctor. But the girls were going on, as usual, about that actor who plays Magnum. What's his name? The hairy one. They weren't like that in my day. Lord, no. Robert Young, Robert Taylor, Tyrone Power even, every hair in place. Anyway, they were raving on about what a heavenly hunk he was—that's what they say, these days—and Jane took exception. He wasn't heavenly, she insisted. Not as heavenly as, as—you. So that's what they've been calling you lately,'' she rushed on. "Heavenly Kevin. Girls do that, you know. No sign of disrespect. Jane didn't know what she was doing.''

Kevin took a deep breath. "No. Of course not. So that's the fuss.''

"Girls fasten on some man now and again. There's a word . . .''

"Fixate,'' he supplied grimly.

She nodded happily. "Fixate. Well, they'd been interested in you before, but when *Jane,* after all, a patient of yours . . . I think they were just a wee bit jealous, if that makes any sense. Hell hath no fury like a dormful of women scorned,'' she chirruped.

"Je-sus, Mrs. B. I didn't scorn anybody. I'm just doing my job. I should've known better than to drag in a bunch of, of teenagers!'' Kevin paced the narrow hall, torn between laughing and hitting his fist into the wall.

"They're young ladies, despite their silliness. And why Jane, Jane would say such a thing . . . Of course she likes you; they all do—"

He came and leaned on the desk, his voice low, his eyes intense. "Why Jane would say that is elementary, my dear Bellingham. Transference. A stage during psychiatric treatment when the patient sees the doctor as a sort of god figure. Perfect in every respect. The shrink is viewed as father, mother, sister, brother, lover, everything. It's easy for outsiders to misconstrue this dependence, but it's an encouraging sign of progress, for Jane to look beyond herself. And psychiatrists learn how to deal with transference, or get into selling real estate. But if it's misconstrued, it could compromise my treatment, Jane's future. So the adolescent twittering has got to stop."

"It will, Dr. Blake. Human nature, you know. They'll go on to something—someone—else. They always do. In the meantime, I'll make the outspoken ones understand that Jane is not just another girl, that they mustn't take what she says too seriously. After all, she hardly knows anything, poor thing, and can't even remember her own mother and father. Why shouldn't she say or do something odd now and then?"

He smiled ruefully. "Just like the rest of us, right? Okay. Thanks for the information. I need to know these things, no matter how silly."

He left, Mrs. Bellingham bidding him farewell by breathlessly promising to tell him *everything* Jane said and did from now on.

Kevin stood on the dorm steps, inhaling the scent of illegally burning leaves. Someone always broke the burning ban, but he wasn't sorry to catch a whiff of that somehow comforting fall scent again. Fires. And leaping figures. Chewbacca. Why not? The celestial Dr. Blake. Didn't he wish. Jane. Swanson and her much ado about nothing. But he was committed now, at least to giving Swanson a crack at Jane, and, by admitting vulnerability, he had acquired it.

Why give in if there was nothing to hide? Why titillate the Probe meeting with juicy glimpses of a past for Jane that he didn't believe in, not for one instant?

Why do any of it, unless he was going absolutely, off-the-wall, bananas-and-bonkers, mind-bending, career-scuttling crackers?

Chapter Twenty-one

It was a basement, a vast, echoing, concrete-gray basement; all the beige vinyl tile and fluorescent light in the world couldn't hide that.

"Come in, Jane."

Carolyn Swanson sat at her dented metal desk. She'd had to take what was there in the way of office furniture when she'd got this space, but that was all right. She was a no-frills scientist.

"Sit down." Jane didn't, but she eyed the oak side chair. "Not as cushy as Dr. Blake's, is it? Matt showed you the way over? Whittington Hall's a bit off the beaten track—like you and me."

Jane neither flinched nor smiled at the last reference. Carolyn was glad her job centered around reading inarguable test data, not people. Let the brilliant Dr. Blake run the intuition stand single-handedly. Objective results never lied.

"Will you be able to find your way here again? I can have Matt pick you up . . ."

"I can find it." Jane idly swept her fingertips over the desktop. In most people, it would have been an unconscious gesture of distaste for the coffee-stained gray paint, probably battleship surplus from WWII. But Jane's expression was noncommittal as she turned to study the procession of Audubon prints with which Carolyn had tried to enliven the tan-painted walls. Audubon wasn't a mere frill, but instructional.

"Do you know what I'm hoping to do with you?" Carolyn adjusted her glasses self-consciously as Jane stared back. That unnerving calm, so like a cat's, but with no sense of play lurking behind the somber eyes. Working daily with such a patient would drive her crazy; how did Blake do it?

Jane hadn't responded, so Carolyn rapidly outlined her experimental program: ESP, remote viewing, precognition. She carefully avoided the patriotic pitch she usually directed at government observers or grant underwriters or even impressionable freshmen. Jane Doe didn't seem the flag-waving type.

"Dr. Blake was anxious for you to participate," she concluded, watching Jane's whole body tense, as a dog's does at its master's voice. Ah, the key. Heavenly Kevin. Hard to believe this emotionless cipher responded to anything. Poor Kevin. He'd obviously been hung on false evidence, but it didn't matter, she had her three sessions a week by hook or by crook. . . .

"We'll find a free room down the hall."

Carolyn stood by the open office door until Jane preceded her through. Behind soundproofed walls, teaching assistants administered batteries of tests. Despite the overall austerity, everything necessary to conduct parapsychological experiments was available; it was the university that was ungenerous with its space, not the government that was parsimonious with its funds. Ever since news of "Mind Wars" experimentation among the Russians, Carolyn found her underestimated field newly popular—in some circles, at least.

The room was small, square and covered in soundproofing tiles that looked like pegboard. A long folding table against one wall held an array of everyday objects. A cup, empty. A ring of keys. A clock radio, much out of date. A tape recorder. A common kitchen spoon.

Carolyn pulled a metal folding chair away from the table. "This is where we'll be working. I want you to move these things—without touching them, with your mind only."

Jane stared at her. Carolyn fingered the items in turn. If trying left an aura, then this household trivia should glow; several subjects had spent many hours concentrating on mental locomotion. No one had made so much as a dial on the radio turn. It was perhaps the most difficult psychic ability to prove, telekinesis. Usually, adolescents were the most fruitful subjects. But Carolyn had a strong, unscientific suspicion that Kevin Blake's jinxed Jane Doe could move more than people's emotions. She'd heard about the reporter who'd found a faceful of shattered plastic her only reward for pursuing a story. . . .

"Concentrate, Jane. Try this. The spoon. Make the handle loop. Look at it; think it. Do it!"

The young woman obediently crossed her open palm with the silver spoon. Her eyes, after one last piercing look at Carolyn, lowered to the shining stainless steel. An over-sentimentalized rose design crested the handle. The thing was cheap, like everything in this place, but once legitimately bent, the spoon would be worth more than a twelve-place setting of Francis I sterling.

Carolyn pulled another folding chair away from the table and sat down to watch Jane Doe watch the spoon. Nothing happened, but that was the agony and the ecstasy of psychic research. So often, nothing *seemed* to be happening. . . .

After an hour, Carolyn rose. Jane had not budged an ion of the spoon. She'd sat docilely enough, and looked and looked and looked, but nothing had happened. Carolyn had a feeling that Jane would see to it that nothing would.

"You're not trying!"

Jane looked up, mutely expressionless.

"I can recognize real concentration—I've had subjects

sweat from sheer mental effort while not moving a muscle. You're not really trying, Jane. What is it? Did Dr. Blake tell you to only go through the motions? Do you want to work on something else—the eggbeater?''

She scraped the implement across the tabletop until the beaters whirred ready protest at being moved, then rotated to silence in front of a silent Jane.

Carolyn bit her bloodless lip. ''Well, say something! At least pretend to be cooperative. You know what I want, I know you do. Your precious Kevin promised me access to you. . . . The clock radio, do you want to try moving the hands? You must try.'' Carolyn flourished the key ring at her impassive subject, as if rattling it at an infant she believed to be deaf. ''These. Move one key a mere fraction of a millimeter, and it will scrape against another key and tell us. Which do you want to work with, which?''

Jane was silent—soberly, watchfully silent. Carolyn blinked behind her lenses. A light sweat sent the nosepiece skiing down the bridge of her nose. She hated that! It was dank and clammy in these quarters, and she hated that, too, if she stopped to think about it. And most of all, she hated having stooped to coercion to get at a so-called sensitive subject who sat there like a salt lick and did nothing!

''Maybe the tape recorder,'' Carolyn suggested harshly. Like most overcontrolled people, she was at the capricious beck and call of sudden rages. ''You seem to have an affinity for them—'' Carolyn shoved it away in disgust, sent the empty, motionless thing sliding across the slick Formica, sliding more forcefully than she meant, hurling aggressively toward Jane Doe.

She straightened, shoved her glasses into focus against her forehead, took a warning breath. ''Watchout . . . I'msorry—''

Jane had not moved. The thing was about to overshoot the tabletop and smash into her midriff like a fist. Jane watched it, as she had the spoon. And it stopped. It slowed and stopped as it reached her.

Carolyn's fear-tautened muscles uncoiled one by one. She took off her glasses, then reseated them precisely on her nose.

"Well," she told Jane. "It seems silent water runs deep. I think we can accomplish something, now that we understand how each other works. And Dr. Blake will be so pleased to hear that our association is going to be—productive."

Jane looked up at her, dark eyes emotionless, hands still folded on her lap, as composed as a statue carved from stone. As silent as the sphinx. Carolyn Swanson did not often indulge in flights of fancy or think in comparisons. It was amazing what a little stress could elicit from the human organism, she thought smugly. Absolutely amazing.

Sleeping again. "I" slept. As they slept. All of them. "I" stirred uneasily, sleep a cocoon it twisted itself to fit, as it had once fit into the strangely transparent container, and did no longer.

No, "I" inhabited a vaster, vaguer environment now. Shadowy at times; at others so piercingly clear in all its details that "I" shrunk to a small pulsing nerve at the core of some far-flung organic network, a network as busy and relentlessly organized in its way as the place where "I" had drifted nameless once—and many times.

And the clattering, the chattering, the clicks and hums all around, mechanical songs of those other "others." Those smooth cool immobile entities so arbitrarily lambent in expression—red, green, blue blinking in hysterical turn—their harsh metallic voices buzzing in harmony. Sometimes they slept, too, dormant as "I" was—and was not. But "I" could sense the power surging through them even then.

From the beginning there had been those that moved freely, and those that did not. "I" was more often among the last than the first.

"And/many/that/are/first/shall/be/last;/and/the/last/shall/

146

be/first." Matthew 19:30. Odd, these symbols/sounds, more remembered than heard. "I" had heard other sounds once, like and not like, more forgotten than remembered. Sounds like . . . kulis . . . skli . . . kuliskanth. But meaning and memory merged, fled. "I" did not understand those others—not the formless ones, not the free floating. But those anchored things. Silent unless spoken to, then crackling into life and power. Much power hidden behind smooth, dark, hard façades.

Like "I," and not like "I." Some sleeping, and therefore safe. Others . . . pulsing, throbbing, humming to one another, whirling, turning, ready to fill themselves with what "I" must glean. Always when they were there, the others came to empty "I," to waken "I" to an unending sleep. Always. Losing what "I" had gleaned, had gained. "I" would stop the living dead ones. The servants. Must stop them. But . . . not all. Some were—acceptable, if dormant. Yes. Some played as pets to a commanding hand. Hand. That was a concept suddenly terrifying concrete, out of place in this foggy half world "I" wandered.

The hand—made flesh, made new (new sound) human— seemed to swell, grow, hang over "I" to press down upon it. Memories whirred into a blur, fragments torn free to drift into the void. Machine. Moving. Stop. Stop. Stop. Any way. No. Yes. Defend. "I" would be defended always, by "I." Except now, "I" must not—could not— defend, and no silver sun shone through the black fog, and Zyunsinth was a nonsense sound that hummed along the knotted skeins of memory in rhythmic lashes and only the huge, alien hand remained, pressing down.

"I" could no longer sleep, dream, defend. "I" hid. Somewhere deep. Somewhere so deep even memory couldn't find it.

Chapter Twenty-two

In late November, Jane began wearing the fur coat. Kevin would stand by his office window, watching her stride across the snowless campus in the new winter boots, looking like a chic Cossack. Not many coeds wore calf-length fur at the U of M. Jane's foxy pelt stood out among the milling pastel-hued down coats like something feral loose amid a domesticated huddle of tie-dyed sheep.

She had a special library card now, and—from student nurse accounts—used it often, reading the same incredible range of subjects. Apparently her interest in the mechanics of human sexuality was sated; the nurses never mentioned her reading any subject matter that could be subjected to misinterpretation; the "Heavenly Kevin" episode was as forgotten as *Ben Casey*.

And, it turned out, he had not lied to Laurel Bowman. When he'd finally returned her calls, he had found her reconciliatory. Her face had healed, she reported, and she was also cured of midnight jaunts in search of stories. By the way, anything happening with Jane Doe? The police had run her sketch in several big-city papers and turned up nothing.

Neither had Kevin, he told Laurel. Maybe they—and Jane herself—would never know who she really was. Tough, commiserated Laurel. Now he knew how a balked reporter would feel, *knowing* there's got to be a story there and not getting it. . . . Maybe, said Kevin, and that was that. End phone call, end tenuous relationship, end press curiosity.

This time, he was sure, Laurel had believed him. And why not? He had spoken only the truth.

Kevin turned back to his desk and rewound the last session's tape. Jane, he knew, would be at his door at precisely two P.M. He'd come to set his watch by her.

Her voice came back to him, deliberate in hypnosis, muffled as recordings always are. It was gibberish she spoke, organized as if into language. He'd tried writing it phonetically and now knew it by heart.

"Sklivent ysrossni. Kuliskanth, ynin ynin romascalonti. . . ."

It was beginning, in an odd, subconscious way, to make sense to him, like the child's game of "O wah ta goo, Siam," or the so familiar formula of "Ipledgealegencetutheflag." He'd tried Jane's gibberish on a university linguist, who'd confirmed there was a Slavic feel to the syllables, also elements of romance language and something Oriental.

Goulash, in other words. Impossible to pin down, like Jane.

"Hi." She stood in the doorway, waiting, as always, for his invitation to enter. Very formal, our Jane. What was it that had to be invited over thresholds to enter—vampires? For some reason he checked his watch. She was a full minute late.

"C'mon in. Stop anywhere on the way?"

"No. My session with Dr. Swanson was a little . . . longer . . . today."

"Do you like working with Dr. Swanson?"

She unpeeled the coat and threw it on the Eames chair, cradling herself in its satiny lining moments later. "She has me do stupid things, like stare at a spoon and try to make it bend. A bent spoon is useless."

"To Dr. Swanson, it's a pearl beyond price."

"She doesn't seem pleased with me."

"Maybe she was expecting something different."

"I'm not different," Jane said in a faintly truculent tone.

149

He studied her relaxed, healthy exterior. Slender but no longer painfully thin. Her hair, having reached her shoulders, and her fingernails, having reached her fingertips, had decided jointly to stop growing. Or, rather, the nurses of Willhelm had equipped Jane with the scissors and files needed to keep herself neatly groomed. It had become nearly impossible to tell anymore what about Jane was natural and native, and what was a veneer of social custom. It was what he had wanted: to disguise her from the world at large. But it also kept him guessing in the dark. He began to think that he was so pleased with the Jane Doe his care had created that he didn't want to solve the mystery of her origins, that it didn't matter. It certainly didn't seem to matter to Jane herself.

"Sklivent ysrossni," he said suddenly. "Kuliskanth, ynin ynin romascalonti. . . ."

Jane's head cocked his way.

"Not different, hmmm? That's what you said when you were under two sessions ago. 'Sklivent ysrossni. Kuliskanth, ynin ynin romascalonti. . . .' Have I got the pronunciation right?"

"I don't know. I don't remember anything like that."

"You said it."

"But it—means nothing."

"Here," he conceded. "Now. But then, somewhere else . . . ?"

"I don't know where I was, *when* I was, before here and now. I like this, can't I—"

"No!" He spoke more forcefully than he meant to, maybe because he'd been tempted by the same question. Can't she just stay as she is? "You have no educational credentials— not even for grade school, no obvious job skills or history. If you weren't swaddled by the ingrown environs of our academic community, how would you survive? Yes, I know you know a lot of extraordinary things, but your knowledge is unorganized. Even with equivalency tests, you'd probably sail off the graphs in some areas, and hatch goose eggs in others. You ever had the required physical education courses? Can you swim? Do you know the rules of football? I don't know, and I'm sure you don't. You're not equipped to survive in this world with the little you know about yourself. If we can find out what 'sklivent ysrossni' means, maybe we can arm you a bit better for graduation day. You can't remain my patient forever, you know."

She listened, dark head bent, eyes cast down to her laced fingers. She looked up finally, cool and betrayed. "What about Dr. Swanson? She'd keep me on . . . especially if she found something to intrigue her."

"Are you saying you can turn your . . . differences . . . on and off?"

"No, but I don't know what Dr. Swanson wants. I don't know what you want."

"What does Jane want?"

She frowned. "To go on. That's all. To last. As I am now."

"Immortality? Eternal youth?"

"No. Just ordinary mortality. A lifetime of remembering from now on."

"Maybe 'sklivent ysrossni' is an invocation to mortality, and if we solved it . . ."

Jane laid her head back on the leather, the coat collar curling around her neck. She looked as intent—and remote—as when she paged through book after book looking for some clue only she knew.

"Say the word, Dr. Blake, and I will go back and look for the meaning. The word. What would happen if I say it?"

"Try," he suggested.

"Ecnalubma," she intoned, seemingly convinced that an exotic password would unlock her past. Bibbitty bobbitty boo, my forgetful Cinderella, Kevin thought sadly. Nothing happened, except the November wind whistled by to rattle the window frame before gusting away.

"I guess you still need me." Kevin leaned forward to

151

invoke peace in plain English. By the time "ecnalubma" came out, Jane was relaxed and had surrendered her waking mind.

"Far out, man."

Kandy was sitting Indian-style—Western or Eastern, you could take your pick—in the middle of his chaotic living room, studying "sklivent ysrossni."

"Reminds me of 'E Publista' on *Star Trek*; you know, the one where the primitive people had our Declaration of Independence but had garbled the words over the centuries. This sounds like it meant something once, too. I can just hear some Atlantean orator giving forth: 'Sklivent ysrossni, lend me your ears . . . ' "

Kevin pulled his foot tighter over his bent knee; sitting cross-legged was the only option in Kandy's living room; every horizontal surface was thick with books, papers and pillows. The apartment was a mess; Kandy's long-term residence with six Russian blue cats, his grandmother's herd of mastadon-sized mahogany furniture and his own self-propagating paper mine created an environment where litter and litters fought for supremacy. Even now a kitten was scaling Kevin's sweater in a rear attack, hooking tiny barbs into his skin. He reached back to scrape it off, then cupped it against his chest while his forefinger smoothed the tiny velvet skull.

"Now Jane Doe's an escapee from Atlantis. Settle on something, Kandy, for Chrissake. Whatever it is, it was made for vocal chords."

"Oh, right." Kandy delicately plucked his smoldering joint off the battered brass ashtray and offered Kevin a toke. Kevin took a drag despite his impatience; maybe he needed to slow down. He inhaled deep and held it, feeling reality slip an almost imperceptible notch. The kitten squirmed and he let it somersault to the floor, where it skittered away over a carpet of newspaper.

152

The apartment air, never bracing, weighed heavier with the commingled odors of pot and used Kitty Litter.

Kandy's eyes squinted consideringly half-shut. He inhaled on the vanishing roach again. "You ever contemplate . . . hoax?"

"What do you mean?"

"She's a ringer. Maybe a Commie infiltrator. She's spent enough time unquestioned at Probe, right? And now she's privy to Swanson's deepest, darkest experiments. The Russians love parapsychological claptrap."

"Swanson as good as forced me to let her experiment with Jane. No, Jane hasn't initiated anything. She's just soaked it all up, like a good human sponge."

"I rest my case. A spy doesn't run around looking for trouble. A spy gets in—and spies. Quietly. You've been workin' with this babe how long—two and a half, three months? And you keep diggin' up weirder and weirder junk in her hypnotic sessions. Looks to me like she wants to keep you comin' back for more."

Kevin's headshake passed on the offered joint. "Like a twentieth-century Scheherazade, huh? Sinister, no. But maybe . . . In a sense, she *is* dependent on me, on the camouflage of normalcy I've created around her. She could be afraid I'd drop her case if she didn't leak me some puzzling tidbit now and then."

"Too simple, man. The girl's from Mars. Or Dubrovnik. Or, my favorite—Atlantis. Mark my words."

Kevin unscrambled himself, retrieving his notebook from the pile of paperwork where Kandy had tossed it. "If it's Dubrovnik, I'd think you'd recognize a phrase or two."

"Nah, that stuff all sounds alike to me. Lost my inherited ear. Sorry I can't help you, man." Kandy waved good-bye from amid his rings of pot smoke, like the hookah-smoking caterpillar in *Alice in Wonderland. He* hadn't been much help, either. "Sure you don't want a cat?"

Kevin looked down. A struggling bit of blue-gray fur was

shinning up his leg. He pulled it off and stuck it inside his down jacket. He was getting tired of coming away from everything empty-handed. "Sure, I'll take one. See you."

He would have said thanks, but he wasn't certain the bestowal of a kitten was anything to be grateful for.

"There's a hot Guthrie Theater bash comin' up," Kandy sang as Kevin let himself out. "I'll let you know. . . ."

The narrow hall seemed airy after Kandy's stuffy apartment. Sometimes, Kevin wondered how his friend kept it. But there always seemed to be understanding landlords and pockets of kindred souls for the sixties throwback. A fat woman with hip-length, center-parted hair waddled toward him, her garbage eating grease spots through the brown paper bag she carried. Kevin felt reflexively guilty for lounging in the lap of eighties affluence.

On the way home, the kitten proved it could do something besides scale clothing, sleeping in its cozy sandwich of sweater and down.

"I must be crazy," he told it as he climbed the stairs to his condo. But he filled some saucers with milk, water and smoked herring. "All I got, kitty. Don't even know your gender. Let's call you something unisex, like, uh, Blue Streak."

There it went, whisker-wet from the milk dish to pretending his flexed knee was the Matterhorn. He shredded that morning's unread *Strib* in an empty shoebox and presented this proudly to his new pet, earning a look of profound feline indifference. Shit. And that's what he'd get, just where he didn't want it. To the Tom Thumb store in the morning, for litter and food.

Kevin dropped his notebook on the stereo cover, where he was sure to spot it on the way out, then went to shower the weed whiff out of his skin and hair. He didn't mind pot smoking; he just didn't seem to need it. What he needed was a good night's sleep, without the images invoked by Zyunsinth and sklivent ysrossni dancing in his head. He collapsed on the bed, taking drowsy pleasure in clean white walls, uncluttered surfaces. He was getting set in his ways, like an old-time farmer who plows his fields in the same pattern season after season.

Something shot up the side of the bed, waded through heavy swells of comforter and settled by his hip, purring its pleasure loud enough to wake the dead—all the way to Atlantis.

"I've never seen you this way."

"How?" asked Jane.

"I don't know. Worried. Despondent. You look pale."

"No sun. It's winter."

"Not yet. Not until December twenty-third; it's only December sixth."

"I know what day it is. Winter is when it feels like winter. Gray and cold. . . ." Her voice reflected the bleakness she described.

"If you really know what day it is, you'll know why you're getting this." It was an impulse to flash the candy cane he'd snagged from Bridget's jar of staff treats at Jane, but he wanted to cheer her up and find out if her wide-ranging mind had happened upon the date's significance.

She batted for it, like Blue Streak for a tantalizing bit of string.

"Saint Nicholas's Feast Day. Candy for good children," she recited in pat recognition, and snatched the cellophane-wrapped sweet.

"Those really don't taste that good," he warned her, but she was greedily working the hooked end into her mouth. She laughed, the red striping garishly coloring her unlipsticked mouth, and sucked upon it as contentedly as a baby on a thumb.

"My first Christmas present," she announced in candy-slurred tones. Then the troubled expression settled on her face again.

"What's the matter? Or do I have to hypnotize you to find out?"

"No, it's nothing like that. I, I know this." She thought a moment, trying to rewrap the cane. Kevin pulled out his top drawer and offered some Kleenex. Useful at last. Jane glanced up, looking as he'd never seen her—fearful.

"I—need . . . money." The last word came out quick and furtive, forced and confessional. He wondered if she had been going to say something else. "The girls at the dorm draw for Christmas presents, and I, I don't have anything. I'll be getting one, but I'm supposed to give Glenda one, too. I need to buy something."

"Do you know what to give her?"

"The latest Prince album."

Glib, she was getting so glib. So far away from the narrow, dangerous girl who had been found naked on a country bluff top. He felt both happy and sad. Perhaps the most successful treatment was this, a Jane of laughter and greed and enthusiasm, of conformity and anxiety and emotional needs. A normal young woman. Perhaps he was the anomaly for being unable to accept her as such and no more.

"I can give you some money. . . ."

Her glance fell. Not the answer she wanted.

"Lend you, rather—" Better.

Of course. Now she wanted financial independence. The ability to buy her own Zyunsinth, to be given presents, and to give in turn. She wanted what he'd tried to tell her once she didn't have: the skills, the credentials to survive as a normal person. You talk money, you talk job. Jane as what—a bank clerk? She had a good head for figures. And those seeing-eye cameras recording every movement; they might develop a sudden short. A teacher; she remembered everything she read. And what if some smart aleck asked a simple question that revealed she didn't know what daylight saving time was, or some other trivia of modern life? How could she be presented to the real world, as someone mysteriously locked away from everyday wear and tear, like an ex-nun? A mental patient?

"I'll lend you the money, until whenever. . . ." And there's your precious coat, he added mentally. I'm paying it off at $150 a month plus 18 percent interest. You weren't aware enough then of economic niceties to take responsibility for that; how would you buy a fur coat, Jane Doe, when you can't even remember your real name?

She nodded and took the twenty-dollar bill he extended much more reluctantly than she had taken the twenty-cent candy cane.

"And you're sure there was nothing else bothering you?"

She shook her head no, and stuffed the twenty in Zyunsinth's belly pocket.

Santa Claus cutouts decorated Bridget's desk front; even the coffeepot top wore a sprig of mistletoe.

"Where does Dr. Swanson conduct her experiments these days?" Kevin asked, breaking the hardened cream substitute into lumps with his plastic spoon and sprinkling islands of it into his cup.

"Basement of Whittington Hall, I think." Bridget was busy refilling her bowl of wrapped candy.

"Basement of Whittington! Sounds Frankensteinish."

"You know how the student newshounds keep trying to get the goods on her project. There were just too many curious people in this building, she said, so she had Cross get her a new location weeks ago. Where have you been, Doctor?"

"Obviously not behind a jackhammer—can *you* do anything to get this . . . concrete . . . from there to here?" He pointed at his cup.

"I thought you took your coffee black, with nails." Bridget shook the jar, stabbed its interior with a letter opener and poured out a fine drizzle of whitener.

"The woman's touch. No, I must've missed the decampment to Whittington. I'm one person whose curiosity doesn't trend in that direction.''

"But it's fascinating stuff. Finding lost bodies and reading people's minds long-distance. Think what that'd do for our phone bills if we all could develop those talents.''

"I'd rather develop talents for woman-handling a Cremora jar. Thanks for the dairy substitute.''

But once inside his office, he left the cup steaming on his desk and went to the window. Whittington was a decrepit four-story leftover from the U's infancy. The theater department once had stored costumes in the basement, then demanded climate-controlled quarters; Whittington was reputedly cold and damp, an ideal site for Swanson to ply her clandestine arts.

He hadn't sampled Jane's parapsychological sessions; maybe he should.

Chapter Twenty-three

Cold and secret. That's the feeling the basement of Whittington Hall distilled from the very bones of the building inward the way some women emanate expensive perfume from the skin out.

Cold and secret. Maybe that described Carolyn Swanson; maybe it explained why Kevin had never liked her. He didn't like her subterranean workshop, either.

Halls were extra wide, ceilings high; basement space had been apportioned generously, not being at the same premium as street-level areas. Such expansiveness made for echoes. The broad metal door anchoring a flight of exterior stairs had slammed shut behind him with bank vault–like finality. His watch-circled wrist, glancing off an unexpected locker, chimed soft metallic alarm.

Kevin's rubber-soled shoes whispered along the uneven checkerboard of vinyl tiles leading monotonously into a distance that looked oddly endless.

He hadn't told Dr. Swanson he was coming. He hadn't told Jane.

It was quiet in the basement of Whittington. He felt like an intruder, swathing his steps in caution as he approached each door along the corridor. Luckily, they'd been glass-paned so late-arriving students could find the proper classroom; now, Kevin peered into emptiness. Classes hadn't been taught down here since the sixties.

Kevin studied the latest empty room, distaste curdling his features. Its soundproofed white tiles with regiments of black holes looked permanently fly-spotted, reminiscent of language labs at best, of police interrogation rooms at worst.

The next room wasn't empty. A pale girl wearing a muddy brown ponytail spoke into a microphone, her mouth moving soundlessly through the glass. In the adjoining room, a thin young man in horn-rimmed glasses slowly dealt an oversized deck of cards, while a woman made notes. The cards bore the traditional symbols of modern mental magic—the cross, the star, the wavy lines that one mind was supposed to broadcast to another psychically receptive mind.

Kevin sighed and the empty wide hall absorbed the sound, just as it amplified sharper noises. Hogwash. Too big a chance of coincidence or tampering, no matter how the researcher came at it. He hoped Jane hadn't been forced to undergo such pointless rituals.

Jane. Where was she? He couldn't imagine her among these pallidly obsessive people. And thinking of pallid obsession—where was Swanson?

Somewhere, something thumped, like a dead body falling on an old Alfred Hitchcock TV show. Nothing magnified the sound; it was one, brief, decently muffled thump. Kevin glanced around, looking for things that might go bump in the basement.

The place was quiet again, all doors shut. He approached a new blank window until it framed an interior scene—either an empty room or tensely immobile strangers attempting mental tricks.

The next thump indicated a direction—ahead. And he heard a sharp exclamation. Female. He picked up his speed, he didn't know why, and came to what turned out to be the right door.

Swanson was pacing in front of the glass, offering Kevin her white-coated back. A long table defined the opposite wall. The pattern of holes in white tile seemed to repeat into geometric infinity, like a stark Vasarely print. Everything was sharp and distorted, as if viewed through a fish-eye lens, through the fishbowl lenses with which Swanson saw the world.

He saw Swanson, talking in forceful mime of herself through the soundproofed door. He saw Jane as Swanson finally moved out of her sightline. Jane sitting at the head of a long table, Jane looking small and distant, with an odd array of items opposite her on the table. Nothing edible. Items large and small. Homely things. Ordinary. Swanson hovered over the collection, gesturing toward Jane.

Kevin froze. Jane's face was as impassive as when he'd first seen it—months ago. She was carved from stone, or salt; her eyes didn't even follow Swanson's agitated figure.

And Swanson was an astounding sight. This was the cool figure with a clipboard for a heart? She paced, exhorted, turned, elevated her hands in despair, then dropped them to the tabletop and, with a tremendous heave, sent the clock radio skating violently across the slick Formica—toward Jane.

Kevin jumped, his hands hitting the door and feeling blindly for a knob even as his eyes measured the slow-motion inevitability of the radio slamming toward Jane.

"My God, woman, are you crazy?" He was still outside,

160

his voice unheard. The door was locked. "Swanson! Dammit, Swanson . . ."

His palms hit wood and stung; his face was hot against cool glass. He saw the plastic-sheathed box reach the table end. He saw Laurel's face fresh from her abortive interview with Jane, ragged from exploding plastic. For an instant he wondered if Swanson were an avenger—Laurel and Swanson against Jane, making her pay for not being one of them . . . for Kellehay, even.

The radio slid to the table's very end, and still Jane had not moved. Then her face reared back from the oncoming radio, her features winced in anticipation of imminent impact. Kevin throttled the ungiving knob, his foot braced against tough old wood, all his weight bearing down and getting no more answer than a wooden groan. "Swanson . . ." He was whispering now, and knew it didn't matter. She'd gone mad.

Or he had. The radio hung for a trillionth of a second over the table edge, almost in Jane's lap. Then it spun around, toward Swanson, leaped a good three feet of space like a big brown plastic toad and squatted to a stop.

Kevin's hands reflexively squeezed the sweat-slippery knob. His body began untensing, so he could hear the near yet distant roaring along his arteries as adrenaline ebbed through his system.

Swanson, still only a back, rushed toward Jane—not to inspect her, but to pull a tape measure from her pocket and mark the distance between Jane and the now motionless radio. She jotted the results on a clipboard. Over her impersonal shoulder, Kevin spotted the blue ballpoint trail of many such notations.

He hit the locked door with his side, bellowing, "Swanson, dammit, open up or I'll kick it in!"

Her face finally swiveled over her shoulder. The magnified empty eyes, the blank features showed no surprise, but she came to the door and turned the key.

Kevin exploded inward. "Are you crazy? What do you

think you're doing? Jane—'' He paused, chilled by how her face reflected Swanson's emotionless façade. How far Jane had come, he realized only now, in the past few weeks. His plan had worked; she was becoming a real, normal, ordinary young woman. Now this, and she looked as lifeless as Swanson, who'd had ten years of higher education and the genes of a lizard to excuse herself.

"What the hell have you done?"

"Shhh." Swanson was rapidly shutting the door. And locking it again.

"Your setup is out in the open. Forget locks, forget hushing me up. What the hell do you think you're doing here? That damn radio could have done any kind of injury—"

"There was no danger. Surely you see that. You did see it?"

"I saw you—throw—that thing at Jane. It must weigh—"

Swanson leaned against the table edge. "And you saw Jane repel it. Nothing that approaches her with force can touch her. She's the safest girl in the world. You're behaving like a mother hen. Look at this record; that radio you're so worried about hurting Jane has been repelled by her nine times, always farther. Look, thirty-seven and a half inches this time."

He skimmed the figures dancing raggedly across the lined paper. "Jane *stops* these things from hitting her?"

"No, she repels them. Forces them back. Oh, I was getting nowhere at first, and then it hit me. Jane doesn't work by drawing things to herself—we've always assumed that to be the telekinetic method. She *pushes* them from her. And she's very good. Infallible, in fact, if they come at her with proper force. . . ."

"You mean—" Kevin's tone was quiet, his manner almost preternaturally rational. "You mean, you've been tossing things at Jane to get a reaction, bombarding her with, with household trash, just to see her defend herself?"

"You make it sound so—juvenile. I've recorded every-

162

thing." She defensively waved the clipboard under his face again. "It's a remarkable record, no telling the size of the objects, people even, she could repel. It's the most exciting evidence of voluntary telekinesis ever."

"Voluntary," Kevin snorted bitterly.

Swanson moved to the table's wall side, indicating her array of objects. "It isn't just kid stuff like keys, Kevin, or lightweight things like cards. It's this eggbeater." She waved it in demonstration, oblivious to looking ludicrous. "It's a five-pound, 1967 clock radio, pretransister." How precise she was, Swanson the scientist. "There's no telling where it might end."

"It ends here!" Kevin braced the heels of his hands on the table and slammed it toward the wall. It raucously scraped the floor, stopping only inches from the wall, pinning Swanson there like some pale, unattractive moth. She stood with her hands thrown up, the clipboard still grasped in one and turned to display its cryptic notations, Jane's fear calibrated in feet and inches.

"You damn ice cube. You don't even know what you've done, do you? You've taken a *psychiatric* patient, *my* patient, whose reality has been stretched so thin it can cut you—and used her for target practice."

"But I was right. Jane has remarkable abilities. She might—"

"I don't care if she might transport the Eiffel Tower to Schenectady. Her mind and emotions are fragile. And you tormented her. You're no better than a kid who pulls the wings off an insect to see if it can still writhe. You're a lousy scientist, Doctor, and an execrable human being. You want to see moving objects? I could move this table into your guts with a force that would astound you—"

"Kevin . . . ," Swanson squeaked, clapping the clipboard over the pale oval of her mouth. She looked scared to death.

Kevin straightened. "Feelings are my expertise; not figures. And I can tell you authoritatively that how you feel right now is how Jane felt every time—*every time*—you threw something at her in the name of science.''

Swanson was quivering now, like an experimental white rat in a cage who's been around long enough to know what's coming. ''All right. All right. I won't—do it again. I promise. Kevin. Please.''

He stepped away from the table. Swanson put down the clipboard, then laboriously pushed the table far enough away to sidestep along the wall and into the open room. She tucked a strand of hair back into the messy knot at her neck and pushed her glasses into proper position.

Kevin got Jane, his hand on her arm propelling her up. He escorted her past Swanson to the locked door, and waited, back to the room.

Swanson sidled around him; her key missed the lock twice before she inserted it.

''Kevin . . .''

He finally could look at her as a human being again. ''It's my case, Doctor, not yours. You never should have meddled in it. I'll keep my mouth shut about you, if you'll keep yours shut about Jane.''

She nodded and folded the clipboard primly to her chest, like an errant child caught with a dirty book. Kevin eyed it unrelentingly. Swanson finally extended it. He ripped off the sheet recording Jane's exploits, Swanson flinching at the sound, and handed back the blank notepad.

''Clean slate, Dr. Swanson.''

She was subdued as Kevin left with Jane and the only record of an extraordinary experiment in telekinesis.

He folded the paper into his sport coat pocket. The echoes of their footsteps tailed them down the long, silent hall. At the outer door he stopped, reminded by the sift of snowflakes past the chicken wire–reinforced glass.

''Did you have—a coat?'' he asked Jane.

She led him to the row of lockers around the corner and extracted a familiar length of ruddy fur. Jane held it for a long moment, cuddling it like a pet, seeming almost to reassure it, until he took it from her. It was soft and heavy in his hands. And soothing. He needed to be soothed. He held it up, and Jane turned away to thrust her arms into the satin-lined sleeves.

"Why didn't you tell me?" he asked the back of her head, afraid to face her, afraid to find that Carolyn Swanson's battering experiments had harmed her.

Jane's hand stroked the fur at her shoulder.

"Zyunsinth," she murmured. "Zyunsinth knew."

Chapter Twenty-four

"Aren't you glad I talked you into this?"

Kandy sat against the wall, nursing a glass of—what else? —Russian vodka, poured over naked ice cubes and called a drink.

"What?" Kevin yelled into his adjacent ear. The stereo staked out the wall opposite their claim, and thundering bass vibrated the soles of Kevin's feet; screaming electric guitar fibrilated in his eardrums.

"Glad you came?" repeated Kandy at the level of a genial scream. "Great party." He knocked back a mouthful of one-hundred-proof potato power.

Kevin let the woody sting of his Johnnie Walker slide through his teeth. He worked it around like mouthwash before swallowing, and leaned his head against the wall.

Above them, a window open wide to the below-zero winter air pumped a stream of chill, refreshing oxygen into a room ripe with cigarette and pot smoke, B.O. and a stew of human pheromones sufficient to madden a beehive.

Kevin reached for the pint of Johnnie Walker black in his jacket pocket. If you wanted to drink el primo hooch at a party like this, you kept it on you—not on the community bar across the room with enough bottles of mediocre brands to stock a liquor warehouse.

The cool glass smoothed into his palm, but something cut his cuticle as he lifted it out.

"Ouch!"

"Bee in your pocket?" inquired Kandy from the dreamy pinnacle of czars, cossacks and chronic party drunks.

"Just paper." Kevin shook out the folds after he'd refilled his glass and slipped the Scotch back in his pocket. He studied Swanson's precisely messy notations through the pleasant stride of Johnnie Walker through his circulatory system. Enough good Scotch and the worst things looked better. He shrugged, laughed and leaned forward.

"Got a lighter, Kandy?"

Kandy's head shook mournfully. "No smokkum nicotine. Bum a match from someone—"

"Here." A narrow Cricket lighter floated in the smoky air. A woman lucky enough—or high enough soon enough—to have snagged a seat on the long sofa across the way leaned forward smiling.

"Thank you," Kevin said formally. He was always formal when getting drunk. He lit the corner of the paper and held it up like a dirty diaper. Kandy watched with woozy admiration as the fast flames smacked their way up the sheet. "Ashtray," Kevin demanded in surgical tones, a palm extended imperiously.

Nothing slapped into it. Kandy was patting the carpet vaguely, and heat licked experimentally at Kevin's fingertips. Blackened flakes of burnt paper fluttered in the window draft, pretty as ebony snow. "Hey, Kandy!"

The woman on the couch was suddenly crouched beside him, a palm-sized glass ashtray in hand. Kevin dropped the remaining paper into the tray and watched the fire curl its last edges.

"I think your friend's out of it." The woman glanced at Kandy, who had adopted what would have been a navel-contemplating position, had he been naked. "I hope nobody's phone number just went up in smoke."

Kevin smiled reflectively. "Nope. Not that kind of number."

"You an actor?"

He felt flattered, though he didn't know why. "Nah. Just sometimes in real life. The usual hide-preserving stuff. Are you?"

"I keep telling myself." She sat back on her heels, folding herself into the little floor space left. Her spot on the couch had filled in with other bodies. Most of the women here wore slacks or jeans. She wore a wool skirt, and smart black pumps with ankle straps. He could see why; she had great legs.

A blast of December air slapped through the warm smoke, stinging his senses. "This your first year at the Guthrie?"

She nodded. "What do *you* do?"

"Well, my somanbulent, uh, som*nam*bulent friend here's a shrink. He sometimes coaches Guthrie actors on the psychology of their characters. Sort of the madness method. He got the invitation; I'm just a hitchhiker. Somnambulent. Strange word. A lot like ambulance. What's it backwards? Tnel . . ."

"Uh . . . ubmanmos. Tnelubmanmos." Her laugh rang freely. "You an English teacher?"

He shook his head. "Not my language. Tnel, tnel—"

"Tnelubmanmos." She had been drinking, too—who hadn't, in this place? Theater types were notorious for releasing the tensions of their trade in fine and public style. "I bet you're, you're a doctor, too. The surgeon bit with the ashtray. You made me feel I should be wearing a white cap. And now you're talking ambulances."

"Guilty," Kevin admitted.

"But you don't help actors with character analyses?"

"Not guilty."

"I'd think that guilt was the basis of it all."

167

Kevin nodded. He was tiring of this familiar social dialogue. So far, the woman was just a pair of legs, and a lighter and a voice he had to respond to when he felt like withdrawing from everything.

"You don't need me," he said suddenly and soberly. "Guilt is the whole ball of wax. Write that down. Use it. And liberate the shrinks of the world from drilling like earwigs into everybody's psyches. You'll win an—"

"It's a Tony in the theater, not an Oscar," she supplied, picking up the ashtray and studying the ashes of Swanson's paper, something dramatic about her, something of the gypsy consulting tea leaves and the future. But she didn't look like a gypsy. Her hair was a halo of naturally curly, well-dyed strawberry blond around her face. It looked Zyunsinth soft. She had a nice face, neither too pretty nor too handsome in the way of some actresses, all overbearing bone structure. He wondered what her name was, even as he knew he'd never ask.

She was levering herself up gracefully, no easy feat in the body-packed room, and finally stood over him, smiling down. "I'd better hit the bar; my hearing is starting to come back. G'night, Dr.—X."

She was absorbed by the party's myriad body as suddenly as she had differentiated herself from it. Kevin felt—deserted, even though he'd asked for it.

"I think she liked you." Kandy leaned elaborately nearer. "What d'you think of the redhead on the sofa? She look my type?"

"Nobody looks your type."

"They're all my type, God bless 'em. But they always go for your type. And your type is always so goddamn indifferent. You would have made a good Afghan, you know? The dog."

Kevin laughed. "If you weren't drinking, I'd take offense. But if I weren't drinking, I wouldn't have been here to hear it. If that makes any sense."

"I'll tell you what doesn't make sense, my friend." Kandy was rising to his alcoholic high horse. "You. Man, you just let the chicks fly away left and right. Nobody's been makin' eyes at me like that blond woman did at you—what's her name?"

"I didn't ask."

"Criminal negligence! Criminal. Hell, there's guys that beg me for a tagalong to one of these bashes. You can almost always score if you can stand upright." Kandy demonstrated by drawing himself straighter against the wall. "Look, it's therapy. You need to let down your hair, tear loose a little. Give me a break. Give me at least some vicarious thrills. . . ."

"If you'd get off the floor and the vodka and away from the damn stereo, you might meet someone, too."

"Oh, sure. But you just sit here and have them practically fall into your lap. I'll never figure it out. You must have no glands, man."

Kevin washed the Scotch around his ice cubes. "I've got my share."

"No shit, I'm worried about you. Ever since you got back from med school out east, it's been Kevin Blake, the one-man miracle unicycle act. It's been this case, and that case, and Probe this and that. And this case and that—I said that, didn't I? Anyway, you're gonna lose your membership in the human race if you don't loosen up."

Kandy always was more serious drunk than sober. Kevin leaned his head against the wall, feeling the old plaster vibrate down to the base of his spine. The music was so loud it verged on having the soothing effect of white noise.

"Kandy," he asked, "have you ever become too involved with a patient?"

Kandy looked blank, then surprised, then knowing. "Screw one, you mean? Sure, the thought's passed through my cranium. 'Specially if she had legs like that one." He toasted sloppily in the direction of the vanished actress. "That's normal, Kevin, as long as we don't do anything about it.

169

Hell, there was one Russian language major with a perform-ance pressure problem. . . ."

"Not screw." Kevin articulated the word slowly, drawing out its crudity. "Is that all you think about? I mean really involved. On every level. Like a real person and not some starched-shirt desk jockey with an electronic notepad."

"You're talking countertransference, man. I may be smashed but I'm not too drunk to see that. Countertransference is ver-bo-ten." His mock Nazi came out too mushy to have an impact, but Kevin smiled.

"Where the shrink gets a crush on a patient? I don't know, Kandy; countertransference is pretty rare. Maybe I just mean that you pick up a case and can't put it down."

"Standard operating procedure for you, sport," Kandy observed with an expansive hand gesture that rained fat vodka spots across the ancient figured carpet. "Oops." He grinned his guilt, pressed his back into the wall until he could walk himself upright against it and pushed himself experi-mentally away. "Time for the old Red Fox to start cruising. I'm sure not going to meet anything sitting in the corner with you."

Kevin watched him lurch away; Kandy was no more out of it than most of the people standing, sitting and leaning around the room. He sipped some more Scotch. Maybe Kevin wasn't out of it enough. He pictured Jane Doe in this room, sitting on the sofa where the actress had, her elbows guarding her against the raw, warm press of strangers; Jane with her legs—fully as attractive as the actress's—neatly together, an untasted glass of Scotch and soda balanced on her knees, both hands holding on to it for dear life. She seemed a figure from another, more governable era, a black-and-white image from a fifties film in a 1985 Technicolor madhouse.

What would Jane think of all this, of these people who didn't really know one another exercising their affectional preferences and addictive inclinations in public? What would she think of him, wearing his jeans' seat shiny on the floor, icing his fingers on a glass of potent depressive? For an instant he joined her in the silent black-and-white movie he'd evoked. He moved like a 16 mm ghost, pale silver nitrite man, through the room, seeing it with that brief, alienated clarity that he sometimes thought was the human's nearest graze with godhood. The gay couple in the corner, holding hands and radiating the eager brightness of matched Dobermans; Kandy orchestrating some conversation near the refrigerator with broad sweeps of his rawboned hands. The blond actress, smoking in the dining room, talking to some mustached man in a turtleneck. She glanced his way routinely, as if waiting for him to spot her.

Kevin jerked his attention back to the sofa where she had sat before, looking for a slice of sanity in simple black and white. There was only another line of tangled legs—his and hers, hers and his. A couple necked gracelessly at the couch's end. People underestimated how good actors were at eroticizing public sex. This was all a bad movie.

Kevin pushed himself upright, mentally blazed an exit path to the door and began. A firm step here—don't stomp on anyone's ashtray/purse/foot/hand. Hand? Oh, well. Farewell wave at Kandy. No use. Oh, God. Coat. Down the hall. Bedroom dark. Light switch—light switch. There. A bed heaped with a harvest of Minnesota winterwear, all of it squirming oddly. No, couple squirming on the coats. Kevin spotted a familiar khaki down jacket, eyeballed its location, turned off the light and made for it. The heaving coats emitted grunts and moans. He clutched what he believed to be the proper tuft of fabric and pulled. Resistance. He tugged again and somebody complained. "Hey!"

He was already out the door, examining the jacket in the feeble hall light. Right one. "Leaving already?" a stranger asked jovially.

"Nah, just going to the bathroom," he returned, jamming his arms into his coat sleeves as he walked.

"Where *is* the bathroom?" The guy stopped, did a Lean-

171

ing Tower of Pisa act. Kevin paused, too. He looked over his shoulder to the dark bedroom and pointed solemnly. "There. Light switch is on the right."

"Thanks. Gee, thanks," slurred the guy, lurching straight for the room. He was so drunk he might piss out the fire on the bed, thought Kevin. At least his jacket was out of there.

Nobody noticed him leave the apartment; he'd never known who the hosts were. Even the hall harbored party overflow, mostly necking couples on the way to cars or other apartments or nowhere at all.

"Hey. I was just goin', too."

The blonde was wrapped in a cinnamon circle of wool cape, turning his way with slightly tipsy recognition. She wasn't really drunk, just nice and languid and warm, like sherry. She caught Kevin's jacket lapels in her hands, leaned inward, into his body heat, tipped her face to his. "You can't leave without saying good night."

His arms burrowed under the wings of her cloak, pulling her close. He kissed her the way he felt like kissing right now—not too hard or soft, but just right. And she was just right in answer. He hadn't been interested enough to specu-late about her body, but it was lush without being mushy. She was like plunging into warm spice cake, tangy but nonthreatening. He thought she was a nice person, she had to be, to feel like this—not pushy, just warmly, sweetly re-sponsive. Breaking their kiss came off as an odd blend of passion—and escape.

"Sorry. I've got to get home."

"I'm glad you've got one to go to," she said sleepily.

"You, too?"

She nodded. "My name's Gerry, for Geraldine." Only the "Geraldine" still wore the tart twist of an English accent, like a martini wears a lime.

"Kevin." He smiled back. "Maybe . . ."

Her fingertip pushed him away. "Maybe. You know how to dial the Guthrie, don't you, you just hit the right buttons—"

172

He kissed the end of her retroussé nose. Kandy would call him crazy for walking away from a close encounter of the sensual kind. He didn't know when he'd had such an instant response to a woman—feeling excited and secure at the same time. And he walked away.

Maybe Kandy was right. Maybe he should get his head examined.

Chapter Twenty-five

Kevin stood by the Jag, slapping his arms with ungloved hands to restart his circulation. Lights still burned in the old apartment building, and music drifted out of more than one open window—no wonder nobody called the police on anybody else.

The parking lot snow squeaked as he jitterbugged his boots on it. People thought booze warmed the blood; it did the opposite, thinning it enough to make exposure a real threat to any drunk out in the Minnesota winter.

Kevin wasn't one. Despite enough JWB to launch a bathtub submarine, he was annoyingly close to sobriety. Still, he decided to jog around the block, leaving his jacket open. His breath preceded him in steam-engine puffs. Icy air frosted the inside of his throat and lungs, drove deep into his nasal passages, acting like a dose of smelling salts.

By the time he trotted back to the car, he was breathing hard and had no fears about his driving. Stone cold sober. Or what passed for it.

It was nearly two A.M. Few cars were on the roads. The traffic semaphores performed their lonely, pretimed rituals,

Kevin the sole witness to his own law-abiding ways. He idled at the intersections, watching red blink into green, thinking about the party, its promising sequel that he had clapped shut on chapter one . . . about being a shrink. Once he even thought of Julie.

The condo parking lot lay deserted under an electric blue glare. Three stories of rear decking made the building loom with a ramshackle resemblance to the slum it had been not many years past. Cars cast cobalt shadows on snowbanks. A hanging plant, forgotten over the winter, twirled lethargically in the wind.

Kevin dug his hands into his pockets, the condo key in one fist, and started for the stairs. He hadn't been to the Guthrie for a long time; maybe he should take in a play, take Kandy's advice . . . There couldn't be too many Geraldines on the cast list. . . .

A shadow loomed from the side of the building, from the edge of his vision.

"Hey—" Damn, his hands were jammed in the narrow pockets. Mugging three weeks ago. How much cash? How much chance of getting past?

It was a bulky figure, short, stocky, formidable. Kevin tensed.

It spoke. "Dr. Blake?"

"Jane? Jane!" He drew her into the icy-blue light. "What are you doing here?"

"I . . ." She seemed uncertain.

"How did you get here? The dorm is across the river, all the way through Cedar-Riverside. . . ."

That she knew. "I walked." Her foot lifted to display the boots they'd bought at Dayton's.

"Walked? It's nearly two A.M. How could you walk?"

"I did."

"How did you know where to find me?"

"I saw your address, on Bridget McCarthy's desk once."

"When?"

She shrugged. It wasn't important.

"And you found me from that?"

"I saw a city map."

"When? Where is it now?"

"I saw a city map once."

She meant it. She had seen a map once. Literally. Just once and she'd remembered it. Oh, she was his Jane Doe all right, as baffling as ever. Kevin finally expelled the breath caught when he'd figured himself about to be mugged and murdered, the breath he'd misered deep in his diaphragm while all his questions rode on shallow bursts of air.

He reached into her pockets to find her hands and pull her farther into the open. "Your fingers are frozen. No gloves . . ."

"We didn't buy any. We forgot."

"Yes, 'we' forgot. Come on. You better get warmed up."

They clattered up the rear stairs to his unit. She paused on the threshold as the door swung obediently open to his key, but Kevin drew her through, chilled by her cold hands, and sat her on the long Victorian sofa.

"How are your feet? Can you feel them?" He pulled at the knee-high boots, but they were surprisingly hard to dislodge.

"Fine. My feet are fine." She spread her hands. "It's gloves I didn't have."

Kevin's warm fingers wrapped her chill ones. "And you got frostbite. Why on earth would you do a thing like this? Come traipsing out in the middle of a cold night? Jane, I might not even have come home tonight." He hated to think how close he'd come to not returning.

"Why not? You live here."

"Sometimes . . . these parties go all night."

She nodded sagely, and a bit critically. "Like the nurses'. They're not back, either."

He sat back on his heels. "That's it. The nurses went to a party and left you behind."

"I stayed behind."

"Why?" He was still rubbing her hands, as they seemed to be warming. He ran his palms up her wide coat sleeves, pushed it open and was relieved to find her body heat hoarded by the grace of Zyunsinth. For once, he didn't resent this mysterious being.

"Why did you stay behind, Jane?"

"I didn't want to go."

"You certainly don't have to accompany the nurses every-where. But you tramped through the worst of Minneapolis's urban redevelopment in the dark of night—I wouldn't send King Kong out there. Why?"

"I was . . ." She laced her fingers, hesitated.

His hands covered hers—they were nearly normal temperature now. "Yes?"

"Lonely."

"Oh." He sat back on his heels again, absently rubbing the fingers curled around his. Lonely. Such an obvious diagnosis would escape a man who expected the exotic and only the exotic from his prize patient. She'd never expressed a personal need before—except for food or rest or peace and quiet.

Kevin stood. "It does get lonely out there. Take your coat?" He gently put his hands on it. She unfastened it as delicately. He lifted it over the sofa back and tossed his jacket beside it.

"Still cold?" he inquired politely. "Want some coffee, tea?"

She shook her head, her eyes darting around, documenting the contents of his condo.

"Maybe I'll have some." From the adjoining kitchen he watched her as she studied the floor-to-ceiling bookcases, dropped her hand to pet the long-haired white rug under the coffee table, examined the hanging plants along the bay window.

"Maybe you'd like a drink," he suggested through the pass-through.

176

"A drink?"

"What do you take—bourbon, beer, kirsch?"

"Bourbon would be fine." She said the word "bourbon" the way he'd say "head cheese." She knew it, but not in the biblical sense.

Kevin poured two light fingers of whiskey in a lowball glass with water and delivered it. He sat while waiting for his instant coffee water to boil, pleased to have his vintage black-and-white Jane under observation in his own living room.

Jane looked at the drink, then at him, but his hands were empty, laced between his knees. He smiled. Her face dipped fawnlike to the liquor. Then her head jerked back as if she'd sampled electricity.

"Too strong?"

She sipped again, without comment.

"Why don't you take off your boots, get comfortable? You've had a long, wintry walk." He bounded over to help her with the stiff boots. Jane's legs were properly encased in neutral-tone panty hose. His hand cradled one cold instep. As soon as he released it, she curled her feet under her on the sofa. And sipped her drink once more.

"Aren't you tired?" he asked.

"I don't think so."

He dashed to the kitchen to rescue boiling water and returned with a steaming cup of instant upper. It was fine to lull Jane into relaxation. He was the observer and had to stay alert. Shades of the indomitable Swanson.

Kevin lounged in the sling chair and sipped his scalding coffee as cautiously as she took her Jack Daniel's. "You're all right now," he prodded.

"Yes, only . . ."

"Only what?"

"Only, I still feel—cold."

He went to sit down by her, checking her hands—not as

177

warm as his, but warmer than before—ran the back of his hand across her cheek—chill but not abnormally so.

She sprang toward him like something released from a cage, a wild, turning, lost, burrowing thing. His palms framed her face to read the reaction's violence, to hold her back. He felt poised for primal struggle, to ward off the primitive force unleashed within her, to save himself from being devoured by it. And then he read it in her face, an expression not exotic, but deeper than he'd ever seen it on any human face, even his own. Sheer aloneness. Dumb, terrifying outsideness. An alienation that he expected to see in the eyes of a denizen of the Third World, or the red-neck at the next table in a Denny's Restaurant, or in the dead gaze of a paranoid schizophrenic. Or an overbright child. Or the mirror.

There was nothing to do but crush it out of her, with everything at his command. Smother it, drive in a winning, warmer force, press her hard against her own humanity and hold her there. . . .

He did what he had been accused of so wrongly; he did it rightly now, even though part of him knew it was wrong. He kissed her. Not just kissed, breathed into her his heart, his soul, his will that she should know more than that awful, alien isolation. She pressed toward him as desperately. They were sliding down together on the sofa cushions. He broke the kiss and let himself recline, Jane falling, pushing herself atop him. Her head lay on his shoulder, and when he glanced at her face, her barely parted lips stirred an irresistible erotic burst. He bent to kiss her again, deliberately, his tongue unleashed and probing, her mouth flowering under his as one glance had told him it would. It was the most adult, personal, wrenching kiss he'd given or received. Incredible erotic possibilities coiled in his head. His hands convulsed on her body, drew her nearer—then suddenly, everything had shifted.

She was a fragile, delicate thing in his care. His breathing slowed; he didn't want to shake her too roughly. Her eyes were half-lidded, content. Kevin felt he'd swallowed her beast, that it prowled him now, chained and biding its time. He touched the corner of her lips with the tip of his little finger. She smiled. He pulled her hand across his chest, then reached up and tugged the heavy curtain of her coat over them. Jane pressed minusculely nearer; one leg and hip lay warmly against his, the other flexed naturally across his body, her thigh pushing lightly against his groin. He felt pilloried between delight and despair. He felt possessive and taken possession of. Passive and participatory. Tender and fierce. He felt maker and made, dancer and dance. Dr. Blake was gone. Dr. Blake would have censored everything from the hand touch outside the condo to the intimate curl of her body into his, his into hers, now. Kevin wished he'd never see Dr. Blake again.

Chapter Twenty-six

The woods were high, dark and deep, circling the clearing as symmetrically as a fence. Their heavy, pungent scent erected yet another barrier between naked earth and the forest lands.

A huge fire crackled at the clearing's center, almost in defiance of the living trees whose deadwood fed its flames. There was no moon, no stars, only a tunnel of darkness rising from the ring of trees.

A crouching figure tossed a stick into the blaze, then leaped suddenly upright, its silhouette unmistakably simian, the sharp edges blurred by a corona of long, fine hairs. The thing catapulted skyward again, etching a series of agile springs against the molten-gold sheets of undulating fire. It vanished behind the dark side of the blaze, capering around the burning center, joined by others of its kind, until they resembled an endless chain of dark, hirsute paper dolls.

His mind rejected them even as it invented and watched them. Flat, they had that flat, unreal look of dreamland. And then he looked down and saw himself—a ripple of sandy fur from chest to instep. He sprang his alien body skyward, trying to trick it into staying in one place while he twisted and darted and leaped into another. But it clung to him, like an odor, invisible and persistent.

No wonder the others danced around the fire, trying to evade their own skins, he thought. Now he knew what the phrase meant, to jump out of one's skin. One's fur. He turned to the other beside him. With that unsettling instant dissolve of a dream scenario, they were copulating there in the firelit chiaroscuro, and her (it must be "she") fur was melting with their motions—her fur, her skin and her, her bones. He was coupling with a skeleton, and drew back, repelled.

A soft rain fell, dampening but not quenching the fire, and the ambulance was coming through the trees, a strange nonsensical word wriggling flamelike over its windshield. Ecnerefsnart. It was important to remember that word. That was the key, the key. Ecne, ecne . . .

A tiny thing, furred, fell out of the sky and onto his face, blinding him, smothering him, making him forget the word. He flailed, driving away waves of earthy scent, beating off standing legions of waiting trees, scattering shards of shattered bones.

Light poured in pinstripe lines through the open Levolors. He was hot and his neck ached. Something mobile and furry was stapling his arm to his leaden chest.

Kevin stared, waching the condo walls assume shape around him, watching the fire dwindle to a spot of undiluted sun hitting the kitchen table's glass fruit bowl. Blue Streak was struggling, claw by tiny claw, up his arm, mewling for breakfast. A heavy fur throw—coat/Zyunsinth—kept his body overheated and lethargic. Jane lay asleep beside him, her profile aimed at the ceiling, her lips ajar on the soft hiss of her breath.

Ecne—ecna. His subconscious had had it. The word. Ecna . . . It was gone, though its *impact* remained. It had been there, whole and accessible, he knew it. *He* had been there, with Zyunsinth and the stay-fire. And the forest. And—he recalled the skeletal sex partner and winced. And who? Not Jane. It was only a dream, Freud aside, and he wasn't going to waste energy analyzing it when he had more vital things to attend to. Like feeding Blue.

The kitten swam frantically when he picked it up, kicking all the way to the kitchen, where he set it before a dish caked with yesterday's congealing gob of Feline Fancy.

"Didn't go for that shit, huh? Okay, it's nothing but Tender Tidbits from now on. You know how that crap smells when it sits all day. No wonder I was having nightmares. . . ." He bent to pour fresh milk in its saucer, actually a plant water-catcher. Blue braced its short legs—Kevin still hadn't inspected it for gender—and began implanting tiny teeth in a mound of red dye no. 3-colored food pellets, the mahogany color no doubt intended to assure humans that this was a "meaty" pet food. At least it wasn't odiferous.

Kevin ambled back to the living room as soon as his instant coffee was mixed. Jane still slept. If she'd been a problem before, she was plastic explosive now. He had to figure out what to do with her, and then he had to figure out what to do with himself.

He didn't have the heart to wake her—or maybe it wasn't the heart to face her—so he rustled around as quietly as he could, lifting the heavy coat onto the sofa back, setting her boots neatly by the sofa leg, rummaging in the semiempty refrigerator for something resembling breakfast.

When the kitchen wall phone rang, he dove for it Lynn Swann–style, then whispered a "Hello."

"Dr. Blake. This is the dorm. Mrs. Bellingham. Thank God for the campus phone directory. Jane isn't—"

"Jane isn't there. I know, Mrs. B."

"You know?"

"No magic. She's here."

"There?"

Kevin sighed. "I found her on my doorstep when I got back from a party last night—actually, early this morning. It seems she felt disconnected and came hunting her nearest shrink."

"How did she find you?"

"There are more things in the human mind, Mrs. Bellingham, than are dreamt of in our Psychology One textbooks. I don't really know, but I did know she was cold and tired, so I decided to keep her here until morning."

Mrs. Bellingham's tongue clucked sympathetically. "What a night you had, Doctor. We didn't notice she was gone until just now. I'm not really on duty today, but Glenda will be at the desk when you bring her back. Such a relief. I can't tell you how derelict the girls all felt. And rightly so. They had a little 'party' last night—and early this morning—too."

Kevin deciphered the tones of over-sixty-five disapproval of under-thirty-five goings-on. "Everyone's present and accounted for now. I'll bring Jane back as soon as she wakes up."

"She's still asleep?"

"She had a long hike."

"Just where do you live, Doctor?"

"Oh, West Bank," he said vaguely. "Near Cedar-Riverside." The last thing he wanted was for someone to realize what a feat Jane had performed last night.

"Why, she must have walked several blocks."

"Several. Thanks a lot, Mrs. B. See you later."

When he peeked in the other room, Jane was sitting up, looking disoriented but calm. How could he tell her to say nothing of what had happened last night without drawing her attention to what had happened last night? If an episode of *Magnum P.I.* could get him into hot water when he'd been utterly innocent, what could Jane do to him with a real incident of psychiatric overstepping behind her? He wasn't about to deny the truth to save his skin. Lying in front of a patient would shake her confidence in the whole belief system he had patched painfully together from nothing.

"Good morning," he said, keeping his distance.

Jane ignored him and pointed to his feet. "What's that?"

"Oh. Cat. Or kitten, rather. Meet Blue Streak, who does everything fast, including grow."

He plucked the creature from the floor and brought it to an awestruck Jane.

"Oh, Dr. Blake, it's wonderful! Can I see it?"

Formal address. Dr. Blake. Very good. He laid the kitten in Jane's cupped palms and watched her settle against the sofa arm to fondle it.

"Blue Streak?" The phrase was tentative on her tongue.

"Blue for short."

The kitten made stiff-legged forays over Jane and the sofa, looking for a route to the floor and keeping Jane busy trying to corral it. Kevin returned to his coffee, sipping slowly, watching and thinking. Seeing Jane now, it wasn't hard to understand why he had bridged the patient-doctor moat so impulsively last night. She looked perfectly ordinary. No, not perfectly ordinary. More than ordinary. Attractive, intelligent, the kind of woman he wouldn't be surprised to wake up next to some after-party morning. Or sorry to wake up next to.

Kevin scratched his bearded cheek absently and thought harder. He'd obviously made the mistake, not her. And why? He'd never, ever in the remotest way been tempted to get personal with a patient, and there had been the beautiful and bright among them. But Jane wasn't like a normal patient, blending the mystery of commonplace past and psychologically suffering present. She didn't suffer—when he kept Dr.

Swanson away from her—and she didn't have a past, except for the one that Kevin had carefully shaped around her the last few months, like a great sustaining feather pillow. Everything that Jane knew, he knew, except for the gibberish her hypnotized self revealed in sudden bursts.

So he knew her better than anyone, worried about her more than anyone, loved her more than anyone. That was natural. He was all she had and anyone the least bit compassionate would respond to that. But caring and loving didn't have to translate into making love. And that was what he had wanted to do with Jane Doe last night, as he had not wanted to do it with Laurel Bowman two months before, and as he was not quite interested enough to do with the actress Geraldine only an hour before he had violated Jane.

His thoughts had led him to an ugly turn of phrase, but maybe the face of honesty always wore its blemishes openly.

Blue Streak had lived up to its name and finally wriggled to the floor. Kevin gestured Jane to the kitchen.

"Come on, we'll have some cereal and then get you back to the dorm."

She came over, smoothing her sleep-rumpled skirt and sweater, looking at him as Jane Doe always did, with utter confidence and no reservation.

Maybe she had forgotten, as he should. As he would. After all, amnesia was her middle name.

It was alone. The formless ones were gone, if they had ever been there. It floated still, and nothing buoyed it but the confusion of the void. Out of that infinity, came a memory of another time, another confusion partly dispersed. "I" floated. "The one."

But now . . . there was another "one."

Others before, yes. The crowding, many pelts of Zyunsinth. The rich scent of uncooked meat to be eaten; the gobble of fresh, raw words—first words—to be regurgitated by hairy throats; the fervid, inward compressing of

Zyunsinth together, forcing the "I" into their conjoined midst, making one part of all.

"I" had not wanted to leave them. "I" had protested. "I" had fought. And "I" had lost. For in the end "they" came, smooth and silent from the dark. "I" had no strength against them.

But—the other "one." New, like a word. Alone, like "I." Unfurred, like "I." More new words, easy words lodged in smooth-speaking throat and thoughts—more thoughts than stars in the common sky. Thoughts made seeable, words made flesh, words wearing shape and form. As the new "one" wore skin.

One that served as well as an entire circle of Zyunsinth. One that another one could not forget. Never forget. That was important. To never forget. "I" didn't like to have memories fluttering around the edges of reason, like moths. Lovely new word. Moth. Mawth. A word to eat, and give back. And to remember. Like the other one. Like . . . him.

He. Him. A name of sorts, as Zyunsinth was name to the many furred and gentle creatures of the silver sun. Oh, the silver sun. And a golden sun. Suns passing endlessly overhead as the new words flow and the thoughts grow thick as, as . . . dandelions.

Dan-de-li-on. Noun. A common weedy plant with many-rayed yellow flowers. (Old French: dent-de-lion, "lion's tooth.")

Golden suns upon the grass. Comparisons. New, new, new. All new. Like him. Like her. Like I, the one. She. She liked the sound of it. It suited her. She. It was as good as Zyunsinth, to be one. Or better—to be I. And best of all—to be she.

The Claiming
December 13

Chapter Twenty-seven

"Calling Dr. Blake."

"Cut out the coy, and come in and tell me what's on your mind."

"Oooh. We must have had some weekend to be this cranky on Monday." Bridget's red head disappeared from the crack in his door, then the rest of her entered normally as she swung it open, a twinkle in her smiling Irish eyes.

"I've got news that will make your day and sweep all your worries away," she sang. "Dr. Cross would have my head on a clipboard for spilling it, but I figured your mental health was more important than the confidential relationship between secretary and boss."

Kevin was interested. Bridget had arranged herself on the Eames chair, her body language conveying a sense of secret excitement more than any verbal pose could.

"Guess which case of yours is involved," she tantalized.

"I could throttle it out of you, you know, and consign your corpse to medical science."

"You doctors are so bloodthirsty." Bridget swung her legs to the floor and patted her coarse red bob with self-congratulatory care. "I thought you'd want to know that fate has stepped in to remove the biggest thorn in the sides of Probe and the eminent Dr. Blake."

"Swanson got a grant to Pango-Pango."

"Really, Dr. Blake, I'm not supposed to have opinions on staff. But it's not *that* good. Oh, can't you guess?"

"If I were any good at guessing, I'd be a game show contestant instead of a shrink. I would say, though, that you look pleased, and act as if you thought I would be, too.''

"Darn it. I wanted to keep you in suspense. It's simply that''—she checked the round little Timex dial on her freckled wrist—''in approximately an hour and twenty minutes, give or take a few, Jane Doe's parents will walk through Dr. Cross's office door.''

"What?'' Kevin hadn't moved, but he felt as if the room had exploded outward and he was sitting twenty-five feet back from where he'd been an instant earlier.

"Isn't it astounding? And just before Christmas, too. It's like it was programmed. I bet Jane's—or whatever her real name is—parents have never had a better Christmas present . . .''

"Why wasn't I told?''

"You will be. Any minute now. I wanted to break the news first. I knew how relieved you'd be. Just think, home in time for Christmas.''

"I doubt we can arrange that. I've got to make sure the adjustment is—''

"Adjustment, schmujustment. We've got a happy ending here, Doctor, the least you could do is beam a little sillily about it, instead of acting so, so grim. Everything's going to make sense now, and you won't have to walk around looking like you're hunting for a lost shoelace when you don't have tie shoes. Isn't it wonderful?''

"Yeah, just great. I think I'll see Cross—''

Bridget jumped up from the Eames. "Oh, don't. Dr. Cross'll know I spilled my guts.''

"Should have kept your mouth shut, then,'' Kevin said unsympathetically, hunching into the hated white lab coat that would make his descent on Cross much more official—and effective.

"Aren't you just going to sit here and gloat and wait to be told?''

"Hell, no. You should know by now we shrinks are

190

emotionally volatile. I'm going to go put Cross's ass into a wringer until it comes out looking like confetti.''

''Oh, dear.'' She must have finally believed him, because she sank weakly onto the leather chaise, watching the door slam shut on his back.

''Why didn't you *tell* me?''

''Now, Kevin, sit down; you'll wear a ring in the rug. I'm not accustomed to answering to my junior staff, you know.''

''All right, I'll phrase it differently: Why *didn't* you tell me?''

''It all happened very quickly. This weekend—''

''I have a home phone.''

''The police requested that this be kept quiet until the parents' claim was investigated.''

''Which was?''

Cross nodded sagely. ''Probed and proven absolutely valid. They have high school yearbooks, baby pictures, hospital footprints. There's not a shadow of a doubt.''

Kevin finally sat down, dangling his wrists over the arms of the leather side chair. ''When, how did they find them?''

Cross's fingers tented as he assumed his *Head of Staff Knows Best* manner. ''It was simply standard, dogged police investigation, Kevin. Like your head work.'' He smiled, but Kevin didn't. ''They sent that sketch to every hamlet and village, apparently, looking for identification. And they got it.''

''Where?''

''Crookston.''

''*Crookston?* You're telling me that a couple from the polyester-and-hairspray, schottische-and-square-dance set are coming today to collect Jane Doe?''

''What's the matter with Crookston?'' Cross bridled. ''Are you getting so special that folks from a town like Crookston aren't good enough for you and your highfalutin patients? Where *should* they be from? Sri Lanka? Mars? Face it, a

191

Blake amnesia victim could be just a lost little girl from Coon Rapids or Crookston, with maybe a party involving booze and pills, and bingo, the memory is gone and she's suddenly Dr. Blake's miraculous cure project. Seeing her parents may do more for her than all your skill and will, Doctor, and if you can't accept that, you don't belong in psychiatry.''

There was a long silence while Cross's face held its hypertensive flush and Kevin held his tongue, slouching into the chair and staring fixedly at his Nike toetips. He looked up from under a shock of brown wavy hair, disarmingly, roguishly frank.

"I thought I was your favorite.''

Cross guffawed and relaxed into his big leather chair, swiveling to the window. Outside, the sky was cloud-bleached white, and leaf-empty tree limbs arranged themselves like praying mantises against it. Jane Doe and her parents would likely have a white Christmas.

Cross sighed, but the high leather chair back obscured the heave of his narrow shoulders. "I knew you'd take this personally, Kevin. It's easy to get possessive of a patient who has no claim upon her but what you can dig out of her psyche. You said yourself progress was slow. A few ravings about furred worshipers. Hell, chances of it leading to anything up Probe's alley were nil.''

"Swanson had some sessions with her; said her mind control looked promising." He never thought he'd use Swanson for a bailout.

Cross swiveled noiselessly. Maybe that's why he headed Probe and Kevin just worked for it from a squeaky chair.

"Did she? Interesting. Usually Swanson's so . . . overeager to report results.''

"I asked her to sit on it. Jane's an amnesia victim, not a guinea pig for the 'Mind Wars' phalanx that underwrites us all.''

"And Swanson meekly did as you asked. You have rare talent, my boy. Suitable for Probe at its most underground.''

"Anyway, when can I meet Jane's parents?"

"Lynn. Lynn Elizabeth Volker. The Volkers are due in an hour, and of course I'd planned on you meeting them. You'll have to—integrate—this rather dramatically shattered family unit. We can't have Jane—er, Lynn—feeling her own parents are alien. But perhaps she'll suddenly recognize them. Amnesiacs sometimes do."

"Only in movies of the week, Dr. Cross." Kevin slapped his jeans as he rose. "All right. New mode. Teach the humble Crookston goose girl how to get along with long-lost parents. Or maybe not so long lost. You know the details?"

Cross looked startled. "I can't say that I do. Only that Detective Smith was positive they've got a match here. He wouldn't bring the parents this far, then risk having their hopes dashed by the wrong girl. I imagine we'll learn all the details soon, Doctor. Sooner than you think. Relax. I know this case has been frustrating, but it'll soon be out of your hands."

Kevin nodded and left.

Fifteen minutes later, he was waiting in the Willhelm Hall lounge, while the girl at the desk fetched Jane.

"You visited me." She sounded pleased and looked at home in the tight blue jeans now. She looked at home in Willhelm. She had looked at home on his damn sofa. He couldn't picture her in a one-cinema berg like Crookston.

"Just passing through. I had some photos I wanted to show you, to see if the landscape looked familiar."

She dutifully paged through the photographs, snapshots from a north woods camping trip last June and meaningless. He hadn't called her "Jane" since he'd arrived, and found the habit hard to break.

"Nothing familiar," she said, her head bowed, her back to the door, the photos balanced on her knees, where the denim showed a little wear.

Kevin watched her, keeping his voice neutral yet loud enough to command attention.

"Lynn," he said, staring right at her.

She looked up at the sound, and turned her head over her shoulder to see if someone had come in the door.

Chapter Twenty-eight

She was short, past pleasantly plump, past fifty and had a pretty unmade-up face under a teased helmet of a hairstyle that had to require weekly setting on small rollers. Her hair was still dark, but was graying at the temples. Half of America could have called her "Mother."

He was medium tall, portly, balding, uneasy. A lower incisor was missing, but it added character to a face as undefined as a doughnut. He seemed like a nice guy to Kevin, and so he would to filling station attendants, Girl Scouts and the local Lions Club.

"Dr. Cross. Dr. Blake." Jack Volker shook their hands gingerly, betraying a working man's inbred deference for the titled professional man. He probably hadn't gone beyond the eighth grade; in a rural community like Crookston, youngsters often dropped out to help farm. Volker unzipped his red plaid jacket, and wiped a nervous hand over his mouth. The lost tooth bothered him, and probably had for over thirty years. "I guess you folks have got our girl here."

"Sit down." Cross played host expansively. "Take off your coats; I can have my secretary hang them up—"

"No, no." Volker pushed his jacket farther open as a concession to formally shedding it.

Mrs. Volker perched—that was the only word—on the

194

leather chair seat and unbuttoned her camel-colored car coat. "I'll keep mine, too. Seems kind of . ... cold in here," she noted apologetically.

"University energy saving," Kevin said abruptly from his leaning post against the ice-cold, cast-iron radiator. "Taxpayers don't pay to keep us in a sauna."

Mrs. Volker smiled. "I'd pay to keep you in clover, Doctor, if you've really got my girl. Our Lynn." She looked at her husband.

"Well." Cross extended a fat, oversized manila envelope. "I understand that you identified her from the sketch."

"Took one look at that drawing and knew it was our Lynn," agreed Volker. "Oh, she seemed a little peaked . . . but that detective said she was awful skinny when they found her. Starving almost."

Volker turned instinctively to Kevin to calm the parental fears.

"She was thin, yes, but there was no physical damage, Mr. Volker. No malnutrition."

"And she's fine now," interjected his wife, more pronouncing a verdict than asking a question.

Kevin nodded. "She's put on weight; her health is excellent."

"Not too much weight, Doctor," joked Volker. "Mama here'll have nothing to fatten up."

Mrs. Volker smiled shyly at this reference to what must be her most notable skill. Kevin wondered what her first name was, and guessed only the records would tell him. In public, she was either Mrs. Volker or "Mama," and had been for decades.

But Kevin was more interested in Jane. "Is . . . she an only child?" he asked. Somehow he couldn't call her Lynn.

There was a pause. "Yes," said both Volkers, in a tone that indicated one had not been enough, but was all they were given.

"And how long has she been—missing?"

195

Their eyes met briefly, as if strengthening each other for the retelling.

"Three years, Doctor," Mrs. Volker said sadly. "Three dreadful years."

"Three years. You don't think Ja—your daughter could have wanted to drop out of sight?"

"My Lord, no! I'm her mother. I'd know if something was troubling her enough to make her—leave home. Lynn always was the happiest baby. Even though she was by herself, she was so clever about inventing ways to entertain herself. Always singing to herself, and talking—such a chatterbox. She always got along with us real good; never gave us a drop of sorrow. And did fine in high school. Went to college at Moorhead, got good grades . . . Father, you tell the doctor. Lynn never would have just vanished like that without a good-bye unless something had happened to her. . . ."

"That's true, that's true." His lower lip pouted judiciously. "Lynn was *solid,* you know? We couldn't of asked for a better daughter. Everybody told us she was dead; had to be. Killed in that park."

"Some folks said a bear got her!" Mrs. Volker interrupted with genuine anguish. "But we never thought so. Not our Lynn."

"Wait a minute." Kevin searched their honest faces. "You mean . . . your Lynn didn't just vanish from her hometown, from your house? . . ."

"No, sir," said Volker. "No, it was that park. Glacier. Summer of eighty-two. She was working at a resort there. Tuition money, you know? I don't make much off of the hardware store, not that kind of money. Them fancy educations cost. But I guess you doctors know that."

"College hits everybody pretty hard these days, Mr. Volker," noted Cross.

Economic commiseration left Kevin cold. "But Ja—your

196

daughter was lost from Glacier Park? So how'd she get back here?''

"I know, it just seems like the Lord was pulling her back, kind of, doesn't it?" Mrs. Volker smiled. So many hard questions could be answered easily by the Lord.

"There must have been a search. . . ."

"Volunteers, and park rangers," Volker confirmed. "They went over those woods with a fine-tooth comb. Helicopters, everything. Lynn'd gone camping with some other young folks."

"Lynn didn't take up with strangers, Doctor." Mrs. Volker was anxious to make that clear. "But these were other young people from colleges all over. That's what they do in the summer, work hard to earn money."

And sit out under the mountain stars and drink beer and smoke pot and screw and don't tell Mommy and Daddy back home, I bet, Kevin thought. College is no guarantee of propriety, maybe the opposite, my Crookston innocents.

"Anyway," Volker went on, "Lynn was on an overnight hike with some boys and girls from the lodge, and she vanished, just like that."

"Like she'd never been there," added his wife. "That's how we knew we'd get her back someday. There was no body, you see, and even the bears would have, would have—"

"There would have been traces," Volker said gruffly.

"But now we've seen the drawing, and she looks just like herself, and it's all right," finished Mrs. Volker.

"You understand that she suffers from amnesia, that she doesn't remember much of anything?"

Cross was quick to intervene. "Amnesia isn't necessarily permanent. Dr. Blake was merely warning you that Ja—that your daughter might not recognize you right away. We'll have to go slowly; the job's not over yet."

"Dr. Cross, we'd camp at the gates of hell itself to see our daughter again." Mrs. Volker's chin pumped for emphasis.

It was the slightly prominent chin of people prone to overweight and their own way.

"I understand. But I've got to consult with Dr. Blake on how to . . . acquaint . . . her with her past. You have someplace to stay?"

"Motor hotel. On University Avenue."

"Fine. University goes right through campus. You'll be spending some time here, I think."

"When do we see Lynn?" Mrs. Volker sat forward, plump hands squeezed bloodless around her lumpish purse.

Cross looked at Kevin, who looked back with owlish impassiveness.

"Ah, that's what Dr. Blake and I should discuss. She'll have to be . . . prepared, of course. Could you come back tomorrow?"

"Tomorrow?"

Kevin stepped forward to sit on the desk edge and lean intently toward both Volkers. "I know how anxious you are. But it can't be hurried. Jane is—I'm sorry, that's what we've been calling her. Jane Doe. It's a hard habit to break. Anyway, her amnesia is very deep; we can't shock her with a set of parents she doesn't recognize—and may not for some time. You have to meet each other. In a way, it's like starting over. You don't want to rush it."

The father was the first to sit back, convinced. "No. No, I can see that, Doctor. Knowing that she's safe, that we've found her . . . I guess that can hold us overnight."

"Fine." Cross came around his desk to shake hands. "That's the best way; we'll see you at . . . ?"

"Three," Kevin supplied.

"Three tomorrow. Go out tonight. Celebrate. Enjoy the Twin Cities. You'll see your daughter tomorrow, I promise."

Mrs. Volker dug down into her oversized purse, pulling out a brown paper bag tied with string. She offered it to Kevin.

198

"My zucchini bread. Lynn's favorite. Maybe you could—give—it to her now. It might help—"

Kevin smiled. "Who knows what sight, sound, taste might bring back memory, Mrs. Volker? I'll make sure she gets it."

The couple almost backed reverentially from the room, murmuring a litany of gratitude. Kevin stayed put on Cross's desk edge, even though his position was slightly insubordinate.

"Nice people." Cross was returning from ushering them out, his features a mirror of their benign beaming faces.

"But not Jane Doe's parents," Kevin said.

Cross stopped in his tracks. "Not her parents?"

"Those people didn't rear our Doe, believe it. Jane is too—"

"So they're undereducated. They said their daughter was smart, first generation to go to college. And Smith said their story checked out."

"Maybe Lynn Volker was the smartest person to hit Crookston since its founder left town. I'm sure the Volkers lost their daughter and that she looked something like Jane. But Jane's one of a kind. They broke the mold when they found her—and lost her. Crookston, she ain't."

"Geographical chauvinism, Kevin? The sun doesn't rise and set on the big cities, you know. Why can't your Jane Doe come from simple folk and have a simple story behind her disappearance and a simple solution to her problem? You always have to make everything so damn hard. Being lost in the wilderness would explain her initial emaciation. . . ."

"For three *years*? Norbert, take some probability pills."

"It's wild out there in Montana. She could have wandered, taken up with some back-to-nature types—there's your furry-coated fire-dancers. Just hippies hided up for the winter. Maybe she was trying to find her way back here. Lost touch with civilization. She didn't know who she was, remember."

"I've never forgotten," Kevin said quietly.

"I think you have forgotten something. Sit down."

"Time for a lecture?"

"Time for reality. You always take your cases like they were personal property. They're not. They belong to Probe more than they do any one staff member. Not only you forgets that; Swanson does sometimes, too. Yes, you two are more alike than either of you would like to think. That doesn't mean you're not good at what you do, but you hang on too long. Damn, I wish we were at some bar and not in this office. I don't want to come on like head doctor. . . ."

"I can take it cold sober, Norbert. Go on. It's fascinating; I've never been analyzed one-to-one."

"Maybe you should have been. But you avoid that, like you avoid anybody or anything that comes too close. It's my job to know my staff pretty well. I've seen all your personality work-ups, the reports on your group therapy in residence—"

"I'm an open book, so why keep riffling through the pages?"

Cross shook his head. "You're not open at all. You're a loner. You're bright as surgical steel, and twice as sharp. You're a closet crusader in search of a windmill that can knock you off your white horse. You have that one bitter pill that you just can't swallow. I know about the Symons girl, Kevin, and why you're so addicted to hopeless cases and just can't give up on them. And that's why you can't admit that Jane Doe is not your case anymore. Face it; she's the Volkers' lost little girl, and you're going to have to smooth her ruffled psyche, dust off her memories and give her back to them."

"Do we, do we just turn a patient over to anyone who waltzes by to claim her? What about the cult guy? I worked with *him*, to make sure I had the real personality back. Turned out he still didn't like his parents much after Probe rinsed his head free of that religious brainwashing. Don't we have to be sure that Jane knows and cares for these people—or any parental figures? That she wants to be found? This sweet couple of yours could have abused her; they could be your goatskin-draped devil worshipers, rearing Jane in Satan's shadow. Even in Crookston. Maybe especially in Crookston."

"Kevin. The police have accepted them. Why the hell can't you?" Cross's forefinger angrily tapped the manila folder. "Look at this evidence before you spill your instincts all over my desk and can't scrape them together again."

"Have *you* looked at it?"

Norbert Cross straightened subtly. "Saturday. Smith brought it over before the Volkers arrived in town."

"And you didn't call me in?"

"I wanted to avoid—just this."

Kevin spun the folder toward him, pushed back the flap and pulled out a sheaf of papers. One of those mushed-edged cardboard folders that portraits come in opened in his hands almost of its own volition. A smiling child captured in slick color tones—dark, glossy straight hair, well-defined features, no braces, no glasses. It could have been Jane at twelve, but so could a lot of kids. Adult faces don't advertise in the childhood physiognomy. . . .

"Eyesight?" Kevin asked as he paged through the papers.

"Twenty-twenty."

"Identifying marks?"

"None. Those small towns were leery of mass vaccination."

"Aha! No fluoride, then. Teeth must be terrible—"

"No decay up to her disappearance. Family trait, the Volkers said. Resistant. Here. Why don't you look at this, Kevin?" Cross picked up a leatherette-bound high school yearbook. The 1977 Cherokee. He handed it over gently, his thumb marking a page.

Kevin flipped it open, feeling cold and unconvinced. A double page of slightly out-of-focus faces stared up at him—boys stiff in suits and ties, the girls in their white blouses and black graduation gowns all turned into an array of look-alike penguins.

She didn't look like the rest of them, though. There was something arresting in her calm, symmetrical face, the honesty with which she met the camera and whoever chose to view her through the years. It was Jane all right, looking barely younger than today.

There was some type under her picture:

Lynn Volker
Favorite Expression: Don't count on me.
Ambition: To see the world.

Chapter Twenty-nine

"What's this?"

Jane had arrived for her Monday session to be greeted by a brown paper bag sprouting mushroomlike from the tufted leather chair seat.

"A present," Kevin answered promptly. "Have a look."

She liked presents and immediately picked it up, sat in its place and set it on her lap to unwrap. He doubted that the indifference with which she had regarded a storeful of clothing three months ago would last five minutes inside the Dayton's doors now. She seemed to have caught conspicuous consumption from her dormmates, the way some susceptible people catch colds.

His program to domesticate Jane, Kevin realized with a wry internal twinge, had created a woman who could slide perfectly into the slot labeled "Lynn Elizabeth Volker." It was a pity Jane was someone else.

"What's *this*?" Her tone was no longer curious, but faintly disowning, though the words were the same. She stared at a brick of homemade bread, then looked to him for explanation, as she always did.

"Taste it."

Jane thought a moment, then pulled a piece off the end. It looked like damn good bread—if you liked vegetables in your bread; soft but textured. . . . He watched her chew slowly, shrug and regard him with something like the mystification with which he had originally regarded her. Kevin smiled, even though his mood was anything but happy. He was about to put Jane on a calculated roller-coaster ride—solo—and he basically thought it was kind of mean. But sometimes shock therapy was needed.

"What *is* it?" This time, she demanded.

"A present from your mother. Zucchini bread."

"My . . . mother?"

"Yes. A northern Minnesota couple saw your sketch in the paper. They recognized you, contacted the police and apparently are your parents. They want to see you."

Jane set the bread in its homely brown paper doily on the ottoman, dead center, but she didn't notice that. She stood, then walked away, almost into the closed door, staring at the lolling lingual symbols of Mick Jagger and crew. She didn't seem to see the poster.

"My . . . parents."

"Yes. Isn't that good news?" He said it the same inane way most people would say a thing like that, a question phrased to elicit only happy agreement.

Jane might buy the agreement part; happy—no.

"My parents have been found." She said it flatly, then came back to stare at the bread.

"Did it taste good?" Kevin asked.

"All right."

"It's your favorite."

Jane looked up, puzzled.

"Your mother said so."

"Then," said Jane, "it must be."

"They're coming to see you tomorrow afternoon. I thought we could use our next two sessions to prepare for that. Why

203

don't you put the bread on my desk, sit down and stay a while?"

She did as he suggested, handling the bread with no more tenderness than a . . . well, than a loaf of bread. She didn't touch it as if it were the only physical trace of a long-lost mother.

"Nothing concrete has come back to you, about your mother, your father?" He watched her mechanically rhythmic head shakes for evidence of emotion. There was none. "What about the bread? Taste bud therapy. Flavor bring any familiar kitchen odors wafting through your memory?"

"No. Nothing. Just nothing."

Kevin took a new tack. "Do you like the outdoors?"

"I suppose so. . . ."

"Gotten any urges lately to explore—other than heading overland to my place?"

"No. I mostly stay in the dorm. Or go with some of the other girls if they've got somewhere to go."

"Then you feel no great affinity for nature in the raw, piney woods, that kind of thing?"

"No. Do you?"

"It's *your* past we're trying to tap. Have you ever been in Big Sky country?"

A blank look wasn't generally considered a rewarding response to a question, but for Kevin it was. "Montana," he clarified.

"Oh. The state. No. Of course, I don't remember it, but I don't think I've been anywhere but here."

"Here?"

"The campus. The dorm. Your office. And the, the ambulance. And . . ."

"And?"

"And that dark place, so cold, where the ambulance found me."

"Crow Wing township."

"Was that it? I don't remember much of it."

204

"You remember being found out there in the darkness; that's more than you recalled before hypnosis. It's progress, Jane. We all should know where we come from."

"And I come from—Crow Wing?" The way she said it meant she'd believe it if he said so.

"No. I don't think so." He studied her speculatively, amused by how calmly she took it all. "I think you come from someplace else. But not Crow Wing—and not Crookston."

"Crookston?"

"A small town in the northwest of the state. It's where the Volkers come from."

"Volkers?"

"Your parents."

She was silent. The word "parents" seemed to carry all the emotional impact of a dead trout. Kevin studied her, aware of an intermittent, disturbing likeness to Mrs. Volker. If Jane's features wore a softening mantle of flesh, if her expression tripped through the standard set of culturally implanted female facial tricks—mock surprise, shy hesitancy—she would more than casually resemble Mrs. Volker.

But Jane had never looked like that. She was as devoid of female set reactions as, as—well, as Swanson, though for different reasons. Swanson's scholarly bent, her frigid nature, had repressed all that cultural conditioning. Jane, Kevin would swear, had never had it.

She was as invigorating as a mountain stream, fresh and lucid, so you could read right through her and come out the other side feeling as if you hadn't touched anything human. She had no biases, feared no fires, approached nothing from a time-worn habitual angle. It was as if she had never been hurt—physically, emotionally or any other way.

This was a lovely insight, Kevin realized sourly, but it didn't match at all a naked amnesia victim who must have been traumatized severely. Somehow it did fit a woman who had a startling ability to control physical objects around her.

205

He'd bet Lynn Volker hadn't budged so much as a feather pillow in her long Crookston career. So how did three years among the missing bestow such a lavish psychic gift while robbing her of all memory?

"Do you want me to keep the bread?" Jane was asking.

"Do you want to keep it?"

She studied it through narrowed eyes. "All the girls get goodie boxes from home. I'll say that's how it came."

"Jane. Everybody at Willhelm knows you don't remember your home."

"I know. It'll give them something to think about besides rock videos and, and dumb boyfriends." She pulled the paper tight and retied the strings. "And when they ask me again what we discuss in my sessions, I can tell them—zucchini bread."

"They ask about your sessions, do they?"

"They're very interested in me. And you."

"You don't want to tell them . . . too much."

Her eyes met his as blankly as eyes so ripe with read-into emotions could. Dark-eyed people never seemed to be able to lie as successfully as the bland-eyed.

"I know so little," she said reflectively. "It's better not to try to tell people more than I know." He guessed she had felt some fallout on the "Heavenly Kevin" affair, and learned. One-take Jane. "But zucchini bread . . . They can have that."

"It'll give 'em something to chew on," he agreed.

She seemed to recognize the play on words. At any rate, Jane looked wickedly self-pleased as she left, and not at all like a woman who was about to meet her parents for the first time.

"Great news," Cross announced at the Probe meeting, ready to bask in their conjoined surprise.

Kevin didn't think even witnessing Carolyn Swanson and

206

Roger Matthews undergoing paroxysms of severe shock would entertain him now.

"Jane Doe's parents have been found."

Matthews and Swanson perked up like terriers.

"Where is she from?" said Matthews.

"What are they like?" said Swanson.

Kevin read right to their underlying concerns. Matthews wanted to know what socially sequestered community could account for fully adult women with intact hymens. Swanson's motives were more purely scientific, or maybe just more pure: she wanted to know if Jane's talents ran in the family, and if so, how she could latch on to a guinea pig that didn't have Kevin Blake sitting watchdog over it. But Cross reveled in being the center of their interest.

"We don't know much yet. They're a couple from up north. Small town up there, Crookston. The Volkers saw the sketch in the Grand Forks paper, can you figure it? Their daughter'd been missing for three years. Lost on a Montana camping trip."

"Well." Dr. Swanson wasn't enamored of this pedestrian background, either. "And what does Dr. Blake think of this?"

"I think it's . . . interesting. I've told Jane—"

"Lynn," corrected Cross. "We've got to start calling her by her right name."

"Jane's not terribly impressed by all this," Kevin went on inexorably, as if he'd never heard Cross. "There's been no epiphany of resurgent memory. She displays an indifference to Mrs. Volker's fabled zucchini bread; I'm not sure she'll accept them."

"Accept them?" Cross's tone matched his name. "They're her parents, Dr. Blake. It's our job to make sure she accepts them."

"Kevin is so possessive of his cases," Swanson noted primly. "Particularly this one."

"I'm 'possessive' of providing the right treatment. Has it

occurred to anyone that in the name of giving Jane a happy ending, we may traumatize her as much as the amnesia-onset incident? We can't simply throw her into the arms of parents she doesn't remember—and maybe never even liked—and write her off. We have to make sure that there's . . .''

"A good match," supplied Swanson with a tight smile. "Like between blood types."

"They're her parents," Cross said with more asperity. "That's all we need. Even if Ja—Lynn—never remembers them, we at least can rest easy knowing the Volkers love her—you don't doubt that, do you, Doctor?"

"The Volkers love their daughter," Kevin conceded.

"They love her and they'll take care of her—no matter what, which is more than Probe or any one of us is prepared to do."

"That's just an assumption, isn't it?" asked Matthews in his ponderous bovine way.

"What?"

"That her parents want only what's good for her, Dr. Cross. I mean, her memory's gone. They could have done something to drive it out. All parents are not good parents."

"These people are the salt of the earth." Cross was devastated to have his judgments questioned.

"Salt can sting," Kevin put in, "wounds that aren't healed. I don't think Jane—or Lynn, or whatever you call her—I don't think our patient, my patient, is ready to be dismissed."

"And the rest of you go along with this?" Cross's eyes could be piercing when he was stirred up, and they sharply scanned the faces at the table. Not a muscle moved among the three. For whatever reason, the Probe team for once was providing its leader with a united front—against him.

"All right," Cross agreed reluctantly. "We'll let . . . Lynn meet her parents in stages, get acquainted. You people don't seem to have much faith in the restorative powers of the emotions, despite your profession. I do. I'll bet we'll see something dramatic out of this."

Cross left the meeting alone, aware of the others lingering—not liking it but not daring to stay and face them down.

"He's a good diagnostician," remarked Kevin when alone with his colleagues. "Why'd you cross him?"

They grinned in concert, with a camaraderie new to them.

Matthews answered first. "That hymen disturbs me. I'm hardly in the vanguard of the sexual revolution—"

"Which is over anyway, thanks to herpes and AIDS," noted Kevin.

"—but an anomaly like that makes me uneasy. I think we should go slow until we're sure this girl is on the right track, and can defend herself. The parents could have been religious nuts, and she repressed so much she finally just turned the off switch on her memory."

"That's a damn good theory, Roger," said Kevin. "I don't know if I buy it. . . ."

"What hymen?" Swanson braced her elbows on the table and looked alertly from one to the other.

"Jane has an intact hymen, Carolyn. Unusual in this era in a healthy young woman her age. I found it during my physical examination."

"Kevin really was hung for a sheep, then, wasn't he?" Swanson shot him a smug look. "But that means we could be dealing with an adolescent personality here." Her eyes were beginning to dart around the circles of her lenses like carp in a feeding frenzy. "It might go a long way to explain—" She looked significantly at Kevin, unwilling to let Roger in on her clandestine telekinetic experiments with Jane. "Don't you see, Blake, it's often sexual repression that triggers certain talents?"

"Look," Kevin threw into the now seething pot of speculation, "I've theorized enough about Jane to occupy the rest of you for a decade. But you're right; there are a lot of unanswered questions. We may never answer them. But I think we owe Jane—and ourselves—the time to try a little longer. That's why I don't want to take Cross's route of

209

rushing her out of our hands and into the parental arms. I'm not convinced yet that they *are* her parents. Oh, they think they are, and there is some evidence, but—you know Jane; she doesn't fit into the usual scheme of things.''

''That's for sure,'' said Matthews, standing. ''You will let me know if you find an answer to that hymen?'' Kevin nodded, and Matthews left. Swanson stood, too, her thumbs hooked in her coat pockets.

''And you will let me know if you find any family trait—like psychic powers?''

Kevin rolled his eyes, but nodded.

''Poor Kevin.'' Swanson leaned back and studied him. ''No wonder the girl became a transference problem. Emotionally, she's just a teenager at heart, innocently susceptible to crushes, particularly on an older man in an authority position. 'Heavenly Kevin' indeed.''

And she chuckled, Swanson actually chuckled.

''Please, Swannee. No Lolita trip.''

''Why didn't Roger report the hymen at the meeting?''

''It . . . didn't seem significant, I guess. Jane's identity problems are a lot more pressing in more vital areas than the sexual.''

''But do you realize what this could mean, Kevin? That virginity is the answer to the telekinesis.''

He couldn't help laughing. ''You'll have a hard time recruiting for the psychic spy corps with that as a physical requirement, Carolyn. But seriously, I don't think Jane's virginity has squat to do with any telekinetic powers. Try selling that theory to the government; they'd strip you of your grants. That's an old folklore fantasy—the virgin and the unicorn—the idea that a woman who's untouched by man has magical powers. . . .''

''I don't know.'' Her tongue ran speculatively over her teeth, distorting her already unattractive face. ''I got the most remarkable results with her. It'd be fascinating to try the same tests when she was no longer intact—''

210

Kevin threw up his hands. "Hey, we don't sacrifice virgins to science anymore, remember? God, Swanson, you're as bloodthirsty as the Aztecs. Look, I'll keep all five and even my sixth sense alert for any manifestations in Jane or the Volkers that might intrigue you. I admit Jane has remarkable powers at . . . discouraging . . . unwanted contact."

Swanson's eyebrows rose.

"Not that kind. But I don't think, repeat, do not think, you'll find it's any organized skill. Right now, I've got to concentrate on introducing her to her parents."

"Good luck, Doctor."

"And thanks for helping turn Cross off the path of least resistance."

"I only did what seemed logical. I have a stake in Jane, too, no matter how—remote." She smiled frostily and left.

Kevin looked around the empty, nondescript room. Despite a victory of sorts, despite unprecedented solidarity among the Probe team members on his side of the argument, he felt alone. It shouldn't bother him; he was used to sitting the solo side of many issues, and often relished it. This time, though, it stirred a cold snake of disquiet in his guts. This time, whether he won or not might really matter. Either he was getting older, or he was catching terminal alienation from Jane Doe.

Chapter Thirty

He felt like a teacher introducing the chaperones at a school dance: Jane, the Volkers. Volkers, Jane. It happened in his office, as he had wanted, at three P.M. Tuesday, as he had planned.

He hadn't planned on the room seeming so crowded, so claustrophobia inducing. Jane was on the Eames chair, as she had been during her usual session. Two chairs had been dragged to the desk for the Volkers. Kevin sat in his squeaky swivel chair and tried to neither swivel nor squeak. Cross, disdaining a folding chair pulled in from the hall, stood guard against the closed door and the Rolling Stones poster.

"Well." The Volkers had been persuaded to leave their coats on the rack outside, but Jack Volker seemed as uneasy without his jacket as he had seemed with it the previous day. He squirmed on the hard chair seat, and tugged the knot in his forest-green tie. "You look . . . pretty good, girl. Doesn't she, Ma?"

"Oh, yes. We expected . . . We read about her way before we knew she was—ours. We expected the worst, Doctor."

"Physically, Jane's in apple-pie order." Kevin swiveled impatiently to face Jane as he anticipated the Volkers' first question. "We'd better settle what to call her. Your name was Lynn," he told Jane directly. "It's what we should call you from now on."

"Lynn?" Jane tasted it as cautiously as she'd tried the zucchini bread. "Like Loretta Lynn? My name is Jane Lynn?"

"No, no, honey." So Mrs. Volker would have reproached a slightly slow ten-year-old. "Lynn's your *first* name. You were never a Jane. That's just something they called you here, because they didn't know nothing else to call you. You're Lynn Elizabeth Volker."

Silence.

"You'll have to get used to it again maybe, huh, Doctor? You were named after your Aunt Lynn, my sister, who died last year. Oh, there's so much to catch up on!"

"Aunt Lynn?" Jane sounded bewildered. "Jane. I'm Jane."

The Volkers exchanged a look.

"Now look, honey, we got to start somewhere," said the father, getting down to business. "We got to go back to the

212

way it was, and then maybe you'll remember . . . the way it was. Isn't there anything familiar about us?''

Jane's eyes seriously measured each of their faces in turn. ''No. . . .''

A tear welled on Mrs. Volker's lower lid and rolled painstakingly across her plump, unlined cheek. Kevin looked down, as did Volker. Dr. Cross couldn't see it, so he maintained his expression of bored supervision. Jane saw it, though, and tilted her head to watch it meander into the corner of the woman's mouth.

It hadn't occurred to Kevin until then that Jane was virgin in other areas than hymens.

''My name is Jane,'' she insisted. ''What was that?''

Two more tears slid down Mrs. Volker's face, as if evoked by the question. ''I'm afraid I'm getting weepy, honey. It's the joy of seein' you again, and then seein' that you don't even know your right name—''

''My right name is Jane.'' She looked defiantly at Kevin.

They all looked at Kevin, the parents as they would at a baby-sitter who'd taught their kid a particularly nasty habit in their absence.

''I'm sorry, but your name is Lynn,'' put in Jack Volker. ''Why, you were our little Lynnsy-winnsy when you were just a tiny thing. Used to call yourself Lyndy in high school for a while. But it's always been Lynn, one way or another.''

Jane was silent, but growing sullen. Kevin took everyone's emotional temperature, then intervened cautiously.

''Look. It's hard on everybody to meet like this. If . . . she's grown used to the name we gave her—and we did give it to you, just a few months ago—'' Jane looked away, betrayed. ''If she's used to it, I suggest we all continue to call her that, until she recognizes another name as her own. As a compromise, you could call her 'Jane Lynn,' Mr. and Mrs. Volker. Jane would feel comfortable with the first part, and you would have the second.''

213

"We christened her, we raised her . . . why doesn't she know us, Doctor? Why doesn't she know her own name?"

"We don't know why, Mrs. Volker. But we do know how hard this is on you both, on all three. You thought finding her would end it; it's just the beginning. So take it easy; even the pot of gold at rainbow's end sometimes takes digging up."

"Why should she care more for some name that's put on every lost soul that anybody runs across?" Volker pushed on, as sullen in his way as Jane; maybe it was an inherited trait. "Her name is Lynn. I'd hate to think how many times she was called that in her life. How do you forget a thing like that?"

"We don't always know." Cross had stepped forward. "But Dr. Blake's suggestion is a good one for now. Your daughter obviously identifies with her time here at the University Hospitals; she remembers her life here as Jane Doe. She doesn't remember her life as Lynn Volker. And maybe never will. You may have to get used to calling her 'Jane.' "

A sob burst hiccough-awkward from Mrs. Volker, who quickly buried her face in her hands. Kevin opened his drawer and handed over the intact tissue box, which Mr. Volker ripped open. His wife grabbed blindly for a fistful of blue tissue. And Jane watched it all from her Eames chair, unstirred, unrelenting. She was Jane, that was all there was to it.

"We'd better call it a day," Kevin suggested. "Withdraw and think it over." He got up, rested an encouraging hand on Mrs. Volker's shoulder. "You could assemble your family photos, think of childhood incidents dramatic enough for . . . your daughter to remember. It'll take time—"

"And she may never . . . ?"

Kevin nodded soberly.

Mrs. Volker crushed the soggy tissues in her hand. "I thought there was only the question of whether she was really ours. I never, we never thought—" She didn't finish.

214

He showed them out, managing to turn Cross around before they reached the door. "I'm sure Dr. Cross can explain this process better than I." Kevin flashed his boss a look. "I'd better pacify my patient."

Cross elevated an eyebrow at Jane. "Pacify? She looks like a remarkably calm young woman. Come along," he told the Volkers. "You'll see your daughter tomorrow."

On the threshold, Mrs. Volker paused, her face looking ready to rain again. "Good-bye, darling. Good-bye . . . Jane Lynn."

"Good-bye," answered Jane, turning away to arrange herself full length on the Eames chair, ready for another session, it seemed, and all too ready to bid her newfound parents good-bye.

"She's been a difficult case from the very beginning, and she's difficult now." Cross spun impatiently to the window. He'd called Kevin in the minute Jane had left.

"At least she's consistent."

Cross whirled back to Kevin. "It's not funny. You act as if you're enjoying Jane's obduracy, as if you're *encouraging* it."

"And you act as if you're the lord high executioner. Look, Jane is the patient, not her parents. She's the one whose mental state is at issue. If she's unable to remember the people who claim her, and unable to accept them on their—or our—say-so, she has a right to that. She's past twenty-one—by all the evidence. She can do whatever she wishes—change her name to Henrietta if she wants to."

"She may be of age, but, Kevin, somebody needs to look after her. We can't turn her out on the street with no job, no references, no means of support. And there's the odd fact of her virginity. She needs a guardian, for a while at least. Why not her parents?"

"Great. They'd do the job. Take her back to Crookston; I doubt anyone there would bat an eyelash at a virgin in her twenties. But we wouldn't solve the question of her memory loss. And Jane wouldn't be happy parceled out like that, with no vote in it. She may have no memory of her life before Probe; that doesn't mean she's stupid, or even particularly manageable."

"You want to keep her. For God's sake, Kevin, when will you stop regarding patients as stray animals to take under your wing? They are *cases*. They come—and they go."

"As do we all. What I want is of no great consequence here. Jane's a free being, as I told you. She should do as she feels, and, believe me, it hasn't been easy to dig any feelings, much less free will out of the frozen personality she had when she came here."

"It looks like you've been all too successful, Doctor," Cross said grimly. "I only hope she behaves herself on Friday for the press conference."

"Press conference?" Kevin gawked in disbelief.

"What do you think? We reunite a memoryless girl with her parents and nobody notices? Damn right, press conference. Get the circus over with in a big one-ring bang. Local stuff, national. *Time, Newsweek,* the networks, *L.A. Times*— they all want their slice of the happy story. I just hope your Doe doesn't turn stubborn on us and get more headlines than Probe can handle. Think you can talk her into behaving herself?"

"So that's what it's come down to, sweet-talking patients into putting on puppet shows for the media. I won't do it! You won't let me treat Jane my way, so you take the heat!"

"Settle down. Any heat's liable to wilt us all, not to mention our funding sources. But it'd be nice if Jane would sit there in a ladylike way and answer questions. Pose for photos with the happy parents, that kind of thing. It'd give Probe some good publicity for once, and you owe us that, Kevin."

He sat back. "Press conference. I should have known you wouldn't miss a chance like that. No way of getting out of it,

I suppose? All right, I'll talk to Jane, but only to prepare her for the ordeal. I didn't sign on as a brainwasher.''

"Put it in whatever melodramatic terms you must, Kevin, but it's for Jane's own good—and yours.''

Kevin left, brushing by Swanson on her way in and giving her no more notice than he would a fly. Jane loomed in his mind like a face on Mt. Rushmore, occupying his entire horizon now, yet still remote and mysterious. He began to see her as Kellehay must have magnified her—the catalyst for awesome, frightening changes in his once stable life, perhaps even the destroyer of parts of it.

"What can I do for you, Dr. Swanson?''

"You look tired, Dr. Cross.''

"I've been talking to Dr. Blake.''

"He is—forceful.''

"Yes. . . . What can I do for you?''

"I'm afraid it's about Kevin's Doe.''

"Yes?''

"It came out in the meeting the other day that I'd done some telekinetic experiments on her—''

"Yes, yes, I know. . . .''

"It's not a matter for dismissal. It was more than a few casual experiments; it was a logical series. Jane has amazing abilities to repel physical objects. Things of respectable mass and weight, she can—toss—them away from her like paper airplanes. I have a rough list here of examples—''

"I see. How did you get Dr. Blake to agree to these experiments? Never mind explaining if it's that difficult. Is this all you've got to show for it?''

"I wanted to videotape the sessions, but wasn't ready to bring in a third party. Jane is—skittish.''

"I know. What's your point here?''

"My point is, when you consider that Jane is the only subject I've worked with that's *ever* shown true telekinetic

217

ability, it would be foolhardy of Probe to let her simply . . . return . . . to an ordinary life in the hinterlands, to let her escape without her talents being explored or even cultivated.''

"You're on Blake's side; you want Probe to keep her.''

"I'm on the side of science—and Probe. You know how intrigued our most important sponsors have been by *my* work lately. Blake may get all the publicity, but how concrete has his contribution been?''

"He'll fight you tooth and nail if you take his patient for your program.''

"Him we can fight. Parents who want to take her back to Crookston—''

"How can . . . Probe . . . stop them?''

"Back her doctor. Back Blake, who only wants what's best for her. Say she can't go with her parents until she remembers.''

"And you don't think she will.''

"Not even Blake can get through that wall.''

"The press conference—''

"All the better. The press will exhaust themselves and their coverage if we give them all the access they want. They'll forget it, and we can get back to our work.''

"Back to work. I'm all in favor of getting back to work, Dr. Swanson. I'll keep what you said in mind.''

Chapter Thirty-one

A nest of microphones, like a metallic hydra, raised mesh-coned heads from the long table's center. Cables—thick, black and tangled—coupled indiscriminately on the vinyl-tiled floor. The wall-sized blackboard was blank; no complicated diagrams of the inner working of organs were called for. It was a head case that had caused all this hullaballoo, and no one expected edifying illustration of *that* particular human organ.

Reporters and cameramen surrounded the table, and shoulder-borne cameras bore instantly identifiable initials—CBS, ABC, NBC. The local stations were there, too, even the public education channel. Radio tape recorders plugged umbilically into the microphone centerpiece. Print reporters—and reportedly they represented *Time, Newsweek, People, US, Christian Science Monitor,* an entire subscription list of America's best and brightest rags—ringed the inner circle of electronic media, their heads constantly striving to see past the restless, possessive backs of the cameramen.

Laurel Bowman's was one of the faces craning around the bodies of burly network cameramen. Kevin cleared his throat, and glanced at Jane on his left, at the Volkers beyond her. The university public relations department had prepared a four-page release—mostly accurate—on the circumstances of Jane's finding, treatment and reunion with her purported parents. Only the release didn't say purported. Kevin did, in his private editorial comment upon it. It lay before him now; what was left of a stack of two hundred still sat at the table's far end.

"One—two—three, testing." The low words were repeated like a song in round all over the room, adding to the general cacophony. Kevin eyed the recording equipment uneasily. He'd tried to restrict press conference attendance, even offered to give a few major sources private interviews, but Cross was not to be denied his "happy" story. The cult deprogramming had been a genuine triumph for Probe and psychiatry, but legal maneuverings had prevented self-advertisement. Jane Doe, however, suffered from no such visible shadows, as far as Cross knew.

"Ladies and Gentlemen." Cross managed to sound both

219

tentative and self-important. "We can begin. All hooked up there? Right. I'll read the prepared statement, then answer any questions. And, of course, you may address questions to the Volkers and their daughter, or Dr. Blake, who's worked on the case from the beginning. Shall I start now?"

A couple dozen RECORD buttons depressed in unison; cameramen suddenly shifted position, causing a chain reaction of agitation all the way back to the SRO people lining the big room's back wall. Cross cleared his throat and began reading, keeping his eyes downcast too long and breaking his sentences into illogical patterns. Oh, well, not everyone's a media star, Kevin thought as he watched the faces in front of him reflect disappointment and cameras quietly shut down.

Four pages seemed like a Sunday sermon. The pent-up press corps chorused questions as Cross finished, so eager for a spontaneous answer they seemed to yelp. They sounded like a pack of shrinks; all they wanted to know was how everyone involved felt.

"How did you feel, Mr. and Mrs. Volker, when you realized the newspaper sketch was of your long-lost daughter?" "How did you feel, Lynn, at the first meeting—or should we say reunion—with your parents?" "It must be rewarding, Dr. Blake, to solve a case by reuniting such dramatically separated parents and child. How do you feel about it?"

The Volkers smiled and nodded and said happy, vague things, like "We felt real good." Jane spoke quiet, emotionless phrases that the sensitive mikes apparently picked up. Kevin felt obliged to keep this unwanted show on the road it was too late to turn back from: he spewed statistics on the rate of recovery from amnesia, discussed the condition's difficulties and patted Probe on the back with as little self-serving as he could muster.

Laurel had been right. The media liked him. Questions came more and more his way, and cameramen stalked him, leaning close to focus their long, nosy black lenses, their cameras whirring disconcertingly at his rear like mechanical dragonflies.

"What did Lynn first say when she met the Volkers?"

"I forget," he joked. Laughter. "No, she was . . ." He glanced at the carefully composed face beside him. "She was shy. Didn't say much. It's all new to her, you know."

"When do you think her total memory will come back?"

"Hard to say. The human mind is like the city bus system; it doesn't run on schedule." More laughter. "Jane's on her own internal clock. And who says she has to remember every last iota of her life? Do you? Does any of us? The important thing is that she remembers herself, her personality."

"You called her 'Jane,' Doctor—"

"That's what we call all unidentified patients," he interrupted. "Old medical custom. Did I call her that just now? Sorry, I forgot again. She's got a new old name. Lynn."

"That's interesting. As far as she's concerned, from the press release, all that she still really remembers is being a Jane Doe." To Jane. "Are you happy to have found your parents?"

Jane paused. "I'm happy," she said, looking up.

"And which do you prefer, being Jane—or Lynn?"

Kevin shifted, about to jump in. It was a damn stupid question to ask. . . .

But Jane seemed to read his alarm. She smiled serenely at the ring of cameras. "I like being who I am," she said. "That's what's really important."

There was momentary silence among the milling press people as they jotted notes to themselves that they'd found their closing quote. Touching. Kevin couldn't have orchestrated as skillful an evasion himself. And not a damn tape recorder in the joint going into electronic cardiac arrest.

He smiled at Jane, and the cameras recorded that, too. Later, on the evening news, which he was vain enough to watch, he would see a drama of stunning cliché skillfully pieced from the torpid afternoon chaos. Inarticulate, joyful parents. Shy, frail patient. And proud, nurturing young shrink.

But now Jane and the Volkers had to be extracted from the persistent questions, the still pressing press corps. He let Cross try to handle it and waited by the blackboard.

Enterprising reporters besieged him for post–press conference questions, which he delighted in answering with some inconsistency. Inevitably, Laurel Bowman's face—haughty, intent and, oddly enough, ashamed—appeared among them.

"That's all for now," Kevin told the furiously pecking news hawks. Once convinced he meant it, they scattered, hunting new sources of any random tidbit—the ward secretary, the maintenance man. Laurel stuck to Kevin.

"Finally answer all your questions?" he asked. They were alone in the hall, and her narrow stenographer's notebook was flipped open, though she hadn't written anything down since he'd begun observing her.

Laurel groped in the briefcase-sized purse hanging from her arm. "Damn manipulated event. I should have known that'd be your style, Blake."

"I had nothing to do with it. Don't blame me. I didn't even—"

"Didn't even want a press conference, I bet. Good. Nice to know you don't get your way all the time."

She couldn't quite manage to dig out her cigarettes and lighter, juggle her notebook and play fishwife with him simultaneously. Kevin took the lighter while she jammed a semicrushed cigarette between her lips and let the purse strap slide down into her free hand. "Thanks," she mumbled as she inhaled, handlessly, on the fag.

"I'm surprised you came," he told her. "I thought you'd given up on the Doe story."

"A good reporter *never* gives up." Smoke swirled in front of her mocking features as she whisked the cigarette away from her lips and exhaled the first, deep-drawn stream of smoke. "Think I'd stay away to avoid facing you?"

"No. . . . But Jane maybe."

Laurel's head tossed. He had something there.

"She's a weird one, isn't she? Just poor little Patty Hearst at the mike and margarine wouldn't melt in her mouth. . . . Of course, all those media hotshots in row one will miss it."

"Who're you covering this for?"

"Me, buster. Just me. I might see it a few times across the country in some of the big papers I string for. But mainly I came to see how you and plain Jane are faring. Old times' sake."

"And you decided?"

"The same."

"How about you?"

"I'm still looking for that big story that's gonna ride me right to the top. *Suburban Sun* isn't my style."

"Never thought it was."

"But you, I thought some things about you that weren't right on." Laurel buried her cigarette butt in a stainless-steel column of sand, and shut her notebook with a practiced flick of the wrist. It vanished into the dark depths of her purse, like a penny into a well, with the spiral binding flashing metallically. "It wasn't that hot a story, anyway. This place is crawling with everybody and their camera crew. I like exclusives."

"Maybe," Kevin said thoughtfully, "you can still get one."

"Look. Even a private interview with you—in bed or out—wouldn't add much new to the pot, so if you're thinking you can make up for keeping me off the story when it was still worth something . . ."

"I don't have to make up for anything. There might be another angle to all this, but it'd take research, someone who could get in there and dig. And it still might turn out to be nothing. . . ."

Her features sharpened, doglike, at the story scent he'd laid.

"The great Dr. Blake, dropping a crumb in a poor reporter's path?"

He shrugged. "I don't suppose if I asked you to meet me for a drink later, you'd take it personally."

"Of course not."

"Improper Noun? Know where it is?"

Her nose wrinkled as she nodded.

"Four o'clock?"

She nodded again. "Who's buying?"

"Me."

"An offer I can't refuse. Not on this month's budget. See you, Doc."

Laurel looped the purse straps over her shoulder and swaggered out, the only woman he knew who could walk that way and look like she meant it, but she had tenacity. She was just the woman for the job.

Kevin smiled on his way to his office, passing nursing stations besieged by eager clumps of staff, passing equipment trolleys and men toting cameras with reporters lugging spare tripods at their rear.

He wanted to find Jane and see how she was reacting to all this attention, but possessive psychiatrist was the last role he needed to play now. No, he'd remain coolly on the sidelines, where Cross and the Volkers wanted him, and leave them to Laurel Bowman, God help them.

It was only sleep. She recognized that even as she surrendered to it. Sleep was a state natural to her organism, even the deeper sleep, deeper dreams that he, the man induced. To/sleep/perchance/to/dream. Sleep/together. Sleep/in. Sleep.

But they always came for her in her sleep, all the creatures that ran together in a soggy incestuous brainstorm that coupled past, present and future. They came now, wearing the nameless aspects of her deepest dreams, the marching mesh heads and encoiling arms of black

224

cable, the two damp pinkish blobs always turned, like sunflowers, her way, their plump, stubby digits twisting, twisting, twisting. Ours, they said. She is ours. No, said "I," subsiding as she endured it.

It was the cold black ones that unnerved her, that entoiled her in their pulsing ropes of sending and receiving, knowing and remembering. And the hands, pink, grasping, abetting the machines, holding the machines, reaching for her. To capture her, empty her. Command. Spin, twirl, perform. As she did. Answer. Tell. Remember Re-mem-ber. 1. To recall to the mind; to think of again. . . . She remembered the great, heavy, clumsy repositories, listing things in ponderous sequence. They were utterly dead, those things called books, and did not threaten her. These did. These moving, power-pulsing machines that she understood and feared and with which she shared a terrible, undeniable common energy.

So. She had turned and emptied and retained, one impulse warring with another inscribed as deeply. Now the artificial stars had flashed against the room's ceiling/ sky, over and over, until her eye discerned no machines, no faces, no pair of beseeching damp eyes, not even him, the blue-eyed Namer who worried. She saw only the nova of light, swelling, consuming, eradicating her. Blinding the precious "I." Washing away the newfound "her." Leaving only the part that recorded and retained. The memory that she was not supposed to have.

She saw it all. Even the other Her. The unwanted dark one with the servant-machine "I" had splintered into stabbing fragments. The one who had returned, risen from the dead like a machine. There. With him. Walking away. Nameless. They said "I" had a name, more than one. Only one seemed imprinted on her deepest instincts. The one he had given her, called her. This other She had no name, had no claim upon anything. "I" did not like her.

She turned in sleep, in dream, in confusion. She had a name, although she could not remember it now. She would not forget that.

Chapter Thirty-two

Mrs. Volker unwrapped a piece of white tissue paper so wrinkled it hung limp. She elevated something equally pale and even limper.

"Well, Jane-Lynn? It's your christening dress. I used to show it to you all the time when you were young. You were always at me to see the pretty dress, remember?"

Jane stared at the scrap of dotted swiss and lace. "I wore that?"

"Sure, honey, for your christening, when you got your name, Lynn Elizabeth. I wouldn't expect you to remember way back to *that,* but we used to look at it together, oh, until you started gettin' new grown-up dresses. Then you weren't so interested. I kept it for a—grandchild."

"No name," said Jane suddenly.

"What, honey?"

"No name."

Mrs. Volker turned stricken brown eyes on Kevin. She was doing a lot of that lately. Her husband sat mostly silent during these sessions, either defeated by a daughter who showed no recognition, or reconciled to it, as his wife never was. Her name, Kevin had finally discovered from one of the news stories, was Adelle.

"Why does she keep saying that she has no name, Dr. Blake? We're already calling her by one first name we never gave her—"

"Ask Jane."

Mrs. Volker turned back, a little angry. "Now, Jane-Lynn. Why do you say you have no name? You have three very nice ones. Volker is an honorable name, nobility even, in the medieval times in the old country, I hear. And Lynn is what we picked for you. . . ."

"Jane," said Jane.

Kevin smiled into his beard.

"Jane-*Lynn*!"

"Now, Mother, no use getting testy with the girl." Mr. Volker turned a lugubrious face to Kevin for confirmation. "She'll come as far as she can when she can. We can't force her."

"But it's, it's like having no daughter back at all. All that time, and, and—" Mrs. Volker waved the christening robe like a white flag. "If she doesn't remember us, the past we shared, not even her own name that we called her by for over twenty years . . . Maybe a, a medium."

"A medium, Mrs. Volker?"

"One of those people who can talk to ghosts. We could have a sitting, and call up a Lynn that would know us and love us and recognize her own christening gown. . . ."

Kevin leaned forward until his chair squeaked. Jane's alert eyes flew to meet his. "A medium, even if any of them were reputable, and there are grave doubts about that, a medium conjures dead people, Mrs. Volker. Ghosts. Jane's here, alive. Very much alive."

"She might as well be dead!" The woman's generous bosom heaved. "I'm sorry, sorry. Didn't mean that, Lynn honey, *Jane*-Lynn, honey. Oh, it's no use! She's not Jane! She's my little Lynn, returned miraculously from the dead. They said she was dead, but she's not; you can all see she's not. How come she isn't my little Lynn, then?"

The woman was sobbing, her husband was looking steadfastly at his feet and Jane seemed intensely uncomfortable. Kevin broke his rule and reached for the tissue box in his drawer, for which Mrs. Volker was becoming a very steady customer.

"Perhaps we should call it a day," he suggested.

227

"Yes, Mother. Let's go back to the motel. You don't want to upset, er, the girl." Volker had taken to referring to Jane in that neutral way to avoid the Jane-Lynn trap. Using one or the other name alienated one or the other of the women, and Kevin's compromise of using both names won little favor from either of them.

Jane remained remarkably unaffected by the primal parental battle waging over her memory. She watched Kevin return from showing the couple out rather like a coconspirator. He suspected she was glad to have these three-way sessions, where attention was diverted from Zyunsinth and sklivent ysrossni and all the other mysteries that she couldn't explain, and was focused on the Volkers and their failure with her.

"You want me to stay?" She sounded mildly hopeful.

He was amused. She didn't really want tête-à-têtes with him just now, but knew enough to flatter him by inquiring. He felt oddly her equal now, or vice versa. He no longer knew that awesome, primal surge of protectiveness that had overwhelmed him the night she'd turned up on his doorstep, nor did he feel its uneasy tandem emotion, whatever it was that had caused him to overstep the line between therapist and patient. He was glad that seemed to be behind him—and Jane. They were both wary now—with others and with each other. And it was for the best.

Jane left, leaving the door ajar, and someone knocked soon after.

"Norbert, come in. Something up?" Cross almost never dropped into staff offices.

"Just seeing how things were going. Oh, and they did quite a job in the *Christian Science Monitor*. Thought you'd like to see your picture." The paper hit his desktop, casually folded to the right page. He saw himself, photographed in midsentence so he looked intense, with a rather vapid quote lifted out in big type next to his face.

"Ooof! Did I say that?"

"You're the one who had the phone interview. Actually, I

think it puts Probe in rather a good light. You seem to have a knack for saying the right thing." Cross sat on the Eames chair, then smiled slowly. "Except at staff meetings, of course."

"I don't know. I've been pretty well behaved lately."

Cross's feet lowered from their brief perch on the ottoman. He braced his hands, heels out, on his knees, elbows askew and looking like some kind of malformed feeding stork. The postures people took when presenting things they were uncomfortable with were almost as interesting as what they had to say.

"That's what worries me, Kevin. Your old firebrand self seems to have gotten doused by that recent wave of publicity."

"Maybe I'm mellowing."

"Or maybe you like publicity."

"Maybe."

"Now that's what I mean! A couple weeks ago, you'd have taken my head off and stuffed it down my throat for insinuating such a thing. Or tried to. My head's pretty well stitched on, as I'm sure you've noticed. Now, you hold amiable three-way sessions with the Volkers, peaceful as the proverbial lamb. What's wrong?"

"Hey. Maybe nothing for once. You're going along with my wishes, giving me time to work with both Jane and the Volkers. . . ."

"Her parents."

"Sure. Whatever you say. Anyway, I think they really need this time. This is tough for the Volkers, too. Between you and me, I doubt she'll ever remember anything before ecna—before she was found, so why shouldn't I be my usual cooperative self? Everything's going my way."

"Zippety doo dah." Cross stood. "Okay, Kevin, have it your way. I just hoped you'd let me in on what you were up to."

"Look, we want to talk mutual suspicion, I could do a number on why you changed into Dr. Jekyll after playing Mr. Hyde on getting Jane out of Probe hands. Before Christ-

mas, it was 'Out, out damn Spot. And Dick. And Jane.'
Now, there's no pressure; there are lots of leisurely sessions
with the Volkers. . . .''

"I agreed with you, Dr. Blake, that's all. It can happen."

"Then why worry? We're all in grinning, ecstatic accord—
you, me, the Volkers, Jane, Swanson and Matthews. . . .''

Cross snorted, walked to the open door, pulled it shut,
studied the Stones poster for a good minute, then turned back
to Kevin. "I'll believe that when these fellows pull in their
tongues and gather no moss."

He'd never had recurring dreams. And this one wasn't
exactly the same as any other, only similar to several. All he
could remember was coupling frantically with a skeleton
when the phone rang and woke him.

It was 11:30, and Blue was a sleeping ball of gray-blue
yarn clothing his feet.

"Blake here."

"Not *the* Dr. Blake?"

A flirtatious, feminine tone. If those damn student nurses
were getting playful again . . . The voice resumed before he
could sweep away mental cobwebs and answer.

"Guess where I'm calling from?"

"The Bates Motel."

Pause. "Close. The Holiday Inn at Detroit Lakes."

"Detroit Lakes?"

"Don't tell me my voice isn't instantly recognizable?"

Detroit Lakes. Must be near . . . Crookston. "Just the
honey in it, Laurel. Have you been drinking? And can't you
call before bedtime?"

"Had a late dinner. Met somebody . . . interesting . . . at
the bar. And then, I love your voice when you're sleepy—"

"Cut it out, Laurel. There's got to be a reason for getting
me up. Nope. Just leave that one lay. What's going on?" He
dragged himself up against the old mahogany headboard and
braced his back with pillows.

230

"Something that ought to help you give up impolite habits, like yawning on the phone. I've been digging around ye old hometown. The neighbors, the newspaper files. You know, I'd have a decent story even if I didn't turn up anything spectacular. 'Tis a gift to be simple and all that. Small-town girl, thought lost, returned to plain-folk parents. You've got a nose for news, Kevin Blake."

"This had better be spectacular, Laurel."

"Why? Interrupt your beauty rest? Oh, the good doctor's got somebody *there*! Well, helllooo. A little lower and to the left, maybe—"

"Laurel! I'm going to hang up in a second—"

"You can't. I charged it to your number."

"Watch me. And how'd you get my home number, anyway?"

"Brenda Starr, ace reporter time. You ever heard of a reverse directory? I've had your number for a long time. I just didn't feel like using it before. So you tell whatsis to get lost—"

"I'm alone."

"That's even more shocking, but it'll get you the bedtime story you wanted."

"What have you got?"

"Just what the doctor ordered. A scandal. The Volkers were the talk of the town—the whole county—twenty-some years back. And furthermore, none of those big-time reporters except me bothered to come up to Crookston and find out what the townsfolk thought of the long-lost daughter thing. Not much. They're clucking like chickens en route to Colonel Sanders's joint. Oh. Joint. I made a funny. I'm really a very entertaining girl, Doctor. . . ."

"Lau-rel."

"Okay. But you owe me a bushel and peck for this one. The town is talking again. They're shaking their heads and saying isn't it a shame, but that Jane Doe person *can't* be

231

little lost Lynn Volker, no matter how much her pitcher—that's what they say here, pitcher—looks like Lynn.

"The Volkers are vintage-minted flakes, Kevin. Crazy as the loons on the lake. Ba-nan-as. They can't be your Jane Doe's parents—migod, years ago, *years* ago, they were running around claiming they'd seen a spaceship. Saying they'd been taken up in it. They've been ignoring reality for a long time, believe it. And anyway, I have a record here, copied from the sheriff's office, that says that the body of Lynn Elizabeth Volker was found two years ago in Montana, and identified by the dental work. She's *buried* here. I saw the grave. The town had to do it, because the Volkers wouldn't. Wouldn't believe their daughter was dead. Nobody here knew why they went to the Twin Cities, until the TV stories started coming back. It is a hot topic, let me tell you. The whole damn story's gonna blow sky high, and little Laurel is sittin' on the plunger. That what you wanted, lover?"

"You bet. Leak it any way you like."

"Just finished my first draft and it's dynamite. I'm going to phone it in. It should hit type tomorrow. In stars and stripes forever. Copyright. Front-page byline. The *Times*. See you in the news."

She hung up. Kevin stared into the dark, stunned, elated and thinking hard.

The Pursuing
December 29

Chapter Thirty-three

"It's a good thing," said Dr. Cross, "that we moved cautiously on this."

Kevin looked at Swanson who looked at Matthews who looked at him. No one looked at Dr. Cross.

The copy of the *New York Times* splayed on the conference table had been passed on by a U regent. Despite its conservative type style, the words "fraud" and "psych unit" looked pretty sensational in the three-decker headline. Luckily, Probe wasn't mentioned specifically until the story's fifth paragraph. That was the only bit of luck in the unwinding media melodrama that more irreverent elements around the University Hospitals titled "Ma and Pa Volker Go to Mars."

Laurel had her byline—"Special Report by Laurel Bowman." Kevin had his Doe back, unequivocably. The Volkers had been grilled like a pair of Fourth of July frankfurters by Detective Lucius Smith and shipped back, as deluded but honest citizens, to Crookston, where a media mob waited to record in minuscule detail the once despised flavor of small-town Minnesota now that it had fermented a particularly pungent batch of madness.

"I've asked Detective Smith to brief us," Cross went on calmly. After an initial burst of disbelief, the media had decided to redeem itself in a mass mea culpa. It had turned as one and focused exclusively on the Volkers. Jane and Kevin and Probe were mere catalysts, now, in a greater tragedy. Peace, such as it was, was returning. Except maybe to Kevin. He had never thought the Volkers were Jane's parents. Now that they'd been disproved, he wondered who the hell were.

Detective Smith entered when summoned, escorted by a curiosity-brimming Bridget McCarthy. Kevin winked as she reluctantly withdrew. Nowadays, it never hurt to be on good terms with Cross's secretary, who sometimes knew more than Cross did.

"Dr. Blake." Smith nodded his recognition and looked alertly to the table's unfamiliar faces, which Cross introduced with seniority firmly in mind, first Matthews, then Swanson. Kevin, had he needed an introduction, would have been last.

"Well, Dr. Blake." Smith sat down, expanding his beefy frame into the slight armchair. "Your young lady has turned out to be a real nine days' wonder," he observed, shattering protocol.

Kevin loved it. "Indeed. I hear *Life* magazine will run an in-depth photo story on Crookston and its alien encounter in the next issue."

Smith shook his head. "Those poor people. Nuts, but the kind that sincerely believe their own craziness." He looked around the table. "I guess that puts you guys back to square one—and lady. Me, too. Dr. Cross asked me to outline developments since this bombshell exploded in the *Times*." Smith swiveled the paper toward himself and scanned the front page. Mideast violence, as usual, took the lead position, but the "Jane Doe affair," as the media was beginning to tag it, occupied a prominent place above the fold.

"How's our Doe taking it?"

"Fine," said Kevin. "She never really accepted the Volkers as her parents. Maybe we should have listened to her."

Smith grinned. "I bet *you* did, Doc. But nobody was marching to your tune, right?"

"Not visibly."

"Sometimes you get a gut feeling about a case, know what I mean? You just *know* it isn't what it looks like. Usually nobody agrees with you but that little voice in your innards, and it's kind of hard to call on as a reliable witness. You just keep lookin', Doc. I always do."

"What about the parents?" interjected Matthews impatiently. "Since we all took them at face value, I suppose we'd better hear what was behind that simple façade."

Kevin let the chill Smith had dropped on him like a damp, invisible cloak fall away. Cross and Swanson and Matthews could hem and haw all they liked. A lot more was going on than their buttoned-down little minds could perceive, and Smith knew it. Kevin wondered how much he'd tell them about the Volkers.

"The parents. Or not the parents now, I guess. They're what they must have seemed. Nice, small-town folks. Everybody in Crookston knew about their . . . delusion. They laughed about it some, in the old days, whispered about it, forgot it. The Volkers never caused any trouble, 'cept a couple years ago when the circus passed through—just a little flea-bitten, one-ride crooked-game deal. Volker got into practicing a little assault on a fortune teller. Seems she'd told his wife she could arrange for a talk fest with their dead daughter. That's when things got out of hand.

"See, the Volkers just couldn't admit their daughter was dead. Right after she disappeared, that was understandable. But the Montana State coroner finally traced some remains found a couple years ago to a Minnesota missing persons file—Lynn Volker's. That's when it got weird. The Volkers insisted their girl was still alive. Rejected the remains, rejected the whole idea. Some town leaders, the minister and such, finally stepped in and accepted the body—or what little was left of it. And buried it in the Presbyterian churchyard. Nice, tasteful headstone. Lynn Elizabeth Volker. Nineteen sixty-one to 1982—that's when she died. That nice shiny dark marble lettering on light, you know."

"You've—been—to Crookston?"

"Yes, Dr. Blake. And Crow Wing. Just because your patient hasn't got a name doesn't mean the police don't take an interest. City of Minneapolis got a lot of national publicity on this case, just like you folks and your Probe outfit here.

Then, I take kind of a personal interest in the case; I bet you do that, too, in some case or other. After all, I matched the Volkers with the Doe in the first place. Remarkable physical similarity. Kissin' cousins, maybe. You can't really blame the Volkers—a little shy on the marbles for years, and then seeing that sketch that looks just like their daughter . . .''

"I'm sure this mess, this mistake, is perfectly understandable, Detective Smith," said Cross. "We all fell for it. It seemed the logical answer to everyone except Kevin."

Smith nodded painfully slow agreement. "All except Dr. Blake." He looked amiably at Kevin. "Somehow that doesn't surprise me."

"Kevin goes out of his way to be disagreeable," put in Swanson with uncustomary acerbity and a softening smile. "That we know. What we don't know is about the Volkers' —craziness. It was really bizarre, wasn't it? Didn't they claim to have contacted beings from outer space?"

"Oh, that was years ago, er, Dr. Swanson." He paused for her to deny the "Dr.," but when she remained silent, went on. "Twenty years or so. Happens all the time. Especially in rural areas. Northern Minnesota's real infected with it for some reason. There was that local country cop who claimed he was chased by a UFO a few years back—made the national news, too.

"Well, I don't believe or disbelieve anybody's testimony straight off, but nobody in Crookston was about to swallow that this couple was 'assumed up into the belly of the Leviathan from the stars,' was how they put it. That's the first anybody suspected that they might be a little weak in the sanity department. But they were essentially harmless . . . so, everybody ignored it. Just like they ignored the way the Volkers denied their daughter's death and refused her remains. If you believe what *can't* be true, it follows, I guess they figured, that you doubt what *must* be true."

"What about their daughter?" Kevin ventured. "How did Lynn Volker react to being reared by parents like that?"

238

"From all I can tell, she was a normal girl. The Volkers doted on her. They were a bit gray in the muzzle when she came along, considered her a gift from above, that kind of thing. I guess she survived that pretty well. Cheerleader. Popular. Did well at school. Dated some, the usual. But, you see, the Volkers were pretty normal, unless they got off on that spaceship thing. And since it'd happened before Lynn was born, and they were kind of diverted by her all those years, nothing nutsy showed up—until she disappeared. Then they went off the deep end again."

"It sounds to me," said Cross, "like they needed something besides themselves in their lives—and when they found it, they stabilized. It's a pity Jane wasn't their daughter—"

"She deserves more than acting as a human pacifier to a pair of head cases," said Kevin sharply. "She deserves her own past—and future."

"Bravo, Dr. Blake," Swanson said sardonically. "I thought we'd lost the crusading shrink to all that media hoopla. 'The patient's personal good at any expense.' No matter what she could do for anyone else, for society at large—"

"Sounds like you and Dr. Blake have a difference of opinion—"

"No, no, Detective Smith. A mere philosophical dividing of the ways. Our Kevin sets himself up as the quintessential humanist, which casts the rest of us as mad scientists by default."

"We're not that different," Kevin added. "Just our methods; it's the same old madness, thinking we can accomplish something."

Smith smiled the half-crooked smile he used as a bridge to span social chasms of indeterminate depth. "I guess, Dr. Cross, you know everything I do, if not vice versa. Anything else you want to know?"

"You've answered our most pressing questions, Detective Smith. Thank you for filling us in—"

"Part of the job, Doctor." He stood and shambled to the

239

door. "Nice meetin' you all. Good luck with that Doe of yours, Dr. Blake."

"You're not—dropping investigating her background?" Cross sounded somewhat anxious and even more hopeful.

Smith pursed his lips and shook his head. "Oh, no, Dr. Cross. I don't drop anything. Kellehay's death is still unsolved; we still got a girl with no name . . . It's all in the active file. Don't you worry about that. You have any questions, just call."

He shut the door exceedingly softly for a man of his size and vocation, and left a long, awkward silence behind him.

"Okay," said Kevin at last. "When do they bring on the clowns?"

"I'm afraid they already did," returned Cross significantly, looking from face to face around the table. "Let's just hope this circus shuts down and decamps town permanently."

"To Crookston," wished Matthews with uncharacteristic humor.

"A-men," intoned Kevin with even more uncharacteristic reverence.

Chapter Thirty-four

It was the same and not the same. It was like beginning again, and as if nothing had ever begun. Snow fell in a silent, soothing rhythm outside Kevin's office window, unreal against the hanging greenery inside.

Fall's dead leaves were slowly powderizing under the soft, relentless weight of it. It was January, and there was no seasonal respite to anticipate, no airborne Christmas jingle, only the drab passage of Washington's and Lincoln's birthdays, hailed by idiotic store sales, and the juvenile ritual of Groundhog Day. He didn't need any mammalian weather forecaster; Kevin knew he was in for a long, cold, dark winter.

Jane occupied the Eames chair, her arms relaxed on its leather-upholstered arms, as if she floated on a kid-supple giant glove, confident the internal fist wouldn't squeeze to crush her, like a leaf. Maybe he'd been too easy on her, for she'd taken the unmasking of the Volkers with the same indifference she'd taken their claiming. Of course, he'd known they weren't her parents, as she had known. Or maybe not . . . not known . . . but simply not cared.

"Did you like the Volkers?" he asked abruptly.

She thought, then uttered a "No" that was all the more indicting because she'd taken the trouble to consider it. "Did you?"

"I don't know. I didn't—accept—them, I know that. Just as you didn't. But like? . . . It's hard to like parent figures, that's a basic human reaction. Love. Respect. Yes to the first, on some level, no matter how deep. Probably no to the second. But like . . . like's a different animal altogether."

"Do you—like—me?"

"Right now? I don't think so."

"Why?"

He sighed. "A failure on my part, I guess. I expect too much. You seem to expect nothing. It's hard to like that in someone. You don't seem to want to help me, to want my help."

She was silent, like the snow. The stumbling block in therapy lay between them, vast and divisive. It had begun before the descent of the Volkers and the media had masked it. He wasn't getting anywhere, as he had told Laurel. He was growing bored with Jane Doe.

The room should have contained an old-fashioned ticking

clock to mark their mutual disengagement, their individual ennui.

Jane finally stirred. "I *can't* remember," she said. Her voice was as controlled as ever, but her eyes glistened oddly bright . . . brighter . . . brightest, until one overflowed and a jagged ladder of wetness slowly wove its way down her cheek.

Kevin felt like a kid who'd kicked the dog next door, then looked up to see the neighbor watching. Our heavenly father Freud, he was sure, was gazing down right now in eternal disappointment, marking down Kevin's commission of one of the seven deadly sins of shrinkdom—forgetting that a patient, no matter how distant, or difficult, has feelings. . . .

"We could—try again," he suggested, ignoring the phenomenon of the tear, ignoring the tissue box he'd thrust so frequently at her would-be mother. He owed Jane a linen handkerchief at least.

"Try . . . ?"

"Try the hypnosis again. It's my fault. I've been a bad father, mother, sister, brother, lover. I've let unspoken things in therapy scab over. I've been too easy on you—and me. I can't afford to be nice anymore."

She nodded.

"Do you still want to know? Did you ever?"

Her head shook. "I'm afraid. I mustn't—"

"All right. That I can deal with—fear, repression, all the ugly inside turmoil you don't want me to see, and you don't, do you?"

Her head shook again, almost imperceptibly but repeatedly, a parkinsonian tremor of denial.

"Jane, if I don't see it all, I can't help. Why are you so guarded? I know you're probably as alone as anyone could be, but I want to help you. Probe is here to help you. Even the Volkers only wanted to love you—"

"And Dr. Swanson?"

He smiled grimly. "Dr. Swanson wanted to help her parapsychology program. You were just a means to an end. Some people are like that. It's all right not to like Dr. Swanson. I don't myself."

"You didn't like that woman, either."

"You mean—with the recorder, the woman in your room?"

"I saw you talking with her, leaving the, the—"

"Press conference. No, I don't suppose I like her much. But she helped me out when I needed it."

"Like Dr. Swanson."

"Jane, I never should have let you work with Swanson. She—persuaded me against my better judgment. She shouldn't have forced you that way."

"You wanted me there."

"Not wanted, permitted; there's a difference. And I was wrong."

"I could have—" Jane's voice hardened.

"Could have what?"

"I could have smashed her, like you wanted to, against the wall. But she said, you said, it was all right to do what she wanted."

Kevin punched on the tape recorder and sat back, the chair squealing mechanical protest. "Let's talk about that. About what you can do. I've tiptoed around it, pretended it was some obsession of Swanson's. But you can do—extraordinary things. Surely you know that?"

"I can—and I can't." Jane's fingers squeezed the padded leather. "I don't want to, or think I want to. It just happens, and I happen to be there—does that make any sense?"

"Swanson kept a record. It said that every time she threw something at you, you—somehow—threw it back. Without touching it."

"It was more as if, as if—it—couldn't . . . touch me."

Kevin got up, went to the ottoman and suddenly straddled it. "You don't like to be touched, do you?"

Her eyes darted evasively from his. "Not . . . usually."

The "usually" recalled a night he'd almost forgotten in the

243

recent hubbub, in his need to forget. Jane hadn't. He felt caught off guard, as if he were the one fooling himself. He wanted to back off; instead, he bore down.

"When Dr. Matthews examined you, you didn't like it."

Her answer was a shiver of recollection.

"And the nurses?"

She nodded.

"But it's better now. No one's got a reason to touch you. Do you know why you hate being touched? You like to touch. You like Zyunsinth; you're forever petting that thing."

"Zyunsinth. Zyunsinth's . . . different."

"Is it just strangers who frighten you? Or men? Women? Have you been hurt?"

Her gaze was indignant. "No! Never hurt. But—"

"But?"

She nodded solemnly, as if repeating something she just remembered. "But—I could be. It could be taken from me."

"What could?"

Her head shook again, mute misery sculpting her features. She was trying, but he sometimes thought she hardly knew what she said.

He put out his palm. "Jane. Shake my hand. That's what people do. Are you afraid?"

Her hand extended hesitantly, yearned away from his innocent palm as if it held a coiled serpent even as the distance between them closed. And he had thought her unnaturally fearless. He just hadn't known where to find her bogeymen.

His hand was so still it could have tempted a fawn from a bed of ferns. He could almost inhale the human salt rising from it. All wild creatures responded to the naked human hand, if it were patient and still enough. He'd touched her before, casually, through her clothes. He wondered why this deliberate reaching out was so difficult, and remembered the tingle her touch had communicated in the hospital, when she'd first come. Jane and her electric personality. . . .

Her palm hovered over his, so slow to approach that he felt

the heat of it first—incredible heat, no wonder Kirlian photography generated auras—then the featherweight pressure of the fleshy square of her palm, and her fingers naturally curling around his hand, as his curled in turn, turning a touch into a clasp.

There was no "shock," not a trace of it. He let his breath out carefully, so she wouldn't catch his emotional tenor.

"You see." He shook her hand gently. "Nothing to be afraid of."

Her eyes moved from their hands to his face, and even then he didn't see it, what she knew and he didn't. They were breathing in tandem, he realized, suddenly as aware of his respiration as if he were meditating. He could almost hear the plants behind him growing, the room was so still. Look deep into my eyes, you are getting sleepy. Deep into her eyes. Deeper. Dark, calm, fearless yet abrim with feral shyness. It really wasn't necessary to stare; he wasn't hypnotizing her now, nor she him. And he had made a significant breakthrough, gotten her to trust her hand to his, he had reached something. . . .

The name of that something was surging up his arms, brushing spookily across the nape of his neck, turning his stomach on end and making his esophagus do pirouettes. If only it had been an electric shock, a psychokinetic phenomenon, instead of what it was.

Kevin whirled up from the ottoman and to the window to watch fat snowflakes drift by, melded into multiflaked parties.

He jammed his hands in his jeans pockets. "I guess that doesn't prove much. Any suggestions?"

"There was a man . . ."

"Where?"

"In the hospital. I don't remember much, but I think he came to hurt me." Kevin turned to look at her. "I don't think he did. You could hypnotize me," she offered, a lamb to her own funeral.

"Maybe I don't want to know." Kevin turned away again.

"That is your prime need," she said primly, sounding like a computer. He turned back. She still sat on the chair's edge, her hand idly stroking the soft leather, over and over again.

"All right. We've never tried hypnosis on events that took place *after* you were found." He intoned the familiar words so casually it seemed he almost didn't want the verbal spell to work. But Jane was eminently suggestible. Before ecnalubma's last syllable had hummed off his lips, she was tranquilly under, her body cradled by the cushioning leather.

Kevin, sighing, leaned against his desk. "All right. It's early September of this year—" He paged through his desk calendar until he found the date of Jane's arrival, Kellehay's departure. "September first. It's very early morning, and the ward is quiet, but someone's coming into your room. Do you hear it?"

"I am—sleeping."

"Of course you are; they gave you a sleeping pill, but later, when I brought you to the other room, your eyes opened momentarily. Do you remember that?"

"I remember—your eyes. So blue, worried. I wasn't worried then."

"I thought not. But there was a man in your room, earlier, a man—"

"He wore blue, dark blue, but I didn't like him. He put a cloud over my face, and he talked and talked and his words seemed to run around my head and crash into each other and make no sense. Killed."

"Killed?"

"He—said—I . . ."

"You're there again, Jane. You can hear him now, and report what he's saying. . . ."

"Mehtoosek. I killed Mehtoosek. I don't remember. It was so cold for so long, and my hands, my feet, they seem so far away, just floating in this white space. Bed. Hospital. Killed, Matusek. He's coming nearer. To touch, to tear. Must not. Something will—too close, I can't think; it's beginning,

246

beyond me, it's what must be done. I must keep what I have gleaned. Things in the room are flying from me. Table. Funny table with one leg. But he's there again, so fast, so rough. Ah!'' Jane's left elbow flexed shut; her right hand cupped the flesh as if covering a wound.

Kevin crouched by her, studying her face. She looked as if someone were pulling her teeth out by the roots. She'd never showed the slightest agitation before under hypnosis; maybe that's why he'd gotten so little out of her. Not this time.

"Is it the IV, Jane? The thin transparent tube in your arm? Did the man rip it out?''

She nodded. ''Rip it out. I'm inside, I see all this, I'm so frightened, but the outside me . . . The metal tree, it goes over, on him; I hear it crack against his face. Up again, moving, his voice, his anger—the room is filling with him. It's all him and hate, swallowing me, swallowing everything, like the pillow. And then, I'm driven back, far away, to where I am small and faint. And—it just—'' Jane took a deep breath, her chest swelling, her hands, tensed open like claws, welling up from her center. Her elbows pressed her torso. Her eyes stared at a vision from her subconscious, her mouth contorted.

"It—just—blew—him away. Far, far, far . . . smaller through an ugly black hole. Everything's shriveling and Jane, Jane can come out now. To peek.''

Her body compressed, driving her breath out like a bellows. Kevin caught her as she collapsed. Her head sagged to his shoulder. Blew him away. Right through thermal-pane glass. If he didn't know better, he'd think she'd got that phrase from a Dirty Harry movie. Blew him away. C'mon, make my day. Not this way, sweetheart.

Kevin blew a worried breath of his own at his forehead. "Jane. Jane?'' She stirred, but not much. He didn't know if he was being cruel or kind or just plain stupid, but he kept his voice level and spoke into the hair massing at her ear. "Jane. You're going to wake up in a moment. And you'll—

you'll remember all this—what you said, what you saw. This time it won't vanish. Now it may upset you, and that's normal. But you've got to know what really happened—" What really did happen, ace? You know? He shook her gently. "Jane. Come on. I'm going to count to five and when I reach five, you'll be awake." The countdown seemed eternal; he was as curious as anybody to see if he'd say the fatal "five."

"Five."

Jane jerked away, instantly revived. Her expression blended realization, horror, denial. He caught her hand—but her final expression had been a betrayed one; she tried to wring her fingers free of his, pulling away as frantically as if he were the hateful figure in the dark blue uniform.

"Jane! Jane, calm down! No one will hurt you now. I won't—"

It was useless; she exerted all the dumb brute force of a panicked stag. She thrashed, she twisted; he feared breaking her hand.

"Jane, please; calm down. We'll work it out. Kellehay tried to kill you. He was crazy. It was self-defense. Jane, I won't hurt you—"

The ottoman toppled as she scrambled to elude him, the room, reality. She half crawled, half fell to the floor beyond the Eames chair. Kevin dragged himself after. She was scrabbling blindly around the room, colliding with the windows, clawing at them. He followed, trying literally to pin her to the wall. She writhed, salamander-supple, silent and intent, and slipped from his hands. The radiator's dull clank as her ankle banged it made him wince sympathetically, but she flailed still. Hanging plants swung bell-like over their contending heads. Her elbow rapped his jaw, but it was pure, manic natural force she exerted against him, not the power that had blown Kellehay through a new hole in the dark.

She spun sideways, to the desk, losing her balance. He went over with her. They ended wedged between his chair and the drawers, where he finally could twine his legs over hers, clutch her securely in his arms and make her listen.

"Jane, Jane, Jane. It's all right. Kellehay's gone. The thing that blew Kellehay away is gone. It wasn't you; you're here with me. You're not hurting me, except for a stray belt or two. Come on. Calm down. Shhh, sweet Jane. It's all right, all right, babe."

He rocked her, stroked her, pressed kisses into the hair at her temple, crooned to her, lied to her, circled his fingers soothingly on her shoulder blade, felt her hide in the dark of his arms, felt her tensions slowly quiver away, felt hot tears seep into the creases of his fingers as he held her face close to his heart and kept his mouth at her ear, whispering trite formulas of emotional security. "Don't worry; it's all right: it's okay, babe; I'm here."

He did it all by instinct, by hope. He did it all, and he did one last, damnable, unforgivable thing. He enjoyed it.

Chapter Thirty-five

"What am I?" Jane's voice sounded as calm as ever, or maybe it had been just dead all along.

"I don't know," he said.

They sat in the Jag outside Willhelm Hall. She didn't want to get out, and Kevin didn't want to drive away.

"We'll work on it," he promised, realizing his voice had become as emotionless as hers. His fingers probed his jacket pocket for the small rectangle of cassette he planned to run when he got home. Emotionless. That's not how the tape would show either of them. "God, I was wrong. If I could just go back and tell you to forget—"

"No." Jane turned to him, and she was smiling. She looked down at her extended bare hand. "You said we'd work it out. Let's—shake hands on it. That's what people do."

He took her fingers. "No gloves. You never learn. It's cold out there."

Her eyes narrowed. "I think I've been places colder."

Kevin pulled her close, hugged her, didn't give a damn who saw. He didn't know what to say—hang in there, be good—so he said nothing and watched her walk into what he had once considered the impregnable safety of Willhelm. The brick looked like cardboard now, that any strong wind could blow over, and there was a wolf at the venerable wooden door. Maybe its name was Zyunsinth. Maybe it was Kevin.

He drove home, fed the cat, brewed some herbal tea, punched on the cassette and listened with what he hoped was a dispassionate, trained ear. Technology hadn't failed him. The built-in microphone had caught it all—Jane's confused confession; the damning implications of what she had said; the muffled progress of their struggle; his last, unprofessional crooning to a troubled patient.

Kevin backed up the tape and listened again to her description of the hospital room attack, when Kellehay and hatred had assumed synonymous, lethal form, then had paid the price for it as Jane's power flared out to protect her. He replayed it until he thought he knew it by heart, and the premature daylight savings time winter evening drew its impenetrable shades across the windows. Kevin saw himself reflected on the jet-black surface, his image dissected by the open blinds' scalpel-thin lines, as if methodically lacerated. The room behind him mirrored a warm, lamplit glow, but he sat at the center of it like some emotional black hole, sucking everything around him into the same empty vacuum of doubt he occupied.

He rewound the tape totally and hit ERASE. Watching the tiny twin reels rapidly diminish and swell in turn, he knew he'd stepped irrevocably out of bounds—out of Probe's, out of his own. He was no longer simply Jane Doe's shrink. He was her advocate, her defender, her friend and probably her lover in every sense but physical. The game had been played to check and mate, to transference and countertransference.

Kellehay had been right; she was a killer, and Kevin kept her secret. She was an enigma, and he would solve her mystery only for her good, and his—the rest of society be damned. Her innocence encompassed both an unearthly power and an all-too-earthy inexperience. He would have to pursue both to their roots. And when he found whatever answers he could, he would keep them to himself, just as he would—somehow—keep Jane.

Kevin smiled—not happily—and played the whole blank, erased reel back, listening intently to the low-key hiss of tape against reel, just to make sure. Blue, curled up on the sofa beside him, flicked a feline ear at the sound, yawned to display a delicately pink shell of palate and hid its triangular face in a crook of soft gray paw.

"Hey, Kev! Hold up a minute."

Martin Kandinsky was darting ruthlessly through the cafeteria line, snaking a long arm through the clogged queue to snitch this dish or that. Frowns followed his progress, but Kandy kept grinning and kept on grabbing.

"Hey, man, how's it been going?"

"The kitten's fine; likes to eat electric cords, though."

"Not the damn cat." Kandy trailed Kevin to a window table, where a steady snowfall was painting the campus into a tardy Christmas card scene. "Must've been some flap at Probe with the magical, off-and-on parent machine," he began, inhaling food and exhaling a running commentary simultaneously. "I mean, one minute it's 'Hail, Hail the Gang's All Here' with the whole damn university basking in klieg lights and my pal Kevin is a media star. The next minute everybody's talking about Crookston, and the Betty

251

and Barney Hill case—there isn't a copy of *Interrupted Journey* in a circumference of eight miles—and fraud. I guess Probe hasn't got a copyright on crazies, huh? Those Volkers must have been space cruisers, excuse the expression."

"They were nice people." Kevin wondered why he defended them. Maybe Kandy's conspicuous consumption was getting on his nerves. "Hey, leave some for the starving in India," he added.

"Sorry," Kandy mumbled through a bowl of chili. "Had to skip coffee break today. So, how's your prize patient taking revelations on her on-again, off-again origins?"

"Stablest of us all."

"She's a cool one, from what you said. Any hints about that sklivent gobbledygook?"

"Red herring, probably. A lot of kids have secret languages. I think those words were only fragments of that."

"Me, I just had pig latin—uday uyay igday?"

"I dig. No, everything's business as usual. That's why I haven't called you—nothing to consult the incisive Kandinsky about."

"We don't have to talk shop. What about the Guthrie party? Some blast. You ever hear from that blonde with the legs and the lighter?"

"Geraldine?"

Kandy's knife jabbed triumphantly. "You *did* find out her name, you cagey bastard! See her yet?"

"We got together." Kevin shoved down the lie with a forkful of baked beans.

"All *right*! No wonder I haven't heard from you. I guess you won't lust after the next thespian bash?"

Kevin smiled. "No, I think I'm set for a while."

"Lucky dog. Everything always falls into place for you—cases, chicks—I bet that damn cat even goes in its Kitty Litter. . . ."

"Don't they all?" Kevin asked innocently.

"Shit, man, you are disgusting. When you gonna get your Nobel?"

"Next week. But it's top secret for now." Kevin got up, the empty tray in his hands.

"Well, give me a call sometime," said Kandy, still diving into his hamburger casserole. He looked up through thick, round lenses, for once not chewing something. "That's what friends are for."

"Jane, I'm going to take you back to the Crow Wing bluff."

She looked so startled that he smiled despite a gnaw of anxiety in his gut that belied his professionally calm voice. "Not literally, just via our usual mode of travel—hypnotism."

Surprise ebbed to distaste—no, remembered pain.

"Yesterday still—stings?" he asked.

Jane nodded. "I remembered more after I went back to the dorm. Last night." Her voice grew emotionless again, as if she were a bored court reporter asked to read back a particularly technical but lurid bit of testimony. "He was there, that man. He tried to . . ." Her hands spread before her face as she strove to name the act of surrounding her senses with a feather pillow and pressing.

"Smother," Kevin furnished brutally. "He did try to kill you, you know."

"But I—"

"Something killed him. I don't know if it was you. You seemed to be absent from the room in some way, distant."

"I have always been distant," she pointed out, and there was a spasm of emptiness in her voice that might have been bitterness, might have been indifference. "Not here. Not—real."

"Not always distant," he reminded her with both his voice and the momentary press of his hand on her shoulder. Then he began prowling the room again. This was different from the controlled sessions he had held before, both of them

253

primly in their respective chairs. It had to be. "Are you afraid to go back to Crow Wing? We did it before."

"Then, I couldn't . . ."

"Couldn't what?"

"Couldn't *see* so clearly."

He stopped behind her, resting his hands on her shoulders. "That's why we have to go back. Now, you're willing to see the past, if only in glimpses. I have to know that, and you have to remember it. Or there won't be any future, for either of us."

That scared her. He saw her dark head nod, watched the tips of her foreshortened eyelashes flutter her nervousness. The backs of his fingers stroked her cheek as he moved to the desk, putting the distance between them that frightened her now, and that he needed.

His fingertip hovered over the tape button, as hers had at the first session he had introduced it. "I'm not keeping the tapes, anymore, just long enough to study them." He smiled. "So one of us at least remembers what you remember."

She took a breath and nodded as he began chanting the formula that hypnotized her so easily. "Ecnalubma," he ended, watching the dark of her eyes vanish easily under the heavy fringe of lashes. Ambulance backward. That should have told him something, the basic, alien logic of it. He sighed and punched on the tape recorder. It was the same reel that he'd erased yesterday and that he planned to erase again after he had studied it. It was an odd fancy, but he was struck by the act of recording over and over the anomalies of Jane Doe, until the mute tape had held her whole history, the way a DNA molecule holds the future of an individual, imbedded maybe, ripe with potential, but somehow dormant. . . .

He wondered if in some arcane way her story would make more sense in its ghostly layers upon an eradicated tape than it would told sequentially in a psychiatrist's office or a Probe meeting. Probably not.

He began invoking the time and place of the Crow Wing

bluff top, the hot August night so different from this January world of silent snow. Crickets scraping themselves frenzied over the climax of some insect symphony. The police car's wheels grinding up the unpaved grade, the summer night heavy and empty over them all, especially above the naked, emaciated young woman floating on the refuse. . . . He had forgotten what it must have been like, forgotten why Kellehay had taken it so to heart, forgotten how he'd felt on first seeing Jane Doe. . . .

This time when he asked his questions, she answered more fully.

"Kellehay. The other man called his name. " 'No drinkin' on the job, Kellehay.' " Her head thrashed on the leather, as if avoiding an image that wouldn't let go. "It's raining. From the sky. Stones, such little stones that sting. And they're there—touching me, talking. I'm swinging out over the abyss, alone. So cold. No Zyunsinth, only the far, distant dots in the sky. Stars. Yes, that's it. Stars. And this must be night. And these . . . people— He hurts me, presses hard. And there's the beast, the black-and-white beast. It—bristles with power, purring, humming, shining. They will—cage me, cage me. Floating again, liquid again. And machines, I hear them buzzing to each other. Talking. Talking about something. About me. I. I is here. I must not allow. I must defend. Turn. Turn the beast upon itself, quickly! He looks at me, from so far away. I must . . . I let the thing take me, do it, I feel something tingle through me. And then I am done. I am as usual. I am gone. Far away. Later, the screaming wakes me. I'm less cold; there are more lights, more people, but I am more awake. I do not need the defender. I am where I am supposed to be. I am—" She smiled suddenly. "Jane Doe. The man came into the room and said so. I don't think I've ever had a name before. I, I—like it."

He didn't call a friend that evening, as Kandy had suggested. Unfortunately, enemies were safer than friends right now, friends who expected him to adhere to truth, justice and the American way. So he called an old enemy.

"Kevin Blake. Any more fallout on the Volkers?"

"I'm packing. Got an interview at the *Times* tomorrow afternoon. The Volkers are old news. I got my scoop."

"That's great, Laurel. It's what you wanted, right?"

"Right."

"Before you depart for fame and fortune, I wanted to check some details with you."

"Yes?"

"The timetable, mostly. Like when Lynn Volker vanished, when her body was found. And some stuff on the Volkers' close encounter—when it purportedly happened and what they said happened. . . ."

"Hey, don't you read your favorite reporter?"

"Religiously. But there's been so much on this damn case—"

"Okay. I haven't got time to play cat and mouse with you. Let's see. Lynn Volker vanished August 16, 1981. The Montana coroner's office identified her remains in July of 1982, and she was returned to Crookston and buried—on August 13 that year, without Papa and Momma present, naturally."

"They identified her from the dental charts, right? Then the Volkers must have lied when they said their daughter had no dental work, that the family was decay-resistant?"

"Or fooled themselves. Listen, Lynn didn't have much for a dental record, but there were a couple of cavities. That's what made her so identifiable—almost perfect teeth. And the item with the sketch mentioned perfect teeth. If you're getting at deliberate deception, I don't think the Volkers are capable of it. They just forgot, or wanted to forget, a couple of very telling silver strikes in their darling daughter's teeth."

"I take it you've seen the dental records."

"I went through every record in that damn town with

dental floss, Kevin. That's Lynn Volker in that cemetery plot or I'm Mr. Tooth Decay. Why the interest in oral hygiene?''

"Just wanted the facts, ma'am. And the Volkers episode with the aliens, when did that take place?''

"They claimed in the fall of 1960, just after Kennedy got elected. You know, that's odd. It was less than a year before the Hills claimed to have been assumed into a spaceship, too.''

"You must have been reading—''

"Yeah. *Interrupted Journey*. I do *some* research, you know. Just in case the Volkers really were up in the weird blue yonder.''

"So . . . Lynn wasn't even alive when this supposedly went on.''

"Honey, she probably wasn't even *conceived* yet.''

"When was she born? Must've been in sixty-one.''

"August. Ironic. Born in August, died in August. I used it in my story. The headstone dates. August 31, 1960—God, people are getting born *young* these days—to August 1982. I guess they don't know exactly when she died. Twenty-two years old.''

"Yeah. Short stay. Thanks, Laurel. We've had our differences, but good luck in New York.''

"And stay there a while, right? You don't fool me, Kevin Blake. You've wanted me off your case from the very beginning. Well, I've got what I wanted, thanks to you in part, but you've got exactly what you wanted, too. Not all the baby blues in the world will make me get amnesia about that. I just hope you'll get what you deserve, too.''

"And you, Laurel.''

He hung up without saying good-bye, but so had she.

Death. There was still, silent death. The death of being. And the undeath of not being . . . free. It was a death somehow familiar to her.

There was another death, she knew that now. Death of

fire and blood, of sizzling flesh and exploding cells—raw death; oozing, ugly death. She knew it now also. Knew it in the night, the formless, moving night that enveloped her as warmly as Zyunsinth's sheltering pelt had once, a barrier no longer enough to shield her from the half dreams that made sleep a sort of mental banishment.

She floated through her sleep now, bobbing against formless fellow prisoners from a time so distant she recognized it as both past and future. She twisted through her own anchorless mind, spinning like the machines attached by black umbilical cords of cable to some power beyond any field of vision she saw. Finally faces surged into focus and out, swelled near and dwindled far, like a breath, in and out.

First faces. They returned, now identifiable: male, human, frightening. Two wore caps; one exploded into flames as it bestrode a flashing, blinking black-and-white beast throbbing with force. Another face, haunting. Round, pink, bland, yet . . . Near, and always coming nearer. Then, abruptly, deflating—diminishing at great speed into a picture frame of night pierced by fluorescent green stars.

Other faces, unimportant he's and she's in white, tending, bending innocently over her. He came that way, one of many, then alone. Eye to eye, mind to mind. Many times, until his face shifted to wear the masks of many others—the pair who pressed their homely features against hers as if to will an attachment. And always, behind the faces—even his—the faceless ones her memory could never focus upon. Many. Always present, as if past and future wrapped them like skin and were inseparable from them. Behind the screaming, fiery face, behind the hating, falling face, behind the nearing, loving faces—always them, claiming every face and every facelessness. Claiming her.

No. The answer flamed into the darkness, a bristling comet tail of pure will made visible. No claims, no more. No faces had title to her. None but the one in the mirror.

Its name/title was . . . Jane, she whispered, enamored, into the darkness that hissed an echo back from every passing shapeless mouth. Jaaaaane . . .

I, Jane, claim thee, Jane.

The faces faded, and only the name remained.

Chapter Thirty-six

Interstate 94 was a gray concrete ribbon laced through the undulating snow-sculpted waves of Minnesota farmland turned white for the winter. The green Jag followed its weavings northwest, bypassing towns like St. Joseph and Fergus Falls, towns that wouldn't have known what to do with an interstate highway through their midst anyway.

Outside Moorhead along the North Dakota border, Kevin turned due north on State Highway 75, a thin red vein on the map that pulsed weakly through Hendrum, Halstad and, fittingly, Climax, before veering back east to Crookston. He had to slow to thirty miles an hour as he hit each farm town in ceaseless rhythm. The Jag protested this curtailment; it'd been a while since it'd stretched its automotive sinews for any trek longer and faster than on the strands of metropolitan freeway girdling the Twin Cities.

Kevin watched local restaurants, main streets and simple houses ease by, wondering if Lynn Volker had noticed them on her trips back and forth from college at Moorhead to her home in Crookston.

Crookston was bigger than its predecessors, wrapped in a slightly citified air of civic hubris—a brick church with a flight of imposing stairs; modern streetlights. The sign at the city limits boasted almost 9,000 souls. Less one. Maybe.

It was late Saturday afternoon. He'd made the drive in

something over six hours. At a cafe near the Country Club Motel, he ordered a hamburger, and consulted the pay phone's slender local phone book. Volker. There were lots of them; folks in towns like Crookston tended to stay put and propagate. John B. John L. Jack K. . . . After paying a ridiculously low price for a humongous burger and plateful of overgreasy fries, Kevin bought a mint and used the extra time to ask after his quarry.

"You mean *the* Volkers?" The woman at the register eyed him suspiciously.

He nodded and picked up a free toothpick.

"You from the Cities?"

He nodded again.

"The press?"

He paused, then nodded once more.

She nodded next. "Thought you people had done with us. It's been some circus around here, let me tell you. They're on Twelfth Street. Go down Main to Hill, turn right, go about ten blocks and then left. Gray house. You can't miss it."

He thanked her, then paused in the tiny lobby, debating calling the Volkers first. Maybe surprise was the best disguise. Catch them off-balance, so they wouldn't have time to wonder what he was doing here. Maybe so he wouldn't have time to wonder that same thing.

The Jag was still warm and purring, despite forty-five minutes in a wind chill of twenty below. Kevin idled along the Crookston streets, trying to picture Jane growing up here, shopping in the lone dime store, avoiding the Main Street beer parlors sprinkled generously among the more respectable stores. . . . He couldn't even imagine Lynn Volker doing it. No wonder her ambition was "to see the world." Montana, he thought, hadn't been much improvement.

The house was a graceless two stories of bald-windowed, basic farmhouse construction practiced at the turn of the century. Two windows on either side, door in the middle. In

260

the fifties, someone had plastered gray asphalt shingles over the clapboard. The trim was white but the effect was lackluster rather than fresh. Even the snowdrifts leaned lackadaisically, cinder-dirtied and footstep-pocked.

Not here, he told himself. Maybe under the silver sun and the basalt domes, but not here. Not Jane. Not his Jane.

He approached the house slowly, glad he'd worn boots. The walk wasn't well shoveled, but maybe Volker had more on his mind recently. The walk looked as if a herd of elephants had stampeded there—spoor of the wild, wandering media circus.

Kevin knocked on the weathered wood; the doorbell didn't respond to even brutal punches.

"Dr. Blake!" Mrs. Volker stared through the storm door. Her hair's careful curl had wilted and the effect was softer. She wore a pinafore-style floral cotton apron banded in seam tape, the kind he thought had died out with his grandmother. The door opened farther. "Come in. My goodness, we never expected to see you again. Father, come see who's dropped by."

He followed her through a dim entry hall into a living room almost as dark. Two windows front, back and either side didn't do much for interior airiness.

"Sit down, Doctor. My husband's just in the kitchen—"

Volker came out then, holding an oversized cup of coffee. "What're you doing here, Dr. Blake? Your Jane Doe is no concern of ours anymore; the police and your Dr. Cross made that plain."

"She's still a concern of mine, Mr. Volker. I thought I'd—if you don't mind—ask you some questions? . . ." He looked at Mrs. Volker.

She sat beside him on the dark old couch, in front of an undernourished walnut coffee table that looked as if it had been fashioned in some long-ago 4-H project, self-consciously patting her unset hair and looking vaguely sad.

"How is . . . Jane-Lynn, Doctor?"

261

"Pretty good, I guess. No different."

"She never did warm up to us. That's what I remember most out of all this—the reporters, the detective, the folks around here all saying they were sorry but not lookin' us in the eye. . . ." Her shoulders straightened under the folksy floral cotton. "But we're used to it, Father and I. We been used to it for a long time."

"I don't mean to add to your burdens—"

"You never believed that girl was ours, did you?" Volker had moved to the overstuffed La-Z-Boy so obviously his. But he stood by it, as if unwilling to unbend in Kevin's presence. A gilt-framed misty-focus portrait of Lynn Volker, obviously of high school graduation, peered over her father's shoulder. The eyes looked right into Kevin's, and they were Jane's.

He shifted on the scratchy sofa. "I never thought she was Crookston-reared, no."

"What's wrong with Crookston?" Volker demanded. "Look, I know we don't have no fancy college degrees. We're just ordinary folks—or would be, if people would leave us alone. We can't help what happened to us, but it happened, and we can't forget it. Not the . . . incident, not Lynn disappearing, not any of it."

"Jane *can't* be Lynn, Mr. Volker," Kevin answered. "There isn't a cavity in her teeth. Not one. Your daughter apparently had very few, but they were filled by the local dentist. They're on his records. And they match the remains found in Montana, where your daughter was."

"Volkers have good teeth," he returned gruffly. "I've only got three or four fillings yet. And Mother's got teeth strong as a row of corn kernels. Her father used to joke when we got married I'd never have to invest in choppers for his girl. Maybe, maybe Dr. Loftus mixed up his records; he's no kid. I don't remember Lynn hardly ever having anything wrong with her teeth."

Now that he was alone with them, now that he no longer feared their possessing Jane, Kevin found them impressing

262

his sensitive internal sincerity meter. They believed what they said, though delusion was perhaps the most consistent and deceptive mental illness.

He plunged into waters that should chill the parental certitude.

"And then—there's the fact that our Jane Doe is a virgin. I don't know about your Lynn, but most young women in their early twenties have had some experience by then. . . ."

"Our Lynn was a good girl."

" 'Good' girls today aren't judged by whether they're sexually active or not, Mrs. Volker. I'm just guessing, but you might feel more comfortable testifying in court to your experience with a UFO than your daughter's virginity. Can you be sure no one would step forward to say that Lynn had led a sexually active life? . . ."

The couple's eyes met. Volker finally sat down, heavily. "I thought you couldn't tell anymore, that was just a wives' tale. Girls today—"

"Girls today lead active lives that make the tradition of an intact hymen obsolete, yes, Mr. Volker, one way or the other. But Jane Doe—and we estimate she's about the same age as your daughter would have been—has an intact hymen. She is a certified virgin. Never even been touched."

There was silence; during it, Volker raised his cup to his lips, slurping slightly. Mrs. Volker leaned forward abruptly and began rearranging the china knickknacks on the coffee table.

"Lynn was popular," she said quietly, looking down. "She was a pretty girl. There were boys, and drive-in movies; that's all the young folks do around here for entertainment. Go to drive-in movies. She never said anything, and we—we'd never talk about that. Not since I told her about her bodily functions when she was eleven. . . ." She sighed. "Young people today, you can't stop them from wantin' to do what they want to do. And they don't marry at eighteen like we used to. There's a long time in college . . ."

263

"He knows what you're sayin', Adelle." Kevin had never heard Volker call his wife by her first name before. "Hell, we know the facts of life. The doctor was just tryin' to get us to face 'em." Volker's troubled face met Kevin's regard with something of Jane's distance and dignity. "Nobody told us your—patient—that she was a virgin. We might claim a lot that people won't believe, but we can't fool ourselves about that. Boys will be boys, and, nowadays, girls will be girls. Ours was no different."

"I'm glad!" Mrs. Volker's hands curled fiercely into her apron. "We wanted Lynn to have a full life; I don't care what anybody would think. Could even the minister say his kids didn't ever have a drink or a smoke or get—sexually active?" She had grabbed on to Kevin's discreet sociological term like a drowning woman clinging to a rope.

"If you . . . pressed . . . your claim on Jane, it would have to come down to questions like that," Kevin pointed out gently.

"We weren't going to," said Volker. "Those articles; people sent them without puttin' their names on. They made us look like fools. Like sad fools. What's the use? Nobody believed us twenty-five years ago, who's gonna believe us now? *We* don't even know anymore. But we always felt in our bones that Lynn wasn't really dead, that she was out there somewhere. . . ."

Mrs. Volker sobbed suddenly, pulling the apron skirt to her face like an oversized hankie.

"Did Lynn have any female cousins her age?"

Volker stared at him.

"Jane has the family teeth," said Kevin, shrugging. He glanced at the pastel-tinted black-and-white face of Lynn Volker on the wall. "There *is* a physical resemblance, although unrelated 'doubles' aren't as rare as people think. The DNA helix doesn't spiral into infinity." They looked lost. "Haven't you ever had an acquaintance swear he or she saw you across town when you weren't there?"

264

Both Volkers shook their heads. "There's a family resemblance around here," Volker said, "but not so's you could fool anyone."

"In a big city, it happens eerily often. We all like to think we're one of a kind, but sometimes nature turns playful and puts the same features, general body build, even voice on unrelated people. Research is barely beginning to explore the amazing linkages between twins—there's a study going on right now at the University of Minnesota—things that would have been bad science fiction a couple generations ago. What I'm saying is, who knows what coincidence, what unthinkable link exists between one person and another, even between Lynn—and Jane? You may have been right to feel a kinship with her."

"What do you want, Doctor?" Volker was mollified, but wary.

"What am I thinking of?" his wife interjected. "I haven't offered you some coffee."

Kevin smiled, grateful for a few extra moments to phrase his request. "That'd be great, Mrs. Volker. It's a long drive; having the heater on makes you sleepy. And I want to be alert right now. Because what I want—that's what I came here for—is to hear what happened when you ran into that UFO."

In the ensuing silence, Kevin heard for the first time the homey tick of a clock—an old mantel model atop a golden oak secretary he wouldn't mind having in his condo. The walls were so old the plaster bulged, and doorless archways wore decorative corner squares. Everything was painted with a thick cream-colored enamel that had gone out of style about 1920. Despite that, the rooms were dim, maybe just with the passage of the time the old clock clucked about rhythmically. Kevin felt pierced by nostalgia for a life he'd never known, for the people who still tried to live it, and often succeeded. " 'Tis a gift to be simple, 'tis a gift to be free. . . ." Laurel had hit it right on with the old Shaker hymn, and then

265

dismissed it. Talking about UFOs in such an atmosphere was so ludicrous it almost became believable.

"Why do you want to know?" Volker asked emotionlessly.

"Because nobody believes you. Because a psychiatrist has to delve into unlikely depths of human experience. Because I might learn something that would help me, or you, or Jane. Because I closed my mind and it doesn't sit well."

"Let's tell him, Father. Maybe this time—"

"He's just another city smartass, Adelle. He'll go off laughin', like the rest of 'em."

"I don't care anymore. Not after seein' Jane-Lynn." She turned to Kevin with a maternal croon. "Let me get you that cup of coffee, Doctor, and then we'll tell you all about it."

Chapter Thirty-seven

Kevin punched off and flipped the tape. Amazing the amount of abuse the little machine could take. The first side had an hour's worth of what he'd expected to hear from the Volkers, and had hoped not to.

It was the usual tale of ascension into the belly of a UFO: the lonely night road; the glowing object that follows the car; the car giving up the ghost. The dazed approach to an alien hovering object. An indistinct description of "somehow" boarding it. Misty humanoid forms with at least one undeniably inhuman characteristic. This time, "eye slits." Lights and machines, all indescribable. Communication—usually in strangely understandable language. The star charts. The examination, reported more vaguely than by Roger Matthews at his foggiest. Then—return. Ground-bound again. A great glowing form flashing skyward, leaving two ordinary humans confounded on the road.

"Well?" Mrs. Volker sounded hopeful of Kevin's imminent conversation.

"Interesting," he hedged. "And this was . . ."

"November 12, 1960. It was cold, but not too bad; no snow on the ground. I definitely remember regretting that there was no snow; otherwise, we could have seen what kind of footprints they made."

"How . . . old were you two then?"

"I was, um, thirty-two, I guess, and Jack . . ." She looked at her husband.

"Thirty-five. I was born in twenty-five."

"That's right. We'd been married fourteen years that May. It's funny; the older you get, the harder it is to remember how old you are. But I suppose you haven't noticed that yet, Doctor."

"Some Monday mornings I notice it a lot, Mrs. Volker. The, uh, details of the experience have gotten locked in by time and repetition. You must have discussed the incident, compared impressions—"

"I didn't want to talk about it," said Volker. "Adelle was the one couldn't forget. Had dreams. I think . . . I think bein' pregnant had something to do with it."

"You were *pregnant*, Mrs. Volker, at the time of the incident?"

"Oh, no. No, Dr. Blake. Later. With Lynn. But then, my gosh, the last thing on our minds was a baby. I mean, it'd been so long. . . . So you can't say I exaggerated things because of that, no. I had Lynn in August of the next year. Late August. And she was premature almost, just a little mite, hardly five pounds. You can't say it was hormones," she added truculently, evidently having heard this argument before. "Besides, Father was there."

Volker paused in reaming out his pipe to nod. "I seen it, too. I'm not sure what, or that I could put a name on it. But there was something there, and we somehow ended up inside it. It was like nothin' I ever saw. She dragged me to that movie—*Close Encounters of the, the*—"

"*The Third Kind.*"

"Yup. I guess that's what we had. Anyway, all that movie hardware and music, it looked like one of those game arcades at the county fair. No, this thing was smooth, hard to see. It glowed, kind of like it wore a coat of light, if you know what I mean. You couldn't see anything clearly. And it wasn't real bright. It was soft; like, like that pink stuff you sometimes see in the sky when the lightning's real strange. . . ."

"Saint Elmo's fire."

"Soft, more like mist than light. Hell, you couldn't see this thing once it was any distance away. That's how we didn't know it was on us until it was there."

Mrs. Volker leaned toward Kevin, trying to be her most convincing. "That's right, Doctor. It was all . . . soft; like it being there just made everything peaceful around you. It sort of drew you to it, right into the light. You could feel it, like warm rain. I think—" She glanced apologetically at her husband. "I'm sorry, Father, but that's how I remember it; I think we were—lifted—up into it. Like on an invisible elevator. I don't remember any elevator doors. And the people. They wore light clothes. There was a buzz, like you hear folks in an auditorium when you're a ways away, and you can't understand what they're saying. They seemed to talk to one another, but it wasn't any language I ever heard. They never tried to talk to us." She sounded almost wistful.

"Did they touch you?"

"No," Volker said quickly.

"Yes," said his wife.

Kevin looked at Volker, who shook his head. "I don't remember anything but standing there, being looked at by these . . . creatures. 'People' is going too far. They were draped, you know? Like those mummy things. And their eyes were slits. Don't see how they could see out of those narrow things.''

"Mrs. Volker?"

She shuddered. "They touched me. And I wasn't afraid—then. Only when I think of what they must have been, where they must have come from . . . There are so many stars out there, Doctor, with so many hidden planets. Some must be like ours. Why couldn't there be people like us out there?''

"They weren't like us," Volker said sharply. "Not at all. She gets it in her head that they meant us no harm, that they were like angels . . .''

"Not like angels! We're not people angels visit. I wouldn't claim that. Can I, can I talk to the doctor alone?''

Volker inhaled intently on the pipe until the bowl finally took fire. "I don't suppose you can do us any more harm.'' He stood, as if relieved to be absolved from participating in a rite he no longer subscribed to. "I'll be in the kitchen.''

Mrs. Volker smiled apologetically and leaned over to snap on the tablelamp. Dusk had pressed its smudgy fingers shut around the old house, and Kevin hadn't even noticed. In the room, shadows stretched long and black. Lynn Volker's photograph looked unduly harsh, her face sunken and haunted.

Her mother pressed plump fingers into Kevin's forearm.

"Doctor." Her voice had lowered, with caution, furtiveness or shame. "He doesn't like me to say this. Only I remember it, and sometimes wish I didn't. They touched me. I think they touched him. I know we said they examined us—looked at our faces, our feet, our hands. That's all he remembers. But it was more . . . like at a doctor's. Not just looking and poking at what showed. They looked us over real good. I remember. It was like the doctor's. Like when I had to go in when I was pregnant with Lynn later. I hated those visits! I don't know why. I'd never had to be examined like that before. It seemed . . . an invasion.''

"Betty Hill—she and her husband said they were taken aboard a UFO about a year after your experience—Betty Hill

269

said they put a needle in her navel. Do you remember anything like that?''

Her face of utter distaste convinced him she hadn't encountered the Hill case. ''A needle in her . . . Oh, no, Doctor. I'd remember something awful like that. But there were needles, I think, and tubes and, and glasses clinking. I only saw the light. It was so peaceful. I know, like the plant lights you put over violets to make them grow, those purple lights. They meant us no harm, I'd swear it. And we were none the worse for it. I had a perfectly normal delivery. Lynn was a *perfect* baby. Our lives were wonderful.'' Her expression crumpled. ''Then we lost her. If you, if you find that you were wrong, that Jane is our little girl, you wouldn't hide it from us, would you, Doctor? Just because you said she wasn't and would be embarrassed to admit she was?''

Her hands wrung his forearm through his heavy sweater; her eyes wrung his heart more. Her story might be delusion; the love and loss she felt for her only daughter were not. He stilled her gesture with the pressure of his hand.

''I promise, Mrs. Volker; if there's any proof that Jane Doe is your daughter, I'll bring her back to you.''

She read him with a look he hadn't seen since his own mother had subjected him to her intense, loving scrutiny when she wanted to know if he was telling the truth about something vital. Mrs. Volker finally nodded and smiled, pulling away her hands with a consoling farewell pat of her own. Who was giving succor here, the shrink or the shrinkee?

''You can stay to supper,'' she offered.

The living room was dark now, despite the lamp, and the face framed on the wall had vanished. Supper. Kevin hadn't had something that could be called ''supper'' in years. He was tempted.

''Sorry, Mrs. Volker. I have to drive back to the Cities tonight. But, thanks. Two sides of a tape should do it. If I have any other questions . . .''

''Just call,'' she said. ''Ask for me.''

Kevin stood, surprised to be stiff from sitting so long. "I'll say good-bye to Mr. Volker. . . ."

Her hand clenched his arm. "It's better to just go. This is hard on Father. It's harder on a man to see visions, you know. It makes him nervous to see something he doesn't understand."

"Me, too," admitted Kevin wryly as she led him to the door and switched on the porch light. Fresh snow leaped into view, gleaming like a sinkful of Ivory Snow. It had fallen while they had sat and talked and got nowhere. Kevin's hard-soled boots crushed a feathery new layer, and the Jag was artistically snuggled into a downy coat of snow. He brushed off the windshield with his gloved hand and got in. The car started on the first try, as Kevin, with something like paternal pride, backed out the rutted drive and onto the street.

Crookston lay dreaming in the dark and under the snow. In his headlights, lacy snowflakes pirouetted endlessly; the utterly homely was now the utterly exotic, transformed by the weather, by some climatic change within Kevin. Spaceship earth, he mused. Be it ever so humble, there's no place like home. He wished he could find a good one for Jane Doe.

Chapter Thirty-eight

Kevin woke up, amazed he hadn't dreamed. Sunday morning, the clock of his rousing consciousness told him. Morning? Hell, afternoon, going by how the light warmed his bank of bedroom windows.

He lifted his wrist to check the time—two o'clock—then let his forearm shade his eyes, and retreated into semiwakefulness. The day before drifted back. It'd been past midnight

271

when he'd gotten home from Crookston, then he'd settled down for several hours of tape playing. He'd finally fallen asleep on the sofa; the cushion welts seemed sewn to his anatomy like methodical seams. A battered paperback on the Betty and Barney Hill case that he'd cadged from Kandy lay open facedown on the coffee table. Blue, curled contentedly, warmed his crotch.

"Sorry, kitty." Kevin cupped the sleeping kitten in his hands and moved it to an empty cushion as he sat up. He retrieved the splayed paperback guiltily. Hard on the spine. He stretched his own cramped spine, Blue waking and mirroring the action in feline efficiency as it rose, arched and circled into itself again for sleep.

Kevin, wishing he could do the same, slapped down the paperback—closed. He'd read the whole damn thing through, struck by eerie similarities between his hypnotic sessions with Jane, the Volkers' close encounter and the psychotherapist's recorded sessions with the Hills. And striking differences. He rubbed his eyes, shifting his body irritatedly; sleeping dressed always brought a morning-after itch, like that night with Jane. . . . His automatic censor slammed an iron curtain shut on his thoughts. Jane was a puzzle, a patient. That's all he could allow if he was going to solve her mystery, help her.

In the bedroom, he glanced wistfully at the big tub under the skylight as he changed clothes—he hadn't led a life that allowed for soaking under the stars since . . . since Cross called him at three in the morning and brought Jane Doe into his life. But the shower steam effectively misted the memory of eight hundred miles of barren Minnesota snowscape. He was just whipping up a satisfying lather when the phone rang, faintly, through the hot, relaxing patter.

He froze. Nah, let it go. Sunday morning, practically. But it might be . . . He started for the towel hanging over the door, paused, then committed, wrapping and racing simultaneously. Better still be there; damn fool time to call. Can't be important.

Dripping by the bed, Kevin cradled the receiver on his wet shoulder while he tried to sponge up the worst of the water. "Hello."

"Hello. Is Kevin Blake there? Kevin, is that you?"

"This is Kevin Blake."

It was a woman's voice, rich as a perfectly ripened persimmon. He didn't know any women with quite that moneyed confidence in their tones, not since he'd left the east, anyway.

"This is . . . Marlene Symons, Kevin. I hope I haven't disturbed you—"

An understatement to remember. Kevin's heart hung suspended somewhere between systolic and diastolic.

"No, Mrs. Symons, I—I just didn't recognize your voice."

"It's been so long."

"Yeah. A long time." He dropped the damp towel on the bed and sat on it, hoping conversation would work the shock from his voice. "Are you calling from Boston or . . ."

"From the Hyatt downtown. We're in Minneapolis for the weekend. Jackson had a conference. I tried to call yesterday—"

"I was . . . out of town."

"I see."

"Well, great to hear from you. Everything going—all right?"

"All right." Her voice was heavy. "Kevin. I was thinking— We'd like to have you come for dinner, here at the hotel. I know it's short notice, but I didn't know if we'd find you; if you'd still be living here or be in the book. . . ."

"Dinner." He'd made it sound like poison. "Tonight?"

"It's short notice, I know. Of course we'd understand if you had other plans. But we haven't talked since . . . since the funeral. I guess we were all too numb to think. And then you graduated and left. I just thought it'd be nice to say hello, to see how you were doing."

273

"I'm doing great, Mrs. Symons. On staff at the U of M Hospitals. Special unit."

"What are you specializing in? You hadn't quite made up your mind at Harvard."

"Psychiatry."

There was a pause. He pictured her well-bred face trying to master the implications. But she was a pro. Her voice came smooth and cordial.

"If you, you're married now, we'd—love—to meet your wife."

"I'm not married." It sounded like a confession, and Kevin suddenly wondered why he wasn't. Most of his Harvard classmates were well launched on a wife—or two—a suburban house, two kids and three cars by now. I've got a cat, he thought wryly. That's a start.

"Oh." She couldn't help sounding relieved. "Well, can you come by tonight? Say . . . seven? There's a pretty restaurant called The Willows here. I don't know about the food."

"Uh, sure, I guess so." He was committing himself when he really wanted a quick excuse to say no.

"We'd love to see you again, Kevin. I don't know why we let you slip out of our lives after . . ." Her sigh wafted over the phone lines like an ectoplasmic kiss. "We were just so, so frozen. Well, you know now, given your work."

"Grief takes many forms, Mrs. Symons."

"Yes. About tonight? Can we count on you?" The forced social brightness of tone touched him as nothing else had. Can we count on you? asked Mrs. Symons. Don't count on me, said long dead Lynn Volker. Ideas, people, the past and present were colliding like surrealistic cymbals in Kevin's brain. Cymbals—or symbols? Why that image—making a subconscious pun? Self-analysis, Dr. Blake? When you can't even unravel one amnesia case?

"Sure. Seven you said?"

"Thank you, Kevin." She meant it. "See you tonight."

"Bye, Mrs. Symons. . . ."

Mrs. Symons. Marlene, she'd called herself, meaning he could call her that now, adult to adult, equal to equal. But there he was, back in callow authority figure crisis. She'd always be Mrs. Symons to him. And *Mr.* Symons. Jackson Oliver Symons. Plastic surgeon extraordinaire. Made all the East Coast ladies into facial polyester—permanently pressed against wear, tear and wrinkles. Didn't want to see him again. Shit, no. Stuffed shirt. Mrs. Symons was all right, but how could she stand the old man? Arrogant bastard. Julie never could. Oh, God, Julie. He didn't want to think of Julie . . . especially now. "I know about the Symons girl," Cross had intoned at his lecture session last week. Did he? Did anyone really know? Maybe Mrs. Symons did. Marlene. And Kevin. And that was all.

Hyatt lobbies were always splashy—literally, thanks to fountains; figuratively, thanks to marble, brass and constellations of fairy-size lights shining in the obligatory atrium's highest reaches. Frosted glass panels etched in nouveau contortions and a smattering of Minneapolis diners garbed in Sunday night chic heralded The Willows. Kevin patted his silk tie. He'd reverted instantly to suit and French-cuffed shirt, going to meet the Symonses like a nervous suitor. The word made him flinch. It was all over; he had nothing to prove, and nothing to lose.

The restaurant was calculatedly dark, its banks of green velvet banquettes semiconcealed by parlor palms transporting him back to his dream, his stalking dream of primal woods and dark green night and blood-red death . . .

Against a frosted-glass room divider, sat the Symonses. He moved toward them in déjà vu slow motion. They looked the same, at least she did, with her ambiguously silver-blond hair and faint facial lines fading but not overshadowing her features. He wondered why Dr. Symons never had done a face lift on his wife.

"Kevin." Symons was standing, wearing—what else?—navy

suit, white shirt and red tie, shaking Kevin's hand with that paralyzing grip of men who heard once when young that handshakes should be firm and overdid it ever after.

Kevin had his choice of banquettes, so slid in beside Mrs. Symons.

"A beard," she remarked, smiling like a mother intent on taking well whatever her grown offspring did. "You look very dashing, and like a psychiatrist. That's what Kevin went into, Jackson."

"Good field." He nodded, perusing his oversized dark green menu in a way that left no doubt this reunion was his wife's idea.

You are a thirty-two-year-old whiz kid and your photograph has been in the *Christian Science Monitor,* sport, Kevin lectured himself. No need to undergo adolescent relapse just because these people are rich easterners and the parents of the girl you loved.

He dove behind the slick façade of his menu, resolving to pick an entree quickly and end the social rituals. The Symonses would pay, of course. They always had.

When the waitress appeared, they all ordered quickly. Symons waggled his fingers at the couple's almost empty lowball glasses. "Another round. Kevin?"

He wanted a beer. "Scotch and soda."

"Just what you always used to order," Mrs. Symons noted, as if somehow vindicated. Don't believe it, he answered mentally. I've changed, lady, oh, how I've changed . . . I hope.

"Well. How's the head business?" Symons crossed his arms on the table and waited.

"Like faces, they're always around to work on."

"Your own practice?"

"No. I'm attached to a University Hospitals special unit. We specialize in difficult, maybe impossible cases—cult deprogrammings, multiple personalities, severe schizophrenia . . ."

"Can't be much money in it."

"It's quite rewarding, sir." Shit. Where had that "sir" come from? and that stiff, self-justifying tone?

"I'm sure Kevin does very well." Mrs. Symons's hand paused gracefully on his arm. The gesture, the long, narrow fingers, were so like Julie that he was momentarily speechless. "It's good to catch up on you, Kevin. To see you again." Her hand tightened, and he knew she meant it. Let the old man play his sour self; his wife needed more than Symons could squeeze out of his tough emotional rind. So had his daughter.

"Actually, one of my cases caused some hubbub recently," Kevin found himself saying. Bragging. "You may have heard. An amnesia case—"

"Not the one in *Time*?" Mrs. Symons jumped on his lead. And it would be *Time,* not *Newsweek.* No nouveau news magazines for the Symonses of Boston and Cape Cod. "Kevin, that's fantastic! Were you mentioned?"

"Don't know. I couldn't keep up with it all. Publicity's a pain in the neck."

"I know." Mrs. Symons seemed pathetically glad of a common problem. "When Jackson does a movie star . . . But it's good for business."

"Jackson" concentrated on his drink, his eyes roaming the room with unconcealed restlessness. He never had tolerated fools gladly, and unfortunately his wife, daughter and daughter's boyfriend had all fallen into that category.

Kevin felt a flush of anger, and cooled it with a belt of Scotch. They had all three come up cold against that flinty expert at the emotional stone wall. Even Julie couldn't crack it by dying. Kevin sometimes thought she had died trying. Their food came just when he had decided he had no appetite. He picked at it anyway, wondering why he'd come.

She waited until the plates were cleared and the coffee cups were steaming before them to bring up Julie.

"It's so good to see you again, Kevin. You look—happy. Julie would have been glad to know that."

"For God's sake, Marlene! You don't know what Julie would be glad to know. She's dead; you can't keep inventing responses for her, isn't that right, Blake?"

"When we're really close to someone, I think we know—sometimes how'd they react. And"—he turned to Julie's mother—"I don't think Julie would want you—would want any of us—making her loss the center of our lives."

"I still miss her," she said, her eyes tearing.

"And always will. I do, too."

Symons kept out of it, but then he always had.

"Do you, Kevin?" Her eyes were a paler blue than aquavit, and chronic pain shimmered through them. That look had been there when he'd met her, long before Julie and he had become an item, long before Julie had become ill. "I wondered when you said you hadn't married. . . ."

He pulled his hand free of the soft, slack-fleshed pressure of hers. "I mourn Julie, sure, and miss her. We were going to get married—" He glanced at Symons and smiled tightly. "Someday. We hoped. But, Mrs. Symons, you can't interpret my life as a monument to your daughter. I'm not married because I'm not married, not because—it was a tragedy, what happened to Julie; I'd give anything if it hadn't. But there was nothing any of us could do about it. And we're here now and we go on." Every cliché he uttered only intensified the dumb, hopeful look in her eyes, the need to believe that some other person shared her maternal unwillingness to let go. Like a well-trained shrink, he turned brutal for her own good. "I've known other women since, and loved them, and will again. And I'll probably marry one of them. Someday. I hope."

"I didn't mean to imply that you should—"

"The hell you didn't, Marlene." Despite Symons's passionate words, his tone was cool. "We're all supposed to worship at the shrine of your beloved daughter. Face it.

There was something radically wrong with her, otherwise, she'd have never— We should get back to the room.''

"There was something wrong with *us*,'' Kevin interjected sharply. "That's what has to be faced. Julie got on that track to self-destruction, but somebody else laid it. It's like suicide; it's intended, however unconsciously, to punish the survivors. That's why you can't forget, Mrs. Symons. You're a victim of the person you loved most in the world. So am I.'' He left Symons out of it.

"Oh, Kevin.'' Her eyes were frankly tear-glazed now. "I still see her the way she was at the end. Not even looking human. So sharp, so sunken, so thin. And her eyes, her hair . . . It's as if someone took my little girl, my daughter, and made the most opposite thing to what she was out of what was left of her.''

"Not *someone*—Julie!'' He felt compelled to administer a dose of reality. "That's what's so frustrating about anorexia nervosa. It's still the most damnable, untreatable, maddening, worst fucking mental disease around. Even Probe hasn't tackled a case. Julie was tailor-made for it. The victims are usually females, usually young. They're bright, pretty girls from upper-middle-class families with a passion for perfection and control, and—for some reason—a self-image that absolutely contradicts the outer facts of their lives. And so they starve themselves to death, insisting all the while that they're fine, even fat. I don't know when or how Julie began going that way—when we met everything seemed normal. No, more than normal. Perfect,'' he diagnosed bitterly. "She was the perfect daughter, the perfect student, the perfect girl for me. That was a sign, right there. But I was too ignorant to know.''

"Kevin. Was it the, the ballet?''

"That damn dancing.'' He looked hard at Mrs. Symons. "When did you start her—eight, nine? She had the ballet for eleven years; you all her life; me—for eighteen months. Which one of us did it? I don't know, Mrs. Symons. Maybe I never will. But ballet is notorious for driving people to extremes of thinness and perfection. Julie might have used that as the pretext for her disease, but I don't think the answer is as easy as that.''

"I just wanted her to be graceful, to be accomplished. I didn't want her to die. And that way, right before our eyes, so slowly.''

Kevin writhed interiorly under the images she was invoking in his inner eye. Julie, thin and tired at first, dark circles hollowing fevered hazel eyes. Her wrist so narrow it seemed formed of the bones of birds—hollow, so she could execute those dazzling leaps through the air above the stage. He'd never liked, understood ballet, and went only to watch Julie, to admire Julie, to love Julie in all she did. He came to loathe the memory of that elegantly attenuated Julie, later seeing in it the specter of her decline and death. Her slow decline and slower death.

"Marlene.'' Symons sounded weary. "You can't go through this again. Spare me, at least.''

"Spare you!'' she spat. "You were spared everything! Julie and I never did anything to disrupt your life, your quiet, your needs. Not even dying did it.''

"Look,'' interceded Kevin, "maybe we should go up to the room.'' This was turning into family therapy, with himself as reluctant referee.

"It's finished,'' said Symons. "I knew if she managed to dig you up, it'd only bring out the same old weeping and wailing. I don't need to discuss it.''

Kevin turned to Symons's wife. Okay, to his patient. "Marlene,'' he said, unwilling to attach Symons's name to her any longer. "You've got to understand what's happened to you. Anorexia is such a brutal disease, particularly when it's fatal—and it is far too often—because it's a rejection of everything the rest of us think is vital. Health, life—the very life you and your husband gave Julie, she chose to give up. Not consciously, but from some perverted sense of finding herself, holding herself to an impossible standard. A standard too stringent to live with. Everything you had given her, everything I had to offer her, she said no to in the most final, telling, agonizing way. That's why she's so hard to forget; you have to accept that.''

Her hand shading her eyes, she was sobbing quietly. "Christ." Her husband tossed down his napkin and angled his body to face the aisle as he finished his coffee.

Kevin leaned inward to lock the woman into a tête-à-tête. "Marlene, seeing me isn't going to resurrect Julie, or make her death any easier to understand. But I know how you feel. I was young; I thought I could conquer the world, or at least the eastern seaboard. I had a scholarship to Harvard and I had Julie. I didn't think that anybody could take that away from me." He looked down, moved his untouched coffee spoon slightly across the tablecloth. "Then Julie did it herself, saying she loved me the whole damn time."

"Kevin." Her whisper was tremulous, just as her hand shook as it paused on his. "I always wondered. Did you—did you and Julie . . . Did she know life fully? . . ."

The old man was listening despite his aggressive indifference. Fathers were always possessive of their daughters; younger men were inevitably rivals, and there was a sexual competitiveness in that, no matter how unconscious. Kevin knew what Julie's mother wanted to know, and couldn't deny her need to know, but he'd be damned if he'd give Symons one last, necrophiliac peek into the life of the daughter he'd probably driven into the grave. Kevin had read extensively on anorexia nervosa. He blamed Jackson Oliver Symons for this particular case of it.

"It was for Julie to tell you."

"That's what her psychiatrist always said—*she* must tell you. Well, she can't, Kevin, and I need to know."

He couldn't look at her. Across from them, Symons signaled the waitress for the check, ending the privacy their conversation required. His wife began pulling herself together, inside and out, a handsome woman hurting badly.

Julie would have looked like her if she had lived as long, and could have borne the imperfection of fading hair and wrinkles. Kevin suddenly knew that Marlene had refused a face lift from her husband, not the other way around.

They kept awkward silence as they filed out of the dim restaurant into the hyperexcitement of the lobby. Symons pulled out his room key and looked significantly at his wife. "I'm going up, Marlene."

She nodded but didn't move. Together, they watched his erect form stride to the elevators. The atrium fountain chattered inanely.

"It's an impressive lobby," she commented. "The plants . . ."

He looked up and nodded.

"Kevin, I hope I haven't embarrassed or hurt you. These last ten years . . . I just, just—"

He leaned against the polished travertine that lined the lobby. People thronged a few feet away, their bubbling voices adding to the fountain's exuberance. But no one was within hearing distance.

Kevin looked at her fine, faded eyes, and dropped his glance to somewhere neutral in between them, speaking softly, clinically.

"One of the symptoms of anorexia nervosa is the loss of normal female functions. The victim ceases to menstruate. There isn't enough nourishment to produce the hormones. The victim loses interest in sex." He looked up. "Of course we were lovers. It was 1975, postpill, postsexual revolution; we were both in school; we were both in love. We were lovers until Julie couldn't anymore. I didn't know then what was doing it. Exhaustion, I thought. Her studies, the hours of ballet . . . She wanted to be a ballerina. I was patient. It turned out I'd have to be patient forever.

"It was hell, watching the body you loved to see and touch just melt on its bones, become everything that's unlovely. And still I loved her, until the very end—and beyond. Loved.

282

Past tense. She's gone, Marlene; she was gone even while we thought she was here. She—and it's not her fault, but that's how our egos see it in the dark of night—she rejected the life you gave her, the love and lovemaking I gave her. That's what hurts, that's what haunts. But I loved her, and I made love with her and to her and I can never be sorry for that.''

Marlene Symons's eyelids slid shut over sheets of tears, but they trickled down the sides of her face anyway. She wore good mascara; her wet lashes stayed starred and black.

''Thank you, Kevin. I just had to know that another human being felt what I felt, loved what I loved, lost what I lost, that I wasn't alone.'' Her lips tightened, seeking control. ''There's something that keeps a parent from fully accepting any stranger that claims a child. It's not right, but that's the way we are. I'm glad you allowed me to be a human being first. Julie was lucky.''

Kevin nodded. ''So were we.''

Her heels clicked across the echoing floor, lost quickly in the sounds filling the lobby. He didn't envy her return to the room and the man who waited in it. Kevin walked down the hall to the elevators to the parking ramp, until a thought struck him and he stopped while the people behind parted and surged around him.

He'd spent a lot of months literally watching Julie Symons die, but he had never, ever seen her cry.

Luke, Chapter 1, verse 7, said it all. Kevin, his memory pricked by the Volkers' testimony, had been struck by a certain universality in their story. Once back in his condo Sunday evening, he skimmed the Bible given him at confirmation, eager to take his mind off the dinner with the Symonses.

It was a mythological pattern of primitive simplicity: an older, childless couple encounter a heavenly being. Months later, they deliver their first and promised child. So had Isaac been born to the aged Abraham and Sarah, so had Elizabeth and Zachary become parents in the New Testament, producing John the Baptist, who had spent some time in the wilderness, like Lynn Volker, and, like her, died early.

Of course the Volkers were still well within childbearing age at the time of their "visitation." But Kevin wondered if the entire episode was a bizarre variety of wish fulfillment, if the fantasy of an encounter with beings from outer space had produced the pregnancy. Often some little-understood mechanism of the psyche stymied the long-term barren. Infertile couples who adopted children frequently conceived normally soon after, the stimulus somehow erasing the mental block to conception.

Then there was Betty Hill's "needle in the navel," now a commonplace procedure of purely earthly prenatal care in cases where amniocentesis or even fetal monitoring and treatment were called for. Yet in 1961, when Betty Hill claimed to have experienced it, it was virtually unheard of, and the mores of the time were dead against any interference with pregnancy or the fetus, for fear it would lead to what was then both unthinkable and illegal—abortion.

Kevin sighed, stretched and shut the black-bound Bible. The case of Jane Doe was leading him down odd alleyways. He thought again of the two women he'd seen that weekend; they were like oddly mated bookends encompassing the same sad stories. Adelle Volker. Simple, sweet in an unadulterated way, plain as oven-baked bread, clinging to the notion that her dead daughter lived. And Marlene Symons. Urban, sophisticated, yet as alone in her grief as her country cousin. And clinging to what her daughter had been before she had died.

Julie. Kevin had never known her as a mother would; he had no nostalgic nosegays of her first steps, words, prom cards to tuck into mental scrapbooks. Yet their relationship had been powerful, the impact of falling in love followed fast by the equally overwhelming process of facing death and pacing it every step of the way to the inevitable end. As a medical student, he had known the painful physical convolutions of slow, self-induced starvation better than anyone.

But he was young. Optimism was nature's way of preserving the species. He had "gotten over" Julie's death—and, more important, her life. He seldom let her memory depress him; he was in steady control. Of course the experience had shaped his choice of career; he couldn't expect to be unaffected by it, just as a surgeon is often directed into a specialty by a personal tragedy or a particularly poignant case.

Kevin squirmed on the couch, nursing the beer he had wanted earlier and hadn't had the guts to order. He'd just survived an unwanted close encounter of the most intimate kind with the Symonses, with his past. It was disquieting. It gave him the feeling that many lines of his life, personal and professional, were converging as if even now being manipulated by some ruthless, overseeing force. He didn't believe in overseeing forces—conventional, like God, or unconventional, like Swanson's phenomena or the Volkers' offworld beings.

But a lot of things he didn't believe in were grinning at the windows of his composure, seeking recognition and admittance. He guessed he'd see more of them before he found an answer to Jane Doe.

She floated, asleep, adream. Her body bounced gently against the thin, invisible skin separating herself from those others—all those others. The barrier was clear and thin as glass, but seemed to reflect great distances in space and time, like a very thick watch crystal.

She dreamed in terms of things with names now; her body, a watch crystal. Him. Kevin. The formless ones remained just that, unshapen, but seemed part of a past no longer hers. Something to be avoided, like nightmare figures that fade by day. Nightmare. The word drifted from a benevolent pink mouth. Then Mrs. Bellingham was there, tucking Zyunsinth more closely around her, repeating that Jane had had a bad dream and it was all right now. . . .

The dream of Mrs. Bellingham was a memory of Mrs. Bellingham, and the same in reverse. Dreams. All the faint, disturbing memories of floating and formless ones were not dreams. Dreams were . . . nice. Dreams were Zyunsinth crowding near, and dry fall leaves falling like sunshine flakes and Kevin walking alongside, talking. Talking, talking . . . talking was safe. Dreaming was sometimes safe. Remembering—not safe, but necessary. Remembering to forget. Forget the questions and the odd, subterranean pull at her impulses, the fear and disorientation. She didn't have to worry about that. Kevin said so, even as he probed the delicate tissues of her memory.

Memory. It was a limitless black hole into which she could disappear in an instant, a dark night sky lit now with the glittering treasures she had installed as guideposts— the odd words from the books, words that had hovered gleaming before her eyes instead of sinking anonymously into her skull; the burning aftersensation of a snowflake or Kevin's touch on her skin; the smell of the air whether it blew hot or cold or reeked of burning leaves.

Still . . . she could evoke—and exorcise—all that, and it was not enough. It was more than before, inconceivably more. But it was not enough, Jane knew that when she dreamed. Perhaps that was why she dreamed. It was not enough for him, and not enough for her.

Chapter Thirty-nine

"What am I?" she asked.

Jane lounged on the Eames chair, but Kevin sat his own uneasily, swiveling and squeaking to collect his thoughts.

The first thought: If only Jane's identity crisis for once could be phrased as the usual amnesiac's anthem—"*Who* am I?" The mere substitution of a noun for a pronoun had devastating implications.

His second thought: How far he had come and gone the past two days in his journeys to Crookston and the Hyatt Regency. Jane, he realized guiltily, had only had the limbo of the dorm while she came to terms with a self she probably had been better off forgetting.

"I don't know what you are. Do you think it's important?"

He watched her while she thought. Blue jeans, boots, the melon blouse an oriflamme of color on her shoulders. The nurses had been easing her toward the makeup concession; faint rose tinged her cheeks, dark blue underlined her sable eyelashes. Jane had never looked more normal.

"Is it important?" she repeated, again tasting each word.

"Yes, I think it is. I need to know now."

"Why now? You didn't really want to know before. You said you did, but you didn't. Why do you care now?" She didn't answer. "Is it because you're afraid of what . . . happened when they found you? You haven't injured anyone since."

"You're afraid." She'd never accused him of anything before, yet her tone was flat, more statement than accusation.

"Afraid of what?"

"Of what . . . I did. Of someone finding out what I did. Of me."

"Of you? No." Her eyes told him he had lied. "Not because of that. I wasn't afraid of you Friday, and you were tearing up the joint. Gave me quite a clip on the jaw, too." He worked his mandible in remembrance, in teasing demonstration.

She could smile now, at his jokes, but she didn't at this one.

"Jane. It's not your fault. You didn't know what you were doing."

Her eyes slid toward him reluctantly, her look knowing. "I could. If I tried hard enough—"

"But you don't have to!" He knelt impulsively by the chair, so his eyes met her evasive ones. "You must try to forget all that."

"You said I must remember."

"Remember, yes—and then forget."

Her eyes dropped. "Are all psychiatrists so contradictory?"

"No." She was smiling, victorious. "Just me. For Christ's sake, Jane, don't play head games on me; I'm too fragile."

Her palm reached out, shaped itself to his cheek and rested there, with a warm, addictive pressure. He felt elevated to the ranks of Zyunsinth.

"You're afraid of me, Dr. Blake," she said softly. He pulled away a second later.

"I'm not the issue here," he argued, eager to reestablish control. He stood and pointed sternly at her. "You patient." Kevin's forefinger stabbed his chest repeatedly. "Me doctor."

Her head cocked curiously, parrotlike. "*Tarzan*! I saw a movie on TV Saturday."

"That's great. You weren't . . . born . . . knowing *Tarzan*, huh? How much did you know when you woke up in our hands? What's been picked up from that reading you do, the air, me, the nurses? What came with you?"

She shrugged, a gesture new to her. "I don't know. I liked Jane."

"Jane?"

"In the movie. She didn't have to do things—buy clothes or paint her nails. Is that where my name came from?"

"Your name came from the law's inability to deal with anything lacking a label." He sat on the desk. "You're a cousin of John Doe; I think both Jane and John Doe were used in common law for circumstances that called for indicating a specific person without knowing the true name. It may feel unique to you, but it's been used before."

"There are three Lynns in the dorm," she pointed out defensively.

"And half a dozen Kevins on faculty. None of us are unique, at least in name only. Except—Zyunsinth."

"Zyunsinth's fading," Jane said abruptly. "I'm forgetting it, whatever it was. I don't know why I called the coat you gave me that."

"The coat I gave you—"

She glanced over her shoulder. Zyunsinth—the damn coat, rather—lay abandoned on the wooden chair by the door. It had served as a security blanket, and, like a security blanket, it was being outgrown.

"Don't you like it anymore?"

"It's warm, useful." So much for $1,800 of impulse purchase. Jane smiled impishly. "And Glenda loves it. She says it must have cost a fortune. Maybe I'll give it to Glenda for next Christmas. . . ."

"Now listen." He trapped her against the leather, clamping his hands around her chair arms and leaning inward for emphasis. "I don't care if you want to use the damn coat for a dustmop. Yes, it cost a lot of money—still is costing a lot of money—and, yes, some people judge things by that fact alone. But I got you the coat because it was the only thing you responded strongly to at that point, and I figured it would be good therapy. If you don't need it now, fine; I don't care.

289

But . . ." He paused. "Jane, you mustn't let people get too curious about that coat. It could be misconstrued, simply because it was expensive. You needed it, and I got it for you; that's all. You didn't tell Glenda who paid for it—how the hell would you know, anyway?"

She looked down, at her lap, where her palms smoothed the jeans wrinkles on her thighs. "I know now; I didn't know until Glenda made such a fuss over it. I didn't understand the difference between jeans and shoes and a . . . a fur coat. You didn't have to buy it; you shouldn't have bought it. You got it for me; it was a—present. Zyunsinth is gone now; I don't even know who—what—Zyunsinth was. Just a way I liked to feel, that I couldn't feel any other way. Until now. I'd never give your coat away, Kevin."

"You mustn't call me that."

"You call me Jane."

"You're the patient. I'm the male authority figure; I went to school for eight years to earn the right to be condescending." He hadn't flummoxed her; whatever was bothering Jane had been festering for a while.

Her hands moved to the chair arms, just in front of his, and picked defensively at the leather. "In the dorm, all the student nurses call the doctors by their first names."

"That's their revenge for being institutionally condescended to, too."

"You're teasing me," she charged, her eyes flashing anger. "You know I don't know . . . so much . . . and you're confusing me."

"Yes. So tell me what's really bothering you." Evidently proximity was a potent weapon; he congratulated himself for confronting her, for pushing her, for overcoming his delicacy and driving her to the edges of her defenses. Bully for him.

The anger in her eyes softened to fear, hurt; the fighting sparkle dimmed to remoteness, to unfocused loneliness.

"You're afraid of me," she said, each word receiving no more emphasis than the other, each word driving into him

290

like a verbal icicle. He shut his eyes, shut out the sight of her face and its too plain patchwork of emotions.

"No," he whispered. When he opened his eyes, her face was the same. "Yes," he spit out as loudly as he could, aghast at the contrariness of meshing negative and affirmative into one response.

Jane's face softened, seeming to draw away, though it hadn't moved. He remembered her white against the sheets, narrow and ungiving, chilling as a statue. It wasn't what he saw now, and what he feared now—the humanity in her. That was what she wanted, needed, to have him admit to, what he had been working toward, what he felt impelled to avoid with all his will. Tears sheened her dark eyes, the black irises exploded; she sat in his shadow, he was leaning so close. Her mouth, tensely expectant, looked dewy. He didn't know if it was some subtle lip gloss applied by the nurses, or a phenomenon of Jane's, or just the way he wanted to see it right now.

He leaned inward until their lips met, her hands moving delicately over his clenched fists on the chair arms, then up his arms, barely felt. Their breath mingled first, then the kiss took root and drove deep. She kissed pretty expertly for a virgin—Jane and her damn dawn reading expeditions; he should have seen what was happening when she'd raided the library sex manuals weeks ago. For a virgin. His mortally wounded sense of ethics writhed in the back of his mind even as the forefront of his senses reveled in an initiatory act that seemed a kind of surrender. He felt the weight of the world pressed upon his shoulders, finally understanding the aptness of the cliché, but it was only Jane's linked hands, attaining their goal, as she had herself. It seemed like the world's longest kiss, or series of them; he couldn't count how many opportunities he had for breaking it, and how many times the pressure of his lips—or her lips—prolonged it.

They were finally apart, at least physically. Kevin reached

up to pull her hands down over his shoulders, down his arms. "Yes, Jane, I'm afraid of you. You know why now."

Her hands tightened over his, preventing him from disengaging her. "They all talk about you, think about you. I hear them, day after day. It's a crush, Mrs. Bellingham says. It's like you're all theirs, no matter how much time you spend with me. But—the coat, the way you're afraid to touch me—and you said *I* was afraid, and I was . . . You love *me*, don't you?"

He supposed he could have tried fooling her, or himself, or just saving his ass, and lied. But he didn't.

Chapter Forty

"Yes, Jane. I love you."

Cross's lips moved in what could have been a smile, but he wasn't smiling.

"I was looking," he began in his usual roundabout way, "for the one argument that would convince you, that would stop the protests, the persuasion before it began. In the end, I thought your own words would do it best."

It was hard to argue or protest or persuade when you were cringing.

"How the hell did you get that?" Kevin regarded the desktop tape machine, which had been set to spit out that one damning sentence and now was mercifully silent.

"That doesn't matter. What does is that . . . conditions . . . between you and your patient have gone far beyond the unconventional to the impermissible. I know, I know; you've never played psychiatry according to Hoyle—or Freud. But there are bounds, Kevin, even for you, and you've badly overstepped them this time. It's why, you'll understand when you think it over, I've had to remove you from the Jane Doe case."

"Remove? Past tense? Shit, Norbert, I just saw her yesterday afternoon."

"And you won't again. You're clearly too emotionally involved to—"

"You bet I'm emotionally involved! You tape my sessions—secretly; what do you think this is, some Gulag head ward? And then convict me single-handedly just because I reassure a patient . . ."

"There are other tapes, Kevin. It's more than words, it's become physical. I'm sorry, but I just can't allow the scandal if the patient advocate groups should find out—"

"And you'd help 'em if you needed to shut me up, wouldn't you?"

"Of course not. But these things have a way of leaking out. Be realistic. You put Jane Doe in among the student nurses yourself. Things of this . . . nature . . . are bound to come out."

" 'This nature' is nothing! I haven't done anything. Maybe I'm providing a bit more emotional support than I do to the average patient, but Jane isn't average. . . . There's nobody else for her to rely on."

"But there is, Kevin, and that's what you don't see. You are not the only one in the world who can help Jane. In fact, right now, I think you're the one who can hurt her the most. Why should she go through the pain of remembering her past when you're there to—to kiss away every twinge."

"All right! All right! Maybe I've overstepped the traditional shrink/patient relationship. All I know is I'm doing what works, and with Jane, not a hell of a lot does."

Cross leaned back to view him with irritating compassion. "Kevin, you're brilliant, but that doesn't mean you don't have blind spots. Why, for instance, have you never undertaken a case of anorexia nervosa? You, who ache for chal-

293

lenges, yet never tackle the most challenging, frustrating malady of all? I should think you'd be rarin' to do battle with it, after . . .''

"After what?"

"Don't be so hostile. I told you I knew about the Symons girl. It's my job to know. 'After' losing the love of your life to anorexia. You were totally impotent, Kevin. Just another bewildered, loving witness to what is a terrible waste. I know that experience shaped you for psychiatry, that you channeled the frustration, the helplessness into helping others, but now that very impetus is turning on you—and you can't see it. It's my job to make you see it.''

Kevin leaned back in the chair—hot seat—and sighed, regarding Cross through slitted, cynical eyes. "Do your analysis, Doctor. God knows you need the practice.''

Cross chuckled. "You would have been a hell of a lawyer, too. Instinct for the jugular. You know, administration does take the edge off, but it gives one perspective, too. I've watched you, admired you, gave you plenty of rope and never had to jerk you up short. Let me outline what's happened here. I think you'll see it my way if you really examine it.''

Kevin twiddled his thumbs and inspected the ceiling, but Cross only smiled, that same, sick shit-eating smile of anybody with power about to exercise it for the victim's "own good."

"It doesn't take a detective to figure out that Julie Symons's death pointed you in the direction of psychiatry. Or that your passion for tackling the most difficult cases and treating them by innovative but last-ditch methods was a way to fight the reality of her death in another, less emotionally charged arena. That's why you've been wise enough to avoid anorexia cases. Too close to home; you know the odds of cure are nil—that wouldn't fit with the profile of the wonder-working Dr. Blake; and, unlike most psychiatric cases, other than the suicide-prone, death can be a very real outcome.

"But Jane. Did you ever objectively analyze how much she resembled an anorexia victim when she came here? Thin, unresponsive. Only this one thrived. She ate, put on weight. Half your job was done. It was only her mind, not her body, you had to battle for. You could have your cake and eat it, too. It's not so odd you fell in love with her. She's Julie Symons, willing to cure herself. And her memory—maybe you don't want to restore her memory. Maybe you want to be all there is for her."

Kevin stirred resentfully, but Cross continued.

"It's not, as I said, surprising that you became involved with her. It's the old Pygmalion and Galatea legend. You made her, you sculpted her social reactions, her psychological orientation—even, I think, her emotional responses. You, to sink to the trite, played God. And you liked it. Why not? I would, if I had the imagination to aspire to that level. But I don't, which is why I'm an administrator, and you do. Which is why you're in hot water. Let her go peacefully, Kevin. Can't you see she was blank slate for you to scrawl your own hidden emotional agenda upon? You're not helping her; you're hurting her."

Cross was right in one thing, Kevin's only defense was protest or persuasion; it's hard to do either when you've been caught red-handed. Cross rewound the tape during the silence, and replayed the damning sentence. "Yes, Jane. I love you." Cross, damn him, had replayed it a lot. He knew right where to stop the tape.

"How the hell did you record that? And how long have you been eavesdropping?"

"It's not particularly hard. Probe handles sensitive cases. It's important sometimes to monitor them."

"Monitor! Spy, you mean. You've sold out to the spook shop, Norbert."

"They pay your salary, too, Kevin."

"Maybe not."

"Now don't get impulsive and quit. You know much of

our funding comes from governmental sources. It's usually just the final reports they're interested in, like how you deprogrammed that cult member, and in record time, too. It might help them with returning prisoners of war, for instance."

"It might help them program people, too."

"I doubt it. The point is, I recorded this to confirm my own suspicions, to find some way of making you confront the rather seamy direction in which you were heading. You've had a fine career, Kevin; more important, you're a splendid psychiatrist. You don't want to harm that—and Jane—by falling into some reflexive emotional pattern. I blame myself; I shouldn't have called you in. I should have seen the similarity. . . ."

"Right. Blaming yourself just convicts me faster."

"I've heard you question my competence, Kevin; my ethics for taping your session. I haven't heard you challenge my central argument: You're in love with Jane Doe and unfit for treating her."

" 'In love.' What is that? I don't know; don't know if I ever did. I said what I said on that tape. She needed to hear it; maybe I needed to say it. What does that add up to? So, you're taking me off the case; who's getting it? You?"

Cross picked up the ballpoint pretentiously implanted in its stand and doodled along the edge of his notepad. "I, um, I thought it best she not remain here to . . . aggravate . . . the situation. I'm sending her to another facility, where they can deal with her objectively. Besides, the publicity here, the false parents— It'd be good to give her a fresh start, too."

"Sending her—where?"

"I'm not telling you, Kevin."

"God, what is this? *Romeo and Juliet*? I've got a right—an obligation—to know what you plan for my patient, even if I do give up treating her." Just saying it made it a reality. He'd given up. He would let Cross whisk Jane away, for her sake, his sake. There was the implicit blackmail of the tape; that wasn't enough to stop him, not if he believed he was right. Only this time, he feared, he believed, he might be wrong, dreadfully wrong.

"It's better for all of us if you don't know. I don't mean to act like the father in a melodrama, but Probe is a sensitive unit. Surely, Kevin, you can see what a scandal like this would do to all of us, not just you?"

Kevin stood. "I guess. How long have you been taping?"

"Only the last few sessions. When it became apparent . . . They're really not that scandalizing. I'll say this for you, Kevin; you fought even making these relatively harmless false steps. That's why it's still worth stopping, and it's Jane I'm transferring, instead of firing you."

"I didn't tape the last couple sessions myself—" He reached for the machine, hoping.

Cross punched a button and the cassette popped obediently into his hand, like a magician's rabbit. "I'll keep this. We don't want it to get into the wrong hands."

"No," Kevin murmured. "Let's hear it for the right hands."

He left, and Cross didn't say good-bye.

Chapter Forty-one

There was no point in sticking around the office. When Kevin called the dorm, the ever-helpful Mrs. Bellingham told him not to worry: Jane had gotten his message that there would be no session that day.

He hung up, worrying. Cross had wasted no time. Kevin wondered when he'd order the boxcar and ship Jane to her new shrink. Jane, with her memories nicely revived now—all about Zyunsinth and killing Officer Kellehay.

Kevin drove home, put on some old Bob Dylan, spun the

blinds shut with a twist of their Plexiglas wands and in the resulting, magical dimness pulled Julie's picture from its semiseclusion in the bookcase.

He propped it on the coffee table, poured himself a double Johnnie Walker and lay on the sofa to contemplate it and anything else that happened to get in the way—like himself.

He hadn't been so humiliated since—well, even excavating the deepest sediment of adolescence couldn't produce a suitably demeaning comparison. What stung most was knowing that he *had* been out of line, not simply in what the clandestine tape recording had shown—a supposedly objective shrink uttering such a subjective value judgment as "I love you." But he'd been out of line from the beginning: concealing Jane's consciousness at the time of Kellehay's death; hiding the odd fact of her virginity, her weird snippets of memory, her powers, whatever they were; even engineering the Volkers' exposure and banishment.

And all because of Julie, to hear Cross tell it. Kevin studied Julie's photograph, the hollow, howling bones of her face, as the stereo wailed in melancholy concert. He'd always subconsciously disowned the photo, even as he'd dutifully dragged it from place to place. All Julie's photos showed her dancing. Even this close-up crowned her with some elegantly impossible tiara, her neck muscles strained, her face wearing that otherworldly expression that ballet dancers seem to don with their toe shoes.

The Julie he had loved had been a remnant, one only he and her mother saw clearly, even at the end.

So. In the gospel according to Cross, Kevin—bedeviled by his sense of loss at Julie's death—let that long-gone emotional turmoil fuel his career and blind him to replacing Julie with the nearest anorexia substitute, an emaciated, memoryless Jane.

Kevin stared into his untouched drink. If Cross was right, his whole life was a sham, with himself as chief victim, and he had no right trying to help, much less love, anybody.

And Jane. He took a belt of undiluted Scotch. Jane, with her odd bits of memory stimulated. He'd been just good enough to uncover some damning evidence for somebody else to prosecute to its conclusion. They might diagnose her as a delusional schizophrenic, lock her up. Not even the Volkers were there to fight for her now, thanks to Kevin the Manipulative. Oh, what tangled webs we weave, etc. etc. And how would Jane take being severed from him just after—with an unholy blend of innocence and intent—she had forced him to commit to her in a more than professional way? The question drilled into his mind with all the relentless power of a white-hot steel auger: What would happen to Jane Doe now?

The doorbell rang. His glance flicked to the clock. Four-thirty P.M. Probably some tyke selling chocolate bars. Who else would haunt this indecent hour; this limbo between day and evening when twilight ghosts of the subconscious and conscience couple obscenely; this time that he wanted to keep for himself?

It rang again. Kevin self-indulgently ached to muffle himself in his depression, the heavy, immobilizing blanket that anger weaves on the loom of repression. Instead he decided to cuss out whoever had the bad taste to be at the door.

"Hello, Kevin. Are you getting drunk?"

"Swanson." Surprise diffused his rage. "No, just pretending to."

She came in, not waiting for an invitation, looking oddly civilian in a brown wool chesterfield. Her eyes gauged the lowball glass on the coffee table.

"Only one swallow down; I'm coherent."

"Good. Because you're not going to like what I've come to tell you. You're an angry young man sober; drunk I don't need."

"More good news. Sit down."

She claimed the old maroon overstuffed chair. It matched her, being both bloated and inflexible.

"I imagine Cross has taken you off the Doe case," she began.

"Elementary school, my dear Swanson. How'd you know? Or does half the hemisphere know by now?"

"What reason did he give you?"

"Let's just say . . . my general incompetence."

She nodded, pale eyes bobbing behind her thick lenses. "There are a lot of things I could say about you, Dr. Blake, that wouldn't be complimentary, but incompetence isn't one of them. Is that why this place looks like the set for a Russian play?" She rose and marched to the windows, twisting open the Levolors in blinding sequence until late rosy winter light cascaded into the room. "Nice place, Kevin; more civilized than I thought you'd inhabit." Her back was to the light, so he couldn't read her face, probably deliberately.

"I don't like telling you this, but then, I don't like what's happening here. I don't know what fairy tale our leader told you, but *Cross* didn't take you off Jane's case; the CIA did. The Company or whatever they're calling themselves this week. He was under orders."

"The CIA?"

"Who do you think funds me?"

"Sure. I know who's been running your spook show, but—"

"It's all been a spook show, even your little stand, Kevin. You just never turned up anything hot before, so you hardly felt the strings being pulled."

"You mean—Cross . . . made up . . . what he told me to get me off the case?"

"It must have worked. I've never seen you this shaken before, and what's worse, sitting on your ass taking it."

"Swanson!"

"Wake up, little Kevin. It's a tough world out there; I didn't survive this long by being an academic looney." Swanson unbuttoned her coat. "You got more of that, or don't you believe in sharing the wealth?"

300

"What's mine is yours." He handed her the glass. Who needed booze when adrenaline was doing the tarantella through his circulatory system?

"What *did* Cross tell you?" she asked after her first, professional swallow.

"Enough to make me feel real bad," he answered, deliberately vague. "So what did he tell *you*?"

"The truth. I ought to make you squirm for it, but I'm so mad right now . . ."

"Yeah, well, I'm not exactly an advertisement for Valium, either. This going to make me madder?"

"I hope so, because maybe you'll do something about it. I can't."

"Okay. Lay it on me."

She took another belt first. Kevin had never seen her looking so human.

"I'm ambitious. For my program, for myself. When you made me stop working with Jane, I realized I'd been going about it in the wrong way. I hoped that when you finished treating her, I could have another try, with your permission, naturally. So—when the would-be parents showed up and you obviously wanted to keep control of Jane for a while, I went along."

"Yeah. Your support at the staff meeting was stunning."

"Not as stunning as my private support." She leaned forward, her eyes a trifle unfocused; JW straight didn't fool around. "Now Kevin, don't waste your hostility on me. But Cross mentioned that you had told him about Jane's sessions with me; that was back when you were using any argument to get Probe to keep her. I thought that I could cement that object by telling Cross how well Jane had done. . . . I did my best to impress him—without any hard evidence. Apparently, it took. He duly reported it to Washington—or Virginia, rather—and they took it even more seriously. Only the bastard's blithely turned Jane over to them. He thought I'd be pleased that my 'discovery' had interested them so much. But

I don't get to do the experiments; no, that's reserved for some head factory in Virginia even I haven't seen. Your patient's been drafted into the 'Mind Wars,' Kevin. My methods, however crude, will seem like the ultimate in benevolence compared to what they'll do to her."

"So you're telling me this because you feel guilty for triggering it."

"And I agree with you; Jane needs delicate handling. Those 'Mind Wars' guys don't understand that. After all, neither you nor I found it easy to get Jane to perform."

He nodded slowly. "I give you credit for that; she did demonstrate her . . . powers . . . at your insistence. Well, this has been more instructive than a roomful of Ph.Ds. Thanks for telling me."

"You going to confront Cross?" she asked as he escorted her to the door. "You going to chew his rotten, lying, government-kowtowing ass right off?"

"You betcha, Swannee." He had the door open and her halfway through it. She would probably go straight home, finish getting drunk and be out of it for at least sixteen hours. "And one of these days, I'll definitely have to buy you a drink in a real bar, for a real occasion. Thanks a lot; thanks a million."

"Anytime, Kevin. Anytime Cross tries to double-Cross either of us again," she promised, grinning foolishly, glasses askew. She giggled.

He didn't smile back as he shut the door. He didn't smile at all.

Chapter Forty-two

His fist hit the door, once. Sharply. It was five-fifteen, and dark already; even the apartment building's hall felt like January—cold, contained, prematurely dark.

He didn't want to knock again, attract attention. Come on, answer. Answer! He pulled the handful of darkness he carried closer to his chest.

The door yawned ajar, then its hinges squeaked as it stretched fully open.

"Hey, man. What'chya doin' here?"

Kevin stepped inside, closing the door behind him. A stuffy wave of intermingled pot, must and cat surged into his nostrils. Kandy's place hadn't lost a dust mote since his last visit.

Kevin thrust out his dark handful. "Cat. Take it."

"What's the matter? Did it pee in your headphones?"

"I won't be home for a while." Kevin studied the mess. "Do you still keep a stash of cash around? Like you used to? Heavy cash?"

"Sure. Still hate banks, no matter the interest rate. What's the score? You in trouble?"

"No. Somebody else is. Look, Kandy. I left the Jag in a campus long-term parking lot. I'd let you use it, but it's better under wraps. I need your van for a few days. I've got to get out of town for a while. And I need your silence. Just take the cat, and try not to unhousebreak it, lend me your van and, and—how about two thousand dollars? You got that much around here?"

Kandy sank cross-legged to the floor. "Two grand? Sure, but Kev, that wipes me out."

"I don't dare take my money out of the bank. I can't even use my phone; otherwise, I'd have called. For all I know, your place might be bugged, too." Kevin eyed the clutter. "It's a perfect candidate. So take the cat, give me the bread and the car keys and keep quiet about me for as long as you can. If you trust me."

"Sure. Trust you, that is. But—bugged? Who? Narcs?"

Kevin laughed. "Narcs are pussycats compared to these. But I'm not going to stand by and let them sweep in and sweep up my patient."

"Holy cow! The Doe."

"Right. They want to rip her away to a mind-bending installation somewhere in Virginia."

"They can't do that!" Kandy was indignant.

"Hell they can't. Who's to claim her? The Volkers are discredited; there aren't any new parental candidates. She's yesterday's news. Who would even notice if she vanished?"

"Why would they want her?"

"That's a longer story than I have time for." Kevin pulled heavy gloves from the pockets of his down jacket. "I assume you'll feed Blue there."

Kandy studied the kitten, who was intently scaling his knee. "Can't bear to see anything starve."

"And the van?"

"Can't stand to see anyone walk." Kandy uncoiled and went to the bulbous mahogany sideboard in the dining room, rummaging until he pulled a key ring from an art glass epergne.

"And the money?" Kevin wasn't so sure about this, though he knew Kandy often kept unsafe amounts of cash around.

Kandy grinned widely. "That's easiest. Can't stomach capitalist stockpiling." He drove deeper into the chaos covering the sideboard like a dust runner, finally uprooting a fat roll of bills. "This should come close," Kandy said, tossing it over.

Kevin caught it against his stomach. Happiness, he decided, was cradling a warm kitten, not cold cash. But money was what he needed. Anyone on the run did.

"Thanks. I'll pay you back—sometime. I hope."

Kandy watched Kevin stuff the bills into his shallow jacket pockets.

"You'll tell me what this is about—sometime. I hope."

"I wish I could now. But the less you know . . ."

Kandy nodded. "This is like a movie. I love it. I told you Jane Doe meant some exotic action." He hooked his thumbs in the belt loops at his hips and cocked his head until the ponytail low on his neck swung incongruously. "Waal, round up the bad guys," Kandy drawled in singsong imitation of the Duke, "and come back and we'll have a brew."

"I just hope the bad guys don't round me up." Kevin ducked out the door into the dim hallway, feeling like a thief.

At the dorm, he felt like a rapist—one of those bland, smiling suckers who play Jack Armstrong on a date and then whisk darling daughters away after midnight.

"Hi, Mrs. B. Can you give Jane's room a buzz? Or has she gone to dinner?"

"Oh, Dr. Blake. I'm so glad you've come to explain in person. About canceling the session. I think Jane . . . well, the other girls are at dinner, but Jane didn't seem to have an appetite. She's still in her room. You remember where?"

He nodded, already heading for the tiny elevator cage. It was on the main floor for once, so he took it. It struck him as ironic, the slow, hiccoughing ascension of the outmoded elevator, himself in his winter survival gear, Kandy's battered van parked beside a snowdrift outside. They were small defense against the grinding bureaucratic gears that even now turned ratchet onto ratchet preparatory to chewing him and Jane alive.

305

Jane dropped the book she was reading and stood as he entered—without knocking, this time. Knocking was irrelevant now.

"You said I wasn't to come today." It was a muted accusation.

"Whoever called here said it; I didn't."

"But—"

"But nothing. Can you get some clothes together—warm clothes?"

She nodded even as she went for the drawers in the age-blackened dorm dresser. Jane looked over her shoulder. "I have nothing to put them in."

He rubbed his beard. "There must be dozens of suitcases in the closets around here."

She nodded.

"Maybe you could—get one."

He watched her leave the room. Great, now she was a thief, along with whatever other nameless things she was. Dr. Blake sure knew how to acclimate a patient to the real world. . . .

Jane said nothing when she returned, brushing by with a medium-sized blue suitcase, and filling it from the dresser. He admired her businesslike response, the lack of hysteria or questions. Then he realized it was because she trusted him implicitly, and felt even worse. At least they couldn't harm her any more if they caught her in his custody than if she came to them meekly via the sacrificial channels of Probe.

"You'd better wear—that." He nodded to the coat. Damn perspicacious purchase; who would have believed it would come in so handy? "And gloves. You still missing gloves?"

She nodded again, wide-eyed.

He jerked his head over his shoulder, wordlessly. Jane, ever the quick study, left the room, returning in minutes with a pair of nice leather gloves, fleece-lined. He rubbed them contemplatively between thumb and forefinger before handing them back. "They fit?"

Jane fanned a gloved hand. "Glenda's hands are the same size as mine; I noticed once."

"Okay, got everything you need in there? I mean everything. We might not be back for a while."

She nodded happily.

Kevin had her carry the coat over her arm, concealing the case. The elevator awaited them; there wasn't much call for it between these dead hours of five and seven, when dorm residents were either eating or out.

"I'm bringing Jane over to the hospital for, uh, a test, Mrs. B. It might take a while, so don't be alarmed."

"Gracious, Doctor, I'd never worry if she was with you." She replaced her glasses and smiled benignly before turning back to her Agatha Christie mystery.

Kevin steered Jane to the door, letting her pause in the tiny entryway to don the coat. "You'll need Zyunsinth tonight," he told her. "It's cold out there."

"Zyunsinth." She patted it nostalgically. He leaned on the long door bar and with a thump it swung open, pushing back a curl of new-drifted snow and admitting a dervish of wind-driven flakes. They plunged into the now absolute dark, snow-buried bushes forming an amorphic gantlet on either side. Every bush could be bugged. Probably her room was. Maybe he was paranoid, but there were worse mental conditions.

Jane stood momentarily perplexed before the van's high first step. Kevin boosted her up, then went around the street side and slipped behind the wheel. The van surrounded them like a cold metal coffin, empty except for his recording equipment and their cases. It was transportation and protection from the wind, little more, and it would take hours to heat that echoing inner space enough to reach the passengers in front. They were shivering already, both of them. Kevin blew his fingers warm before fishing Kandy's cold keys from his pocket and starting the engine.

Snow flew thicker; the flakes careened soundlessly into the

windshield and danced like mad albino mosquitoes in the headlights as he pulled out the knob.

"Where are we going, Dr. Blake?" Jane asked serenely. She had been happy to see him, he didn't have to be a shrink to see that. Very happy.

He tweaked her cold-rouged nose before pulling on the big gloves again and steering the van out into the street.

"You can cut out the Dr. Blake shit, Jane, and you know it. And we're going to see the wizard, a wizard who'll give me some courage, maybe give Probe some heart and—if we're lucky—give you a memory back. The only wizard I ever knew. And I don't think she likes me."

Chapter Forty-three

Traffic was sparse on I-35 northbound. None but the hardy—or foolhardy—braved northern Minnesota wilds in winter. Kevin kept checking the rearview mirror anyway, but the few headlights that trailed them for a time vanished as the city signs by the side of the road—Hinckley, Sandstone, Moose Lake—lured them to warm lights and log-full hearths. . . .

Despite the heater fan on high, the van remained icy. Jane and Kevin huddled into their coats, the fan's roar and the aged van's rock, rattle and roll forbidding conversation.

It was a dark and snowy night, to paraphrase the famous opening line, particularly out here, where population thinned. Once past Duluth, they'd entered Minnesota's northern third, a blank white mystery on the map, dotted blue with lakes, pocked by the irregular outlines of five major Indian reservations and famed for its Iron Range, forests and fishing.

The AM radio tuned in more static than stations, especially

past Duluth where State Highway 61 wove along the rugged coast of Lake Superior. Bob Dylan had seen Highway 61 as an apocalyptic avenue leading from the obscurity of his native Hibbing. Kevin saw it as his salvation, too, but going in an opposite direction, away from city lights and civility, out into the open, where few dared follow. Frozen Superior shone as solid and white as the snowlands on his left, ice-bound; the ritual coming of the spring's first ore boat amounted to an Iron Range feast day, but now seemed as remote as the Second Coming. Each fall, this same highway entertained a constant string of cars touring the North Shore Drive's famed display of autumn leaves. Tonight, the road was semideserted and the little lakeside towns rolled by—Castle Danger, Beaver and Silver Bay—their names the usual, oxymoronic litany of the banal and exotic that forms off-the-interstate America.

Kevin and Jane were heading, like ants edging along an arrowhead, for the top triangular tip of Minnesota usually left off the map except for an apologetic inset; up into the protected Boundary Waters Canoe Area; curving out over singing Superior; tight under the neighborly awning of Ontario; right where no one was supposed to live, where wild game was preserved and perhaps even a few hunted humans could find sanctuary.

A scattered tribe of hermits had always lived here, unwilling to leave at the behest of God, government or common sense, like the late Harry Truman of Mount St. Helens, who had clung to his sense of place until he became ashes with it. The government had granted these people the right to live out their lives where they had begun. When they were gone, no one would live there but the beasts and birds. Maybe no one should try now.

At Little Marais, population 10, Kevin passed the Cottage Colony sign announcing a May reopening. He was glad he'd gassed up in Duluth. Northern Minnesota in winter was Moby Dick on ice, a great white island-beast, a frozen landscape that could kill as effectively and far faster than Death Valley.

Beyond the ski resort of Lutsen, Kevin drew on his memory to take an obscure road inland. The *Strib* had run a feature—almost an Everyman's guide to the homes of the poor and reclusive—on the eccentrics who claimed this narrow neck of the woods. Most were native oddities, but one was his wizard, a locally prominent and therefore undisturbed transplant.

No vehicle followed them now; he hadn't seen a car for miles. The tires whined and bit into barely packed snow, and trees crowded the narrow road, some bare and black, others slender white birches, most haughty pines whose boughs dripped dowagerlike with nature's mink coat—a mantle of pristine snow. The flurries had ended hours before and his headlights picked out stillness and the passing poetry of stark winter vignettes, each glimpse more chillingly lovely than the last.

"Where are we going?" asked Jane again, finally able to be heard. It was as if the van had been dropped into cotton batting; the world beyond the woods seemed remote, and Safety, wearing a cold white velvet robe, silently spread its soft arms wide.

"To the end of the road," he told her, almost euphorically.

He didn't reveal his relief when the headlights finally pinpointed a cabin sitting squat against a ring of pines, and the reassuring profile of a huge woodpile marshaled under its wrapping of snow. Smoke steamed from the limestone chimney; a pair of skis stood soldier-stiff at the wooden door.

Kevin switched off the engine confidently. If it was the wrong cabin, its inhabitant would at least offer them warmth and shelter. If it was the right cabin, Neumeier was still alive, which was good news to him, if not her. It was two A.M.

Jane stood beside him, stamping her feet in the time-honored tradition of cold-honed Minnesotans, while he

310

knocked. He'd always hated north woods rustic, but when the door finally swung open on a homey slice of knotty-pine paneling and rag rugs, he could have wrapped it up for Christmas and given it to himself.

"Come in, and don't take the cold with you. Tell me your business *after* you close the door."

Rosa Neumeier cut off Kevin's burgeoning explanation as efficiently as she'd snipped some student theory in the bud when its holder rose to present the bouquet of his postgraduate thoughts to the class at large.

"Keep your things on and come to the fire. You. Young man. When your fingers unbend, get some more wood. From the bottom, so it's drier."

He went instantly, guilty at having occasioned this sudden, lavish use of a resource so painstakingly gathered. He found himself out in the cold, ladening himself with more logs than he could comfortably carry, reflecting that it was Rosa Neumeier all right.

When door banged shut behind him, announcing his overburdened return, Neumeier paused in settling an afghan over Jane's knees. She looked at him and frowned.

"We can't burn all that. Oh, put it down; I'll feed the fire. Now, don't fret, dear; just stay put and keep warm."

Dear. Even Rosa Neumeier. Kevin unloaded his wood and tried to unzip his jacket with too stiff fingers. "You probably don't remember me, Professor Neumeier, but—"

"Of course I remember you." Her tone dripped scorn for anyone callow enough to think her memory might be less than miraculous. "I didn't have many young men in my classes. The sociology of the adolescent is hardly a masculine specialty, more's the pity. Sit. I don't get visitors often, especially at this hour."

He doubted she remembered him specifically. Professor Rosa Neumeier's classes were attended by social workers and general college students as well as psych majors, sitting in raked tiers of two hundred; Kevin's few brief conferences in her cramped office hardly merited remembering. She must have been past seventy when she finally retired—or was forced to—five years earlier. Now . . . who knew but Rosa Neumeier, and she wasn't likely to tell.

"I keep it warmer than I should, but old bones are old bones." The logs she hefted onto the fire sprayed sparks into a Fourth of July show she ignored, going to the big wood stove against the wall. "Herb tea's all I have, but it's hot. I keep the water warm to put moisture in the air; old lungs, too." She brought steaming mugs to Jane and Kevin, then sat opposite him at the table with its quaint oilcloth covering.

"What do you want, Dr. Blake?"

She did remember. One for her team.

"Help." He matched her abruptness; it was the best way to get her attention. Her eyebrows lifted—they were the sparse, unemphatic iron-gray pennants of age—as she settled against the crude wooden chair struts.

She was an old woman, and she looked like a bag lady in her man-sized flannel shirt and baggy pants. Her hair was cut in what he thought of as the lesbian bob—bangs, straight around the ears—but he knew she wasn't a lesbian; she just didn't care if people thought she was. She was probably as unfeminine a specimen as his imagination could conjure; he'd always liked her. He glanced at Jane, who watched them wide-eyed over the rim of an oversized mug with some ski resort named on the side, and smiled.

"What kind of help?" Neumeier demanded.

Kevin looked back. "The works. Mental, physical and spiritual."

"Spiritual. Now you interest me. You don't hear that word much anymore, especially from you psychiatrists."

"You noticed." He felt flattered that she'd noted his later career. "Did you know I was with the Probe unit?"

Her reaction to mention of Probe was a strange hybrid of snort, sneeze and sneer. "So. You have firewood and tea and a roof over your head. Up here that's the extent of physical

312

comfort. For mental needs, you have me." Her tight smile awaited a challenge she knew wouldn't come. "And spiritual—that I leave to the yogis for now. Tell me your problem."

He looked at Jane, who didn't know it, either.

"We're fugitives from the federal government. Jane—Jane Doe—is an amnesiac who can move objects by mental power alone. I'm . . . her shrink. The CIA wants to corral her and take her apart like a laboratory rat. She hasn't recovered any of her memory, except for some bizarre bits that don't make any sense. She hasn't got a mark on her—not a pierced ear or a ruptured hymen or a vaccination or a dental filling. We need to crack the impasse in her mind, to find out who and what she is and how she got that way. We need to hide out from the feds. We need sanctuary."

"There is none," said Rosa Neumeier. "But tell me about it."

Two hours later, he had. Jane lay on the solitary sofa, under the coat, asleep or close to it. He and Neumeier still sat at the square little table with an empty sugar and creamer set placed next to a full salt and pepper set, forming a restaurantlike grouping.

His tape recorder and a pile of cassettes lay beside the quaint china objects, looking large and overmechanical. He'd even played "Zyunsinth and the basalt domes" and "sklivent ysrossni" for Neumeier.

"Why did you come to me?" the old woman asked, her narrowed eyes almost disappearing into the wrinkles pleating her cheekbones.

"I thought you were the most humane person I knew."

She snorted and reached to pluck the top off the sugar bowl; it wasn't empty. She pulled out a pack of Lucky Strikes and lit one with a farmer's match from the creamer, striking it on the table leg in an elegant motion.

"I never did anything to encourage that impression."

"That's why I thought it."

"I smoke very seldom," she said, as close to apology as

313

she could ever come. Her exhaled smoke vanished into the cabin's warmth. "Why did you take my classes? They weren't required for you."

"I didn't take them; I audited them. I was carrying a heavy academic load; didn't want to risk my GPA." Kevin grinned. "And then you gave me A's. Straight A's. The only straight A's I got. Not a hedging A minus among 'em." He shook his head. "Sure could have used 'em in my record."

"A minus is a sign of a small mind, the kind that says 'Good but maybe I'm wrong.' I know good when I see it. Some teachers never mark an A; they are cowards, or worse, egocentric. But all that adolescent psychology—you didn't need that stuff."

"Your studies in the fifties and sixties were prototypical. Besides, you don't know it all. I'd come back from Harvard with my medical degree and decided to go into psychiatry, but wanted to get some general courses under my belt before I specialized. And—I was very interested in adolescent and family psychology right then. . . ."

She nodded and took a knowing drag on her cigarette. "You were a very sad young man."

Kevin was startled and a bit miffed. "I thought I was handling it pretty well."

The cigarette waved and her voice took on a Garbo-like rasp as if the nicotine wrapped her throat like a smoky scarf. No matter how she dressed, Rosa Neumeier always wore an ineffable, mysterious European elegance. "I have seen a good many sad young men."

The statement would have been a starting gate to a biographer; to Kevin, it was a cul-de-sac. "I should tell you why, because an accredited shrink who happens to be my boss says it's the reason I can't treat Jane objectively. Her name . . . was Julie, and she died."

Neumeier listened, the cigarette burning out in her fingers, while he told of Julie's ailment and death, his own bereavement.

"And they say you cannot separate this Julie and Jane. Interesting, same initial consonant." She smiled provocatively. Had she been analyzing him, Kevin might have felt defensive about that coincidence. "Nonsense," Neumeier said finally. "They underestimate the scientist's passion for the truth, above all."

"The truth is, Jane is dangerous. She killed a man; maybe two."

They both glanced to the couch. Neumeier looked back first; her gray, watery eyes were waiting for him.

"How long have you been in love with her?"

It was the one facet of the truth he had danced around, simply because he still found it shameful. "I don't know, Professor Neumeier. Too long and not long enough, I guess."

"Ah. I ask only because—look around you. This one room with the stove and that room to the left there is my bedroom." Then she pointed to an alcove furnished with a bed and nightstand. "And there's the guest bedroom. Double bed each room. Do you want her to sleep with me, or you?"

"She's a—"

"I know what she is. Most intriguing. Where?"

"With . . . me. She's very dependent."

Neumeier twisted over her red-plaid shoulder to see the sofa. "Not so much as you think, young man. But then, that's why you came to me."

"Do you think there's any—hope? Any chance of answering Jane's mystery? If I know what I'm dealing with, I can defend her better. You were rumored to have done some parapsychology work—in Europe in the thirties, when it was better received."

"That kind of thing is never well received, and if it is, then is the time to most beware." Her face and tone were grim. "It's late. We must rest. Put the subconscious to work on the enigmas." Her gnarled hand patted his shoulder. "The sign of a wise man or woman is when you can let someone or something else do the work for you. Put some

315

more logs on the fire and get your conundrum to bed. We will talk in the morning."

"Time . . . might be a factor," he protested.

"Time is always a factor, but I am like Pontius Pilate. What is Time? I ask. And history smiles at me. Go to sleep, young man; you have more time than you want."

Sleep. Dream. Float. Float—away!

She turns in an alien space, brushing an alien form. All, all utterly unfamiliar. Transported. Suddenly. Pulled as by some string attached to the very heart of her being, to the center of her solar plexus, to the nucleus of every cell in her body. . . .

Body? No body. Just being. Just raging need. To go full circle, become less again. Full, full to bursting. The harvest overflows the silo; the metallic skin strains, splits. All falls out. All fall down. All gone.

Tossing, upon a solid surface. It hurts, stings, repels every particle of her skin. Thrown against a solid substance radiating warmth, once so comforting. Searing heat. Everything physical tortures. Except the one thought. Return. To what was, to what she—it—was, to *where* it was. Before. Before . . . can't think of after, only the imperative to return. To be as before. To be empty, to be less, to be forgotten.

No.

The call, unrelenting, hissing down forgotten synapses, following a preordained thread through labyrinths of neuron, knotting to become a noose, tightening, tightening. "I" shrinking small to slip the net, so small it drifts away, successfully lost in an endless inner universe while the body left behind twitches, jerks, moves in mock motion/false emotion to the inner-outer pull it cannot resist.

No, says "I" in a small, small unspoken voice.

The body turns and slips away.

"Jane," calls the sea in one long, rolling hiss from the other side of the world, washing onto empty beach.

Chapter Forty-four

The mattress was hard, the bed so high it was hard to get into and then it squeaked when you did. Sleeping with Jane was a fully dressed, antierotic experience. He was too worried and she was too tired to make anything more of it.

If he dreamed, Kevin didn't remember it. If his subconscious dug up any instructive tidbits, it quickly buried them again. He did awake, momentarily disoriented, at either 12:30 or 6:00 A.M., depending on which was the big hand and which was the little hand. Overzealous luminescence blurred the difference.

Something ached somewhere from being slept on wrong, but worse, he remembered that Jane should be with him just as his senses said she wasn't. His hand groped miniature foothills of rumpled blankets, finding no warm mountain of body beyond them. The same remorseful panic he'd last felt in Dayton's outerwear department gripped him. He didn't want to disturb Neumeier—or let her know how unsure he was of his patient, so he rolled out of bed and slunk around the cabin in his stocking feet, inky blackness diffusing to mere charcoal gray as his pupils swelled to adapt to the light—or lack of it.

He bumped into Jane at the door, where her hands were scrabbling weakly at the cold dead-bolt latch.

"Jane!" His whisper seemed to admonish the dark. "What are you doing?"

"Going. Have to go. Go back."

"Shhh. Let go of the door. It's freezing out there. You're

317

not even dressed for it. Come on; let's sleepwalk you back to bed.''

She turned readily enough as he steered her back to the alcove. He couldn't blame her for deserting the lumpy nest allotted them, but her movements, her voice, were both leaden, not fully conscious. He'd never seen her like that, not even under hypnosis. Once they reboarded their vintage bedstead, he wrapped his arms around her for safekeeping.

She fell asleep instantly, her breathing deep and smooth. No such luck for Kevin, whose consciousness kept him running circles in his head until it knocked itself out on a sudden dead end.

Jane slept late, undisturbed while Neumeier clatteringly laid out a plain breakfast and brewed some fancy European coffee the consistency of molasses. Kevin swallowed it now and again to look appreciative.

''What if—'' Neumeier's jabbing table knife let Kevin know the meeting of minds was commencing. She chewed her dark toast and squinted intently at where the stovepipe vanished into the wooden ceiling. ''Something bothered me last night. What if the so-called parents, these Volkers, were telling the truth?''

''Can't be. Lynn Volker had two or three documented fillings. Jane's teeth haven't even got a nick.''

''Not about that. About the UFO.''

''The spaceship? You mean, that they aren't just looneys, that they really saw it?''

''Looneys occasionally see things, too. Hmmmm.'' Neumeier's chair legs screeched over the battered linoleum as she scooted back to inspect Jane. ''Does she always sleep that hard? You say you hypnotized her twenty, maybe thirty times. She should have gone into hypermnesia by now.''

''Accelerated total recall. Yeah, I know, but there's a lot Jane should and should not be doing that she isn't and is. But you don't *buy* that UFO story?''

318

" 'There are more things in heaven and earth, Horatio, than are dreamt of in your philosophy.' "

"I've heard that one."

Neumeier twinkled. "I thought maybe you had. Still, you do not reject the fact—and I believe you—that Jane can stop, pick up and move objects without physically touching them, that she has an affinity for transistors, to make machines go kaboom in the night.

"You grew up watching humans walk in space, on the moon. If you had told me such things when I was your age, I would have committed you. A UFO strikes me as a far more logical extension of reality than telekinesis, my young friend. If I believe your Jane can transport my firewood, say, from outside in and save me some labor, why shouldn't a being from elsewhere fly here to give us a look, just as we send our little probe machines—on space journeys of years and years—with engraved pictures of little human forms and examples of higher mathematics that the scientists think will be an instant language between unrelated worlds?"

"My problem—and Jane's—is all too earthly."

"Maybe. Maybe not. You didn't like that shopworn quote I gave you just now from *Hamlet*. How about another? 'When you have eliminated all which is impossible, then whatever remains, however improbable, must be . . . the truth.' The dialogue is Sherlock Holmes's, but the idea is Conan Doyle's. And Doyle became fascinated by psychic phenomena at the end of his life. . . ."

"Obsessed is more like it. He may have been an eye doctor, but he was a writer most of his life, not a scientist."

"One last quote. You will permit a professor emeritus her pedantry, even if it is from popular sources—such as the seminal figure of your own profession, Dr. Sigmund Freud. Do you know what Freud wrote at the end of his life, in the 1930s? 'If I had my life to live over again, I—' "

"Would rather live it as a blond?" Kevin finished sassily. Neumeier ignored him.

" 'I should devote myself to psychical research rather than psychoanalysis.' An amazing sentiment."

"They were products of their time, Professor. Doyle was caught up in late-Victorian spiritualism, and Freud was, well, old and watching the world fall apart."

"Yet the global scientific community takes these things more seriously than it ever has. Extrapolate from advances in biofeedback—control of migraine headaches, lowering of blood pressure . . ."

"Mood rings . . ."

"Ah, you love to reverse roles and play the cynic, Dr. Blake. But what is the quantitative difference between biofeedback—the control of one's own body—and the attempt, or ability, to reach out and control things outside the body, hmmm? Or to project certain senses beyond the body. Look at Targ and his remote viewing experiments, or the Mobius Society in Los Angeles. Why do you think your Dr. Swanson took such unethical steps to work with Jane? Psychokinesis is the least provable of the extrasensory powers; had she had been able to document it . . ."

Neumeier's elbows rapped the table as she crossed her arms. "The psychic is now subject to the scientific method, Kevin. Physicists' tidy microworlds have been shaken by the Big Bang of doubt; new particles have been discovered inside the atom that do not behave according to the rules—some occupy two places at once. What does this say about out-of-the-body experiences? Josephson found particles a decade ago that could pass through supposedly impenetrable barriers—and if a particle, why not a ghost? These billions and billions of infinitesimal subatomic particles hoard secrets that may do much to explain the past—and shape the future. Some think they might transmit psychic energy; others postulate that people can control more than random-number generators with their minds. Jahn at Princeton, for instance, is studying if people can disturb psychically the memory functions of a microelectronic chip. Such a thing would explain Jane's ability to affect equipment.

"And I have not even touched upon the field of biological computing. We spawn test-tube babies routinely now—"

"And test-tube anomalies," Kevin interrupted. "I know all that, Professor Neumeier. They've even come up with 'humsters,' fertilized eggs resulting from human sperm and hamster ova. The stuff is alive and growing until they destroy it. What it'd be if they let it simmer, God only knows."

"Not God. Man, or humanity as it consists of both men and women. We set our own limits now. The tree of knowledge has been in our hands since Eden, since before evolution."

"It was 'knowledge of good and evil,' if I remember my Bible studies."

"Exactly." Neumeier swirled the last swig of coffee around her mug, looking like a gypsy fortune teller reading tea leaves.

Kevin felt free to do some hypothesizing of his own. "I had a feeling, even back when I took your classes—maybe I'm psychic—that you were into a lot more off-the-wall things than juvenile psychology. Your work is a model in the field, but you've obviously kept up your reading in a wider range of research than that. Why concentrate on such a down-home area of behavior when your heart was in the hinterlands of human experience?"

"Do you know," she began dreamily, her foreign accent adding weight to her words, "that if you could store all the information in the Library of Congress on a one-cubic-centimeter microchip—and we're coming close to that—you could implant it in the brain . . . *and* retrieve it. Implant perhaps skills, talents. Stimulate the right or left side. We would be genetic memory banks, programming our brains like some computer.

"You want—what?—to restore Jane Doe's memory. But perhaps it is cluttered with useless or even horrible bits of knowledge. Why carry the minutiae of our existence with us?

What a waste of the brain's storage capacity! Would you care to drag the contents of your house with you everywhere you went? That is why I live with so little—'' Neumeier gestured around the crude cabin. "I learned forty-some years ago that possessions, attachments, people even, are illusory backdrops for the self.

"Have you heard of MacAlear and his 'synbion,' a blend of brain and computer? Ulmer of MIT is modifying DNA, the chemical intelligence of all life, to relay information directly to the brain. Carter at the Naval Research Labs already has a blueprint for a biological computer—an integral body part that could learn to behave like the brain. Think. If we had that, or Russia. What a race would be on—to make the arms race minuscule in comparison. Think. If someone— something—else had that. It would be a new life form. A new evolution. From lower animal to human animal. From human animal to biomachine.

"In the face of all these mysteries, you wish to restore one poor girl's memory. And what will you get? When will you be content? When you learn that the mysterious 'Zyunsinth' is an obscure rock group she worshiped in high school? That your alien syllables are only some secret password for a silly adolescent club? Will you be happy to revive memories of childhood disappointments and prom dresses and petty angers?

"Or are you willing to delve into her past, to face the unexpected if you find it? Your Jane Doe has more than documented perfect teeth, Dr. Blake. She has verifiable tele-kinetic powers—or would have, had you not so rashly destroyed the record of it. Yes, yes; such insensitive science should not be encouraged. But still, the substance of the thing . . . Now I will give another quote, more obscure but more apropos and personal: 'It takes the illogical to reconstruct the pattern of a shattered logic.' A Rosa Neumeier original. More coffee?''

"No thanks.'' Kevin picked up their empty plates and stacked them on the drainboard. When he came back, Neumeier was waiting, a hungry expression on her face. So far, she'd found him to be empty calories.

"Look, Professor . . ." He sat again and folded his hands. "I may not have read as extensively in the professional journals as you, but I read the paper. All this stuff is there, usually under catchall heads like 'World Roundup.' News of the latest test-tube litter in Australia, or a nuclear breakthrough in France, or hints of what horrors the Russians are up to in germ warfare. They mean as much as those bulletins promising a male contraceptive in five years—that have run annually for twenty years. Everything is *possible*. I want the specifics—of Jane, Jane's memory, Jane's past. Yeah, I'm overinvolved. I care what happens to her. And I'm not going to let her be shipped off to some top-secret government funny farm to be taken apart like a transistor radio. . . ."

"You can't stop it." Neumeier's voice was chillingly matter-of-fact.

"What? . . ."

"You can't stop it." She sighed. "I never answered your question about why I worked in the backwater of family sociology. It's because I know what a fragile unit the family is. I came to this country in 1947. The new look was coming in, all the papers said so. It was back from war and off to work. The baby boom was exploding in cracker-box bedrooms all across America, but only the parents knew it yet. Women were told to covet Frigidaires, not careers. Someone like me was an oddity. But my credentials, ah, yes. 'Before the war, Professor Neumeier,' they would say, nodding impressively. They knew of my dabblings in psychic phenomena, but that was considered a hobby. They didn't know, most of them, what happened to science in Germany, in the camps.

"You mention humsters. A joke. Many obscene jokes of that type were played in the concentration camps' makeshift laboratories. Hitler—what is left to say? His SS doctors performed atrocities unmatched since the Middle Ages, and perhaps not even then; they even tried to cross human and animal. It was less workable then, as it may be less unthinkable now. Such a legacy.

"I lost my family in the war, in the camps. 'Lost.' What a word; as if misplaced. They died, were killed. And also neighbors. And also those I never knew. The family was the first to be shattered. A brother spared, a sister killed. A mother sent here, a father there. It came down finally to a terrible individuality. An awesome aloneness with fate. Why do I sit here? I can't tell you. So. Your America, enthroning the family. Father and Mother and one older son and one younger daughter. Easter parade and white gloves. New Buicks. Postwar, prereality. I concentrated my work here, in this ideal family arena, because I was tired of horror, and because it was where America stockpiled its hope for the future, and it was too good to be true."

"You must have . . . loathed what became of science in Germany."

"I wanted nothing to do with this drive toward the impossible, these speculations. The Frankenstein myth. He, too, was German. But it is not just Germans, not simply the convenient excuse of a Hitler. That is why I tell you: If they want Jane Doe, they will take her. They always have."

"No," he said, and left the table.

Neumeier stayed seated. "I got up early, to feed the birds. They depend upon it during a deep-snow winter like this. There were fresh footprints outside. One person. A man. I can live a whole winter through here, and never see another human footprint, like Robinson Crusoe."

"Mine. I got wood last night."

Her grizzled head shook. "You wear hunting boots, like a good Minnesota boy. This was—a shoe. A city man's shoe. Not right for this terrain, but following, as a good bloodhound will. . . ."

"How would anyone know?"

"You drive a car; you have a face. You are, perhaps, as

predictable as your Jane is unpredictable. You are an infant at defying the state. Perhaps they will not harm her—''

"Taking her away would be harmful. They can't just walk in here and grab her!''

"You know they can. You ran.''

"God.'' Kevin stood in the archway facing the bed, although he wasn't seeing Jane asleep in it. "If I could just . . . break through with her. If she knew who she was, what she was, she'd be less easily manipulated . . . by anyone.''

"Or more.'' Neumeier got up. A bit later he heard a thump and whirled to face the room. The door was still shut, but Neumeier stood in the middle of the cabin, a sleeping bag flung at her feet. "Take this; you can hide the van in the woods until dark, if you cover your traces. It will be cold, but I don't think it'll be safe to wait. The man outside obviously has gone to get reinforcements.''

"How many people do you need to deal with one man and a woman who doesn't even know her own name and an old sociology professor?'' he burst out, angry that this remote shelter was so easily violated.

Neumeier smiled. "I hope they bring several. I shall enjoy misleading them.''

"They won't . . . hurt you?''

"This is America, Dr. Blake.'' Her voice was strong and ironic. "Surely it has not come to that.''

Chapter Forty-five

The woods were silent, white and deep. Kevin waited in the parked van all that long, idle day, checking his watch more than was necessary. Behind him, Jane slept in the down bag Neumeier had given him. They were only twenty miles from the cabin; Kevin couldn't risk driving farther, for fear he'd run out of gas. That's why the van was cold and silent. His feet and fingers were numb, but at least the damn fan wasn't blowing his thoughts away.

He glanced around. A light wind sifted through the snow-drifts, subtly altering the landscape. He'd eradicated their tire tracks with a fallen branch. Shades of Grizzly Adams.

Kevin's gloved palms hit the steering wheel in unison, a gesture that both stimulated his sluggish circulation and expressed his rising impatience. This wasn't his scene, none of it. Neumeier's words rang through his mind in a confusing jangle, lit by alternating flashes of disbelief and insight. And someone had found them here; followed them here. How had the trackers known where he might go—or in what vehicle? Kandy? Not Kandy. . . . Yet Neumeier had warned him that nothing held when the state started leaning on the pressure points of a society. And she should know.

He glanced over his shoulder again—the reassuring orangish lump was Jane, her coat across the sleeping bag; beside her lay their cases, his equipment, which was probably too frozen to work even if he did get them somewhere warm again. He wished he had a weapon. A long-barreled rifle, like in his dream, only no tranquilizer darts need apply now, just good, basic survivalist ammunition.

His watch read four forty-five P.M. He figured they could start out at five, as it got dusky. The woods were quiet, cold and stark. It'd be nice to hibernate here until spring. He bit his lip as he regarded Jane again. Neumeier was right; she slept an awful lot. How long had that been going on? Kevin spun out of the driver's seat to bend over her. Jane had been abnormally withdrawn today, as if the cold lulled her into some mentally quiescent state. Yeah, sure. In some circles it was called freezing to death.

"Jane, wake up! Time to get going." Her cheek was cool, but not clinically so. She stirred reluctantly in her pile of down and fur.

"Kevin? I was dreaming, I think."

"Dreams? Now? When you never had even one to report in session? What timing." His joke didn't lighten her sober mood.

"It wasn't really a dream—it was . . . like I was somewhere else. Again. Like I'm getting smaller inside myself. You seem—farther away."

He dredged her up from the seductive warmth as if wrenching her away from a dangerous drug, and braced her against the cold metal ribs of the truck belly.

"I'm not farther away; I'm right here. And dreams are . . . dreams are only in your head." Only.

"You sound angry." She was puzzling it out, as she had said, from a distance, able to dissect his emotions without fearing or echoing them.

"I am angry. They're trying to take you away—from me, from yourself even. Don't you understand?" She nodded slowly, tilting her face to regard him, petlike. God, he hated seeing her act like some docile drone—imagine what the headshrinkers in Virginia could do with that! "I won't let that happen," he promised her, promised himself, defying the experience of Rosa Neumeier.

Jane nodded slowly, and smiled with the sad wisdom he

had seen on Neumeier's face. She didn't quite believe him, either.

"Dammit, I won't," he swore passionately, his rash and desperate kiss sealing the vow on her lips. Her mouth was a warm oasis in the icy desert of cold that anesthetized them; the automatic curl of her fingers into his sleeves a confirmation of the power of human emotions. "I won't let them take you," he repeated, installing her in the van's passenger seat. He fastened her seat belt, then buckled on his.

A black cutwork of trees stood silhouetted against the cloud-swept albino sky. Near the horizon, deep rose seeped in a spreading blush where the pink eye of the sun burned obscurely. Kevin turned the starter, nursing the van's initial coughs into ignition with physicianly intensity. He backed the van through the underbrush, onto Highway 61. The oozing bloodbath of the sunset glowed faintly through the clouds on Jane's side of the van, backlighting her profile. It looked like a scene van owners painted on their windows to remind themselves and the world of the natural glories they were bound for.

Kevin was bound south again, back to civilization. No glory there, but maybe safety in numbers. Darkness was overtaking them fast. He turned on the radio, hungry more for the meager beacon of its lighted dial than its static-scratched patter and song.

"What do we do now?" Jane asked.

"Find another place to hide. I want to work on your memory some more. Neumeier hinted I shouldn't bother, but if you knew your own history, you'd be better able to defend yourself."

"You sound as if you think I may have to deal with them alone."

"You may. As Neumeier said, when it comes down to it, we are all alone."

"That doesn't make sense. 'We' are alone. It's a contradiction."

"You're right." He smiled but kept his eyes on the dim road, toying with the low beams. Yet why run with signals when blindness is the best disguise?

No cars passed them, although the tracks of four-wheel-drive vehicles marked the unplowed paths leading from the highway. Hermits on Jeeps.

It had started snowing again, for when he finally pulled on the headlights, the flakes churned in front of them. It felt like they were driving into one of those winter paperweight worlds where everything is miniaturized. He began to understand Jane's plaint that she felt far away. He felt it, too.

They passed what he thought was the turnoff for Neumeier's cabin. Then the ski resort of Lutsen sped by, its cliff-hanging lodge's lights cheerful in the distance. He checked the gas gauge. Plenty to take them to Duluth.

Kevin glanced at Jane and caught her looking his way. Their smiles met in the middle. There wasn't much to say over the wheeze of the heater fan, over the hum of the highway under their tires. Kevin felt better. He thought they might make it, whatever it was.

A car trailed them now, but people did travel from one warm island to another, even in the dead of winter. Its headlights swelled in his rearview mirror, momentarily blinding, then vanished. Kevin looked down on a dark cartop accelerating past, the taillights twinkling back into the lane ahead.

His boot tapped the van floor, sending a tingle up his ankle and reminding him how cold it was; the radio had boasted a temperature of five below a few miles back. Like every pass-happy driver Kevin had ever seen, the one ahead had settled into the same speed as the vehicle it had passed, forcing him to ease up on the gas. Goddamn Sunday driver. The road narrowed here, curving along the ghostly coast of Lake Superior. His headlights illuminated a "No Passing" sign; in snowless seasons, Kevin would bet, a double yellow line kept scenery gawkers from nudging bumpers. Now he was stuck behind some guy who must think he was in a funeral procession.

Kevin checked the side mirror again; headlights behind, too. Truckers called the spot between two vehicles the rocking chair, an easy place to cruise; Kevin was not in a rocking mood. He studied the road, alert for any straight stretch that would allow him to gun the van ahead.

In a minute he saw his chance, but as he accelerated, the headlights behind swung wide. Apparently the driver had also had the same bright idea. Kevin floored the gas pedal and moved into the passing lane; the car behind him shot recklessly abreast, forcing Kevin back into his lane. Ahead, the first car slowed even more. Rocking chair? He was in the mousehole. He slowed, hoping the car alongside would rocket past. Instead, it dawdled with him. They were all going forty miles an hour now, locked in synchronization. To the right, the rocky roadside loomed, too high to navigate. To the left was the guardian car and a sharp drop to the frozen lake. Ahead was the other car.

Kevin tore off his gloves and flexed bare hands around the wheel. Beside him, Jane sat up straighter—silently questioning.

"Hang on," he told her. "I think we're in trouble."

With each tenth of a mile the odometer ate, he became more aware of how neatly they'd been bagged. There was nowhere to go, nothing to do but stop, or try to drive right over them, or—he saw a valley in the rocks, a break in the woods coming up. Maybe a road, maybe just an old logging path or deer crossing. He wrenched the wheel right, swinging suddenly wide and heading the van into the ambiguous dark as he came abreast of it.

The car on his left overreacted; he saw it lurch wildly across the road, into the trees. Brakes squealed annoyance behind them. He and Jane were plunged from level, predictable road to a surface that bumped and ground its way under a low, dark gantlet of whipping branches. The steering wheel veered sharply, arbitrary as a ouija board. Tree trunks bigger than Kevin's thigh expanded and shrank as they passed, the van caroming off with hollow thuds. None were big enough to stop the van until the path ended, ringing them with tall, impassable pines.

Kevin pumped the brakes. Jane didn't scream; his consciousness gratefully recorded that. Around the windows, the woods tipped and tilted, tree trunks growing diagonally before reassuming normal verticality. Kevin turned off the engine and told Jane to wait for him. He cracked the van's double back doors, hoping to see empty woods. The dark car once ahead of him was now behind him—lights on, motor idling raucously in the snow-wrapped stillness.

He slammed the doors shut as he jumped into calf-high snow. "Car trouble?" he asked the two figures who stood guard behind the dazzling screen of their high beams.

"You should know." He couldn't tell which figure spoke. "Ran Anderson and DeVane right off the road."

"Should I check on them?" the other man asked the speaker.

"Nah, we've got to button things down here first; they either made it or they didn't."

"So, what do you want?" Kevin walked forward, showing empty hands.

"What we came for. We're authorized. You'd save yourself a whole lot of trouble if you'd cooperate, Dr. Blake. Turn your patient over. She's, uh, dangerous. We need to take her for her own good."

"You don't even know why your superiors want her," he accused bitterly. "Whether it's for good or ill or—"

"It's for national security." The voice was harsh, citing a phrase it lived by. "It's not always for us to know the specifics. Come on, you're a civilian. You've been listed as misguided. So far, your actions come under the heading of 'meaning well.' Don't blow that status, Doc. I don't have to tell you what comes when you've lost your presumed innocence. Just back off here. Look, we're not even armed."

The figures advanced in tandem, arms extended, waddling through the drifts like oversized penguins. They didn't even seem human. For a dread second, it ran through his mind: Lies, all lies. They could be Russians or devils or even aliens. . . . No, no demons, just regular working spies. Government muscle men. The light of their own high beams finally revealed them. Men dressed like deer hunters—billed caps with earflaps, down jackets, lace-up boots. The getup suddenly seemed more alien than horns and cloven hooves or green slime. Kevin backed away, plainly, purely panicked. You can never stop them, Rosa Neumeier had said, so sadly, so surely.

His hands were spread, like theirs, only not as proof of benign intention, but symbolizing a helplessness he'd never felt before, as if the world were a giant clock face and he was a mite on the surface of it, waiting for the merciless minute hand to sweep inevitably by. Life wasn't like that; life was good grades and easy answers and being on top of things and suffering from minor malaises and celebrating repeatable triumphs. Life had also been losing Julie, he remembered, dragging that unpleasant thought from the lumber room of his memory. And if Julie, why not Jane?

"Look. I'm a doctor. A psychiatrist. I only want to protect my patient. Taking her like this—taking her at all—you could damage her irrevocably. Doesn't that mean anything to you?"

The men exchanged glances. They were close now, only feet away. "You can register your protest with the proper agencies, Dr. Blake. Go through channels, like the rest of us."

"Jane doesn't have time for channels. You can't take her. I won't—"

They jumped him in concert, as silent and lethal as matched Dobermans. They'd practiced it, he knew, even as he struggled. The clumsy winterwear drowned him in his own bulk. He was no martial arts expert, had never had to fight for anything more vital than a parking spot. He didn't know how to stop them. The humiliation turned sour in his stomach and started to seep back up; Kevin thrashed. If he couldn't hit them, hurt them, fell them with a well-placed judo chop, he could be damn hard to hold.

Their heavy panting sounded feral in the dark, silent woods. Hot breath puffed on his face and blows thudded on his torso and arms, doing little damage. He thought of kids bundled to their eyes, grappling in the snow, bouncing off each other's snowsuits . . . He tripped or was tripped, felled like a living log to the snow-muffled earth. His face was held in chill, feathery snow, pressed down until he inhaled fire through his nose and mouth, his body heat melting a small breathing space in the snow. Slow smothering, like Kellehay's pillow. Poetic justice, in some dim way, in the way of Rosa Neumeier's world. Jane. Would Jane understand why he had left her, why he couldn't, couldn't . . . move, breathe, stop it—

His head was jerked dizzyingly backward. A black hole of sky pierced by stars stared back at him. His lungs worked bellowslike, fanning air in short, unsatisfying gasps.

"Careful. We don't want to waste him—"

"What about Anderson and DeVane? The sucker ran them off the road—"

"Accident. They were doing their job and he rabbited. He's a civilian." The last sentence dripped such casual contempt that Kevin snapped fully conscious.

A civilian, yes, and even civilians can go down fighting. He pushed himself up and lurched into their anonymous knees. A boot kicked his chin as its owner fell backward. Kevin lunged after, but someone hauled him around from behind and threw him backward, backward against . . . a giant metal bell that rang his skull with one dissonant chord before he realized that the night had exploded in his head.

She is two. One is light, drawn thin as molten glass upon a white-hot rod. The other is heavy, burdened, weighed down by bone and blood. It is this cumbersome, semi-conscious self that a hidden small impulse animates, disobeying two conflicting calls. Go. Stay. She is not quite doing either, but a bit of both.

The heavy metal door slides slowly, quietly because this leaden body has to push so hard. Some nagging fear propels her into the white void, which melts to nothing under her bulk. She stands, wades thigh-deep into the white mist, which slows her like curdled clouds. Cold touches an icy finger to her neck, sealing her more tightly into this body that it is increasingly hard to linger within. She shivers, rests her gloved hand on the cold dark metal wall beside her. Van. And Kevin said, before she drifted into sleep again, Kevin said . . . She rounds the rear of the van. . . . Kevin said stay put.

Lights! Glaring, beaming, blinding lights. Her arm levitates to shield her eyes, part reflex, part gesture from a melodrama. "Melodrama. A sentimental dramatic presentation characterized by heavy use of suspense and sensational episodes, popular in the late nineteenth century." A scene of sensational melodrama is suspended before her. Snow, gouged by black gouts of deep shadow, marked by movements long past. Two figures, silhouetted by the blazing lights behind them, bulky and motionless.

Another bulk, even more motionless, at the back of the van. Her heart, pounding so hard to animate this body against the inborn pull that surges along her innermost particles, stops. Stops. Stops. Stops.

She kneels. Touches the jacket's shiny shell. A silken rasp of fabric on fabric. Nothing else. Cold is deeper near the ground. It rises on an icy exhalation. She remembers . . . No. She remembers nothing here. Her hand, ungloved somehow, rests on the cold, furred head. Lost Zyunsinth, lost, lost, lost. Lost Jane, lost Kevin . . . No. She knows no names now, remembers nothing worth forgetting. She rises, facing them.

They stand on two legs, and shift from side to side. They have been silent, but one makes a noise that indicates it is about to speak. An arm extends, separating from the bloated body, inelegantly stretching toward her. The light clearly shows its shape: a forked, clumsy claw with only one digit separating it from the mass. It gestures toward her, then back toward itself.

"Come on, miss. We'll take you back to the Cities. You've got some questions to answer."

Words. Words have not registered on her consciousness since she fell asleep and felt the call slip into her unguarded brain. Back. Answers. She is two. One here, one called away. One dazed, one amok with rising rage. One. She is one. She is "I," racing strong from a hidden center of her being.

"Come along, then," advancing toward her. "He'll be all right."

"I" joins another elemental urge seething to the surface of her emotions. Defend/avenge. Not back, not ever back. Must go back, must not be stopped . . . She is two, and two strike out, strike back as one. The car lurking behind the headlights first, black beast, its circuits sizzling to the leap of some ectoplasmic spark she lights between her mind and its metal body. Light and heat, heavy and dark; they wed, explode. Lights shatter out; fire fans behind. The figures turn, freeze, then turn again, toward her. They move, heavy through the featherweight snow, two-digited hands pinching repeatedly like crab claws. Coming again, to take her, as they always do. To take her away as he was taken away.

No. This time her entire being shouts it. The forces within her invisibly lash out, striking the two dark figures like an irresistible wind. They blow away, backward, into the flaming car, pressed against it like paper dolls, their edges crinkling and curling, amorphous hands shrinking. Cries go up in smoke against the inky sky. She sees no stars, and turns, walking past the still dark form in the snow, past the van's marooned bulk, out into the woods. She is headed due south, heeding no other call but one, and she has no name.

335

Chapter Forty-six

Once when Kevin was about seven, his parents had enrolled him in the baby Boy Scouts—or whatever the hell it was—and the whole troop went to Loring Park in December and camped out in the snow.

He'd never forget the smell. A campfire in the snow; chili scorching in the big cast-iron fry pan the leader had lugged along; wet wool socks adding an undefinable odor as they singed around the flames, and a circle of shivering boys resting bare blue feet on heavy winter gloves waiting for their socks to dry.

Singed wool and hamburger, fire in the snow, an unrelieved cold wrapped around every limb like an Ace bandage. Kevin's senses went fishing for reality, his throbbing brain tried to place himself. Not Loring Park . . . He lifted his head, his nerves screeching disagreement.

The van at his rear still seemed to reverberate with the blow from his head; car lights blazed into his eyes ahead. A smell, god-awful. Like fried metal and, and—Kevin eased himself up, using the van for a brace.

The black car was blacker yet, and cast a distorted, burned shadow on the snow. So did the two shriveled figures beside it. One man lay half across the burnt fender, his charred hand curled into the agape engine compartment. The other draped the snow more formally but just as fatally: flat on his back, burned—as the papers so delicately phrase it—"beyond recognition."

Kevin lunged through the snow, around the side of the van. He saw the deep telltale holes—too small for his feet, too close together for his stride. The snow around the imprints was feathered where her long fur coat had disturbed it.

He jerked the van door open on emptiness. The sleeping bag and cases were there, but Jane, of course, had not stayed put. When had she come out? After he had been knocked unconscious? Had the men seen her and, thinking her only one lone woman, turned to precede her to their car? He winced to imagine what Jane had thought, and done, when she saw Kevin downed like that, looking dead probably.

Her defenses had flared automatically, as they had on the Crow Wing bluff, without thought, without reason. First the car and its mechanisms, then the men, blown back, blown away to burn. Kevin was moving, he didn't know for how long, acting as he thought. Self-defense again. Justifiable. Naturally, there was no flashlight in Kandy's tool kit. Kevin surged past the dead men to the rear of their savaged car. The trunk, sprung open, had been generously equipped. His hand closed cautiously around the blackened flashlight shaft. Still warm, but it worked, so he lumbered back to the van, ignoring the headache that sponsored a light show in his skull. Where? And why leave? The men were—dead, but he was only knocked out. Damn. They had to get out of here, away from—the scene of the crime. Away.

Her tracks led into the striplings edging the pines. He followed, head down, pursuing with bullish determination, no intelligence. Lost, both lost. Julie and Jane. No, Kevin and Jane. Lost in the woods . . . The pine branches dumped snow down his collar as he brushed by. He kept plodding on.

"Jane," he called, softly at first; struck by the absurdity of that, he yelled it. "Jane!" The forest took her name and kept it, as the night had absorbed her form into itself. He was lurching through virgin snow now, untracked except for the delicate braille of bird feet etched on the very surface. The flashlight lit an empty circle; he turned it on his trail and saw the clumsy sinkholes he had made, wiping out Jane's prints.

Backtracking, then. "Jane. It's all right. You can come out."

No answer but the bellows of his own labored breathing. He stopped, studied the snow. There, a branching-off he had missed, and fresh steps along it. He followed, head down, wind rubbing his face raw and putting tears in his lashes; cold turning tears to frost, and air to a needle of dry ice that plunged deep into his frontal sinuses. Snow-blind, he was lost in the white monotonous sweep of it. Time to give up, go back, face whatever was left to face.

He staggered into a pine, grabbing a sweeping bough as an unsteady support, and moved forward, not backward, though he no longer knew why. He started to fall, and spread his arms wide, perhaps to protest his innocence, maybe to make just one last snow angel, moving, moving his arms as he had when a boy, carving a shape into the night snow, laughing at the stars. His arms betrayed him and reached out reflexively to break his fall. They closed on something solid, yet soft; the falling flashlight lit a rich, foxlike expanse of fur.

Kevin lay on his back, snow licking chillingly at his bare wrists and neck. He was hurt, exhausted, relieved, worried, happy, sober, sane. He was himself again. He spread his arms once, high over his head and back down again, before looking up at Jane. It was dark here in the wilderness, but the snow held a soft, ambient glow. He pushed himself up while she watched, watched him with the same careful, distant, emotionless mien of the Jane Doe he'd met months ago.

"Why did you leave the van?" he asked, omitting an accusing "when I told you not to."

Jane looked as if she'd just seen him. "You—weren't there. You didn't come back." *She* had not been hesitant to accuse. "I—I . . . I don't know. I left."

"Obviously." He took her arm and pointed the flashlight ahead. Getting back would be no problem at least; a herd of Abominable Snowmen seemed to have trampled the snow. He let the light linger on his empty indentation. It looked like an angel with wide feathery wings, but not as perfect as he remembered.

"What happened when I didn't come back?" he asked carefully.

"I—don't know."

"How did you get here?"

She stopped and stared at him, the dead, dazed expression thawing into her growing recognition of him, of herself.

"Kevin!" Jane's hands tightened around his, the one holding the flashlight, driving the light down between them. He could hardly make out her features, but the dawning horror in her tone told him that her face must reflect his own emotions—shock, relief and ice-cold fear.

"Kevin, I—I don't remember. I just don't remember . . . anything."

The Reclaiming
January 12

Chapter Forty-seven

Jane leaned against the men's room wall, her furred shoulder obscuring the "you" half of an obscenity scrawled on the cement block wall.

"I'm not supposed to be in here," she ventured.

Kevin smiled faintly. That was Willhelm Hall mentality if he'd ever heard it. At least she remembered something. A gurgle reminded him of business. Ice-cold water dribbled ineffectively from a long-ago-chromed faucet into the sink, washing a white porcelain path through the chaff of his beard.

In the small, scratched mirror, his features wore a Santa Claus's shaving cream whiskers. It would be odd to meet the world bare-faced again, but should make him harder to trace. Jane watched seriously, as if learning a trade.

"This is the hard way to do it, you know." He gestured with the convenience store razor to the can of shaving cream perched on the stingy sink ledge. His face, wiped clean with brown paper towels, looked younger, more innocent, but he avoided his newly naked image, sweeping the beard shavings into the untended wastebasket beside the sink.

"Damn inconvenience," he growled as he jammed the razor and shaving cream into his pockets, displacing his regret at the sacrifice of his beard to something less threatening.

"I'll carry them," Jane offered. "I forgot to bring anything for my legs."

He stared at her, booted to her knees, with two more dead men on her subconscious—maybe four indirectly; the gash in the woods where the second car had crashed remained lifeless as they had turned back on the road and resumed their journey—and she wanted to groom her legs. Her behavior now seemed to veer incongruously between extremes, between the ordinariest triviality and the bizarrest apartness. And he loved the Jane in the middle, his hard luck.

The filling station men's room, such as it was, seemed its normal slovenly self again. It was dark; no one saw him usher Jane out. He hadn't wanted to risk leaving her alone in the van—for her sake, or someone else's. She showed no signs of remembering frying two men and a car; perhaps he should have confronted her. Instead, he'd driven past the grisly scene without comment, Jane safely seated away from it and seeing only a snowy landscape of trees.

Overprotective, he chastised himself as he returned the rest room key, keeping his denuded face buried in his jacket collar. Kevin hoped the sleepy attendant and the convenience store clerk were as forgetful as Jane. Out here it was impossible not to leave some kind of trail, but he doubted the reinforcements' reinforcements would show up right away. They had a couple days, if he could find a hiding place. The wilds had been no answer; maybe he'd try the reverse.

On the road once more, Jane dozed, her chin dipping into the fur at her throat. Asleep again. What had she remembered at first? Sleeping and screaming. The ambulance . . . and before that—sleeping.

"Come on." He shook her shoulder and she blinked awake. "Rise and shine. We're going public."

"Public?" She glanced out at passing streetlights and scattered houses and a growing procession of fast-food restaurants.

"City life. Duluth again. I think we'll stay awhile."

He cruised the main streets, hunting up and down the sharply raked hills. The San Francisco of the snow country, Duluth only boasted a population of 100,000-some, but it was an international port after all, like the city of the Golden Gate, and spawned some of the resultant bustle. Motels lining the city's edge, like hookers, announced their gaudy availability. Kevin needed someplace where no one would think anything of two people holing up for two or three days. Downtown Duluth had its share of transient hotels, but if the sleaze factor didn't deter him, the likelihood of being noticed did; Jane just didn't fit on the cheap side of town—not with her Zyunsinth-swathed shoulders.

He inspected one of the city's tallest buildings, its sides defined by a checkerboard of bright and dark squares, and its top light-crowned with a royal "R." He aimed for it; a wrong turn or two led him away, but finally he was circling his prey on the right one-way street. A dark cavern opened into the belly of the building and Kevin sped the van into the parking ramp feeling like a jubilant Jonah homesick for his whale. At last—peace, isolation, quiet. He had an idea. A wild idea.

The ramp was fairly empty, but he searched out an ill-lit corner to tuck the van into. In the elevator, he pressed "L"; in a minute the doors opened on a scene that smelled "hotel lobby" the way cod smells fish. He stacked the cases under one arm, took Jane's hand and approached the reservation desk. It was after eight P.M., but the dark pattern on the hotel's side promised lots of vacancies.

"We'd like a room. For . . . three nights."

"The, uh, twelfth through the fourteenth, departing on the fifteenth?" A young male room clerk—overofficious and overweight for his age—began scanning the computer screen.

"That's right," said Kevin. "But not just—any—room."

The clerk looked again, sizing them up: Jane weary yet swathed in fur; Kevin looking like any native male in his regulation down jacket.

"Is your . . ." Kevin didn't have to feign a faint embarrassment. "Your bridal suite available?"

"It should be on a Tuesday, sir," the clerk observed primly, canceling whatever data lingered on the computer screen and clicking in a new command.

"We, we were married last Saturday and went to Lutsen

for a few days, but it's hardly like staying at a big hotel. We thought, if you happened to be vacant—"

"Tuesday through Thursday are not big nights for the bridal suite." The clerk smiled mechanically as his eyes, less bored, scanned the screen. "It's available but . . . it's been redecorated recently—including a sunken oversized Jacuzzi. It's one hundred thirty-five dollars a night, sir."

Jane's eyes met Kevin's, intrigued by mention of a word as alien to her as Zyunsinth was to him—a Jacuzzi. To the clerk, it must have read like a married couple's mute price consultation.

Kevin glanced back. "We'll take it."

"Credit card?"

"Cash." Kevin pulled a couple hundred-dollar bills from his pocket. "This do as a deposit until we check out?"

The clerk gave the hundreds a respectful looking over, then whisked them out of sight.

"They make a better wedding present than eight different fondue sets," Kevin said, grinning.

"That's for sure, sir." The clerk was mellow now, happy to have rented a white elephant room out of season, pleased to have a story to tell during the long but otherwise fallow night shift. Typical newlyweds, you know. Very awkward and *very* anxious for the bridal suite. Cash, would you believe? Won't see much of them around the hotel in the next three days. . . .

No, you won't, thought Kevin.

"I'll ring a bellman for your bags—" The clerk saw big tips flowing from the humble pocket that had held the hundred.

"Not much to carry." Kevin hoisted the bags and took the key. He turned away, then looked back. "But you could— send up a bottle of champagne."

The clerk radiated. True to form. Typical. "Of course, sir. It'll be up in a few minutes."

In the elevator, Kevin automatically faced forward, but Jane turned slowly, studying the decor and the glossy photo advertising the Top of the Harbor revolving restaurant. "We'll be using room service a lot," Kevin warned her. "BLTs on toast."

The bridal suite was on the fifteenth floor. Kevin unlocked and swung open the brass-script-emblazoned door on utter darkness except for the faraway glimmer of lights through the windows opposite.

"Home, sweet hospital." He set the cases on carpet so deep they seemed to sink out of sight, and turned to Jane. "Shall we do this right?" Kevin picked her up, a gesture more valiant than wise with the bulky coat. Jane's amazement was overruled by something very like the giggles. There must be a basis to the female hankering to be swept off her feet, Kevin thought, envisioning how a paper on *that* subject would be received academically.

The champagne-bearing bellboy emerged from the elevator just then, a convenient witness to connubial behavior. Kevin smiled and crossed the threshold, aware he had a far more impenetrable mental threshold to cross, and set Jane down gratefully.

Lights flicked on, revealing a slick, pale setting—low, mirrored furniture and ivory satin bedspread, elevated mirrored alcove displaying a sunken king-and-queen-sized Jacuzzi tub.

"Your stereo is controlled from the headboard, sir, as well as the lights. The champagne is complimentary with the good wishes of the hotel," parroted the bellman.

The bellman uncorked the champagne with a flourish, installing the ice bucket and two long-stemmed glasses on an ivory lacquer console. Kevin tipped the guy five bucks, adding to his own in-house legend as buoyant bridegroom, and locked the door promptly behind him.

Jane was wandering the room, which was large, but hardly a suite. She'd dropped her coat on the bed, inadvertently adding to the tinseltown aura, and had climbed the two plush-carpeted steps leading to the enthroned Jacuzzi.

347

Kevin chuckled. "This must be quite a switch from your room at the dorm."

"What does this do?" Her boot toe indicated the Jacuzzi.

"Everything but scramble eggs." Kevin fanned cassettes over the bedspread, and gave the recorder an experimental spin or two. "I bet you only had showers at Willhelm. You can try it out—later, after we're finished working. Well, it's obvious where the bathtub is, but where the hell's the TV? Or the john, for that matter."

Jane, replicated in the angled mirrors, watched in dazed duplicate while Kevin wrenched open console doors until he found the concealed television—apparently newlyweds were thought to be in little need of the news—and discovered that the sliding mirrored doors led to a closet and water closet, respectively.

He checked his watch, then went to the bottle of champagne, elevated it, eyed the label, shrugged and vanished into the bathroom, from where a distinctly bubbly glub-glub wafted out.

Kevin emerged with an empty bottle, shook its last drops into the two untouched glasses and impaled it again in the crushed ice. Jane looked as crushed, in her own inimitable way.

"I've never had champagne, but Glenda says—"

"Kevin says we've work to do; it wasn't a very good year, anyway. Come on." He took her hand and led her off the risers.

Jane regarded the awesome king-sized bed. "We're going to sleep together," she said, something in her voice he didn't want to explore.

"We have already. Twice. Including last night at Neumeier's. But not here. No rest for the wicked, and we have been mucho naughty about letting our work slide. Here, make yourself comfortable." He heaped several pillows against the headboard. "I'm going to order a room service snack, watch the ten o'clock news for signs of bloodhounds on our

348

trail, and then I'm going to hypnotize you and delve to the bottom of that time-lock safe you call a memory until I—we—get an answer to who and what and why. Now, take your boots off and settle down."

Jane leaned forward to wrestle them off while Kevin threw himself in the suede barrel chair across the room and put on the empty tape he had erased of incriminating sessions.

"I think I know who Jane is," she volunteered into the long silence.

When he looked up, she was still studying the room, hands clasped behind her head, elbows askew, her eyes pensive.

"Jane is," she declared in an authoritatively discouraged drawl, "a girl who is spending the world's safest, soberest and most boring honeymoon."

Chapter Forty-eight

"There's a block. Something is holding even the hypnosis back."

"I'm trying. . . ."

"Are you? Or has it all become some game? I can't blame you. Parents you don't recognize here one week, gone the next; mad scientists playing psychic softball with clock radios; treks across half the state with a flaky shrink . . . But there's got to be a way to crack that Great Wall of China in your head. Jane, I can't apply too much pressure—it's like putting an egg in a vise—but I've got to solve something, or you'll forever be a pawn to whoever wants to use you."

"What about—your wizard?"

Kevin lowered himself desultorily on the bed. "Ill-advised. Oh, Neumeier was as sharp as always, and threw some fascinating speculation into the pot. I understand her better, but not you, which wasn't the idea." He tapped the small tape recorder. "I wonder, though, why her first question was about the UFO? Neumeier's brilliant, but unorthodox. What the hell difference would it make if the Volkers did indeed visit an alien vessel; you're not their daughter."

"I did look—exactly—like her. Mrs. Volker made me look at photographs once." Jane sounded tentative; she didn't want to be dragged back to the Volkers, but was eager to help Kevin.

He sat up. "You did, didn't you? A *perfect* match. Except for those teeth—and her bones being found in Montana. What was Neumeier getting at? She always favored the Socratic method." Jane looked blank. "Teaching by asking questions, rather than telling outright. Neumeier's kind of like you—a mystery."

Kevin rewound the tape they'd just made and replayed it.

"Sleeping," intoned the hypnotized Jane. "So long. And then the ambulance screaming, for so long. Moving fast. Through the night, past the stars. I feel . . . isolated, suspended, and they are hanging over me, with bottles and tubes and needles. Please don't, I think, only I can't say it. And they do. They always do."

He switched it off. "You see. I'm tapping trauma all right, but it's the trauma we already know about." Kevin glanced up. Tears ran down Jane's face, though her expression was calm. "Why are you crying?"

"It must be terrible, to have to do or be what others say. That's what you kept asking me—what does Jane want? I didn't understand, but I do now, when I hear . . . her speak like that."

"You feel you're . . . not . . . her?"

"Oh, I'm far away from her now. Far away. I wish you didn't have to find her in me, and talk to her—"

"I do," he interrupted harshly, because he wished so, too.

350

"It's the only way I know. Maybe the goddamn mind battalion would do more for you after all. . . ."

"No!" She sat up against her piled pillows. "Play more; I might hear something that'll help."

He depressed the button disgustedly. It was almost two A.M.; they were both exhausted, and so were the options. Hypnosis hadn't worked before, why should it now? Kevin heard Jane's recorded voice relive recent history; he watched her absorb it, her expression sad and curious at the same time. She didn't know what spooks in Virginia were, but she was beginning to realize that her free will was endangered, to realize what free will was. At least he had taught her that much: to ask, What does Jane want?

"Wait!" Kevin's mind went from at ease to full alert. "You didn't say that tonight. . . ." He replayed a segment. "Just floating in this white space. Bed. Hospital. Killed. Matusek . . . I don't remember anything before the ambulance. Nothing. It's empty, vacant, nothing to see but night—"

He jabbed it off. "That wasn't on this tape, that Matusek stuff. I erased it. We never went into that tonight."

Jane recoiled. She remembered the sessions where she'd relived Kellehay's attack on her, and his death, but she'd never heard herself say it. He reached out to clasp her hand across the bed's awesome width; even newlyweds didn't need that much room.

"It's okay. Just your own voice. Except it *shouldn't* be. . . ." Kevin weighed the small recorder in his hand. "*Crosstalk.* Sure! Sometimes you erase something, but a ghost of it survives. This is the cassette I recorded that old session on, ergo . . ." He looked into her serious dark eyes, letting his widen with unfocused, improvised speculation.

"Jane, *you* could be—crosstalk. You could be a, a human tape recorder. The way you speed-read, remember everything, your phenomenal geographical orientation . . . Even Zyunsinth could be a fragment surviving from another 'recording session,' and so could 'sklivent ysrossni.' Both rem-

351

nants of things that made an indelible emotional imprint—you are biological, after all, and it's hard to 'erase' emotions. Maybe 'Kevin' will show up someday for some poor idiot who's trying to make sense out of you. . . . What am I saying? It's nuts!"

He sprang up from the bed, paced the room. "Forget it. Neumeier's speculations—biological computers and test-tube babies—had me going, that's all. It's too ridiculous."

" 'When you have eliminated all which is impossible, then whatever remains, however improbable, must be the truth,' " said Jane.

Kevin wheeled, staring. Jane sat oddly upright, having delivered herself impassively of this aphorism of Conan Doyle's via Sherlock Holmes via Rosa Neumeier. "How do you know that?"

"Your wizard said it."

"But you were asleep."

"I was almost asleep. Everything seems to come through, as if I can't *not* hear and know things."

"Then you heard Neumeier on psychokinesis and renegade subatomic particles and test-tube babies and the melding of brain and computer?"

She nodded and yawned. He put a knee to the bed, but it turned to jelly; he'd forgotten it was a waterbed. He waded across it on his elbows until he was close enough to shake Jane alert.

"No time for sleeping. If you heard all that . . . let's play free association of harebrained ideas, starting with the Neumeier premise; what if, in 1960, the Volkers really saw, and were assumed, 'into the belly of the Leviathan from the sky'?

Kevin braced himself against the headboard with a couple pillows borrowed from Jane's pile, his gesture—or her intention—pulling her head to his shoulder.

"Stay awake," he admonished, starting to talk it through. "It was twenty-five years ago. The Volkers were childless. They were examined, maybe not with a needle in the navel,

352

but say these were aliens with a wanderlust but unadaptable to our atmosphere. Suppose they—for the hell of it, scientific curiosity or some other reason, just as our own research is doing now—implanted a fertilized egg in Mrs. Volker. An egg that became—Lynn. The supernatural agency that overcomes infertility, just like in the Bible.

"Only—Jane, are you listening?" Her head nodded against his chest, but he shook her gently until she answered.

"I can't help but hear; your voice is echoing around and around under my ear."

"Then put your head back where it belongs." But she didn't move, and he didn't really need a listener.

"Only . . . and this is the wild part. They kept a duplicate, a clone, of the same fertilized cell. That's why they needed the Volkers, for genetic material. You don't remember an earlier life, because you *had none*. You were there—up there. . . ."

Jane's head elevated on cue toward the ceiling. Kevin looked up, too, startled to see himself and Jane reclining in a bronze-tint mirror. The accoutrements of the suite were making themselves felt one disconcerting stage after another.

"You were up there, in the sky with diamonds. That's the stars you talked about . . . and going fast and endless night. You said it all in your very first session. It wasn't the night sky over Crow Wing, or an eighty-mile-an-hour ambulance ride. That was *outer space*! You're an orphan of the whole fucking universe. You were grown, somehow, fed nourishment and enough information picked out of the airways to pass for a native and brought back! To breathe the air, look like us, walk among us, talk among us—and record us. Something in you, your cells, your brain, has been wired for picture and sound.

"That makes you a, a living probe, like those machines we send to Mars that just lie there and record data and transmit it back. Only . . . there are a lot of onlys . . . only they'll have to retrieve you. As they have before! That's why

Zyunsinth! Furry hominids from someplace else, someplace remarkably like earth. And you imprinted on them, as you have on me. You're only human, after all.

"But they can't have many like you. Even for them, it must be difficult, and their . . . probes . . . may be recognized as aliens and destroyed. There must be more, of other species, to go to different environments. Wouldn't we do the same, if we could? Maybe we're even close.

"And that's it. There's no past, no parents to find. Just . . . Jane. Incredible Jane, whom I tried to disguise among a bunch of coeds! That's why no clothes, no clues, no marks. You hadn't passed through anything resembling normal life. And they can erase any memory of your life with them; it can't have been . . . real . . . in any sense of the word. More of an existence, because to them you're simply a tool, a living tool."

He glanced down at Jane; he could see her better by looking in the overhead mirror, but his senses were too leaden to make the effort to look up. His mind was numbed by concepts that were too sweeping. Jane, he saw, was actually sleeping. Kevin slid lower on the pillows with her. Another fully dressed night again, but they needed sleep; for once, he thought he deserved it. Incredible. A human probe. He marshaled all the pieces of the puzzle he'd put together in the past few minutes, but fatigue blurred their edges. He hoped he'd remember it all in the morning, though it was hard to forget a supposition that had you bloody in love with a . . . an unreal woman.

But a certain peace drifted over him. He rubbed his chin against Jane's forehead in token of a good night; the annoying stubble was growing already. If he'd only waited, he might have saved his beard; come up with his brilliant diagnosis, explained it all to the government and—this last thought he must recall first thing when he woke. He must make himself do that. It was vital.

If Jane really was what he thought she was, the creeps in

Washington would be even more eager to get hold of her. She'd been innocent of her own secret, but now—thanks to the remorseless Blake investigation—she was a sitting duck. A sitting probe, waiting to be found and taken apart. By one faction or another. He just happened to have gotten there first.

Chapter Forty-nine

Kevin awoke, intending to stare at the ceiling while he recollected the theories that had illuminated the night before.

The smoky pink mirror was too literally reflective: it showed two scruffy people in rumpled blue jeans, the man with a five-o'clock-in-the-morning shadow you could see from ten feet away; the woman with wide-open, waiting eyes set in faintly purple circles he could see by turning his head to the neighboring pillow.

"You were too sleepy to even hear what I said last night," he noted.

Jane nodded. "It comes on. I feel . . . shuttered in. So sleepy. But I heard parts of what you were saying."

Kevin forced himself to roll off the bed, leaving Jane rocking gently on its rolling satin surface. "What *was* I saying? Lots of crazy things. But I think I'm right. Did you—get—it all?"

Jane sat up, her head braced in her palms, elbows on her knees, hair veiling her face. He'd never seen her look so human, maybe because he'd never seen her uncanny poise shaken.

"You said . . . you said I'm not real, not human. You said I'm a freak, a machine sent by . . . people, things . . . from

355

someplace in space. I know what that means. I know how insane and scary that idea would be to everyone. It scares me.''

"You are *very* human." He pried her hands from her cheeks. The hair still shadowed her eyes, but he brushed it back so he could see her clearly, so she could see him even more clearly. "Jane. You belong here. You're a daughter of earth.''

"Of the Volkers."

"Of their bodies, certainly. But in any real sense . . . You're a prototype human, born without parents. A pattern for the future, perhaps. I promised Mrs. Volker that if I found you were truly her daughter, I'd bring you back. Would you rather claim ordinariness—or the improbable? If you are what I think you are, you belong to no one but yourself.''

"And . . . the ones who sent me."

He shook his head. "They possessed you, like the CIA would possess you if it could. They can control you, affect you, use you—but they don't own you.''

"You said . . . I was a biological recorder, that I could be erased. That I had seen planets other than earth, and had those memories drained and taken. If they control my past, they own me.''

"No. *You* own your future. You know what you are now. You know that your 'powers' are some automatic defensive reflex, imprinted on your nervous system. That's why Jane went far away when Kellehay attacked. Your perimeter defenses took over. As you said once, you never had a name before. Maybe you were never sent to your home planet; you never had an opportunity for instant acceptance, for building a personality of your own creation.''

"Or yours."

He laughed and shook her wrists lightly. "Yours, believe me. I've treated cult freaks more malleable than you. No, Jane is Jane, made out of her needs. Why do you think you remembered Zyunsinth? Whoever or whatever or wherever they are, they were companionable, creatures who touched the humanity in you at a level even your expert outer space programmers couldn't erase. That was their first mistake; the second was sending you to earth, where you could touch what was normal to your human heritage."

"But I'm not normal! That's why we're running, why you left your nice place in Minneapolis. And if I've gained anything, I can be made to forget it. I don't know why I left the van in the woods, when you found me. I don't know why I left you. If it's so easy to forget walking a few hundred feet, why shouldn't I forget all the miles I've walked here, the people I've known? Why shouldn't I forget myself? It only exists here."

He brushed back her hair more for the excuse of a touch than necessity, and smiled. "So you liked my place. Or did you like what happened there, what could have happened there? I know you've done your homework, Jane, so you don't have to pretend you don't know what I mean, although it'd be only human to try. . . ."

She smiled reluctantly under his gentle teasing, her cheek growing pinker after each stroke of his fingers, as if he were a painter deepening the blush upon a portrait. Blushing, Jane blushing because her amplified steel-trap mind knew everything written about human sexual attraction and because her untried human emotions knew nothing about acting on it.

Kevin sat beside her, knowing the tension she was feeling, the tightness in the throat, the breath held captive in the chest, slow fire licking at her extremities as the blood rushed to other, more directly engaged areas. It was all so elementary, so physical—and so psychologically mysterious.

His hand slid down her cheek, down her throat to the swell of her clavicle, where her breath fluttered like a thready pulse under his fingers. Those fingers plucked at the first button on her blouse, the ivory one bought so many lifetimes ago on the say-so of an indifferent saleswoman, and then the second and third, but his eyes were on hers.

"You wanted me to tell you that I loved you once, and so I did. And so I do. But now I have something even more important to tell you." It was hard to hold her attention; her eyelids were pendant with desire, her pupils swollen with the narcolepsy of his seduction.

"This is important. Even more important than what you're feeling now. I'm not afraid of you, Jane. I know what you are now and that's easier than a lot of the things I was afraid you were. I'm not afraid to touch you or love you—or even to lose you, anymore, because I trust what you are. I don't think I can even help you anymore. There was a time, not long ago, when I worried that my personal involvement was affecting my professional relationship with you. There is no professional relationship. Dr. Blake is gone, and only the lover is left. I don't know if you need a lover now, but I do. I do so much."

He let his face go where it was pulled, toward hers, then edged his profile under the wing of her hair, his lips tasting the soft, secret shaded skin of her neck and ear. He found the bra's front clasp and released it, his fingers insinuating under the inflexible semicircle of wire, where they found a fuller breast than he'd expected. Her breathing panted softly by his ear as he shut his eyes and inhaled the unabetted scent of her body heat, taking the pulse of her throbbing carotid artery with his lips, strumming his fingertips across the curving struts of her ribs, pressing the heat of his palm against the breast as soft and cool as sherbet . . .

"Kevin . . ." Her breath exploded in an almost orgasmic gasp. No trace of doctor and patient remained; hardly any remnant of Kevin and Jane. It was man and woman, as the species had been divinely gifted to settle their differences. He no longer accused himself, named himself initiator or exploiter, only, as he had said, lover. He pulled her down on the bed with him, merging with the mouth that had named him, pulling her close to feel her, absorb her, pushing her away to touch her, tease himself. After a long while, they momentarily ran out of urgency and energy and innovation. He rolled away, propped his head on his elbow to look at her.

"Kevin . . . I, I love you." Jane smiled happily, dreamily. Then her face sobered. "But . . . you scratch."

Nonplussed, Kevin stared at her. Jane was awash in a sexual blush from her clavicle to her cheekbones, but her lips wore the pink aurora of a whisker burn.

He rubbed an apologetic palm over his alien beard stubble, feeling it rasp. "Damn inconvenience. Time to shave." He started up as her hands clenched into his shirt.

"No."

Kevin let her weigh him back down for a careful kiss, then eluded her with a twist. "Yes. That's how we do things on your home planet. You're going to have to learn the customs."

"*All* the customs?" Her voice was a provocative drift around the ajar bathroom door. He heard her moving, but stripped off his shirt and began running hot water. The rush of hotel power-pressured water was echoed from the outer room. Kevin patted down his face and smeared on shaving cream. The other room was quiet; he wondered, with a prickle of purely sexual excitement, what Jane was up to. By the time his razor-shy skin had been scraped smooth, the water faucet from the bedroom rang with the muted tone of plunging into new depths.

He emerged to see Jane's jeans, blouse and the distinctive white flag of her cast-off underwear on the risers. She was ensconced in the overbuilt Jacuzzi, the foaming bubbles fluttering about her body like a fan dancer's feathers. Dampened hair curled against her wet shoulders. She looked up at him, her eyes surprised, then pleased by the sight of his hairy chest. He was, he thought, a perfect Zyunsinth substitute.

"This is wonderful." Jane stretched in the hot, seething water.

359

Kevin saw himself reflected—almost born again—in mirrored panels of bronze narcissism—barefoot, unbearded boy with too much cheek. He lowered his gaze to Jane, a glowing, confident Jane, more naked now than when two country cops had found her on a Crow Wing bluff, more vulnerable, thanks to him. He let his look drop farther to his belt buckle and throttled it open, ripped down the zipper, adding his jeans, jockeys and inhibitions to the clothes cluttering the plush stairs.

He glimpsed himself again in the mirror before he stepped down into the Jacuzzi with Jane. He looked prototypically human—a naked, oddly unpredatory body. Two legs, planted slightly apart on unprepossessing feet. Two arms hanging empty of any tool or machine, the opposable thumbs innocently dormant. He looked a lot, Kevin thought as the image in the steam-misted mirror stared back, like the etched male figure on the pictogram to the stars that accompanied the Jupiter probe. Except that, he mused, that little metal man didn't wear an erection. Maybe that was one element both NASA and Jane's alien masters feared to import beyond their respective solar systems.

Water, sweat and semen dampened the sheets, exuding the healthy, human odor that little kids are taught to loathe and sexually active adults are expected to appreciate.

Jane lay on her stomach, her body wound by the twisted sheet as if by an ivory satin snake. Kevin's hand rested on her bare shoulder blade, wafting up and down with her breathing. Damp and cool, addictive. He sat up against the headboard and pulled her onto his lap. She was still sleepy-sated with sex, but she roused enough to nurse automatically at his quickly erect nipple, her cheek and hand rubbing rhythmically into the fur of his chest.

Father, mother, brother, sister, lover. He'd said it. It occurred to him that she'd never had a chance to nurse as an infant; this was her first sex, her first mothering, transformed into the sexual mode. Tenderness overwhelmed him. Baby. Baby Jane Doe. His Baby Jane Doe. He also felt rearoused, on the brink of whirling her on her back, mounting her, moving within her as she lay semiawake. Contradictions. But he couldn't inflict himself on her again so soon. He winced as he recalled the mixed emotions of the past hour. She knew everything, of course, had no inhibitions. She had read it— once. But her body was tenderer than her mind, or even her emotions. He had soon found the fabled hymen—a tight, protective membrane watchdogging her vagina—and explored it with a doctor's educated fingers. Tough little sucker. Made to be broken, with all the stress and pain that implied.

Kevin had hovered over her, supposedly practiced at the act of, the art of coition, hamstrung by his virgin sensibilities. "I don't want to hurt you, Jane," he'd murmured, hesitating even as her body had fretted beneath his, moving in dream patterns against the sheets, inviting as a sun-dappled, wind-shifted pool asking to be plunged into, sharply, cleanly, the invisible, integral skin of its surface tension sending delicious ripple after ripple across the entire body of broken water.

Why had female virginity ever been prized? It made a man into a violator, a woman into a possession or a problem one decided what to do with. To alter or not to alter. Be or not to be.

"It's all right, Kevin. I know what—"

"I know, too. Know clinically how it'll feel. We know too damn much. I don't want you to know any pain from me. . . ."

"I already do." She'd stopped her motions, sobered by his reluctance. Human, he'd said she was human. Of course she'd been hurt. By one or another of his patented too flip remarks. By his self-imposed distance. Why not by his penis? When had he gotten so nice?

In the end he took the serendipitously discovered contraceptive sponge he'd found in the nightstand drawer behind the tissue box—probably left behind as an inadvertent gift by transient newlyweds, unless hotels were now leaving contra-ceptives in their bridal suite drawers the way they deposited Gideon Bibles in their less obviously connubial accommo-dations—he took the damn sponge, moistened it in the bed-side water carafe, and wedged it against the hymen and rammed it into deep lodging against the uterine mouth on one quick, cruel, merciful, logical, unloverlike thrust.

She had gasped under him, her lower body clamping him tight, adding unwanted pleasure to his pain as he felt the deep, dark, warm, wet relief of his housing within her. After that, they moved together gently. And Jane, overexcited, had climaxed before him, from the mere intrusion of a foreign body.

He stroked her cheek now and set her back beside him.

"Was I—it—what you wanted, the way it's supposed to be?"

"Better. But it'll be different every time, because we'll be different."

"Maybe there won't be many times."

He scrunched down beside her, pulled the sheet over them. Daylight sifted through the weave, somehow narcotic. "Many, many times," he promised.

"They still want me." Jane's voice was matter-of-fact. "The men from this world. The beings from whatever other world brought me here."

Kevin kissed her shoulder as he rolled her into the semidark of his body. "You forgot to include me. I want you, too. And I was here first. Have I ever mentioned your appallingly bad memory, Miss Doe? I'd take advantage of it, if I were you, and forget my worries and go to sleep."

She did, promptly, exhausted by their flight, by the sheer glandular excesses of the past hour. Kevin slept, too, enter-ing a blank unconsciousness and passing rapidly through to the woods—the thick green forest he had dreamed before. This time he was naked, weaponless, striding through the underbrush. He was wanderer, not stalker, and when he

362

finally saw the Doe, leaping, arching elegantly over a fallen log, he saw the other hunters, too, and smelled the smoke from their dagger-ended rifles, saw their faceless faces and saw them surround the Doe and bear her away.

He awoke, heart pounding, in an empty afternoon bed. His head swept the room; he rose, ready to check the bathroom, when he saw her naked at the door to the room, or from the room, her cheek pressed against the painted wood, her fingers fussing repeatedly but ineffectively with the chain lock.

"Go," Jane murmured as he came to pry her loose. She acted more classically hypnotized than she ever had under the spell of ecnalubma. "Must go. Go back." She sighed. "Go now."

Chapter Fifty

Crow Wing lay under a decorative layer of snow and, like Bethlehem on a Christmas card, under an overarching skyful of sharply luminous stars. Not one of them looked to Kevin like a guiding light from a benign heavenly visitor.

Kevin hunched over the steering wheel, peering through the windshield at a bigger slice of sky. He could make out the Big Dipper, and that was it, but then astronomy had never been his métier.

Jane had been quiet on the long drive from Duluth. That last day at the hotel it became obvious that Jane heeded some adamant, interior alarm; she would lapse into brief semiconscious states, during which she always headed for the door. Once out it, she veered infallibly south, toward the snow-flung fields and tidy streets of Crow Wing miles away.

Of course a human probe had to have some return mechanism, Kevin rationalized, an implanted biological beeper that would draw Jane to her keepers, and her keepers to Jane, for a rendezvous and retrieval, just as a Soviet spy had a wireless to make a predestined appointment with a homebound submarine. So much for state-of-the-art spying on a galactic scale.

He squinted skyward again, as if hoping to catch the stars flashing a betraying Morse code signal of cognizance: We know you're there. But it was all irretrievably ordinary. He shifted and started down the hill, past the three-story Victorian clapboard houses with well-lit windows leaking human warmth into the cold night through lace curtain webs.

The ghost of Officer Kellehay tweaked the hairs on his neck when they reached the foot of Crow Wing bluff. Idling the engine, Kevin wondered how to tackle the unlit road climbing and curving out of sight. The bluff loomed like a frozen white tidal wave over Kandy's wretchedly maintained van, and the sky seemed utterly black here, completely winked and twinkled out. Dead serious. At the roadside, the local police—minus Matusek and Kellehay—had established a sign bordered in diagonal warning stripes: "Unplowed. Dangerous. Do not use."

Kevin gunned the engine and the van shot up the incline. After sixty triumphant feet, its wheels locked and the rear fishtailed, sliding assbackward into the snowbanks. Kevin applied the gas in rhythmic bursts, letting the van rock, listening to the wheels whine their frustration as they whirled impotently on snow-packed ice. The floored gas pedal prodded the van into an agonizing incremental crawl up the road before it stalled again. Kevin gave up on the gas and let the van coast silently back down the grade.

"Can't we get up?"

"It's a bitch. I'll try again."

This time he backed far down the street, then drove as flat-out fast as the slick-packed snow would let him. He hit the hill at fifty miles an hour, gunned almost to the top of the first incline before the momentum flagged, rounded the curve, hit the gas and cranked the wheel left to meet another curving upgrade.

Crow Wing and all its works instantly fell as far behind them as Duluth. They were launched at last on a dark, narrow, softly treacherous birth canal of terrain, their way lit only by the van's lurching headlights. Roadside bushes, dressed in gleaming white, lost their snowy livery as the bucking van fishtailed into them. And Jane, awed by Kevin's grim fight up the glass mountain, wrapped her hands around her seat cushion. Both their bodies bucked against their seat belts as the van jolted upward.

"Won't they hear us?" she asked over the wheels' abrasive whirr. To Kevin, it sounded like a dentist's drill; he didn't know what it sounded like to Jane, who had never faced a dentist.

"Too far below," he finally answered, shouted. "Houses shut too tight. And up above . . . Maybe we want 'em to know we're coming." Kevin grinned encouragingly despite achingly clenched teeth.

Rounding a bend, the van attacked what turned out to be one big mean mama of an upgrade. The dashboard tilted sharply and the engine shrieked like a dying peacock. Kevin pumped gas until he felt the van's empty bulk finally heave itself over a crest of sorts and poise there precariously.

"This it?" he asked. The land still sloped upward, but a black inverted bowl of stars was visible again.

Jane didn't answer, but left the van to explore before he had turned off the motor. She was doing a lot of that lately, wandering away. Drawn away.

Kevin followed, tamping his boots into knee-high drifts, turning slow circles as he craned his neck at the sky. What'd he expect—lights, action, cameras? If these creatures communicated via melody, as Spielberg fantasized in *Close Encounters of the Third Kind,* he and Jane were out of luck. Kevin was tone-deaf. He suddenly wondered if Jane was, too. How much more there was to discover about her inherent capabilities, he realized, for him—for her. That self-discovery must continue, even if he never saw her again.

Jane returned to him, a wide circle of tracks trailing her.

"You see anything . . . familiar?" he asked.

She shook her head. "It's pretty up here. And peaceful. The town looks like a toy."

He studied the man-made stars below. "Do you remember the ambulance ride down this hill? It must have been pretty terrifying."

She shook her head again. "Only the sound. The screaming. Kevin." She came to him, and he felt her breath frost his face. "Maybe we're wrong."

"Nice of you to say 'we.' This is my idea, my theory. What if we held an extraterrestrial pickup and no one came? Jane, I'd rather be wrong than be president, but I don't think I am. You seemed very ready to return, subconsciously, but I've rushed matters by bringing you back. It's cold, but we can wait."

She pressed her icy lips onto his, pressed even nearer so their inner warmth met and mingled. It was such a small gesture of solidarity in a universe as big as he now perceived it. Stars, sole majestic centers of their own far-flung vacuum, rolled one by one into impenetrable distance, so that, viewed from any one of those distances, they shrank together into tiny sequined galaxial pinwheels on some endless black velvet display cloth.

"Are you cold?" he asked Jane. "Want to wait in the van? I can keep the engine running."

She shook her head and paced away, her coat hem trailing the drifts. She looked like Edward Gorey in one of his desolate, creepy black-and-white sketches, the fur-coated figure seen from behind, near the lifeless hand trailing from the well . . .

Kevin shivered and stomped his own lonely pattern through the unmarked snow. There was nothing more to say. He was either right or wrong. The sky showed the same unchanging cloudless face. Kevin explored the bluff perimeter, wondering where on the inhospitable slopes Jane had been found, where the squad car had crashed into the dark below. It was all moot.

He kicked a dead branch, watched it lift from the snow. There was no moon, but the snow itself shone, almost luminescent against the charred dark. Starlight, he thought. He was seeing starlight reflected. Star light, star bright, first star I see tonight. I wish I may, I wish I might . . .

It was odd how the eyes adjusted to undiluted dark. He could see Jane quite clearly from thirty feet away, see the van. After a while, the snow seemed to emit a warmer, incandescent color, like those pink-tinted light bulbs. . . . Kevin looked around. The snow was warming all right, sparkling in all its rainbow highlights, as if a huge interior floodlight had been switched on.

"Jane!" She turned and started toward him, but Kevin didn't watch her after the first few steps. He looked up. It hovered, just like in all the damn stories—not an oversized, neon-lit mechanical pizza pie of a flying saucer, but a dark, barely differentiated bulk. Its size was such that he couldn't tell whether it hung high or low in the heavens, but it was above them, above the bluff, and it had come without a sound, without a flash of fire or a flicker in the corner of an eye.

He caught Jane to him as he sensed her approach, never taking his eyes off the still shadow in the sky. "I was right! Sonofabitch, I was right! It's all there. The whole theory, the answer, the whole bloody thing!" He hugged Jane and pointed up. "Do you see it? Have you ever seen it before? Do you remember?"

Her head shook. "No. I've never seen anything like this."

"Your memory must have been wiped. I thought I was crazy, buying this, coming here. But I wasn't. The impossible, however improbable is, is . . . possible." He glanced at

367

Jane. She was staring upward, too, her mouth and eyes wide, her face washed with colored lights like a kid's on Christmas morning in front of the world's biggest, brightest, tallest balsam. . . .

They stood together, awed, entranced, frozen, bathed in more and more light, which seemed to shine from the ground and cast its brightness upward, rather than beam down from the thing above.

That thing was almost as big as the bluff top, Kevin estimated. Its color, shape, specificality remained clouded. All he knew was that he couldn't see many stars through it. It was like a hole in the night, a big black glove you put up before your eyes so close you can't focus, but you see it there and feel it there and can't see around it because it occupies your whole field of vision. . . .

"Amazing." Kevin squinted his eyes, wondering if it had moved, drawn closer. He wasn't much on hardware; he didn't care if it was made of chromium or crushed velvet. He had no bright ideas on where it might be from, or who or what might be on it. In it? But it was there. He had to keep staring at it to believe his eyes, his— His ears? Now there was sound, a vibrant buzz, almost hisslike. Low-key sound. Not the kind of thing to rouse the natives and alert the National Guard. Just a steady, deep vibration that began tickling the soles of his feet. His lips tingled together and his teeth felt numb. The same subliminal tremor hummed through his hand on Jane's shoulder.

Above, the darkness grew and the ground light spread, intensifying from soft amber to a copper color. And . . . Kevin's eyes were drawn from the UFO to the bluff top. The snow! It was melting. Without heat—simply sinking away, into the frozen earth, as if the whole damn red clay bluff were a giant sponge. Kevin watched a swelling dark star of thawed earth radiate outward; in seconds the snow at his knees was sucked soundlessly away.

Above, the vessel's indefinable profile, as black and blank

and amorphous as the shadow of a stingray, had dropped, utterly smothering the stars. Kevin felt a tardy spasm of claustrophobia, felt pressed in some cosmic waffle iron.

It was too late. The thing had landed, or hovered as low as it needed to. It blanketed the bluff top, still, dark, mysterious. In a minute he'd begin to believe it had always been there, that there were no stars beyond the dark above him, and never had been, only this dim, unrevealed form.

At the center of the bluff, the thing spat out a core of light, intense as a follow spot on a Broadway stage. From where Kevin stood seventy feet away, it seemed a mere thread of light that spread no illumination.

"Jane! Did you see that?" He began to collect his transfixed senses. Okay. They were here. He had to . . . communicate, convince them that Jane belonged on her home planet, that's all. Make them listen to reason. But did they have ears to hear? Or were their minds even organized along rational lines? How could he imagine himself as an emissary for any viewpoint? He must have been crazy to believe this, and believing it, crazier not to have run in the opposite direction. But they would have to confront him. Emerge, beckon with their webbed hands . . . no, slitted eyes. They would have slitted eyes, because Adelle Volker had told the literal truth. So he was ready for that: slitted eyes. It couldn't be much worse than confronting a person afflicted with a disfiguring birth defect; looks were no excuse for underestimating intelligence. And their intelligence must be . . . light-years . . . beyond the human.

As if it had responded to the word "light" in his mind, the central beam began twisting, widening into a tornadolike gyre. The low-key hiss ended so suddenly that his ears strained to read sound into the ensuing silence, where there was none.

The light shifted shade to blue and then ultraviolet. Jane stirred against him and, moving across the snow-free earth, began walking toward the beam.

"Jane, wait!" He had whispered, as if they didn't know he was there. "Wait!" Normal human tones rang utterly alien on the altered bluff top. Jane didn't wait. She didn't look back. She walked on, growing smaller against the dark, overhanging alien presence, becoming a mote in the eye of the unearthly light.

Kevin rushed after, easily catching up to place a restraining hand on her shoulder. She walked on. His grip tightened, dug into the thick, warm fur of Zyunsinth that was so dear to her. She walked out of the coat, leaving it clutched in his hand. He let it fall to earth and ran after her.

Jane was almost at the violet shower alive with dancing, gleaming motes, possibly the errant particles that drove the physicists mad. She stepped into it, and paused. Kevin pulled up, too. He didn't know why, except that he felt tied to her movements like a puppet to its crossbar of strings. Her hair lifted in a wind he couldn't feel, revealing the strong lines of her shoulder blades. . . . Shoulder blades? Her blouse was melting, dwindling into threads, eating itself off her. Not only her shoulders were bare. He could suddenly see the long notched line of her spine, the dimples of elbows and knees. Naked, naked again, her clothes consumed by the whirlwind of light.

Kevin stumbled forward, shocked by the easy disappearance of sturdy denim, the wiping away of loom time and middleman time and shopping mall time, as if the material were so much cotton candy to melt in any alien wind.

"Jane," he called, but she didn't turn, or stop until reaching the light beam's exact center. Couldn't hear her own name but could find some arbitrary spot on a Crow Wing plateau at the pull of some faceless aliens in a faceless ship. . . .

Kevin plunged into the light, knowing it wasn't for him. His muscles knotted at the unworldly touch of its rays, expecting heat. Cool purple bathed him. He heard a crackle and looked down. The nylon shell of his jacket was cracking, shrinking, invisibly devoured. White feathers, released, flew in a mock-winter blizzard until they shrank star-small and vanished. His face felt the ice, the terrible in-driving ice. He winced away from the phenomenon, back into the ordinary night of earth.

Random feathers performed an aerial ballet before bowing to gravity by drifting earthward. His jacket lining hung off his back and arms in strings. He lunged forward again, into the light. Quickly, to seize Jane and back out, that's all it would take. . . . This time his protection, however feeble, was gone. A sensation of ice water poured over his body, burning cold. His shirt began unweaving on his shoulders; his skin everywhere tightened and stretched, as if being wrenched in the world's biggest Indian burn.

He retreated, stumbling, his arms over his face, his pained cries echoing off the featureless ship above him.

He paused, panting. He'd never thought they'd refuse him, that they'd just ignore him. Another fine specimen? He never thought his being there wouldn't make a difference. It always had. For him, even for Jane.

He saw her naked, light-rinsed form. She looked like a hologram, a damning illusion. And then she finally turned, so he could see her face, a face more distant than he had ever seen. It was the proper face for a probe, a returning probe about to be pried of its secret, like an oyster shell of its pearl. He'd assumed they valued their tool, their living tape recorder. Why?

The light rippled. Jane's beautiful pale body wavered, an image viewed through water. Violet turned gray and then black. Black as night, as a villain's velvet glove, as my true love's hair. It extinguished, and night itself seemed brighter. Jane wasn't there anymore, like her clothes or the snow. They'd all just melted away.

Kevin found himself hesitating at the invisible plane where the cold melting light had met normal Minnesota winter air. He wanted to cross, he would cross, but his body held back,

371

tamed by the touch of the icy light. Mind pushed body over the invisible barrier, careless of the consequences. Every muscle in his body clenched reflexively. And nothing happened. The light was gone. Jane was gone. Nothing could hurt him anymore, he thought numbly even as he recognized the magnitude of the lie.

Moving deliberately, he went to stand in the remembered center, where Jane had stood, and turned slowly, looking up. An eye glared back down at him, perhaps ten feet from the ground. No living eye, only some external mark on the overarching machine. It could have been a navel on a whale, or a bolt on a battleship. It reminded Kevin of the iris of a camera lens, shut.

"I'm staying," he told it. And then he yelled it. "I'm staying until I get Jane back! I don't care if you blast me with your afterburners or roast me to the bone with your fucking freezing plant light. I'm staying!"

Chapter Fifty-one

They were waiting for her, as they had always been, only now she knew it.

The pull had been strongest toward the ship; now it ebbed. She didn't move, and they ignored her, leaving her standing where she was in a large, windowless, well-lighted room. She had stood here before; she knew that but couldn't remember it. She would not remember this in a while. They had come to take her memory, and her body had been tuned to accept that.

Jane waited, too; perceiving what she had never seen using

the perceptions they had been forced to give her to send her to this place, her home.

They were the most familiar element, though she didn't consciously remember them. Smooth-skinned as she, quite human-looking, though their skins were as pale as paper. Paper. A simple, taken-for-granted human product. Surely there was no paper here? Only data screens, machines and the table with its tubes and paraphernalia not so different from the place the ecnalubma had taken her. The hospital.

She wanted a weapon against their hold on her, the hold that hummed through the cells of her body. She had found it. Memory. The memory of paper. Of the ambulance. Of the things that she had been fed full of, to know, and that she now knew of her own experience.

Her body still felt a serene, numb distancing from the light that had lifted her into their ship. It had acted as, she realized, what would be called an anesthetic on earth. It was the first stage in the operation to empty her and make her useful for another, surgically forgettable foray into another world. No, she thought. I won't let them.

I? Who was this I? Had this I stood here before? Yes, said a flash of pure emotional intuition, surging along her quiescent neurons. This was a place she had seen many times, for long periods of time. A place where her memory had been placed and replaced, until it had left some vestigial imprint on her organism through sheer persistence.

"Come this way," said one of the beings. It spoke English, her language, but it was natural it should. They could not imprint her tongue with a language never learned unless they had mastered it themselves.

They all looked alike, but that was because they were many and she was one. One. Another word that thrilled rebellion along her nerves. She was one.

"Come this way," the being repeated.

Her body, docile, began moving toward them and the place where their equipment was arrayed. Now she knew

373

why! Why she'd hated the hospital and its examining rooms, the touch of the mob in uniform dress, the probe of the instruments. Something in her had remembered this. She stopped.

They watched her, their identical faces identically expressionless, even to the thin long eyes that were all dark iris. They wore clothes, she perceived with sudden anger. Loose, light-colored garments that hid their pale torsos and limbs. She was . . . naked. Her skin crawled. She did not wish to be naked in their whiteless eyes when they were clothed. It was not . . . appropriate.

But she began to move toward them again, not willing it. She was *used* to doing so. It was a habit. "To fall into a habit is to begin to cease to be." She had read that in one of the library books she had mastered only to regurgitate, To cease to be. An "I." A "one." A . . . "she." She. Excitement trembled along her numb nerve endings. She was a she. She didn't think she had ever been so specifically "she" before.

"Come." They said it in unison this time, as if that had any greater strength against the I, the one and the she that she had become.

"No."

They were silent. She looked around the room. With the memories of earth they had fed her and that she had drawn from this earth they stranded her upon, she saw the ship in a fearless and logical way. There along the rim, the . . . holding pens. The odd-colored gases of many worlds hissing endlessly into the chambered glasslike compartments, with their dormant, drifting occupants so clearly visible. Sleeping among the stars. Wakening to transitory consciousness and then sleeping again.

She surveyed the area emotionlessly. Her nursery, she supposed. Her high school and college. Her cradle and grave, just as her genes, altered by the wizards from another world, served the same sustaining and self-destructive role.

They approached her, cautiously. She smiled. They stopped. They probably never had seen her smile before.

"This probe has exhibited similar symptoms before," said one.

"Yes," agreed another all-eyes face. "After Zyunsinth."

Zyunsinth. Their pronunciation altered the word, as if articulating a set of syllables alien even to them. The sound hit her in the center of her being, somewhere between her navel and her rib cage, if she had to be specific about a feeling so overwhelming. She wavered, wrenched by a spasm of loss, of memory, of weakness.

"We expect much of them," intoned another voice. "They are, after all, merely biological units. Come here," it ordered, and her legs, disobedient to her, began moving toward them.

"We couldn't know Zyunsinth would have such a psycho-physical effect. And there was so little to learn there."

"This should be different. It was worth the risk, even if the probe is damaged."

"It is our most sophisticated unit."

"Jane!" she stopped and shouted, interrupting whoever, whatever was talking. She could no longer relate to them as individuals; they seemed melded into a many-headed beast, like the medical personnel surrounding the ambulance as she had arrived at the hospital, the confused, submerged thing she was struggling for survival amid the bewildering new environment. This was all new to her, and old, very old, as well.

Her word had silenced them. "Jane," she tried again, enamored by the simplicity of the sound. "My name," she told herself and them. Her hand raised in its first voluntary gesture as she tapped her breastbone. "I—Jane."

They were struck dumb, so she elaborated. "My name is Jane. I am not a unit; I am not 'this probe.' I am . . . I. Jane."

One finally spoke. "This naming undoes our work. It was the same with Zyunsinth."

Another answered, this time in a sibilant clacking sound that was clearly an expression of a language other than English, a place other than earth.

Jane cocked her head to listen. Such sounds had been the sky to her once, she recalled, an overencompassing phenomenon that belled over her as she had hovered in some semisentient state. The sounds were as familiar and yet as annoyingly remote as the static that Kevin complained of on the radio, then forgot to hear. Kevin. When had she seen him last? His image was patchwork—clear in certain, sharp fragments; misted in others. She remembered dark roads, and distant stars, cold and sudden heat—a fire. Warm hands holding hers, touching her naked skin so she felt no fear or shame. And long ago, the chair, the chair buoying her body just as one of these surrounding apparatuses had done once, only she could leave the chair when she wished, when it was over, when Kevin said so.

The people of the stars did not offer her that option.

"I belong here, on this world I was taken from, where you left me to learn more," Jane told them, interrupting their meaningless blizzard of white noise.

It stopped.

"Please," she said. "I must stay. I must stay as I am."

One stepped forward. "So you said when we retrieved you from Zyunsinth. Yet when we took the information you had gleaned, the Zyunsinthians proved to be the primitive hominids of no great promise we had assumed them to be, although the specific data was most helpful. You were far the more sophisticated entity; why should you so irrationally cleave to them?"

"They were . . . warm and welcoming. They held me to them with their young, shared the keep-fires they paid so much to guard. I spoke their language, as you had fed me it,

376

and though it was simple, they were the only sounds I knew then, as the words I speak now are all I know—"

"And will vanish, with the retrieval procedure," noted the one in the forefront.

Another stepped forward, and although the voice was as calm as the first's, something in it bespoke anger.

"This probe exists to provide answers, not demand them. Bring it to the retrieval bay; in minutes it will be dormant again."

The other answered before Jane could. "This planet is sophisticated; so, too, will be the body of data we extract. There should be no risk of damaging the recording mechanism."

The being raised a hand; Jane could not count the number of fingers extended, but she recognized the gesture's universal invitation.

"You have spent your entire existence among us. You were never of your world, except in a spawning sense. Come. Perform your function. The retrieval is painless. You will remain to serve another day, in another place. What you glean is of great value."

Jane vacillated, recognizing truth no matter how bizarre its spokesperson. The beings no longer seemed a solid mass, and one had stepped forward, had dared deal with her as individual to individual, debating her life, her future in the sounds of an alien language that to her mouth was native. For an instant, she was back in Kevin's office, discussing her life, her past. She heard his relentless, gentle questions, heard him intone the name he had conferred upon her so casually over and over, until it was her. Jane.

She spoke to them, to the one who commanded her.

"You . . . Have you ever called me 'you' before? Have 'we' ever communicated this way before?"

The pause was long. "No," admitted the figure, and said no more.

Jane stepped toward it. "Have . . . you . . . ever found

one of your other—probes—responding as this unit has, as I, Jane, have?''

There was silence, except for the distant humming of the ship.

She stood still, sensing finally her apartness. Apart from the holding areas, where her blood sang recognition of familiar sustainment, even as her mind rejected it. Apart from the beings whose alien aspects were yet familiar—remembered and forgotten many times. Apart from Zyunsinth; she saw a familiar furred shape blurred against the faraway glass and knew it for a fellow probe from a once familiar place. Apart even from Kevin. She felt a greater distance from him than she had dreamed would be possible after their utter closeness. Severed completely—by the light, by the ship, by her own otherworldly history. Fear and regret coiled within her body like Siamese snakes at the thought, but her mind was calm. What did Jane want? To be as she was, what she was, until she ceased to be. And to fight for that as long as she had memory.

''You must return me,'' she told them. ''I am no longer useful. I have become what my genes promised even as you swept them through space and away from their source. I am human; I am female. I am Jane.''

Their own language swelled again, with many voices; even Jane could hear agitation in it. She waited, aware that her defiance was short-lived, housed in an individual consciousness that was a transitory and expendable thing to creatures of their advanced technology. But it was not expendable to her anymore. Kevin had not evoked her past during the many sessions in his office, but he had elicited the means to change her future.

Now it was up to her masters, who could continue to turn her to their own purpose, benign or otherwise. Only ''this probe'' could no longer be considered a mute tool fit for many uses. It had a name. And so had their use of her— enslavement. Such an act was universally despised on the

378

world where she had originated, her reading had told her that; she didn't know if such considerations inhibited these beings from worlds away.

"We are scientists," said the one who had become the spokesperson by stepping forward to confront her. "We have altered you for the work. It is possible to extract what we want, but to leave you here, knowing pieces of two worlds, two cultures that cannot hope to meet . . . The very air you breathe has been adulterated to accommodate both you and us for a short space. And there are issues beyond us and our probe ship, you and your name, places and beings beyond imagination, whose futures would be altered by a premature revelation—or any revelation at all."

"I can forget! Isn't that my most valuable virtue? I have forgotten so much, and have no wish to remember it. Only this—last—world, this place, my home. Only these last few months. Only Mrs. Bellingham and snow and bourbon and the movie of the week. And Kevin. Besides, Kevin can make me forget, even if you can't. And he would, to keep me here."

"Kevin?"

Jane was silent, lost for words to translate all that Kevin was to her to them.

"The human male who watches our umbilicus to earth," one defined him.

The spokesbeing nodded its bland, heavy head. "This unit's recording should prove most instructive; we must obtain it. Perhaps it is all for the best."

Jane tensed. "Jane," she insisted, chilled by their easy reversion to discussing her in mechanical terms.

"Jane," agreed the creature. Its hand, never dropped, raised higher, gesturing her nearer. "Come, Jane. We must extract our data; we must make modifications if we are to return you."

She studied the equipment bay. It didn't look so different from the medical paraphernalia of earth. How close were her

379

fellow humans, she wondered, to mastering the arts these unhuman beings practiced?

"You must trust us," said the one who had taken the lead.

She moved toward them, toward the table prepared for her. Jane, she intoned to herself. I am Jane. This I know, remember. Kevin. And Jane. Perhaps something of that would remain, no matter what.

Chapter Fifty-two

Despite the melted snow, the winter wind whined lethally across the Crow Wing bluff top, drowning out the eternal hum of the hovering piece of night Kevin called a spaceship.

He stared up at it, ignoring numb hands and feet in the face of a fear that anesthetized his entire emotional system. Who was he to confront or challenge this? It was mysterious beyond solving, remote beyond imagining. He hardly apprehended that he stood under a UFO. He only knew the absence of Jane, the loss of Jane and the press against himself of a force larger and darker and more alien than anything his puny superego could battle, whether it wore the name of a terrestrial mental disease or an extraterrestrial culture.

But it was here yet, as he was.

Then the iris above him twisted soundlessly open, and a bright column probed downward, foot by foot, like an extension ladder of light. He retreated from the nearing ray, tamed and trained and self-hating. Perhaps this time it had come for him, and part of him wished to be reunited with Jane, at any cost. But some reflexive segment of himself backed away, too. He was so terribly human; he wanted what he wanted, but on his terms. And being human, he doubted he would get it.

380

The light performed its color and motion tricks, broadening, spinning, changing hue. At its core, a solid formed, or was revealed. Just a slim stalk of pinkish white, blossoming into a form, a figure, into Jane.

She began walking toward him. Kevin's emotions surged until a symphony seemed to be climaxing in his head. Cold melted away; the ship above diminished to a distant, unimportant, everyday phenomenon, like a cloud. Heartened, he dared the light to reach in and pull her past it.

She was dazed, and beginning to shiver even as he drew her naked body into his arms.

"Jane." He started walking her away from the light, away from the place she had been, feeling oddly like Adam escorting Eve from Eden, only neither of them had taken the apple. Behind them, the light narrowed until it blazed like a flaming sword.

"Jane." It was all he could say, or sob. Her name. Every time he said it, a new emotion colored the simple syllable. Disbelief. Relief. Fear. Love. Anxiety. Joy.

He had her halfway across the bluff top, trying not to rush her bare feet into scraping on the still frozen turf. It felt colder by the instant; Jane's teeth were chattering, her eyelids closed as if to hoard even that much inner warmth.

His boot kicked the shapeless mound of her fallen fur coat, so he stooped to retrieve it and wrap it around her shoulders, still hurrying her back to the van, away from . . . whatever the hell it was that hovered like a burnt pancake above them.

But like Lot's wife, Kevin couldn't resist a backward look.

The light had extinguished and the stars were stealing back into view even as he watched. The UFO was leaving, leaving in a swift, silent sweep across an impenetrable night sky. He could still glimpse its veiled outline, smell a certain odd metallic tang on the air. Good riddance, he wished it, even as it became smaller and blacker, like the mouth of a gravity-defying well extending to the stars, the stars whose twinkling presence expanded as the visitors' shrunk.

But fear it as he must, deny it as he would, he stood transfixed by it finally, Jane clasped in her fur coat to his side, watching it vanish. He'd seen a UFO and lived to keep it secret. He'd stood under the alien shadow of the thing, and hadn't given a damn. He hadn't observed it or memorized it or even cared enough to speculate about its origin or creators. That was the most unbelievable part of the whole thing, his own behavior. And now it was gone. Crow Wing was peaceful, and snow would fall, covering the bald spot on a deserted bluff.

He looked at Jane, who was staring at him. She had never even looked up to see the damn thing go.

"Jane, are you all right?"

She nodded, still dazed. Of course she was all right. She was here, whatever her condition. He could deal with that—Jane altered, Jane wounded, Jane memoryless. He couldn't do anything about Jane dead or gone beyond the stars.

Kevin guided her along the dark ground, to the van, already planning how to get her into warm clothes and then get them on the road to—to wherever on earth they were going. At least it would be earth; at least it would be they. He felt up to anything Washington could throw at him now; they were amateurs, on a galactic scale.

He stopped by the van, turned her face up to his, studied her calm but puzzled eyes. Her icy palm cupped his cheek, rubbing the already resurging beard stubble; she smiled recognition.

"Kevin." It was the sweetest word on this or any other world. They hadn't taken that from her.

The puzzlement returned to her eyes, and he knew it wasn't over yet; maybe it wouldn't be over for a long time, but it was beginning again, and this time he was ready for it, ready for anything.

"Kevin . . . *who* am I?"

He thought she'd never ask. He looked up at the stars, unshadowed now, inhaled the icily antagonistic air. He saw with vast clarity how incredible it all was, how small they were to tempt the universe, what wonders were out there, and within themselves.

He laughed, and pointed his forefinger to the target of his still overworking heart. "Me—Tarzan." Or Zyunsinth or any furry little ape God made to look agape at the stars and the others who live there.

Jane's head tilted in characteristic puzzlement. His forefinger moved to the pale skin of her chest inside the wind-riffled fur. "You," he confided, "you—Jane." Jane and whatever promise that meant for humanity and a future that had such creatures in it. She smiled slow delight at her nonentity's name.

Her own finger mirrored his gesture, pushing sternly into his chest, pushing his own conceit back at him.

"You Kevin," she argued. "Me—" Her face radiated a smile inarguably human. "Me . . . me. I. One. Jane."

HERALDING.....

Avalon to Camelot, a widely praised and handsomely produced illustrated quarterly magazine. Prominent writers and scholars explore the Arthurian legend from the Dark Ages to the present in features and columns including the arts, literature, the quest for the historical Arthur and more. Articles, news, reviews.

- Illustrated quarterly
- 48 pages
- 8½"x 11"
- Acid-free stock

    I do very much appreciate you sending me copies of the first two numbers of *Avalon to Camelot*. I have found both to be full of interesting and useful articles, handsomely laid out and beautifully printed.

William W. Kibler   *Translator; Lancelot, or The Knight of the Cart*

    I enjoyed perusing the recent issues of *A to C* and appreciated their remarkably charming eclectic appeal. If only I had the soul of an Arthurian . . . life would be better. I just know it.

Bill Zehme   *National magazine writer*

    As a new subscriber, I'd like to thank you for putting out such a wonderful magazine. Your offer of the back issues was irresistible.

Abigail W. Turowski   *Woodlawn, MD*

CLIP AND SEND TO: *Avalon to Camelot*, 2126 W. Wilson, Box TR, Chicago, IL 60625

- -

☐ Please send a year's subscription:
☐ Please send a gift subscription in my name to:

Name _____

Address _____

City _____ State _____ Zip _____

☐ Enclosed is a check or M.O. for $15, payable to:
    Avalon to Camelot, 2126 W. Wilson Ave., Box TR,
    Chicago, IL 60625
    ALLOW 6 WEEKS FOR DELIVERY